PRAISE FOR BESTSELLING AUTHOR

LORI
FOSTER

"Lori Foster delivers the goods."
—*Publishers Weekly*

"A master at creating likable characters and placing them in
situations that tug at the heart and set your pulse racing…"
—*Romance Reviews Today*

"When it comes to delivering sexy and sensual romance,
author Lori Foster is in a class by herself."
—*Romantic Times*

LORI FOSTER

first published with Harlequin in January of 1996 and has since sold over fifty books with various different publishing houses, including categories, novellas, online books, special projects and, most recently, single titles. Lori's second book launched the Temptation Blaze miniseries and her twenty-fifth book launched the Temptation Heat series. She is a Waldenbooks, *USA TODAY, Publishers Weekly* and *New York Times* bestselling author. Lori has brought sensitivity and sensibility to erotic romances by combining family values and sizzling yet tender love. Though Lori enjoys writing, her first priority will always be her family. Her husband and three sons keep her on her toes.

LORI
FOSTER

Tempted

HARLEQUIN®

TORONTO • NEW YORK • LONDON
AMSTERDAM • PARIS • SYDNEY • HAMBURG
STOCKHOLM • ATHENS • TOKYO • MILAN • MADRID
PRAGUE • WARSAW • BUDAPEST • AUCKLAND

ISBN 0-373-83628-7

TEMPTED

CONTENTS

LITTLE MISS INNOCENT?   9

ANNIE, GET YOUR GUY   171

MESSING AROUND WITH MAX   315

LITTLE MISS INNOCENT?

To Bonnie Tucker
Your caring, your openness and your incredible humor
are so very much appreciated. It's easy to see why
you're a friend to so many, and why I'm so glad
you're a friend to *me*.

Chapter One

No. It couldn't be. Daniel rubbed his eyes and tried to deny the highly sensual sight that faced him. But when he looked again, Lace McGee still filled his vision.

It had been a long endless shift, in an even longer endless day. Now it was nearly nine o'clock. Time for him to go home. Though the emergency room still roared with chaos, his brain felt numb, his body dulled with fatigue. He wanted to walk out the sliding-glass doors and to his car, but there *she* stood, blocking the way by her mere presence. Just the sight of her seemed taunting and tempting. She was a thorn in his side, a pain in the butt... Hell, there didn't seem to be a single part of his anatomy that Lace didn't bother in one way or another.

He would simply ignore her, he decided. He stepped away from the front desk and waved goodbye to a group of nurses who hustled past, sending him spoony sidelong glances. They were ever persistent, but gently so, with discretion, respecting his wishes as a bachelor to remain a bachelor. Not like Lace, who forced her way into his thoughts whether he wanted her there or not. She didn't like it when he tried to ignore her—as if any man actually could. She was too damned intrinsically female, too...*noticeable*.

He didn't mean to, but he glanced at her again, and then

he couldn't look away. His palms began to sweat. His glasses fogged.

The cold evening wind sent her dark cloak swirling as white snow blew in behind her, making her entrance seem dramatically staged. Was she here to harass him again, to tease him until his body warred with his brain and his resolve crumbled? His heartbeat quickened as it always did, even as his customary scowl fell into place. He would not let her win.

Then she stepped farther inside and the doors whispered shut behind her.

Without the winter night as a backdrop, he realized Lace wasn't standing as tall as usual. Her face seemed pale rather than radiant, her white-blond hair looked bedraggled, and as he looked lower, he saw a large tear in her black slacks and blood covering her leg. His heart gave a painful lurch at the sight of that slim pale leg, and he jerked out of his stupor. A nurse had already reached her by the time Daniel roared up to her side.

"What the hell happened?"

The nurse looked startled, but Lace only gave him her patented killer grin, though it didn't measure up to her usual knock-him-on-his-can standard. "Hello there, Danny." Her gaze skimmed his face, then his body, and her voice lowered to a husky whisper. "My, you're looking in fine form today."

She deliberately threw him with ridiculous compliments, and he always allowed himself to be thrown, damn her. But not this time. Not with her so obviously hurt. He took her arm to steady her, then reached to lift her cloak and look behind her where most of the damage seemed to be. She slapped at his hands, but his determination overrode her efforts.

He dropped the cape and in a softer, more controlled tone asked, "What happened, Lace?"

She leaned into him—which he expected since that was another of her ploys to drive him insane. This time he didn't step away from her, but held her a little closer. Her body felt warm and soft against his. When she looked up at him, her expression was serious rather than flirtatious. He didn't like it; this wasn't the Lace he was used to.

Lace didn't seem to notice. "I got bit. By a big stupid neighbor's dog."

She looked shaken and he said easily, offering her more support, "The neighbor is big and stupid, or the dog is?"

"Both."

Without missing a beat, he turned to the nurse. "Notify the police and health authorities, then join us." She nodded and hurried away. Daniel's gaze came back to Lace. Damn, but he didn't want to feel concern for her. He didn't want to feel anything. He didn't even like the woman.

He merely *lusted* her.

Her pants were a mess, shredded from just above the back upper thigh, to the front of her right knee. Another nurse had hurried forward with a wheelchair, but Daniel waved her away. "I don't think she can sit." Then to Lace, "Should we get a stretcher, or can you make it to a room?"

Her beautiful eyes narrowed. "I can make it."

He recognized that stubborn set to her jaw. It was the same stubborn look she wore whenever she wanted him to see things her way, which was usually whenever she got around him. And because she was his sister's best friend and they were a close family, that seemed to be more often than not lately. Which explained why he was slowly—and painfully—going crazy.

With his arm around her narrow waist, and his other hand supporting her elbow, he took her to the first empty examining room he found. "Where, exactly, did you get bit?" He had to control his tone with an effort. The idea of an animal attacking her made his gut clench and his heart pound. He didn't like her, didn't approve of her, but she was a delicate woman, more feminine than any he'd ever known. The thought of her soft flesh being torn by sharp teeth was obscene.

Amazingly, her cheeks colored and she looked away. "In the butt."

Daniel knew embarrassment when he saw it, but he'd never have expected it of Lace. Good grief, the woman was a sex therapist, renowned for her books on sexual enlightenment and her late-night radio talk show. A self-professed expert on male/female relationships, she talked openly and without hesitation about every private subject known to man. Of course, as a doctor, he'd known plenty of other therapists. But Lace was different. She was certainly no Dr. Joyce Brothers.

So surely being bitten in a less than auspicious place couldn't be what bothered her. Daniel didn't even try to understand her. He'd done that numerous times, and it only raised his blood pressure and gave him a headache.

Exasperated with himself, he took off his glasses to polish them on a sleeve, giving himself a moment to think. "Tell me what happened."

"I had just come in from a late appointment—"

"An appointment, huh?" He shoved his glasses back onto the bridge of his nose.

"Get your brain out of the gutter, Doctor. Or was it your libido that went slumming there?"

He scowled. She always had some smart remark that thoroughly outdid his own, and she never explained herself. Not that he really expected her to, but still...

"I put my purse away then went down to the lobby to check the mail. And somehow a cat had gotten into the building. It ran behind me, the neighbor's dog tried to go through me and, like an idiot, I turned to see if the cat was all right, giving the mutt a prime target. But he'd never acted aggressive before, so I didn't really consider that he'd bite me."

"Damn. Hold still."

"No." She twisted around to stare at him, and panic edged her tone. "What are you doing?"

"Cutting these pants off you so we can see the damage."

"We?" There was so much nervous sarcasm in her voice, he almost hesitated. "Are you using the royal vernacular now? Because you're the only one looking. I sure as certain can't see a thing."

"Hush, Lace. The nurse will be right back."

"I don't want to hush!" Her voice rose to a squeak as he peeled the bloody pants away. "I demand a different doctor!"

"Well, you've got me." Daniel winced at the damage done to her beautiful skin. Whatever color her panties had once been, they were now stained dark by Lace's blood. The dog's teeth had punctured several places, and then actually torn through her skin, probably when she pulled away. He carefully swabbed at the blood, making certain to wipe away from the wound. His hand shook and he hated himself for it. He'd seen plenty of female bottoms, but none had been hers. Of course, all those nights when he'd dreamed of being this close to her bare, perfectly rounded backside, Lace had been beside herself with desire—only for him. She most certainly hadn't been in pain.

He swabbed at a particularly vicious tear and Lace howled.

Daniel spared her a glance, but his attention remained on caring for her. Past grievances seemed to drift away. Seeing her hurt made him hurt, as well. But she was his sister's best friend, so he reasoned that was acceptable.

"Shh. I know it stings. And you're definitely going to need stitches. The wound is too large to leave open, especially over a stress point like this."

"Damn you, Daniel, stop looking at me!"

"I have to look at you to assess the damage. Whatever modesty you're trying to protect is still intact, I assure you."

"I want a plastic surgeon!"

That gave him pause. "Lace, the scarring will be minimal, and being where it's located, it won't even be seen by the…casual…observer."

He ran out of words and his insides twisted. "Surely it's not that big a deal. Even the briefest bathing suit will cover it.

But then, that's not the issue here, is it?" He watched her face, keeping his own expression carefully impassive. "It would be awkward, but I imagine if two lovers were very creative, the scar might be seen. How often do you intend to be displaying this part of your anatomy for male appreciation, Lace?"

She'd gasped with his first words and now her color rose. "That's certainly none of your business, you damned lecher!"

The nurse walked in and came to a dead stop at Lace's accusing tone. To Daniel's relief, Lace snapped her teeth together and held back any further barrage of outrage. She turned her face away, crossing her arms over her head, and Daniel imagined her stubborn little nose pressed hard against the stiff, cloth-covered table.

He tried for patience—which always seemed in short supply whenever Lace McGee came around. She had a knack for bringing out the worst in him, and he hated himself for allowing her that advantage. He'd learned control long ago; he'd become a master at hiding his feelings and taking care of business because it had been vital to do so. After his mother had died and his father had fallen apart, someone had needed to see to his younger brother and sister. Daniel had elected himself.

But years of self-training and rigid discipline seemed to melt away whenever this particular woman showed up. He took a deep breath and nodded to the nurse.

"Finish getting her pants off so we can make sure there's no other bites. I'll be back in just a minute."

Lace made a choking sound at his order, but kept her thoughts, and her words, to herself. Just as well, he decided, because objections in this case wouldn't have done her any good. He was a doctor, now her doctor, whether she liked it or not.

He stepped out of the room and collapsed against the wall beside the door. The fatigue had left him. He felt wide-awake, charged, full of determination and renewed purpose, and the reason didn't sit well with him at all.

She was a liberal—a sinfully enticing, sexy liberal and a horrible influence on his sister Annie. After twenty-five years of being a sweet-natured tomboy, Annie was suddenly stubborn and willful and more often than not when he saw her, she looked too...female, too...

His brain shied away from the word *sexy* when applied to the sister he'd practically raised on his own.

But he knew it was true. Annie now attracted men in droves, and he didn't like it. But Annie did. Just recently, Annie had gotten pulled into a melee when a brawl had erupted at a local singles' bar. She'd been picked up by the police. Before that, she'd never even been in a bar. He still didn't know what the hell she'd been doing there.

But he did know that it was somehow Lace's fault. She'd turned his sister in a willful femme fatale and she'd affected his libido to such a degree he didn't recognize himself anymore. Hell, she could probably adversely affect the morals of the whole human race with her candid, brassy way. She talked openly of sex, flirted with him outrageously simply to provoke him, and dressed for effect. She enjoyed making him squirm. They were opposites in every way, and she loved driving that fact home whenever it would make him most uncomfortable.

But what she didn't realize was that he'd become addicted to her unique form of torture. After all, he was a man, and he couldn't help reacting to her as such. When she wasn't around, he thought of her, dreamed of her. Yes, he disapproved of the lifestyle she led. As a rational, intelligent, responsible man, he abhorred sexual promiscuity—yet she epitomized that standard with her every breath. When he allowed common sense to guide him, he disliked her immensely.

But that didn't keep him from wanting her. Of all the women in all the world, he wanted Lace McGee so badly he could no longer sleep at night. He burned with wanting her, and resistance became more difficult every day.

And now, for the first time in his life, he hadn't been able to remain totally detached when treating a patient. With the very fiber of his being, he'd been aware of touching Lace, seeing Lace, worrying for Lace. That fact struck at the bone of his professional pride. He should get away from her now, while he still had his integrity.

But he'd be damned if he'd let anyone else in there with her.

LACE WISHED SHE COULD HIDE somewhere, anywhere. Under a mossy rock would do just fine. Of all the doctors to be on call tonight, why did Daniel have to be the one to see her first? And why, when he so obviously disdained everything about her, did he insist on taking care of her? If he knew the depths of mortification she suffered by the circumstances, he'd be more than a little amused. The damn Neanderthal. The damn *gorgeous,* uptight, prudish Neanderthal.

Lace tightened her fingers in her hair and winced when the nurse tugged her slim-fitting slacks over her backside. "So, you and Doctor Sawyers know each other?"

That almost brought a grin. Here she was in the most ignominious position of her entire twenty-seven years, and the nurse displayed signs of jealousy. Lace knew the gossip would be all over the hospital in short order, but at the moment, she didn't care. She lifted her head to face the nurse and noted that she was a pretty woman, young and dark-eyed. Lace narrowed her gaze. "Dan is my best friend's brother." *And a totally obnoxious fellow.*

"Doctor Sawyers prefers to be called Daniel."

Lace dropped her head back onto the table. "Yeah, well, I prefer to annoy him. So I call him a variety of things."

"Then you two aren't...involved?"

Ha. Fat chance of that when Daniel thought of her as a loose woman with no morals. She could still remember the first time she'd met him—not because she was still hurt over it, she assured herself. Only because narrow-minded judgment angered her.

Daniel hadn't shown the kindness or politeness or intelligence Annie had bragged of. No, the big oaf had turned up his nose at her and drawn an immediate and erroneous conclusion based on her career and appearance.

She was used to men doing that, though most of them assumed she was easy and tried to put the make on her. She'd learned over the years how to quickly correct those assumptions.

But Daniel had decreed her unfit and not only hadn't he wanted her in his bed, he hadn't wanted her anywhere around Annie. Lucky for her, Annie had a mind of her own, and she gleefully disobeyed big brother's orders.

Which gave Daniel another sin to lay at her door—the corruption of his twenty-five-year-old *baby* sister.

Of course, Lace hadn't helped to dissuade Daniel from his ridiculous notions. At first, she'd allowed him his beliefs because it rankled her that he thought so little of her simply because of her profession and her flamboyant looks. As if she could help the way she looked, she thought with a self-directed snort. She had her mother's vivid coloring and curvy figure, which had caused her endless grief but no shame.

Her work, on the other hand, was important, and as much a source of pride for her as his own profession. She helped people with their traumas. She made a difference, the same as he did. *Not that he'd ever see it that way.*

The nurse cleared her throat in impatience, and Lace replied, "No, we're not involved."

"I'm glad." The woman's voice was suddenly lighter, friendlier. "Just about every single woman in this hospital has tried to get his attention. But he's always so serious. Not that any of us has given up hope."

Actually, Daniel went beyond serious. Lace would have described him as funereal. Teasing him had become a form of retribution, turning his crank and pushing the buttons that got him steamed. Especially when he tried to be so somber and sophisticated about his anger. But lately, it had turned into a contest. Just once, she wanted to elicit an emotion from Daniel other than cold disdain and sarcasm. She wanted him to yell passionately, to react with fire. But that would never happen. The good doctor had a patent on sobriety.

"You know…" Lace twisted so she could see the woman better, and an evil thought took root in her brain. It was terribly mean, but he deserved it, the self-righteous prig.

"Dan doesn't particularly like shy women. And he pretends to be a stick in the mud, but I know better. He likes an aggressive woman who isn't afraid to say what she wants, to tell him how she feels and how she wants to make him feel. Maybe all of you have just been too subtle."

"Do you really think so?"

Lace grinned at her hopeful tone. "Trust me. Give him your best shot. He'll love all the attention."

Daniel walked back in then and, without a word to Lace, began preparing a shot. She could feel the cool air on her backside and gave a sigh of grateful relief when the nurse, now watching Daniel with a calculating eye, pulled a sheet over her. She stared at the back of Daniel's dark head. "What are you doing?"

"I'm going to give you an injection of lidocaine to numb your…the area, and then I'll stitch you up."

"Daniel…"

"Do you have the name of the dog's owner? The police will want to know and we need to fill out a dog-bite card."

"Forget it. I know the guy and I know the dog, and he's not really a bad dog, he just got overly excited."

"Lace." He turned to face her and his expression was grave. "What if the dog got excited around a kid? What happened to you could have been ten times worse with a small child."

"You're right. I'm sorry."

Daniel looked surprised at her quick agreement. His dark brows raised a fraction, and then he nodded.

Lace pondered the problem. Something had to be done. Just the thought of that dog sinking his teeth into a child chilled her to the bone. But though the dog was a pain, always barking and obviously too undisciplined, she also knew the man was lonely, the dog his only friend. "What will happen?"

"I'm not sure. First we'll make certain the dog has had all his shots."

"He has. The owner hurried to assure me of that after he got the dog to turn me loose."

Daniel winced. "Damn." His expression was unreadable, but Lace thought she saw a bit of sympathy. Impossible.

"I can't believe you're not mad about this." As Daniel spoke, he moved behind her and lifted the sheet. Lace wanted to die. She wanted to tell him to close his eyes, to wear blinders; she did not want to be vulnerable with this man. She began chattering to distract herself.

"I'm not happy to have gotten bitten, but it was an accident. The dog isn't normally vicious, in fact, it's still more a puppy than not. It's just so darn big. Maybe it should go to an obedience school or something. He's usually such a nice big ugly dog. And— Ouch!"

"I'm sorry."

He didn't sound sorry and she gave him a suspicious frown. "That hurt."

"You'll be numb in a minute." His gaze, damn him, remained glued to her backside. "So, how did you get here, by the way?"

Though she knew he asked only to distract her, she appreciated his efforts. It wasn't like Daniel to treat her with consideration, but then she supposed this was his doctor mode and he took his work very seriously. "This nice guy who was close by gave me a ride. I couldn't drive myself, and he had a big back seat, and vinyl upholstery in his car, so I figured I couldn't do much damage…"

"You rode in here with a stranger?"

The nurse was all ears, so Lace couldn't say precisely what

she wished. She wanted to slap him, hard, for his damned presumptions and biased opinions of her. She did the next best thing. She grinned at him.

"Yeah. He was a real sweetheart. He offered to stay and wait for me, but I told him not to bother. He took my number so he could check on me later."

Daniel stared at her, his expression a cross between outrage, disbelief and sheer disgust. His lips were flattened together and his dark brows lowered behind his glasses. His disappointment was plain, but resigned, as if he expected no better of her. Lace tried to laugh, but couldn't quite pull it off. Damn him for always judging her. The man who'd given her the lift had to be around seventy and he'd had his wife of a similar age with him. She'd seen them both in the apartment complex many times, and on the trip to the hospital, they'd doted on her as if she'd been their only grandchild.

His censure hurt, and she heard herself saying, "It's not really like you think—"

But he cut her off. "It doesn't matter, Lace. How you live your life is of no concern to me."

She should have known better than to try to explain to him, the discriminating prude. He didn't want to know the truth about her. And until this moment, she hadn't cared. She decided it was the loss of blood that had temporarily rendered her sensitive to his censure. He was only a man, like many other unenlightened men, and his opinion didn't amount to a hill of beans.

In a sweet tone she said, "Did you expect me to limp in, Daniel, trailing blood in my wake?"

He ignored her. "When was the last time you had a tetanus shot?"

His lack of reaction deflated her. "I have no idea."

He took care of that in short order, only this time she didn't even flinch. Daniel still scowled, but there was also a look of concern on his face and Lace wondered at the seldom seen view. She knew what an excellent doctor he was. Not only did Annie brag on him constantly, but Lace visited the hospital often with her—especially if she knew Annie would be seeing Daniel—and Lace had witnessed the amount of respect given him, the way patients responded to him. He was a wonderful doctor, a sinfully handsome man, and he disapproved of her mightily.

At present, he was busy studying her bottom in great detail. Her eyes nearly crossed at the discomfort of it.

"You're a real mess, Lace. We'll need about fifty subcuticular stitches—"

"Excuse me?" That sounded rather horrific and it unnerved her enough to counteract her embarrassment. She twisted her head around to watch him.

"Stitches in the underneath layer," Daniel explained, his fingers lightly exploring though she couldn't feel a thing, could only watch as his large hand coasted over her exposed flesh. "Another fifty on top. You won't be able to sit for a while, and you should try to keep any stress off the area."

"No deep knee bends, huh?"

Nervousness made her something of a smart-ass, but she couldn't seem to help herself. Daniel didn't appear to mind this time. "I'll give you a prescription for pain and one for oral antibiotics. I'll need to see you again in forty-eight hours to change the dressing, then after that, if all looks well, you can change the dressing yourself. The nurse will write out instructions for you to use a mixture of half-strength hydrogen peroxide. You'll want to watch for signs of infection, increasing pain, redness, swelling. There's going to be a lot of bruising."

"There goes my photo shoot."

Daniel made a sound of disgust, and Lace hid her smile. He'd started to sound too detached there for a moment, but she'd easily brought him back around.

They sat in silence for few moments, other than Daniel and the nurse murmuring to each other as he put in the stitches.

Lace tried to think of other things. Unfortunately, every other thing she thought of still involved her with her pants off and Daniel looking at her.

"So if your savior left already, how do you plan to get home?"

The suddenness of his voice, the growling tone, made her jump. "I hadn't thought about it. I was more concerned with getting here at the time. But I don't look forward to throwing myself facedown in the back of a taxi, if that's what you want to know! Especially given the fact you ruined my slacks."

"If you recall, it was the dog that took a hunk out of you and your pants, not me. But I can give you some scrubs to wear home. That's not a problem."

He stared at Lace a moment more while she struggled to turn on her side and keep the sheet in place at the same time. He looked annoyed and angry and then he threw up his arms. "I suppose I'll just have to drive you home."

Lace stared, not at all amused. "You're kidding, right?"

"My shift actually ended just as you came in. I'm ready to leave, so it won't be any bother. And as you've pointed out to me many times, I drive a disgustingly sedate sedan with a *big back seat*." His gaze scanned her from head to toe. "You'll fit."

Lace didn't know what to think. On the one hand, Daniel was a very conscientious fellow. It could just be that he felt somehow obligated, regardless of his personal dislike of her, to see her settled safely. After all, he'd made her his patient, and she and Annie were very good friends, despite his edict to the contrary. He loved his little sister like crazy, so he wouldn't want her upset. But somehow it felt like more than that. And under no condition did she want to be alone with Daniel when she wasn't up to snuff. He'd make verbal mincemeat out of her, and she couldn't accept the defeat. Right now she ached all over, and she still suffered lingering humiliation. She wasn't in proper form to do battle with the big bad doctor.

"I could call Annie instead."

"Annie and Max have gone Christmas shopping. The malls are having a midnight sale, and Annie will make Max use every minute till then."

"Oh." Max was the middle brother. A real Lothario, but also a sweetheart, when someone understood him. "I forgot."

"Then you already knew?"

She nodded absently. "Max had invited me along." Then she slanted Daniel a look, realizing what he would say and wanting to beat him to the punch. Usually, that was her only defense against his criticism. "Max fancies himself in lust with me, and evidently isn't hampered by your scruples. Your younger brother isn't one to give up easily."

Daniel looked ready to explode. His neck turned red, his frown became fearsome, and he stalked away. He stood with his back to her for long moments. But when he faced her again, his expression was controlled. He pulled off his glasses and polished them on his sleeve. "Max has a little maturing to do yet. He'll gain a finer sense of judgment with age, I'm sure."

"Ouch." She feigned a grimace. "Going for the jugular now, are you? And here I am, a lady in distress, without the means to fight you." She batted her eyes at him, just to make certain he'd caught her double entendre.

Daniel frowned at her, then spoke to the nurse. "Fill out the dog-bite card, then get Ms. McGee some scrubs and help her into them. I'll pull my car around to the front."

Lace would have kicked him if she was sure she wouldn't hurt herself. "I haven't agreed to go with you, you know."

He never paused on his way out the door. "I don't recall asking you."

She sighed. Now she was in for it. Even her taunting hadn't turned him away, as it usually did. Why would Daniel do such a thing? It unnerved her, but then, the man himself unnerved her. Still, she liked the way he polished his glasses, the way he held his shoulders so straight. Actually, on some basic, primal level, she liked a lot of things about him.

Too bad he was such a rotten chauvinistic jerk.

Chapter Two

"YOUR CAR SMELLS like you, Daniel. All spicy and manly and—" she drew a deep breath "—nice."

Daniel had to use all his concentration to keep them on the road. Ever since he'd settled Lace—very gently—into his back seat, she'd been hitting him with little comments like that. They were getting tougher to ignore. His touted self-control held only by a ragged thread.

He glanced into the rearview mirror and saw her resting on her side, managing to look elegant and sexy in a pair of worn scrubs with her black cloak tossed over her like a blanket. The blue color of the scrubs seemed out of place on her. Lace wore black almost without exception. She did it for effect, he was certain, and he had to admit, she always looked striking. The contrast of her pale blond hair and bright green eyes against the black made a very enticing picture.

But then, she'd look every bit as enticing with no clothes on at all.

He chased that errant thought right out of his mind and cleared his throat with difficulty. "That's the leather you smell. My car may be sensible, but it's also top of the line."

"Like you, Daniel?"

He managed a scoffing sound. Damn her, why wouldn't she let up on him? Usually her little barbs and sexual innuendos were well timed, not issued with the rapid-fire succession of a submachine gun blast. He tried to change the subject. "How're you feeling? You holding up okay?"

"Don't worry about me, you'll give me a stroke. It's not what I'm used to from you. The shock could well kill me."

"Lace…"

"I'm fine. Just a little drowsy."

She sounded drowsy, sexy and slumberous, and his undisciplined mind supplied erotic images of her first waking in the morning after a long night of lovemaking. He had to grind his teeth together. With a slightly deeper tone to his voice, he said, "I'll have you home and settled in soon. You're in pain and you need to rest."

With a little sigh, she shifted and he again looked in the rearview mirror. She tried to hide her discomfort from him and that angered him. He didn't want her to be stoic, didn't want her consideration. He wanted to relish his dislike of her, to think only on what he knew was right and true about her.

He'd written her a prescription for pain pills, but now it struck him that she had no way to get them. He and Annie no longer discussed her, since it seemed a bone of contention, but he knew enough about her to know she was alone here in Ohio, with no family close by to lend her a hand. She couldn't very well go after the prescription herself, and with Max and Annie unavailable, she might not have anyone she could call if she needed help. The next few days would be rough for her.

For now, at least, she needed him.

Just that quickly he decided to fetch the pills for her to make certain she was able to settle comfortably. He was off tomorrow, and he had nothing more important planned than his own gift shopping to do. With Christmas only two weeks away, he was running out of time. But he could spare a day or two for Lace. After all, his male intellect reasoned, his sister thought of Lace as family. And though they were at odds a lot more these days thanks to Lace's interference, he cared a great deal about his sister.

Daniel pulled into the lot in front of her apartment building and turned off the car. Once before he'd been here, to pick up Annie when her car had died. Though he hadn't gone inside, his brain had memorized everything about the location of Lace's home. He knew which apartment was hers on the second landing, and now he realized there was a long flight of steps inside.

He looked over the seat at Lace while she shoved herself more or less upright, balancing on her uninjured hip. The effort caused her to pale and grimace in pain and he silently cursed her stubbornness even as he ordered, "Sit still, Lace. I'll carry you up."

He heard her strained laughter as he got out of the car, but it didn't matter. He'd made up his mind, and he knew his duty, repugnant as it might be. He shook his head at himself. Touching Lace wouldn't be the least bit displeasing. He didn't like her, but he wasn't dead, and as a man, he was more than a little aware of her allure.

When he opened her door, his intent obvious, she gave him a wary look and said, "Daniel, really, this isn't... Don't you dare! *Put me down!*"

He didn't give her a chance to argue with him. He tightened his hold and carefully scooped her up, making certain to keep his arms high on her back and low on her thighs so he wouldn't add to her pain. He hefted her out of the car while she made a loud and furious ruckus.

"Good grief, are you nuts?" She gasped and sputtered and tried to twist away. "What will my neighbors say?"

"I don't give a damn what they say." He bumped the car door shut with his hip, jarring her slightly.

Lace made a small sound, then wrapped her arms around his neck and held on, her grip almost painful. "You're being totally ridiculous, Daniel."

"If you'd stop clucking and carrying on, no one will even

notice we're here. Quiet down and hold still before you hurt yourself."

They entered the building—and ran into three neighbors. Lace hid her face in his neck. Soft hair brushed his cheek and he couldn't help but breathe in her musky feminine scent. She felt warm and sweet and…right in his arms. Her plump rounded breasts pressed into his ribs and her thighs felt womanly soft draped over his arm. Damn, but he would not allow his physical attraction to her to override his common sense.

He stared at all three people, daring any of them to ask.

One man stepped forward, twisting his hands together. "Is she all right? Lace, honey, how bad was it?"

The dog owner, Daniel decided, and his scowl deepened. The man appeared to be in his mid-forties, had at least three thick gold chains around his neck, and obviously enjoyed lifting weights. Daniel tightened his hold possessively—not that *he* was possessive. "She got close to a hundred stitches. The dog was reported, of course."

Lace bit his ear. He almost dropped her he was so surprised. It wasn't that it had hurt, because she'd only given him a small nip, but it had nearly buckled his knees. The feel of her open mouth on his skin, the touch of her sharp little teeth, her warm breath, had felt very like a lover's nibble, and suddenly every male hormone he possessed screamed an alert. It took every ounce of his flagging control to keep his expression impassive.

Lace leaned away from him, sending a smile to the other man. "Hello, Frank. I'm going to be fine, so you can stop worrying. And I've decided not to press charges this time. But I will have to insist that you check into some training for him. He can't just go around losing control like that. And from now on, make certain he's kept on a leash."

Relief spread over Frank's face, despite her stern tone. He appeared ready to fall at Lace's feet in gratitude. "I'd already decided the very same thing, Lace, honey. And I really am sorry. I swear I won't let him loose again, now that I know there's a problem. I just don't know what got into him."

"The cat that tried to use me as a shield enticed him beyond his endurance, I'm sure."

"I know he was after the cat, but he's never so much as even growled at a person before."

Lace reached out to pat his shoulder, leaving it to Daniel to balance her weight. "I'll be fine, Frank, really. The important thing is to make certain it never happens again."

Frank turned to the other two men, both older, but still not *old.* "We've been talking, and if there's anything you need, just let one of us know. We'll be glad to help you out while you recuperate."

Daniel finally found his voice. Here was the perfect solution, a way for him to leave her, in familiar hands, so he could go home and retire after his long day. He opened his mouth and said, "That won't be necessary. I'll take care of her."

Silence fell. Daniel heard the words, knew he'd said them himself, and almost shook his head to deny it anyway. He didn't want to take care of Lace. Good grief, he didn't even like the woman. He vigorously *disliked* her! He disapproved of her and her immoderate effect on him. He racked his brain for a tactful way out of the predicament he'd just put himself in when Lace leaned back to see his face.

She looked shocked and ready to protest, which irritated him even more. Perversely, he decided he *would* hang around and there was no way she could stop him. "Not a word out of you, lady. And if you're done socializing, I'd like to get to your place. You're not heavy, but then, you're no featherweight, either."

The men scrambled away, saying hasty good-nights as Daniel started up the stairs. Lace grinned and rubbed her fingertips over his nape. He felt the caress all the way to his suddenly tight abdomen.

"Putting a strain on your back, am I?"

"No more than you strain my patience," he muttered, and

added, "All that male adoration piled on your beautiful head was enough to make me ill. Now I know why you chose this apartment. Are there any females in residence at all?"

Lace cupped his cheek, forcing him to look at her. "Beautiful head? By any chance, was that an actual compliment I just heard, Daniel?"

His foot paused on the next step and he blinked at her. Her smile teased him and her fingertips were gentle on his jaw. His glasses slipped down his nose a fraction of an inch.

"I didn't mean it," he growled, then stomped the rest of the way up the staircase. When they reached her door, he asked, "Where are your keys?"

"In my cloak pocket. Just a minute." She fished them out, then leaned over and unlocked the door. She didn't turn the doorknob or open it, however. "Thank you for seeing me home, Daniel. I appreciate it. Now when your sister sings your praises, I suppose I'll have to agree just a bit—on rare and specific occasions."

She smiled at him, and Daniel only stared back. Irritating female. "Open the door, Lace."

Her brow puckered and her look became wary. "You can put me down now. I'm perfectly capable of walking in on my own steam."

"Open the door. I've gotten you this far, I might as well see it through. Besides, you'll need some help getting settled."

"Oh? And do you escort all your patients home from the hospital and give them personal assistance?"

It was a strain, but he managed to keep his tone even. He would not let her provoke him. "Only the ones who ingratiate themselves on my family. Annie would never forgive me if I left you to fend for yourself. Now, open the door."

"I don't want you in my apartment."

She'd looked down when she said that, and suspicions grew in rapid succession. He imagined mirrors on the ceilings, sex manuals strewn about, maybe a man or two tucked into the corners awaiting her direction. For some reason, his temper simmered and he reached past her for the doorknob.

"Dammit, Daniel, this is my home and you're not invited in!"

"Hush, Lace."

"That's a reoccurring tune with you, isn't it? Any time I inject a little reason into this bizarre situation, you tell me to hush."

She stiffened in his arms as he stepped inside—and stopped. This was not the home he'd envisioned for Lace McGee—love expert, sex guru, relationship connoisseur. There wasn't a single black item to be seen, no obvious suggestive reading material, nothing to indicate the woman he knew—the woman he held in his arms—might abide here.

This looked like a grandmother's retreat. Doilies covered every surface of the battered antique tables, and Tiffany lamps sent soft glows of color everywhere. The couch was overstuffed, brightly floral, soft. Handwoven rag rugs decorated polished hardwood floors.

Daniel stared and then stared some more. For the moment, he forgot he held Lace. "I've just stepped out of the tornado and into Oz."

She squirmed in his arms. "Shut up, Daniel, and put me down."

She startled him out of his study. Slowly, he let her slip down his body, his gaze on her face. Her cheeks flushed and her beautiful green eyes avoided his. He held her carefully until she'd gained her balance, favoring her injured side. "Does your mother or some distant aunt live here with you, Lace?"

"I don't have a distant aunt."

"Lace?"

"Of course not." She still wouldn't look at him, which irked his temper again. First she baited him with endless sexual innuendos, and now she played shy.

"Then who decorated this place?"

She hit his shoulder with a small fist. "I did, you idiot. And there's nothing wrong with my home, so stop gawking."

She turned away and started—with an awkward hobbling gait—down the hall. Daniel looked around once more, and followed her. "But there's so much...color."

"Yeah, so? I enjoy color."

She sounded her most belligerent, and he frowned. "No, you don't. You like black. You always wear black. Your car is black. Even your luggage is black, for crying out loud. I bet your panties are even black, though I couldn't tell since they were covered with so much blood."

She glared over her shoulder, sending him a look of acute dislike, then tried to stalk into her bedroom. But with her recent injury, the effect was minimal. The numbing would have worn off by now, and it had to hurt like the very devil. Daniel followed her, thinking to explain that he'd go get her pain pills. He walked into her bedroom and stopped cold in his tracks. No, it couldn't be. If the living room had been a surprise, this was enough to jump-start his heart.

At least a dozen small velvet pillows in a variety of soft muted hues were tossed atop a candy-striped bedspread with a dark pink dust ruffle. The sheer gauzy material that served as window coverings in a variety of pastel shades flowed across the glass in no particular order. He could easily imagine the room bathed in a pastel-hued rainbow whenever the sunlight shone through.

She wasn't the neatest of people. There were clothes—all black—strewed over a rocker and the end of the bed. And peeking out from the under the bed... Daniel bent to pick up the gleaming material, then held it in the air. Panties. Tiny, shimmering, lime green panties that probably weighed no more than half an ounce. He tried to imagine her in them— and managed only too well.

Lace snatched the panties out of his hand with a low growl. "Okay, Daniel. I'm home. I'm settled. I'm going to change clothes and go to bed and try to forget about big-jawed dogs and arrogant pushy doctors. You can leave now. Your *duty* is complete."

"You wear lime green underwear?"

"Oh, for Pete's sake!" She looked apoplectic. "What do you care what color underwear I wear?"

His brows pulled down tight enough to give him a headache. Confusion swirled, his world tilted. And it was all her fault, the little witch. Why did she keep doing this to him? "I don't understand, Lace."

She huffed out a breath and glared up at him. He stared right back. He was bigger, so therefore it stood to reason he could be twice as stubborn. Finally she gave up. "I'm horrible at matching stuff up, okay? Look around. It's like a circus on the Fourth of July in here. But I *love* color, I really do. All colors, every shade, deep and sinful, light and playful. I need color. It's just that I could never get the knack of putting clothes together, and since I have to appear in public a lot, I just decided it was easier to stick to simple basic black. That way, when I'm in a hurry, I can pick out my outfit without worrying whether or not I'll match or be put together properly."

"You wear black because you have no fashion sense?" His poor suspicious brain couldn't quite assimilate all these new notions, not when they went against everything he thought he knew about her. "It isn't because it's dramatic and adds a special effect to your blond hair and green eyes?"

Slowly, her most provocative smile appeared and she looked at him through her lashes. "Why, Daniel. You've noticed my eyes? And my hair? Was that another compliment, by any chance?"

He took two steps back and his jaw clenched. "I didn't mean it." She continued to grin and he sought a safer topic. "I'm going to run out and get your prescriptions while you get settled in bed. No pajamas."

"Are you suggesting I sleep naked?"

His hands shook and he wanted to smack her for planting that sizzling mental picture firmly into his beleaguered mind. "Put on a gown." His gaze went to the panties she still held. They looked like a bright neon beacon, calling to him, and he added, "Forget underwear. It'll only irritate your wound."

"I never sleep in underwear."

His heart tripped against his ribs and he felt her purring tone clear to his groin. With strong resolution, he kept his gaze on her face. "Do you need any help, Lace?"

"I can manage. But take the spare key off the wall in the kitchen. That way you can let yourself back in. I'll just get myself settled in bed—to wait for you."

Damn her, she was really enjoying herself now. He should just leave. She deserved a little discomfort. Eventually someone would get the medicine for her, and she could get her jollies torturing some other poor male instead of him.

But he couldn't do it. Lace needed him, curse her headstrong, sexy hide, and he told himself his decision to look after her had nothing to do with any personal lust for her. It was just that he was used to protecting and caring for others. It had become a habit, started the day his mother was buried and his father made it clear he couldn't overcome his own grief, much less that of his children. Someone had needed to hug his little sister at night when she cried. And someone had needed to reassure his brother Max when he'd become so withdrawn and sullen.

Annie and Max had needed him then. They needed him still. They looked to him for guidance, almost as a father figure, and Daniel knew they cared about Lace as a friend. He was a doctor, and the patriarch of the family despite his father's flighty presence. It was his duty to see Lace situated as comfortably as possible.

His reasoning sounded lame even to his own ears, but he wasn't about to delve any further for motivation. Therein lay personal disaster and he knew it. He took one more glance around at Lace's bedroom, then stormed out, overcome by mixed feelings. This was either the worst idea he'd ever had—*or the best.*

"I FOUND AN OLD BLACK T-SHIRT to sleep in so I wouldn't further lacerate your expectations of my wardrobe."

Lace waited for some response, but Daniel only nodded. He'd been withdrawn and almost wary since returning a few minutes ago. Very unlike his usual confrontational self. His cheeks were ruddy from the cold, and his dark hair was mussed from the wind. He pulled his glasses off and polished them on his sleeve, removing a few snowflakes. She enjoyed the sight of his light brown, thickly lashed eyes, how intense they could be, how serious. He slid the glasses back onto his straight nose and went to get a glass of water from her kitchen.

Lace kept the bedspread pulled up to her throat. She was on her back, with a pillow propped beneath her leg on her injured side; she felt vulnerable with Daniel there, aware of her awkward discomfort. But when Daniel leaned down to hand her the pill and the water she noticed how rigid he looked, and it annoyed her. He always acted as if he expected her to sexually accost his poor male body at any given moment—and like he'd hate it. Unaccountable prude.

Pain pulled at her, but still she managed a small taunting smile, knowing how he'd react to it. She made a point of letting her fingertips graze his palm as she took the pill from him, and rather than hold the glass herself, she held his wrist, which forced him to tilt the glass to her lips.

He stared at her mouth and his nostrils flared. The hypocrite. He might disdain her supposed lack of morals, but he fantasized the same as she did. It was men like him that kept her profession thriving. His antiquated notions of what was right for a woman, in comparison to the acceptable standards for a man, made her furious. At least half her calls at the radio station dealt with issues over the double standard of sexual freedom for men and women.

She gave him a sloe-eyed look and smiled. "Mmm. Thank you, Daniel."

"You're welcome."

He sounded like a frog, and Lace had to bite back her satisfied chuckle. "I never noticed before what big hands you have." She pretended to study his hand—then came to the realization he really did have big hands. His fingers were long and blunt and smooth. A doctor's capable hands. She shivered with a newly awakened awareness.

"Are you cold?" As he asked, Daniel pulled away from her. "I could get you another blanket."

"I'm fine. Will the pill make me sleepy?"

"Probably." His gaze darted around her room again. He kept looking at everything, and every time he ended up shaking his head.

His disapproval was obvious, and she should have been used to it by now. In her mind, there were two major groups of men. Those who wanted to take advantage of her *expertise,* and those who discounted her expertise as ludicrous simply because she was a young woman. Her mother had always had a similar problem with men who wanted her only for her money and men who thought her money would never buy her any class. Still, her mother had kept trying. Lace had no intention of making that same mistake.

She understood Daniel and his attitudes. By her own design, she courted his disdain. She used it as her defense against him, and Annie had backed her up, respecting her wishes to present herself in any light she chose as long as she didn't have to lie to Daniel. But since Daniel never bothered to ask for the truth, Annie could leave him to his ridiculous beliefs. Daniel would never really know her. And that fact made her a little sad, because she loved Annie. She was the closest friend Lace had ever had. Even Max was okay once you got a handle on him and his robust disregard for propriety. The middle brother did like to shake people up, most especially his big brother. Lace rather liked that about Max. It gave them something in common.

But Daniel... He continued to look around her room, his expression almost comical in its fascinated study. "I didn't leave any other unmentionables laying about."

He turned back to her, shaken from his engrossed examination of her room. "What?"

"If you're really that curious, I keep my panties in the third drawer of the bureau." She waved in that direction. "Feel free."

A red flush stained his neck and his brows snapped down. "You really don't possess a single ounce of decorum, do you?"

"Me?" She'd gotten her desired result, but now her own temper ignited. It was very late, she was tired, and it had been an eventful day. "You're the one who keeps gawking! You're the one who forced yourself into my home and picked up my underwear and keeps looking around like Sherlock Holmes trying to find some wicked evidence of my sordid love life."

He seemed stunned by her outburst—but no more so than she. Generally, she was even-tempered and almost never raised her voice. She'd honed the knack of cutting obnoxious men down with a single sneer or a well-chosen phrase. Daniel, however, tended to bring out the worst in her. She scowled at him, then grumbled, "I'm sorry."

Daniel shook his head, his gaze glued to her face, probing and serious. "No, it was my fault. I didn't mean to make you uncomfortable, and I certainly didn't mean to...gawk. It's just that I never expected..."

"I know. You thought I hated color."

He pulled up a chair and sat beside the bed. "I like your apartment, Lace. It's pretty."

"And colorful."

He laughed. "Well, yeah, but in a nice way."

She studied his handsome face in some surprise. It was the

first time she could ever recall him laughing with her. "I like the way you laugh, Daniel. You should do it more often. Annie assures me you're a happy fellow, but you always seem so staid around me."

At first he looked defensive, and then he sighed. "I suppose I am overly serious at times. But then, that's the life of a doctor, especially in the emergency room. There's not a lot of time left for goofing off."

Lace thought about Daniel's life. He hadn't had an easy childhood, not with his mother dying when he was so young. Annie said he'd decided to become a doctor then. According to Annie, Daniel had been twelve years old when he'd sworn he'd learn how to save people. Perhaps that was enough to take the gaiety out of anyone's life.

Her own mother had never had it easy, and her vulnerability had added to her troubles, especially when it came to relationships. But at least she'd grown up with a mother, and she and Lace had enjoyed a unique life together. Not always a happy one, but it had its special moments.

On impulse, Lace reached out and took Daniel's hand. It felt warm and strong, and she sighed. "I don't make it very easy on you, do I?"

He looked down at their clasped hands for a moment, his expression very contemplative as his fingers curled around hers. "You like to make me a little crazy, I think."

"Actually, I love it." She grinned, feeling almost drunk from the pain medicine and a little too relaxed. "You're so easy to provoke."

"So you love color and you love tormenting me. What else do you love, Lace?"

He was very serious now. Lace realized that for the first time, in some very minute way, he was actually trying to get to know her. Caution warred with the need to share herself, to erase the misconceptions between them. But she didn't dare. Regardless of what she said to him, they'd never see things the same way. They were simply too different.

She settled on keeping things light. It wouldn't be safe to share herself with a man like Daniel. He'd always disapprove of her, and she couldn't get involved with a man who didn't trust and understand her. She shrugged. "I love little children, their honesty and their laughter and their chubby pink cheeks. And I love commercials. They're much better than most television programs."

"Baby cheeks and commercials, huh?"

She could hear the laughter in his tone and she smiled. "I love sunshine and swimming, but also the purity of a first snow. I love talking with people and maybe sometimes helping them. I love thick cotton socks that keep my feet warm on a cold day, and sheets fresh from the laundry, and warm spring breezes. And most of all, I love Christmas carols."

Daniel tightened his hand on hers and looked…disturbed. His tone was very low and deep when he spoke. "I like Christmas carols, too. My mom used to start singing them in mid-October and kept it up till the New Year. I have just about every Christmas CD ever produced."

"Do you sing along with them?"

"When there's no one around to be offended by my less than sterling voice."

"Me, too. At the top of my lungs."

His thumb rubbed over her knuckles, then he said softly, "You don't have a Christmas tree."

Uh-oh. Just that quickly they left the lighthearted stuff and entered into the emotional. She pulled her hand away, using the excuse of smoothing her blankets. Her head felt muddled with fatigue and medicine and the newness of speaking so casually with Daniel. It was dark outside with only a little moonlight coming through her rainbow-sheathed window. Quiet surrounded them, his expression was intent. And he'd seen her bare backside. Suddenly things seemed far too intimate.

Without looking at him, she said, "A tree seems like a lot of fuss and bother for just me." She hoped she sounded casual, not maudlin. Christmas was a hard time for a person alone, but she didn't want him to know it. Regardless of this moment, they didn't like each other, and she couldn't give him future ammunition to use against her.

"You don't entertain on the holidays? You don't have any family to visit with you?"

"My mother lives in Florida but she travels over the holidays, visiting all her...friends." The reality of that hurt, and she closed her eyes to hide her emotions from him. The medicine pulled at her, numbing her wits, and she heard herself whisper, "I know you won't believe it, but I really don't entertain all that often. I'm not much of a partying person."

He didn't say a word, and she finally opened her eyes to meet his gaze, though forcing her lids to lift wasn't easy. Rather than seeing the disbelief she expected, he looked thoughtful. "Daniel?"

His name sounded slurred, and she frowned. Daniel reached out and smoothed a lock of hair away from her temple. The tender touch sent her pulse rioting. Her head pounded, her stomach felt jumpy.

A reaction to the pain pills, she decided. She never did react well to medication.

"Go to sleep, Lace. Just give in to the pills and relax. Everything's going to be okay."

She didn't understand that cryptic comment, but her awareness was fading without her permission.

Her eyes closed and her body seemed to sigh into the mattress. She heard Daniel say softly, "If you need anything, I'll be here."

"Here?" The word emerged as a mere whisper, barely heard by her own ears.

"I'm staying the night, Lace." His fingers touched her cheek, her chin. "I don't want to leave you alone."

She struggled to open her eyes again, to get her mouth to work. She didn't want him in her apartment all night, didn't want to be indebted to him. Most of all, she didn't want to be vulnerable, to have him watch her in her sleep, explore her home without her awareness. But it was too late.

She fell asleep with his promise still in her ears and his large strong hand holding her own.

And surprisingly, she felt comforted by his presence.

Chapter Three

THE SORENESS WENT BONE DEEP, tugging at her, making her temples pound. It hadn't been a restful night, despite the pain medication, but Daniel had done his best to assist her. Maybe that was the problem: Daniel.

Throughout the night, whenever she'd so much as move, Daniel would suddenly be there, at her bedside, tending her, speaking to her in soft, soothing tones. So unlike the Daniel she knew. *So tempting.*

Walking was a definite chore this morning. Even her back and hips hurt. Probably from the awkward way she'd positioned herself in the bed. She found a robe, a pale pink, soft cotton piece of nonsense that fueled her sense of whimsy and completely hid her black T-shirt. She stared at it, wondering if the soft color or the sweet ruffles would lacerate Daniel's sensibilities. He did seem to have a thing about mixing her with color.

Shrugging, she slipped it on and tied the belt tightly. After brushing her teeth and washing her face, she made her way cautiously to the kitchen to start the coffee.

On her way past the living room she heard a soft snore and froze. No man had ever slept in her apartment; no man had ever even *been* in her apartment. How it made her feel now, to have Daniel snoring on her couch, couldn't quite be measured, not first thing in the morning, without coffee and with too little sleep.

Investigating, she inched farther into the darkened living room, following the low sound of deep male breathing until she stood beside the short, fat couch. Daniel, overflowing the squat piece of furniture at every angle, lay on his back, his shirt gone, his belt removed and his pants unbuttoned. His bare feet, long and narrow and sexy really, when she took the time to look at them, hung over the opposite arm of the couch. His face was turned slightly toward her, his lips parted, his silky brown hair mussed and falling over his forehead. Beard shadow darkened his face and his thick, gorgeous lashes rested on his high cheekbones.

She forgot her pain. She forgot her coffee.

He had a lot of soft-looking, light brown hair on his chest; she liked that. His shoulders were hard, the flesh pulled smooth and taut over bone and sinew and muscle. With one arm propped behind his head, she could see the flex of his biceps, the thickness of his forearm, his obvious strength.

But she'd always known he was strong, at least, in the most important ways. He'd cared for his family when no else would or could, and continued to care for them, even now when they were all grown. He handled crises at the hospital every day in his sure, confident manner. He had conviction and deter-mination down to a fine art. She admired him, even though she didn't want to.

Seeing his physical strength now shouldn't do this to her, shouldn't make her heart flutter, or her stomach curl tight. But it did. She looked from his chest to his flat belly, not ridged with muscles, just lean and firm and manly. Through the open clasp of his pants she could see the start of a dark, silky line of hair, the elastic of white briefs, and below that... She in-haled thickly through her nose.

"Good morning."

Startled, she jerked her gaze to a more appropriate place,

like his face, and then from embarrassment because he watched her so intently, to the kitchen. "I was going to start some coffee."

He didn't move and his voice stayed deep and lazy, amused. "You were looking at me."

"You snore."

Chuckling, he rubbed his face and stretched like a big, confident cat, and once again her gaze roamed over him. His dress slacks were badly wrinkled and without his glasses, he looked… She liked his glasses, but he looked softer without them, not as stern. It unnerved her.

He sat up and she noticed the flex and roll of muscles in his chest and shoulders. He yawned hugely, with no sense of his polite, restrained manner, and then grinned at her. "This couch makes a terrible bed."

"Maybe that's because it was never meant to be a bed."

"After last night, I can understand why." He stood, and when she didn't back up, their toes almost touched. Reaching out, he tucked a wayward tress of hair behind her ear and stroked her cheek. "Did you finally get any sleep?"

She could smell him, a deep, dark, musky male scent that was delicious and enticing and forbidden. Why was he being so nice all of a sudden? Was this part of his solicitous doctor mode? Somehow, she didn't think so.

"I slept fine." Her voice sounded like a croak.

"Liar." He took her shoulders and moved her gently aside. "You shouldn't even be out of bed. You should have awakened me if you wanted coffee. That's what I'm here for." He urged her toward the cushions he'd just vacated. "Lie down and I'll get you a pillow."

She started to protest, but he still held her, and never in her life had she felt so tongue-tied. "Daniel…"

"Shh. How do you like your coffee?" He lifted her legs carefully up onto the couch, putting a soft cushion beneath her, situating her as if she had no strength or will at all. "Strong, I hope. I need the caffeine."

So did she. The damned couch was still warm from his body, and on it, his scent was strong, stirring her, making her think ridiculous things. The urge to reach up and pull him down with her was so acute, she had to resort to sarcasm to save herself. "I'm not an invalid, and you're not my great-aunt, so you can stop the coddling. I'm fine."

He scratched his belly, distracting her once again, before slipping on his glasses. He finger-combed his hair, and Lace watched the silky strands glide in and out of his fingers. "You're not fine. I want you to take it easy—*very easy*—for at least forty-eight hours. After that, we'll see."

"You may be used to bossing Annie and Max around, but you're not my brother."

"Not your aunt, not your brother." He touched the tip of her nose without smiling, his expression intent. "Believe me, I've never felt remotely brotherly toward you."

He turned his back on her and went into the kitchen. Lace heard the running of water, the clink of the glass carafe, the opening and closing of a cabinet. She sighed and flopped her head back to stare at the ceiling. How strange it seemed to have Daniel Sawyers in her kitchen. Beyond strange, it seemed bizarre, improbable, ridiculous. Maybe she was imagining the whole thing. Maybe...

"I'm going to take a quick shower. Sit tight. I'll be done before the coffee is."

Her eyes widened and her face felt stiff. Daniel in her shower? Naked? She'd never be able to use that shower again without wicked images invading her mind. How unfair of him to shove his way in, to dominate her thoughts and take over her home.

Used to taking care of herself, she wasn't about to let him run her life. She waited until she heard the shower start, then limped her way into the kitchen. Pain or not, she refused to be a burden, and she refused to allow Daniel to get one up on her. Who knew when he might use this damned weakness against her?

She found a refrigerated package of cinnamon rolls and put them in the oven. The coffee was almost done so she got out two large mugs, spoons, sugar, cream.

"What the hell are you doing?"

She jumped, almost dropping the napkins and jarring her leg enough that she winced in pain. Daniel, his wet hair brushed back from his forehead, his chest still damp, his lashes spiky, stood in her kitchen scowling at her. For some insane reason, she almost felt guilty. She simply couldn't reconcile this scenario with reality. No man had ever stood half-naked in her kitchen after his shower, but she could have imagined almost any other man in such a position easier than she could Daniel.

He saw her grimace of pain and moved toward her, slipping his arm around her waist. The dampness of his skin, the warmth of his bare chest, caused her to stiffen even more.

"Do you need me to carry you?"

She needed him to go away so she could stop acting like an idiot. "No. Don't touch me."

He laughed. "This show of shyness from Lace the Sex Expert? Lace the Uninhibited?"

Her head snapped around and she glared. "This show of concern from Daniel the Ice Man? Daniel the Discreet?"

The barest trace of regret clouded his eyes before he released her, his expression impassive. They stood that way for long moments, each watching the other, until finally Daniel sighed. "I understand how you might feel, Lace. I really do. I know you despise me. But right now, there are other factors involved. One, I'm a doctor, your doctor, and I'm telling you that you have to take it easy. That means staying off your feet and keeping as much stress off the injury as you can. Two, you're my little sister's best friend. I can't ignore that. Annie would have a fit if I just left you alone right now. And three, we're both adults. Surely you can behave like one."

Lace narrowed her eyes and tucked in her chin. An impressive repertoire of scathing comments, one right after the other, tripped to the tip of her tongue. She opened her mouth to blast him with her cold disdain, her well-rehearsed verses reserved for obnoxious men, and said, "I don't despise you."

He blinked twice, rapidly. She imagined she looked just as surprised. That was not what she'd intended to say. Not at all.

Daniel narrowed his eyes and rolled in his lips, his brow drawn. "Then…"

"I have things I have to do, Daniel." Escape seemed her only viable option now. "Mail to read and answer. A show to prepare. Appointments."

"You can't go out. No, Lace, don't go all stiff-faced on me. As a doctor, I'm telling you that you have to take it easy. It's icy outside. If you slip and fall, there's no telling what damage you'll add to your wound. And that's in addition to the harm you'll cause just by trudging through the snow and frigid wind. As far as your mail, I can bring it to you in bed. I have a laptop computer you can use if you'd like."

She hesitated and he seemed to explode. "Dammit, don't be an idiot! Your health is at stake here."

She slumped. "I have phone calls to make, my laundry to do…"

"I'll help you."

The laughter erupted and she clapped a hand over her mouth, then peeked up at him. "I beg your pardon?"

A red flush started at his neck and worked its way to his ears. "I'm off today. I'll run home and get a change of clothes, my laptop, and I'll pick up your mail and something for us to eat later for lunch. While you make your phone calls, I'll go downstairs and throw in some of your laundry."

She fanned her face, pretending a near swoon. "I think I need to sit down."

"No sitting. Come here. And don't shy away from me like that. Just pretend I'm one of your admirers." He hesitated. "Or lovers."

"Ha! I'm not quite that creative." She didn't add that imagining any lover was well beyond her capability.

Grinning, he said, "I know. It does stretch the boundaries of inspiration, doesn't it?" He took her arm and once again led her to the sofa. "Lie down. *Stay* down."

"I'm not a disobedient pet."

"No pet would dare be this disobedient or I'd take it to the pound. Now, I'm going to get you a few more pillows and if you need anything else, please, ask me."

Her head swam. She tried to reconcile why Daniel would be doing all this, why he'd willingly give up his day off to hang around and pester her. No logical reasons presented themselves to her bedeviled brain.

He came back and slipped one of her lemon yellow pillows under her head, another under her leg. "How's that? Are you comfortable?"

Unable to meet his gaze, she nodded. She'd never in her entire life had anyone pamper her. The feeling was unsettling, to say the least. "Thank you."

"Lace."

Lace lifted her gaze to his, confused, nervous, words beyond her. With him still leaning close, one hand on the back of the couch, the other on the cushion, they stared at each other. For long seconds their gazes held, and Daniel slowly, almost imperceptibly, leaned closer. His attention moved to her mouth. Lace parted her lips to take in a deep breath, allowing some necessary oxygen to reach her brain, and got stung by reality.

"I smell something burning."

Daniel paused. "Hmm?"

Oh, that low husky rumble. Lace realized now how dangerous this whole situation had become. Somehow in the space of a single night their antagonism had mutated into something much more elemental between men and women, something she'd never thought to deal with. Something she suspected had been there all along.

She cleared her throat. "I put rolls in the oven. They're burning."

Daniel jerked back, and with understanding came a look of appalled fascination. Lace continued to stare. She felt as though she couldn't quite breathe, as if the world had gone totally hazy. She knew better, had learned early on the ramifications of making such a horrible, ridiculous mistake. But she couldn't deny it any longer. As ill suited as they were, as much as he annoyed her and as much as she enjoyed annoying him, she lusted after Daniel Sawyers.

It was probably the fault of her new revelation that she didn't pay any attention when Daniel went to retrieve the rolls. He asked, his voice only slightly gruff, how she liked her coffee and she answered him, without thought, that she wanted it sweetened and with cream. He carried the cup to her, along with the rolls, already iced. They ate in a kind of unsettled, stunned silence.

Whatever intimacy had existed a minute ago was gone now, replaced by propriety and common sense and belated panic. Lace sipped her hot coffee and reminded herself of all the relationships that had gotten started on such a shaky foundation as lust, relationships she helped to redefine as part of her profession. She remembered all the emotional pain her mother had put herself through, trying to build on something as insubstantial as physical need. She thought of Daniel's cursed opinion of her.

And still, she wanted him.

"You're in pain again, aren't you?"

Her thoughts disrupted, Lace looked at him and shrugged. "A little." Actually more than a little. The dull throbbing discomfort in her backside had increased to the point that she didn't want to move, because moving caused a definite sharp pinch of pain.

"You need to take another pain pill."

She hated to admit he was right, but she didn't relish playing the role of the martyr, either. She started to rise, but he halted her. "I'll get it, and then I've got to get going. Promise me you'll take it easy until I get back."

So he planned to just ignore the preceding moments of passion? That figured. "You're sure you don't mind doing this?"

"I believe I was rather insistent."

"All right. Suit yourself. It's not often a girl gets to be treated like a queen. Maybe I can even find a small bell somewhere that I can ring when I want you. I'll just pretend you're my erstwhile slave, awaiting my meanest direction. What do you think?"

"I think you're pushing your luck."

Lace chuckled. "Just teasing. I'll be a good queen and rest here while I make my phone calls. That should take me at least an hour."

He brought the phone, her phone book, some of the correspondence that required a personal call, and a pen and paper to her. Lace wouldn't have been surprised if he'd set a glass and water pitcher beside her, he seemed so diligent in his efforts to please.

He turned to her as he shrugged into his shirt. She found the process fascinating. Men did things differently, moved differently, even breathed differently. Seeing Daniel in the act of something as mundane as dressing proved fascinating when compared to how her own body moved while performing the same duty. She wished she could watch him shave, though he looked good, rugged, with whiskers on his lean cheeks.

"What do you like to eat? I'll pick something up for a late lunch."

"Mexican," she said without hesitation. "Something hot and spicy and with lots of sauce."

Daniel laughed. "At least that doesn't surprise me. Somehow I knew you'd be a spicy kind of woman."

Lace tilted her head and looked at him with lowered brows.

He pulled on his shoes, still grinning. "No offense, Lace. Just a joke."

"What about you? What will you eat?"

"Mexican is fine by me."

"Ha! Now that does surprise a body, doesn't it? I mean, I definitely *never* thought of you as a spicy kind of man."

He stood and slipped on his coat. On his way out the door, he stopped to look at her over his shoulder. "One of these days, I may just surprise you."

Lace felt her mouth fall open, but he was already gone, the door closing softly behind him.

"It all comes back to how you feel about the whole thing, Renee. If you like him playing the dominant role, if it satisfies you, then there's nothing in the world wrong with it."

Daniel froze one step inside the door. Lace glanced at him, waved a short hello, then gave her attention back to the phone. Dominant? What kind of conversation had he walked in on? *One typical for Lace,* he realized, disgusted with himself.

He closed the door behind him and set his load on the foyer table. Lace had a ton of mail, much more than he'd anticipated. He'd really had no idea she received so much correspondence through her profession, or that she'd become such a popular personality. Hanging his damp, snow frosted coat on the coat tree, he pretended not to listen to the conversation.

"I know it's 1998, and women are supposed to take a more active role, be more decisive and aggressive. But that's the whole thing, choices. What works for one woman, or for a couple, doesn't necessarily work for another. You don't want to let society standards restrict you, any more than you want your mate to. Only you know what feels good to you, what satisfies you. Don't worry about whether or not it's in the 'norm.' If you're comfortable with letting him dominate in your marriage, that's all that matters."

His glasses fogged and he had to turn away. How was it every word out of Lace's mouth sounded like a purr of seduction? As if she said those things specifically to rile him, to arouse him? Irritated, especially given how soft he'd been feeling toward her when he'd left her apartment this morning, he stomped into the kitchen to put the Mexican food in the refrigerator. He'd made certain to have it packaged in a way that he could microwave it later and it would still taste fresh. He'd thought of her satisfaction at the banquet he'd compiled, the spicy enchiladas, the chili, the fajitas. He'd been so pleased with his efforts. Now he had his doubts.

Lace hadn't changed just because she'd been hurt. She wasn't suddenly vulnerable and needy just because she liked Christmas carols but had no one to share them with. She was still the same woman, the liberal who'd transformed his baby sister from tomboy to femme fatale. Her idea of entertainment was to harass him until his mind fogged with lust and his body reacted independently of his brain. He'd have to remember that.

Determined to provide the help he'd promised her, Daniel went in search of dirty laundry. He tried to ignore the ensuing discussion, but certain words jumped out at him, key words that told him all he needed to know about Lace McGee, sexual icon, vamp extraordinaire.

When he walked into her bedroom, he heard her voice raise in a squeak on the phone. Seconds later, she came hobbling in behind him.

"What are you doing?"

He glanced up, pretending to be impervious to the way her pastel robe draped over her slim shoulders, to the way her moon-colored hair curled in disarray. How her bare feet looked pink and small and so very feminine. She stared back nervously, tucking her hair behind her ears and glancing around her room as if she suspected he might have stolen something.

"You're a slob. I was only picking up the laundry so I could go get it started."

Lace scowled. "I can pick up my own laundry."

"No, you need to take it easy." He reached for a T-shirt, then a lacy sock. She snatched them both out of his hands.

"Dammit, Daniel, I don't want you rifling through my things."

"Rifling? I hate to break it to you, Lace, but your dirty clothes aren't all that interesting to me."

"They were last night."

"Don't look so smug. Last night you took me by surprise. I expected your place to look…different. To reflect the woman you are."

Her back stiffened. "You don't have an inkling of the woman I am, so how could you possibly have had an accurate preconceived notion of my housing?"

He whistled through his teeth. "Wow. All that, huh?" She growled and he leaned back on her dresser. "What makes you think I don't know you?"

That stumped her. She opened her mouth twice, only to close it again.

"Well? Nothing to say?" She stubbornly shook her head and he knew he saw a measure of hurt on her features. It had to be physical. He refused to believe his opinion of her caused her a single moment of grief. "Dammit, will you lay down? Use the bed, that way you can watch me and you won't have to worry about me *rifling* through your things."

With her mouth tight and her expression rebellious, she did as he asked. Once she was settled on her side, she peered up at him and gave a sigh. "How come we're arguing again?"

"Damned if I know." Then he sighed, too. "Did you get your phone calls taken care of?"

"Most of them. That last one took longer than I thought. She was very upset."

"A disgruntled woman who's into bondage? Is that where your valuable time is dedicated these days?"

He knew even as he said it he wasn't being fair. It was just that she made him so confused with what he felt and what he ought to feel. How she spent her life shouldn't matter to him, but it did. He wanted her, more than he'd ever wanted any woman, and he knew he shouldn't. He didn't feel any real affection for her, much less the overpowering love people often spoke of. And he didn't believe in uninvolved sex. He'd had his share of sexual relationships, but he'd always liked the women and, more importantly, he'd respected them.

He thought about apologizing. Before he could even work up a good way to start, Lace burst out laughing. She laughed so hard, she fell onto her face on the mattress and he was left with the view of her trim backside, curving round and soft beneath her thin pink robe.

Daniel stepped closer, his arms crossed over his chest. "What is so funny?"

"You!" she gasped, then went off into another peal of laughter. "How you can pretend to be so righteous when your mind spends so much time wading through lascivious gutters I'll never understand."

She wiped tears of mirth from her eyes and laughed some more—at his expense. Confusion hit him. "I'm not the one who was discussing sexual vagaries on the phone…"

Lace rolled onto her back, yelped and went back to her side, still chuckling. "'Sexual vagaries'? Is that what you thought?"

Her bright green eyes were alight with humor. She looked beautiful and happy and… "You were discussing domination."

"Not in bed, you idiot." She softened the insult with another chuckle. "Renee is an older woman who's always allowed her husband to have financial say in their marriage. Now her friends are telling her how he's taking advantage of her, how she should assert herself. It's hogwash, of course, because she doesn't want that responsibility. She's happy letting him handle the major decisions in their lives, and from what she told me, he loves her very much and always puts her best interests first. It's a case of reverse discrimination, and women do it to each other all the time now."

Daniel felt incredibly stupid. "What you were saying had nothing to do with sex?"

"You must think my every waking thought, my every action, centers on the physical!"

He shifted. "Well, yeah."

That started another round of hilarity that continued to the point where Daniel wanted to strangle her. He sat on the edge of the bed and stared at her in dry annoyance. "Aren't you overdoing it just a bit?"

She hiccuped and gave him a teasing, watery-eyed smile. "Oh, but overdoing is evidently what I'm known for. Indulgence. Gluttony, even. Why, I never tire out."

"Lace…"

She rested her head on a pillow and smiled at him. She looked serene, freshened by the laughter. Sweet and innocent. "Why are you so repressed, Daniel?"

"I am not repressed." At least, he didn't think he was. No, certainly not. "Just because I show a modicum of restraint rather than your…*flamboyance,* doesn't mean I'm not a sexual person."

He winced as soon as the words left his mouth. He sounded defensive, and idiotic. And now she'd laugh at him again.

But she didn't. She tipped her head and continued to study him. "Do you think it just might be possible we both have a few misconceptions to iron out?"

"I'll concede the merest possibility could exist."

After a moment she stuck her hand out at him and he took it. "Have I thanked you yet for helping me out today?"

"Not exactly." Her hand felt soft and smooth and small in his own. A woman's hand, offered with integrity. He wrapped his fingers around hers and held her firm.

"Then consider this my show of gratitude. It's the truth, I don't have a lot of family I can rely on. I have no doubt I could have muddled through on my own today, but I'm glad I didn't have to."

The emotion in her gaze unsettled him, touched him to his masculine core. More important than her touch were her words. She'd given him a small piece of herself, trusted him not to turn her words back on her, and he felt ridiculously blessed, as if he'd been given the greatest gift of his life.

He felt so pleased, it scared him.

Daniel released her and stood. "Think nothing of it. But, Lace? You know you can count on Annie as family, and Max."

"And your dad, and Guy?"

He hadn't realized she even knew Guy Donovan, though he should have. Guy was his best friend, practically a brother. He worked at Daniel's father's small local company, fulfilling the spot of oldest son since his dad's rather early retirement, a position Daniel had never aspired to. Guy was close to them all, had even lived with them a good portion of his life, so of course Lace knew him.

With the faintest twinge he had to admit was jealousy, he nodded. "And Dad and Guy."

"And you?" She lowered her gaze, her fingers toying with the lace on a pale blue pillow. "Can I count on you as family?"

He wondered if she deliberately played him. Suspecting she might, he narrowed his eyes and answered more bluntly than he'd intended. "I'm here, aren't I?"

"Hmm." She didn't look as though she believed him, but she kept her thoughts to herself. "I'll get my laundry together tomorrow."

"No, I want you to take it easy tomorrow, too. I'll do it, and no more arguments." He put space between himself and the bed, and while he picked up various pieces of clothing, he felt the warmth of her gaze on him. The last thing he lifted, a sheer red bra that made his vision cloud, unearthed a gilt-framed photo. Daniel studied it a minute and, even before

Lace spoke, knew who the woman in the picture must be. The resemblance was very strong.

"That's my mother." Her tone changed, no longer light with humor or teasing. Now she sounded cautious, distant.

"You look a lot like her."

"My cursed coloring, you mean? She loved it, though for me it's been nothing but a hassle."

Daniel snorted. "You're beautiful and you know it."

"Another compliment? I think I'm losing count." He started to take it back, but she jumped in before he could. "It doesn't matter, Danny, not a bit. What my mother considered her greatest asset has been my biggest handicap. And don't pretend you don't understand. Your attitudes reflect those of the masculine masses. No woman can look like me and be taken seriously."

Lace slid off the bed, her face drawn in real anger, surprising Daniel with the suddenness of it. "Lace..."

"Never mind. I don't even care anymore."

"Then why did you bring it up?" he asked gently, sincerely. She seemed like such an enigma, so hard to fathom, impossible to ignore.

"Because your pain medicine is making me maudlin." She headed for the door, causing him to frown in sympathy over her awkward, faltering gait. "I have calls to make. Try not to eavesdrop this time, okay? I wouldn't want to traumatize your fragile sense of propriety with my blatant sexual discussions."

Daniel watched her limp out, and this time he felt no anger at her disdain, no urge for rebuttal. He felt...sympathy. Something had happened with her mother, something that had possibly helped to mold her into the woman she was today. He wanted to find out what it was, wanted to get to know her better.

He wanted to make love to her until neither one of them could see straight. He just didn't know how to overcome the walls he'd set up between them—but he was now determined to try.

Chapter Four

LACE HEARD A THUMP in the hallway and went still. She tilted her head to listen, but all she heard was silence. Just as she started to type again, she heard a low curse. Daniel? Had he somehow injured himself while going to the basement to do her laundry? Sometimes the steps were slippery from people trudging in and out through the weather.

Once he'd left the apartment again, she'd washed as thoroughly as she could at the sink and dressed in a loose-fitting caftan of lemon yellow and purple. On her feet she wore thick white socks.

The pain medicine hadn't made her quite so sleepy today, but it did work wonders on relieving her pain. She was even able to sit up in bed, with a soft pillow cushioning her injury, while she worked on Daniel's laptop. She knew she looked ridiculous, but Daniel hadn't said a word. He'd only asked her if she was comfortable.

"Daniel?" She called his name softly, but received no answer. Slowly sliding out of bed, feeling a smidgeon of worry she didn't want to acknowledge, she went to her bedroom door and peeked out. She could now hear muted shuffling, but couldn't quite pinpoint the sound.

"Daniel?"

"Sorry, Lace. Didn't mean to disturb you." He appeared a

moment later, his hair sprinkled with snow, his cheeks ruddy from the cold, breathing just a tad too quickly, as if he'd been hurrying.

A sort of truce had fallen between them, like two hostile hostages who decide to work together to make the best of a bad situation. Lace had finally begun to relax, to accept his overwhelming presence filling her home, but now, seeing him again, the thrumming feeling returned and she tingled from head to toe. How did he do it? How did this one particular man affect her so easily—without even trying?

She realized she was staring at him stupidly and blushed. "You've been outside?"

"I, ah… Shouldn't you be back in bed? It looked like you had a hundred letters to answer."

"No, only about thirty and I'm almost through."

"You answer every letter personally?"

"Of course." She studied him, and knew in a heartbeat he was up to something. "All right, give."

He raised one brow, looking his most autocratic. "I beg your pardon?"

"Now that would be a sight—you begging."

He started to speak and she said, "I want to know what you were doing outside, Daniel. For that matter, I want to know what you're doing in my living room."

"It's a small room, have you ever noticed that, Lace? Not a lot of space for maneuvering or rearranging."

"Why in heaven's name would you want to rearrange anything? I have things exactly as I like them."

"Well, as to that…" He hedged a moment longer as Lace leaned against the doorjamb and crossed her arms. He made a sound of disgust. "All right. Ruin the surprise, why don't you? I had to make room for the tree."

"A tree?"

"A small one. A Christmas tree. I bought it when I went out earlier." When she only stared at him, he continued in a defensive tone, "It doesn't seem right for you to not have a tree, Lace. It's Christmas."

She felt the color wash from her face. She pushed around him, but he stayed on her heels, crowding her, and when she came to a staggering halt in the entrance to the living room, he almost bumped into her. She felt his hands settle on her shoulders.

"I haven't had a tree since I was... I can't remember the last time I had a tree."

Quietly, his tone almost a caress, Daniel asked, "Didn't you decorate a tree when you were a little girl?"

She shook her head. "For a long time, my mom was married to this rich guy and he had professional decorators come in and fix a tree that was easily ten feet tall. I was afraid to get near it because I thought I might mess something up and everyone would know. Each bow had been placed just so, you see, and if I moved something, or touched something wrong..."

Daniel squeezed her shoulders again. "We used to decorate our tree with stuff Annie and Max had made. Guy and I would supervise after we'd put on the lights and the star on top. It was funny, because until Max and Annie got big enough, all the ornaments would be around the bottom branches and the top of the tree would be bare. Guy and I would wait until after Annie and Max were in bed, then we'd rearrange things a bit, but we never told them, and they never noticed." He hesitated a moment, and she could feel the humor in him, the fond remembrance. "It was a great tree, full of hodgepodge ornaments."

She turned to face him. "Where was your dad?"

Daniel gave a long, weary sigh, his hands falling to his sides and his gaze directed inward. "After Mom died, Dad couldn't cope with the holidays. He'd give me money and ask me to buy presents for the kids, and I could charge our Christmas dinner at the local market, but he didn't join in with us. He'd stay hidden away, usually up in his room, sometimes he'd even take a vacation away from us, like he does now. I tried to make sure Annie and Max didn't notice that he wasn't there. I tried to sort of fill in, make everything so busy and fun that it wouldn't hurt them."

Lace wondered who had made sure he wouldn't hurt. No one, evidently. Her throat felt tight and she swallowed. "I don't have any ornaments or lights or anything."

"I know. I picked up some stuff."

He stepped around her and sat on the couch. Out of a large bag, he pulled multicolored twinkle lights and several boxes of ornaments. Almost too many, she thought, for such a small tree. Lace crept forward, afraid to delve into how she felt at that moment. She perched carefully on the seat next to him.

"I did my own tree with white lights, but considering how much you like color, I thought you'd prefer these."

He took them out of the box and reached to the right of the couch to plug them in. Lace smiled at the rainbow hue of colors. She felt tears but fought them back, busying herself by picking up a box of ornaments. They were small glass balls in gold and silver and red.

"This is better than Christmas morning." The words felt inadequate to express her feelings, but the silence was killing her, making it impossible to dredge up conversation. Memories rushed back, painful and filled with longing.

One by one, Daniel pulled things from the bag. A package of red bows. A bright silver star for the top. Several strands of multicolored glass garland. Slippery silver icicles.

Lace choked on a deep breath, then laughed at herself for behaving so foolishly. "Now I do feel like a queen."

"I'm glad. Are you up to helping me decorate? Or would you rather just watch?" He spoke quickly, as if his surprise, his words, embarrassed him, and she wanted to hug him tight, to kiss him all over. "I wanted to have the tree in the stand before I showed you the other stuff. Just so you couldn't say no. I wasn't sure…"

"I love it. All of it. I'd never say no."

The words hung in the air, and Lace knew he was thinking of things, other circumstances when he might ask and she might say yes.

Her belly tightened and her breasts ached, as if she needed to wrap her arms around herself—or around him. Daniel bit his upper lip, his gaze glued to hers. He'd shaved when he'd gone home to change clothes, and now she touched his jaw, surprised at how that simple touch made her feel.

"Thank you."

He continued to watch her, and she knew the exact train of his thoughts, because they were her thoughts, as well. He wanted to kiss her—and she wanted him to. But she knew better. Every day she dealt with the relationships, the broken hearts, that had started with a single kiss.

She searched her mind for a topic to break the sexual tension, but only one unpleasant subject sprang to mind. "My mom hated Christmas almost as much as your dad."

Daniel stepped back. Rather than look disgruntled by her choice to halt the tentative progress of their romantic urges, he seemed intrigued. He knelt by the small tree only partially secured in the stand—a tree no more than four feet in height. As he tightened the bolts that held the trunk, he glanced back at her. "Tell me more about your mother."

Too late to withdraw, Lace prepared herself to divulge personal hurts while watching Daniel tackle the tree. "Mom became something of a pariah in the social standing she aspired to. She married a rich man because he could pamper her, could erase every worry from her brain, and my mother really hated to have to fret over anything. She thought he loved her. I always knew she was only a trophy to him, a much younger woman who looked beautiful and sexy on his arm. I suppose, had he lived, it would have been an even trade. They both got what they wanted.

"But then he died, and everything changed. Mom wanted to go on the same way, to find another man who treated her as gently, who patronized her as richly as he did. But somehow that relationship never transpired. Men saw her in one of two ways, and neither of those ways was overly flattering or involved legitimate caring."

Daniel carried the tree to the corner he'd cleared. Lace stopped him. "You probably know a whole lot more about this tree business than I do, but what would you think of sitting the tree on that small marble-topped table? Wouldn't that make it more noticeable?"

Daniel grinned. "Of course it would. Do you have an old towel or something we can put underneath so we don't scratch the marble?"

It took a few moments to get the table situated, and already Lace regretted speaking about her mother. The anger she felt on her mother's behalf, and the pity, left a churning pain in her stomach. She didn't want to ruin this special moment, but already her head ached with the memories.

She thought Daniel might have let the subject go. But as soon as he had the tree steady and secure, he brought it up again. "How did men see your mother, Lace?"

He wasn't fooling her with his casual disregard. She knew his attentive mode and this was it. She'd seen it many times with Annie, when he cared a great deal about the topic, but didn't want to overreact. It didn't matter that he was busy stringing the lights on the tree, or that he hadn't precisely looked at her.

What would happen if she confided in him just a bit? Nothing in the past day and a half seemed real any longer. Certainly not her relationship with Daniel. And if he stopped despising her so much…what then? Maybe her relationship with Annie wouldn't be so strained if Daniel accepted her.

With a bracing breath, she forged onward and hoped for the best. "My mother found men in two separate classifications. One group wanted to marry her for her money, despite her humble beginnings and the very obvious fact that we'd never fit in, that we weren't in any way part of the rich elite.

The other wanted nothing at all to do with her. They turned up their noses and treated her like a tramp, accusing her of marrying for money, of being mercenary enough to be glad her husband was dead."

"It must have been very difficult for you."

Lace pondered that. She hadn't often thought about the way it had affected her, she'd been too filled with remorse for her mother. "She's never stopped trying to find another true love. And I don't have the heart to convince her one doesn't exist."

Daniel stopped what he was doing. He stared.

"What?" Lace felt uncomfortable with his scrutiny. "You're looking at me as if I've grown an extra head."

He smiled. "Was I?" He stood and brushed off his hands, then reached for a box of ornaments. "Actually, there's two things. You said your mother has never stopped looking for a true love. Do you mean she's still looking?"

Since the placement of the ornaments looked simple enough, Lace picked up a box of her own and went to help. She placed the first one on the tree tentatively, waiting for Daniel to explain that she was doing it wrong. But he didn't say anything, just went about his business, hanging more and more until the tree began to look heavy with color and the ornaments rested in clusters.

"My mother travels every holiday. Actually, she travels almost year round, but especially during the holidays. She says she's lonelier then, and believe me, there's always one man or another more than willing to take advantage of her generosity. After all, it's a free vacation, right?"

Lace knew the sarcasm hung thick in her tone, but she didn't care. Daniel didn't seem to mind. He never once looked at her.

"Mom travels in the best circles, with the ritziest accommodations. She never wants for company, but she always comes back more dejected than ever. I've tried to explain to her that she can't buy love, but she doesn't know any other way. When her husband widowed her, he left her with a group of people she'd come to know, to count on as friends through his association. But they've demolished her self-esteem with their condemnation and criticism. They've ostracized her, and she's still doing her best to find acceptance in the only way she knows how."

"Was it hard for you, as a young girl, to accept your mother's choices?"

Lace shook her head vehemently, with certainty. But she lied. Of course it hurt. There just wasn't anything she could do about it.

"Lace…"

"Okay, so it used to embarrass me a little. She'd drag me to gatherings with her, happy that she had her daughter and her new man at her side, and we'd all be ridiculed. But then it struck me how unfair I was being. Men do it all the time, exchange lovers like worn shoes. Why shouldn't my mother do the same if that's the lifestyle that suits her?

"People have to deal with their loneliness and heartache in their own way, despite the ramifications involved. Now it only embarrasses me that society is so ridiculous, that a woman is judged harshly by a double standard as outdated as the one that claims she must be pure, while a man is only more appealing with experience."

"Is that why you condone sexual freedom?"

She rolled her eyes. "It's why I condone personal choices, made by mature, responsible adults. You make it sound as if I advocate orgies and indiscriminate lechery."

Daniel considered that, watching her, his eyes thoughtful and his expression intent. After a moment he nodded, but Lace had no idea what conclusions he'd drawn.

"Another thing." He draped some garland across a branch, then stood back to admire it. Lace admired it, as well. "You said you didn't have the heart to convince your mother that true love doesn't exist."

"It's not my place, even as her daughter, to offer advice when it's not asked for."

"I understand. But the part that stumped me is your assumption that love isn't real."

She tried a laugh, but it sounded forced even to her own ears. "I've seen plenty of relationships begin on the misconception of love, but nothing that could substantiate real love existed. Not the mythical stuff that lasts a lifetime, through thick and thin, sickness and health and all that. All I've seen is an illusion that falls apart easily enough, over the most trivial of things, leaving broken people behind. Lust is real, affection and friendship and common ground. But love…" She shrugged, feeling helpless with the way he watched her, feeling inadequate to explain what she knew as a truth.

Daniel actually laughed. "You're wrong, you know. Love is there, and it's all-consuming. I just want no part of it. It does cripple people, when things don't work out. Look at my dad. He loved my mother more than anything."

And, Lace thought, *even more than his children.* To the point where he couldn't be bothered with them once she'd gone.

"Don't get me wrong. And don't feel pity for me or my family. Dad's there, and he's as involved as he can be. We all know he cares. It's just that I don't think he'll ever really be able to cope with the loss of my mother. He was always flighty, and she was the one who kept things grounded. They were like two halves, each dependent on the other. Now one half is gone and he isn't whole anymore."

"And you think that constitutes love as a dangerous thing?" She thought about it, about his reactions, and nodded to herself. "It could explain why you're so constrained. You're a product of your environment. I can understand that. Children are often influenced by…"

"Don't be a fool, Lace." He thrust his chin toward her, his entire demeanor belligerent.

Familiar ground, she thought.

"I am never foolish, and I only meant—"

"What? To charge me off the clock for a free evaluation? I can't afford you."

Her face reddened. "I don't charge people! I'm not a psychologist. I'm a—"

"I know what you are. And believe me, I don't need to be psychoanalyzed."

She shoved a red bow onto the tree, nearly knocking it over. "And I don't need you to patronize me. Just because I'm female doesn't mean I don't know my business. I have a master's degree in sex education. I graduated at the top of my class. My radio show is one of the most popular around." She tapped a finger against her chest and leaned toward him. "I'm one of the best in my field, despite my gender or age."

Daniel caught her hand and curled his own around it. His knuckles brushed her breast and she stilled, going mute in a heartbeat.

With his nose nearly touching hers and his expression black, he said, "I wasn't trying to discredit your abilities. Believe me, I know the influence you have over others. In Annie's case, you have too much influence." She started to speak, but he laid a quieting finger to her lips. "My turn to talk, okay? Without interruptions."

She nodded since he gave her no other option. The feel of his finger on her mouth, firm and warm, did funny things to her insides.

Slowly, he lowered his hand, allowing it to rest at the side of her neck, causing more reactions to erupt in her belly as he curved his fingers around her throat. His scowl softened and melted away to be replaced by a look of scrutiny. "I've never discriminated against a woman in my life."

She knew that. Time and again she'd seen Daniel show respect and admiration for women and their abilities. He treated all his professional colleagues the same, despite their sex. That attitude, she realized, appealed to her as much as his delectable physical appearance.

His other hand lifted, until he cupped her head between his warm palms. She forgot to breathe, to move away.

"I like touching you, Lace. I'm even finding that I like being around you, when you refrain from dissecting my character, or slicing me to ribbons with your wit."

"You're easy to banter with."

He grinned. "Translated to mean, you can always get the best of me and you like that."

She pursed her lips, modestly holding back her agreement.

"At least we agree on some things. Neither one of us wants anything to do with love. Correct?"

Lace nodded, though she wasn't sure she agreed anymore. She'd told him she didn't entirely believe in love, not that she didn't crave it. At the moment, with him touching her, it seemed like a moot point.

"Will you also agree we've both changed? That this day together has changed us?"

She wanted to agree, but not without verification first. "Explain what you mean."

"I understand you better now, Lace. I know that you're not mindlessly promiscuous, that you're only reacting to how you've been raised, the examples you've been given by both men and women."

Heat rushed up her spine, making her temples pound, her hands curl into fists.

"Don't misunderstand. I'm not judging your mother, I swear. I'm only attributing her with a due amount of influence on your life. As you just said, children react to the environment they're surrounded in—"

"I think you'd better let me go now."

"Lace?"

"I'm warning you, Daniel." She could barely get the words out through her stiff lips. "You're in serious danger of me laying you low."

He rubbed his hands tiredly over his face, nearly knocking his glasses off, then pressed a fist to his mouth and studied her. He dropped his hands and shrugged. "You're snapping like a wounded pup, and there's really no reason. I'm only trying to be honest with you, Lace."

"Ha!" She wanted to smack him, but held herself in check. Barely. "You're trying to fit me into the little niche you've assigned me. But I have to give you credit, Daniel. You've stepped away from the masculine pack, finding your own unique logic to look down your nose at me. You see, like my mother, I've known two types of men. Those outside the professional field who see me and immediately decide I'm easy, based on my profession and my damned *flamboyant* appearance."

Daniel winced, probably a mixed reaction to her barely repressed outrage and her use of his description said with such contempt. "I didn't mean..."

She ignored his scowling interruption. "And men *within* my professional circles totally disregard me as a flake. I'm beneath their exalted notice. My credentials, my experience and accomplishments can't possibly matter because I'm a young attractive female and everyone just knows young females aren't to be taken seriously."

"Lace..."

"But not you, Daniel. Oh, no. You don't want me sexually, because that would make you as real and alive as the rest of us mere mortals, no better than me." She felt sick suddenly and groped for the couch, holding on to the padded arm and doing her best to keep her tone level. "At least you don't deny my intelligence or my influence. No, you think I have so much sway, I'm capable of corrupting your poor little innocent sister!"

"Sit down, Lace."

"Don't you tell me what to do!"

"I am telling you, dammit. You're overreacting and you're ready to collapse." Without her permission, he took her arm and lowered her to the cushion. Very quietly, he said, "I didn't mean to upset you, to start another argument."

"No? What did you mean then? To explain to me why I lack morals so I could look at you, my benevolent instructor, with heartfelt gratitude for straightening it all out for me in my inferior female brain?"

He growled, twisted his fingers in his hair and tugged. Lace watched, bemused and fascinated.

He stared off toward the tree, and Lace looked, too. The tree looked lovely, though sad. Half finished, without the illumination of the lights, it appeared to be an incomplete project.

The silence dragged out until finally he crouched on the floor beside her. "Look. All I meant was to show you understanding." His gaze captured hers and refused to let her look away.

"Understanding of my sordid way of life? Save it, Doctor."

He took her hand and held it tightly when she tried to yank it away. "I'm sorry. I know how badly I hate it when others try to dissect me—which is exactly what you started to do."

"And you practically snapped my head off!"

"I know. I'm sorry. It stands to reason you wouldn't like it any better than I do. The times when I was younger, when my father more or less abandoned me, though I hate to call it that...they were awful, lonely and scary and uncertain. I think it was probably the same for you. Only you were alone. At least I had Max—trial that he was, and Annie. And Guy was there, helping out."

Lace thought it must have been harder on him because he had people who relied on him. She was free to throw herself into her studies, without outside responsibilities to distract her.

His thumb rubbed over her knuckles and her frown faded away. His mouth tilted in a rueful smile. "I wanted to...comfort you, I suppose. Though that seems ridiculous now because you really are an independent, intelligent woman. I don't suppose you need my comfort."

She needed it now. And she thought he might need a little, as well. With her free hand, she smoothed his hair away from his forehead. "I've enjoyed myself today, Daniel. Except for the arguing, of course. But it seems we can't be near each other without haggling. Being professional doesn't automatically endow us with a common ground. And it seems like I no sooner see you than my thoughts start toiling on a way to push your buttons."

One side of his mouth kicked up in a crooked grin. "You do have a most agile tongue when it comes to putting me in my place."

"You don't do so badly yourself."

He hesitated a moment, then forged onward. "There was something else I wanted to do."

Her heart began to thump erratically, knocking against her ribs, making her tremble inside and out. She waited for him to lean toward her, to press his mouth against her own. To kiss her...

"I wanted to invite you to my house for Christmas."

Once again, he'd dumbfounded her. An invitation to spend more time with him was the very last thing she'd anticipated.

"My only excuse for making such a muddle of things is that, well, you confuse my brain, Lace. I think you have since the very first time I saw you."

Slowly, the smile came, and this time she felt it deep inside herself, making her warm and content. She confused his brain? *That sounded like a good thing.* "By any chance, is that another compliment?"

He opened his mouth, snapped it shut and frowned. "The invitation is genuine. Now will you say yes and put me out of my misery, or do I need to remain on my knees all night?"

She shooed him away with her hands. "Off your knees. Even us queens can only take so much abject devotion." When he was standing once again, looking gorgeous and as confused as she felt, one contrary thought after another skittered through her brain. She held her head, then heard herself say, "I'll come for Christmas. If you're sure that's what you want."

In his most officious tone, he said, "Of course I'm certain. I asked, didn't I?"

Lace thought he looked very uncertain, but she held her tongue.

Daniel nodded. "Very good. I'm pleased with your verbal restraint. Now sit back and watch while I put the finishing touches on this tree."

When he plugged in the lights, Lace was so distracted by the beauty of it, the soft glow of a dozen different colors mellowed in the depths of the green tree, she didn't even notice him tack a piece of mistletoe in the arched doorway leading to her kitchen. Not, that is, until he stood beneath it, dogged resolution darkening his features, a crooked finger beckoning her closer.

Chapter Five

EVERY MUSCLE IN HIS BODY pulled tight, including the most vital ones, when Lace slowly, deliberately, came to her feet. He wanted to tease, to claim kissing under mistletoe as a family tradition, which it was, but he was afraid if he tried to speak, he'd only groan. Or maybe confess how much he craved her.

She came nearer and nearer in her injured, halting step, still so feminine, so sweetly sensual with her every movement. She made him want to hold her close, to swear to her nothing would ever hurt her again. He held still until she stood only an inch or two from touching him. Common sense warred with basic need. Need won.

His fingers lifted to her hair. It felt so soft, like Lace herself, and looked so pale he'd often wondered if the shade was real. Finding out would be more fun than his poor afflicted heart could endure. It was also an event greatly anticipated.

He no sooner thought it than he pulled back. His heart wasn't involved, not in any way, only his groin, only his masculine genes and his libido—which raged with encouragement. He wanted her, a simple, straightforward physical reaction, a circumstance suffered by all men.

Only there was nothing straightforward or simple about Lace McGee, or his reaction to her.

As an adult—a *responsible mature adult*—there would be

nothing wrong in the two of them deciding on a brief affair. Or rather, a long, hot, gritty affair. Getting Lace out of his system wasn't going to happen overnight. And he wanted her out. Didn't he?

Lace stared up at him, one slim eyebrow cocked. "Are you going to kiss me or not?"

So much impatience. He smiled. "I believe I am." Her mouth looked rosy and ready and anxious. He tightened his thighs and braced himself to keep from throwing her on the couch and showing her just how badly he wanted to kiss her, to eat her alive.

She smirked. "I don't mean to rush you through whatever masculine ruminations you're presently pursuing, Daniel, but I do wish you'd hurry up with it. The suspense is about to kill me."

He laughed, despite the gravity of the situation, despite his now painful arousal. "You have such a way with words."

"You hate my way with words."

He shrugged. "You're starting to grow on me."

"Moss could grow on you, you move so slowly."

Chuckling, he asked, "Is that a hint?"

She heaved a huge sigh, and his gaze was drawn to her breasts, loose beneath her clothing. He forced his gaze more northerly, to avoid a loss of control.

"It's a statement, telling you I'm about to get bored and walk away."

"We can't let that happen." He leaned down, watching her go still and breathless, and he brushed his mouth over hers, teasing himself, barely tasting her when he wanted to taste her so badly. He wanted his tongue in her mouth, their teeth clashing, her body pressed flush against his so he could grind his hardening flesh into her soft belly. He shuddered with the thought and subsequent reaction of his body.

Such a dangerous game, one that could trip him up and leave him flat on his face. For months now he'd been vehemently trying to prove, both to himself and to her, that he didn't want her. He'd played at being immune when in truth she affected every pore in his body. Even his teeth and toenails ached in need whenever Lace entered the same room as him. Lately, whenever he even thought of her.

But all mankind knew the power of male pride. How could he claim to just change his mind, to give in, without making it look as though he'd been wrong all along? How could he claim to want her sexually without losing his male consequence? He stared down at Lace, pondering the problem.

"Is that it? Is that the best you could do?"

Daniel laughed, but quickly sobered. She was serious. She hadn't even realized the deliberation of his kiss, the temptation of moving slowly, the finesse involved in teasing so delicately. His awesome style was totally wasted on her. Well, hell. Her brow puckered and her eyes were alert, if a bit disappointed.

Just that quickly, a plan took root, an ingenious way for him to salvage his ego and still have her. He tried to wipe the elation off his face and strove for a look of consternation. "You didn't like it?"

She gave a rude snort. "I got kissed better than that when I was in first grade."

"Started young, did you?"

She opened her mouth and he said, "Forget I asked." Once again, he brushed his mouth against hers, this time making all efforts at a lackluster effect, doing his best to restrain the fierce urge to devour her with his mouth and tongue. "Better?"

"Uh, no. Not really."

He had to bite his lip to keep from chuckling. "You're not one much for false flattery, are you?" Before she could answer, he plastered his mouth to hers, keeping his lips closed, barely moving, but damn, she felt good, tasted good, smelled good. He wanted to devour her, to thrust his tongue deep and feel her breasts against his chest, to hear her choppy breathing. To kiss her mouth, her throat, her breasts and her belly.

His heartbeat thundered, reverberating through his body to collect in a single pounding pulse in his groin. He forced himself to pull away before he lost his meager control. Ridiculously, his hands shook.

"Daniel," she moaned, and her arms went around his neck. For the briefest instant he forgot his new game and held her close, his mouth opening on hers, his tongue touching her bottom lip, the edge of her teeth. She groaned again and he wanted, in that instant, to have her naked, warm and willing, beneath him. He wanted her eager and involved. He wanted to experience firsthand everything she knew and condoned about sexual freedom, and he wanted her to beg him to show her what he knew.

But she was injured and any involved intimacy would have to be put off anyway, so there was really no reason for ruining his plan.

"Do you like your tree?" He spoke in a hushed, husky whisper. Getting the words formed in his muddled brain took nearly all his concentration.

"I love my tree." She tried to find his mouth again, but he turned his face toward her neck, nuzzling the soft skin there, breathing gently in her ear.

He felt her trembling increase. *"Daniel."*

"Time for lunch." He made the announcement at the same time he eased away from her. Damn she was good. But then, he'd already known that.

He didn't want to hurt her, her wounded body or her delicate emotions, so he had to move with care.

"Lunch?"

He couldn't look at her or all would be lost. He held his control by only a snippet of a thread. "You need to eat while taking the pain medication and the antibiotics, and with all you've been through, you need to keep up your strength."

She searched his face and her breath still came too fast. "Of course. Food. I was just about to suggest the very same thing."

He kept a straight face with much effort. "I'm going to run down and check on the laundry, then I'll warm everything up. Why don't you finish your correspondence?"

"I only have a few more letters to see to." So saying, she slipped on down the hall, her entire countenance dejected.

Daniel could finally grin. He had her now. She cared about the people she helped, that much was plain. He'd watched her frown her way through tough decisions, ponder for long moments her every reply. She took her work as seriously as he took his own.

He rubbed his hands together, anxious to become one of her cases. She already thought him repressed, and heaven knew how chaotic and busy his life had always been, between med school and tending his brother and sister. It wasn't beyond the realm of possibility that he might be sexually inept. Highly unlikely, but not impossible. So he was thirty-five? Age meant nothing. It certainly wasn't proof that he'd have a wealth of experience at his disposal. And his ego wasn't so tender that he couldn't *pretend* to need help in order to gain Lace's trust.

He'd always been very discreet, not wanting to set a bad example for Annie. Plus, he'd needed to counteract Max's lack of discretion. His younger brother seemed to sow more than his fair quota of wild oats. And with his travels, he'd probably sowed oats in more fields all over the country than any three men put together.

No, Lace would find no evidence of his expertise. He'd let her lead him, gently, into intimacy. He'd give her complete control over his body. The mere thought was enough to make him howl with lust.

He was still considering all the finer points of his plan when he hurried back to the door of Lace's apartment. The laundry basket in his arms all but blocked his vision, and suddenly he bumped into a body coming out of the stairwell.

"Excuse me." He lowered the basket, took in the stunned, familiar face peering up at him, then immediately tried to raise the basket again.

Annie didn't let him get away with it. She snatched the basket out of his hands and dropped it on the floor between them. A pair of turquoise panties tumbled out onto the floor, landing on top of Daniel's shoe. They both stared at them a moment, until Daniel snatched them up and put them back on top of the basket. His sister gaped.

"Dan!" Annie looked from him to the basket and back again. "What in heaven's name are you doing here?"

With a wry grimace and an inward curse at fate, he waved at the basket. "Laundry."

LACE WONDERED WHAT WAS keeping Daniel.

Then she wondered at that kiss. Not that she was any expert on the actuality of the subject, but something hadn't seemed quite right. With the way she'd always felt around him, she'd been expecting to be swept off her feet. And in one regard she had. She'd loved the feel of his mouth, the drift of his breath on her cheek, the warmth of his large, strong body so close to her own. Warm, tingly feelings had stirred in her lower belly and her nipples had felt tight, too sensitive. Strangely enough, she'd wanted him to touch them, to touch her.

But he'd seemed...tentative. Unsure. She'd always known Daniel had a hang-up where she was concerned, but she'd never considered his attitude might stem from inexperience. Now she had to reevaluate.

He was simply too gorgeous, too worldly, too...sought after. Somehow she couldn't imagine a woman looking at him and not wanting him. And somehow she hadn't thought he'd always refuse.

Well, no one had said he was entirely without experience, but surely, even a *little* experience would have taught the man how to kiss. And rigid? He'd held himself like a pike, not moving, barely breathing. He sure wasn't the romancer she'd expected him to be. She felt terrible for teasing him for so long, potentially compounding his problem with sex.

In one regard, she was glad he lacked hands-on confidence. At least it meant he wasn't a hypocrite.

In another way, the thought of him being inexperienced made her giddy with excitement. She wondered how he would react if she set out to educate him. She thought she could probably manage it with a little luck and a lot of forethought. And assisting him could be just the excuse she needed to appease her overwhelming desire.

Having Daniel in her home had changed everything, had shown a different side of him, a more human, considerate, understanding side. She could no longer fight her own natural desires. But she didn't want to look as if all the antagonism between them hadn't mattered, and she simply couldn't concede the contest of wills, not when he'd made such erroneous assumptions about her character.

When she heard a noise at the door, she decided to test him just a bit with a taste of verbal innuendo. She lowered her voice to what she hoped was a sultry, sexy tone, then called out, "Daniel? Is that you, finally? It's really unfair of you to stir up my appetite and then leave me waiting." She giggled at her own ridiculous verbiage before adding, "I'm starved!"

She wondered if he'd assume she meant the food he promised, or if he'd detect the sexual undertones of her words. She heard approaching footsteps and laid her head against the pillows in what she hoped represented an inviting pose. Much of the pain had eased and she could once again use her backside for the purpose intended—sitting. But she had to be cautious and the seat needed to be soft. Unfortunately, she didn't think Daniel's lap would qualify.

With her head tilted just so and a winsome smile on her mouth, she waited until he came through the doorway, then murmured, "It's about…time…"

"Ha!" Annie laughed out loud, her blue eyes dancing. A thick braid held her long dark hair, which hung down her back, swishing near her trim hips. Her parka was unzipped to show a close-fitting red sweater and dark jeans. As always, she looked pretty and vibrant and happy. Daniel had done a good job with her, Lace thought.

Lace jerked upright, only to have Annie rush around the bed and shove her back again. "No, don't you dare get up on my account. Daniel told me what happened. How awful for you!" She glanced at Lace's bottom half, then asked in a whisper, "Does it hurt?"

"Not anymore—"

"I'm so sorry I wasn't home when you needed me! Especially after all the help you've given me." She embraced Lace, and over Annie's shoulder, Lace saw Daniel step into the room and set the filled laundry basket on the floor. He stood in the doorway, took in his sister's effusive regret and rolled his eyes.

Lace pulled herself together. "Annie, really, I'm fine."

"No, no, you're not. Daniel told me *everything*."

Uh-oh. "Daniel has already explained?"

"Yes, and now this proves what a sweetie he is. Didn't I tell you he was just the most *wonderful* brother? Maybe now you'll believe me."

Daniel cleared his throat. He didn't look particularly sweet at the moment. He look disgruntled—and back to his former aloof self. "I'll let Annie put your things away while I get the food heated up."

Because it hurt to see the distance back in his expression, Lace turned to Annie. "Will you stay and eat with us?"

"I suppose, if there's enough. What are you having?"

"Mexican. Hot." Then she turned to Daniel, her look pointed. "What exactly do we have to eat?"

"A little of everything. Fajitas, tacos, burritos, nachos. Lots of salsa and cheeses. And lots of jalapeños and red chilies."

Annie's eyes widened. "Yum! I'd love to join you."

Lace slanted Daniel a look of smug satisfaction, determined to goad him out of his mood. "Your little sister likes *spicy* food as much as I do."

Annie agreed. "I love it, now that Lace has gotten me hooked on it."

To Lace's disappointment, Daniel left the room without a single comment.

"So, tell me. What's really going on?" Without reserve, Annie began opening drawers and closets, shoving clothing inside. Annie was not exactly the epitome of domesticity. Household chores often escaped her realm of understanding.

Lace cleared her throat and took her time gathering up her correspondence. "I don't know what you mean. What did Daniel tell you was going on?"

"He said you got hurt, there was no one else to take care of you, so he stepped in. He said he knew I'd have his head if he left you here alone, and he was right."

Lace frowned. So he didn't want Annie to know he'd kissed her. Probably because he didn't want to corrupt her poor little impressionable mind by letting her think he'd cavort with a woman of Lace's ilk. The big jerk.

Annie patted her hand. "I know there's more to it than that, though."

"Oh? How so?" Lace hoped she looked suitably confused.

"I offered to stay with you, to let him go home now, but he refused. He said I wasn't qualified to take care of you." She snorted. "I can toady for a person as easily as he can."

Lace winced as Annie crammed her T-shirts into a drawer. "Daniel isn't *toadying* for me."

"He's doing your laundry, for crying out loud! What would you call it? And that tree. I saw it the minute I came in and thought you'd finally softened and gotten one. But when I commented on it, he told me he'd done it. He mumbled it, like it embarrassed him or something. Wasn't that sweet of him, Lace?"

The sisterly admiration on Annie's face wasn't to be refuted. "He's been very kind. At select and individual moments."

Daniel called them in to eat, and Annie helped Lace out of the bed, even though she didn't need help. Once they were in the kitchen, Lace felt stymied. There was no way she could sit in one of the hard-bottomed chairs. Daniel touched her shoulder.

"Hold on just a second. I'll be right back."

He went down the hall to her bedroom and returned a moment later with a fat bed pillow. He placed it on the chair, then took her arm. "See how that feels."

Annie watched on as if fascinated while her brother solicitously seated Lace. Once she'd lowered her bottom onto the soft pillow, he pulled another chair forward for her to prop her legs on.

"Keep your leg elevated. It'll help to keep the pressure off the wound."

Then he served her a plate.

Lace felt like an inconsiderate witch, especially with the pleased admiration shining on Annie's face. Daniel had waited on her all day, made certain she'd taken her antibiotics and her pain pills on schedule. He'd fed her and teased her and given her a tree. He'd even washed her dirty laundry, which went well beyond the realm of consideration. She wanted to cry. She should have been more grateful, not resentful that he wanted to keep the kiss between them private.

When she took her first bite of chili, she nearly did cry. Her mouth caught on fire and she fanned her hand in front of her open mouth. Daniel handed her a glass of water, and she knew if she looked at him, he'd be wearing a smug expression. Spicy indeed!

She'd told him she liked her Mexican food hot. Well, it couldn't get much hotter than this.

"Wow!" Annie was the next to suffer from the jalapeño peppers liberally mixed into everything. She grabbed for her own glass of water, sputtering and choking.

Daniel looked at them both with teasing contempt. "Tenderfoots." He wolfed down his own food with a distinct show of relish for their amazement.

Both Annie and Lace laughed at his uncharacteristic display. Lace saluted him, then doused her own food with plenty of salsa and cheese to mellow it enough to be edible. Altogether, it was so delicious, and she ate so much, she knew she wouldn't be hungry the rest of the day.

The meal lingered, mixed with conversation and laughter, for more than two hours. Lace watched Daniel and Annie interact. The way he smiled at his sister, with unconditional love and acceptance, amused by her every word, made Lace ache inside. She couldn't begin to fathom the depth of their dedication to each other.

"I bought you the perfect gift, Lace. You're going to love it."

Lace froze with her fork in midair and her mouth open. "You bought me a present? Why?"

Annie laughed at her in amazement. "It's almost Christmas, silly." She winked at Daniel. "I love buying gifts almost as much as I like getting them."

Daniel shook his head. "I haven't even starting shopping yet, Annie, so stop giving me that look. You'll have to wait until Christmas morning and be surprised like the rest of us."

Lace listened to them with half an ear. It made her uncomfortable to know she was now honor bound to do her own Christmas shopping. She hadn't purchased holiday gifts for anyone in too many years to count. For the most part, she'd always ignored the holidays. Now she wouldn't be able to. She wasn't at all certain if that was a good or a bad thing.

"I have a few more errands to run, but I'll come back and spend the night with you."

Before Lace could find the right words to refuse Annie's offer, Daniel spoke up. "She needs her sleep tonight, Annie, and I know how women are. You two would sit up all night gabbing."

Lace could have debated how well he knew women, given the demonstration she'd had so far, but she truly did want some time alone.

"Really, Annie, I'm fine now. I won't be hopscotching any-time soon, but I can manage."

"You're sure? What if you need something?"

"If she needs you, she can call. Her phone is right by her bed."

Annie stared at Daniel, and he shrugged. "I'll make certain she's settled before I leave this evening, Annie. There's no need for you to worry."

Lace felt all too conspicuous with them speaking about her. She interjected in what she hoped was an aggrieved tone. "All I really need is a hot shower to work out some of the stiffness from sitting around all day, but I think that's out of the question."

Daniel retrieved Annie's coat for her. As she slipped it on, taking the not-so-subtle hint with good grace, Daniel turned to Lace.

"If you really want a shower, I can arrange it."

"A magician, are you? I specifically heard the nurse tell me not to get the stitches wet for a while."

They both walked Annie to the door. "You could use an aqua-guard, a plastic adhesive patch you put over the stitches to keep them dry. I wouldn't want you to soak in a tub, but a quick shower should be okay if you apply the patch correctly."

Annie smiled and mouthed the word, *Wonderful*, behind Daniel's back, then gave them both a hug goodbye. "Promise you'll call me if you need anything, Lace."

"I promise, but I'll be fine."

"I trust you to take good care of her, Dan."

"I intend to."

Once the door closed behind her, Lace felt self-conscious.

The memory of their kiss hung in the air between them. Daniel hesitated a mere second, then pulled her close, gently curling her into his body until she felt surrounded by his heat and his strength and she realized how much she'd missed it since the last time he'd held her. She'd grown addicted to his touch in such a very short time.

She tipped up her face and he kissed her again.

This kiss was a little less awkward, but still very brief. He touched his mouth to the bridge of her nose, her forehead; his cheek rubbed hers as he ran his fingers through her hair, over her skull, cupping her gently. She felt lulled, enticed.

Lace moved back enough that she could see his face, the tenderness in his expression. It moved her so much, she closed her eyes to guard against it and parted her lips, silently asking to have his mouth instead. He nipped her bottom lip, surprising her and making her eyes snap open again.

"The aqua-guard might be a little difficult for you to put on yourself."

His tone was gentle, low. Lace tried to reconcile his words with the mood she presently floated in. "Aqua-guard?"

"The plastic patch I told you about. So you could shower. Given where the dog bit you, it might be difficult for you to get it on properly."

Lace jerked back. "You're not suggesting I let you help me with it?"

He stared at her mouth. "Why not? I'm your doctor. I'll have to check it again tomorrow sometime anyway. And when the stitches are ready to come out."

"Not on your life." Lace had no intention of returning as a patient to the hospital, or of baring her injury to Daniel's interested eyes.

Daniel chucked her chin. "Don't look so appalled. If you think you can manage, that's fine. But do it now while I pick up the mess in the kitchen so if you do have a problem, you can let me know."

"As if I would," she muttered. Lace turned away, horrified by the mere thought. Daniel stopped her with a hand on her arm.

"Come with me to the kitchen. When I got your prescriptions filled, I picked up a couple of the patches just in case."

Lace trailed behind him, feeling the heat in her cheeks. She imagined the ignominious position she'd have to be in to apply the patch, and knew he could easily imagine the same. She covered her face with one hand.

"I'm a doctor, Lace. You have no reason to be embarrassed."

"That little truism helps not one iota."

It wasn't easy, but she did manage to get the patch in place. As she quickly showered, she wondered just how long he intended to hang around. He couldn't spend the night again because he had to be at the hospital very early the next day. She needed him to go so she could sort out her feelings and the strange, seductive plan she'd almost reconciled herself to.

Could she actually give Daniel Sawyers, the epitome of sobriety and discretion, lessons on sexual expression?

She'd never know until she tried. And there was never a better time than the present.

DANIEL PACED, WONDERING how exactly to initiate his newest strategy on Lace. He supposed he could just fumble around enough that she'd take pity on his inept methods and insist on taking the lead. But somehow it seemed better to come right out with it, to get her agreement up front.

He went through her CD collection as he listened to the water running and imagined Lace naked in the shower, her slim body wet and white and so very soft. He groaned. Damn, but she made him nearly crazy. His errant thoughts skipped ahead, erotic images forming in his mind of her naked, sitting astride his hips, giving him direction.

He'd gladly do anything she asked.

But first he had to get her to do the asking. How to do it?

He put on a country classic Christmas collection he'd

brought in earlier from his car and while he listened to the music, he let his mind wander. He jumped a good foot when Lace suddenly touched his shoulder.

Whipping around, he sucked in his breath and every plan in his tormented mind fled, replaced by raw need. She looked beautiful, damp and warm and rosy cheeked. Her wet hair had been combed straight back from her forehead, emphasizing her high cheekbones and her narrow nose, the bright green of her wide eyes.

She'd changed clothes again. It seemed to him she switched outfits often, and every colorful ensemble she put on made his wits numb and his body hungry. This time she wore a long, straight mauve gown with fitted sleeves and a scooped neckline. A hostess gown, he thought it might be called, though where that errant thought had come from he couldn't imagine. She stood there staring at him, looking more enticing by the second, and he couldn't wait a moment more.

He pulled her close and kissed her. At the last second he remembered to botch it, and he let their noses bump, let his glasses get in the way.

Lace huffed in frustration. She shoved him back a few inches and looked him in the eye. "Are you deliberately trying to make me crazy or what?"

Blushing on cue would have been impossible, but he felt his neck turn red, which he supposed could only assist his efforts.

Trying to look downcast, he said, "I'm sorry. I know I'm not very good at this."

"This?"

He gestured at her, down her body and back up again. Then because he couldn't help himself, he kept on looking until Lace cleared her throat, demanding his attention. "Responding with a sexy woman," he blurted. "I suppose you expected better of me?"

He peeked at her and saw her frown. Excellent.

Then she sighed again. "Not really."

He faltered, forgetting his act and giving her a double take. "No?"

"So far, everything about you has indicated you're not very at ease in sexual situations."

He didn't quite know how to respond to that. A show of masculine outrage would be out of place, given his plan. A demonstration of his sexual ease would ruin everything.

His hesitation prompted her to words. "It's all right, Daniel. I understand."

Humph. She didn't understand anything, least of all him or his sexuality. He cleared his throat. "Most women don't. It's the truth, Lace, my love life is in terrible shape."

He could feel her concern, her caring, and he almost felt like a cur for misleading her. But determination and blind need overruled his finer sensitivities and he stuck with his plan.

Her small hand touched his shoulder, and just that, a simple touch in the most innocuous of places, made his pulse thrum.

"Daniel?" When he didn't answer, she said in the gentlest tone he'd ever heard from Lace McGee, "Look at me."

He did.

"There's nothing to be embarrassed about."

"Ha! It's not every day a man has to admit he's no good as a lover."

Her eyes widened and he wondered if perhaps he was laying it on a bit thick. Not many men would ever admit to such a thing. The realization came too late.

Lace's expression softened, and she smiled at him. "What makes you think you're no good?"

"Hoards of disgruntled women?" He hadn't expected her to doubt him, only to help him.

She laughed. "Hoards, huh? Well, I'll let you in on a secret. This is the time of liberation. A woman is responsible for her own pleasure."

She spoke without embarrassment, much the way he'd

been told she spoke on the radio. Lace discussed everything imaginable, to hear others tell it, and never once showed a hint of inhibition. Suddenly the thought inflamed him.

She stroked his shoulder. "If a woman is dissatisfied, it's up to her to tell her lover why, to instruct him, to guide him. Men aren't mind readers. And every woman is different."

Fascinated, he asked, "How so?" just to hear her keep talking. Listening to Lace orate on sexual issues was like extended foreplay; he felt stroked by her voice. How he'd ever last until she was recovered from her wounds was going to be his greatest hardship. He wanted her to start her instructions now. He'd gladly sacrifice his body for the lesson.

"Women all respond to different things, different games, touches, intensity. Some women like subtlety, others blatant advances. Tenderness can be a big turn-on, or rough play, or raw sexuality or…"

Daniel groaned. He'd tortured himself enough for one day. He reached for her—and was interrupted, or perhaps saved, depending on how you looked at it, by a rather loud knocking on the door.

Even as he cursed the fates and silver-tongued women bent on seduction, Lace went to answer her door.

Chapter Six

LACE PULLED HER DOOR OPEN and Max Sawyers whisked in. "Hello, sweetheart."

Lace started in surprise, then gasped when Max jerked her close in his brawny arms and bobbed his eyebrows. "You're under the mistletoe," he said, and Lace looked up, seeing the most ridiculous hat perched on Max's handsome head, a long wire suspending a sprig of mistletoe away from the hat to loom above her.

"Good grief, Max, wherever did you get that thing?"

"Good favor shone on me last night while I was shopping, buying your Christmas present. I saw this hat and knew it was just the thing to get you where I wanted you."

"And where's that?"

He grinned, a roguish tilting of his sensual mouth that probably made female hearts flutter with great anticipation. But Lace was immune, a fact that continued to nettle Max and prod him onward in his amorous pursuit.

He leaned close, still grinning, and whispered, "Right here, in my arms. Ready to be kissed."

Lace flattened her palms against his chest and stiffened her arms, putting as much space between them as she could, even as she laughed. He whirled her around, lifting her off the floor so her feet swung in the air behind her and she lost her balance. She landed hard against his solid chest. Her gasp of pain sounded just as Daniel unglued himself from the living room floor and stormed up to his brother.

"Dammit, Max, knock it off!" He grabbed his brother and pulled him away from Lace, then put his arm around her waist to support her. She sagged against him, relieved to have his rescue. To Lace, he asked, "Are you all right? You're as pale as a ghost."

Lace managed a nod, though in truth Max's actions had sent pain singing up and down her thigh and bottom. She could barely stand on her injured leg.

Max stepped closer, his brows pulling down. "What's going on? What's wrong with Lace?"

"She's injured, you idiot."

"Well, how was I to know?"

Lace held up a hand. "Please, it's no big deal." Briefly she explained the dog bite to Max and he whistled, twisting around and trying to get a look at her bottom. Daniel scowled, physically manuevering her so that Max couldn't see a single thing.

"Damn, that's horrible. I'm sorry, babe."

Daniel's arm stiffened around her and Lace pulled away to prop herself delicately on the edge of the couch. She watched the two brothers, aware of the outrage about to erupt and helpless to defuse it.

"What the hell did you think you were doing, busting in here and attacking her?"

Max lifted his brows, eyeing his brother curiously. "I didn't attack her. Well, not really. And I was only trying to steal a kiss, like I always do."

Any minute now, Lace expected to see lightning to match the thundercloud of Daniel's expression. He transferred his glare from Max to her. "Do you have something going on with my little brother?"

"Of course I do." When Daniel blanched, she added, "It's called friendship, you idiot."

His mouth fell open; seconds later he snapped it shut and a red flush ran up his neck. "I'm sorry."

"Sure you are. Sorry that I'm not proving to be the stereotypical nympho you've envisioned?"

Max looked on with interest. "You want Lace to be a nympho? Come to think of it, that's not a bad—"

They both snapped "Shut up, Max!" at the same time. Max held up his hands in a placating gesture, and his mouth twitched as he fought a smile.

"I can't believe you honestly thought I'd sleep with your little brother."

Max stifled a chuckle, then stepped backed when they both glared at him.

Pointing a finger at her, Daniel turned back to Lace. "I never said—"

"You thought it! And what about Guy? Is he safe from my evil, lascivious clutches? As far as that goes, is any male safe? I mean, it's obvious I have no sense of discrimination, no standards to uphold, no—"

Daniel loomed over her. "That's enough, Lace."

"Why? You don't like having your own nauseating misconceptions thrown in your face?"

Max cleared his throat loudly, interrupting the sudden silence in the room. "Hey, I've never been in here before. Nice place, Lace."

Somehow she couldn't quite force her gaze away from Daniel's. They stared at each other, and it was like touching, a physical, tactile thing that left her energized. "I'm glad someone likes it."

Daniel growled. "I like it, all right? How many times do I need to say it? I like your damned apartment."

Lace crossed her arms over her chest and looked away. Max started backing toward the door. "Look, I think it's time for me to leave. All this hostility is bad for a man of my young impressionable years. Lace, I hope you're feeling better

soon." He saluted his brother. "Dan, I hope you shut up before she kills you." Then he laughed and hurried out the door.

Lace could feel herself heaving, her breath coming too
fast, her turbulent emotions boiling near the surface. She
felt...vital, alive and invigorated. The way she always felt
when she sparred with Daniel.

She'd never before realized how easily she spoke with him,
how comfortable she was saying anything at all to him. She
held no reserve with him, no boundaries. Even his insults no
longer seemed so important, now that she thought she understood him. And as she thought of it, she considered the possibility that he might have been a little jealous of Max.
Heaven knew, he could take lessons from his little brother
when it came to seduction.

"I'm not going away, Lace, no matter how hard you wish it."

She turned to him. "I don't wish any such thing."

"No?"

She shook her head. "Would it really bother you so badly
if I got involved with Max?"

Instead of answering, he went perfectly still and asked,
"Are you considering it?"

"No, never."

He immediately relaxed. "Why?"

"Because he doesn't know what he wants. He's unsettled.
Max is not who you think he is."

Daniel stepped closer, encouraged by her casual tone and
lack of vehemence. "No? Then who is he?"

"I don't know yet, mostly because he doesn't know. I think
he's confused by his role in the family. He's not the oldest son,
the responsible one. And he certainly can't compete with
Annie as the youngest and the only female. Guy has become
your best friend, taking over your place in the family company. I think Max is still trying to figure out where he fits in."

"Max is my brother, my only brother. He doesn't need to
fit in."

"Of course he does. He's twenty-seven years old and he needs his own position in the family. Something with more stature than the overachiever's brother."

Daniel didn't deny being an overachiever, but he did frown.

Lace felt encouraged. "That's why he's always so outrageous. Because he doesn't yet know what to with himself, and being outrageous is a way of covering that up."

"Lace?"

She stared up at him.

He lifted a hand to her cheek. "I don't want to talk about Max anymore."

"What do you want to talk about?" Her skin felt too warm, as if added heat pulsed just beneath. A sweet, tingling sensation swirled low in her belly, pulling tighter with every second that Daniel watched her. Every place his gaze touched on her, she felt it.

"I want to kiss you again. Hell, I want to make love to you and hear you groan." He cupped her face and his hands trembled. "I want you to whisper my name and scream in pleasure."

Lace sucked in a breath. Daniel's brown eyes had softened to a golden glow behind his glasses. She licked her lips and heard him make a small sound of pleasure.

"I...I think I want that, too."

He shook his head. "I don't want to screw up with you."

She knew what he meant, and his sexual insecurity removed her own. "I'll help."

His nostrils flared and his thick lashes swept down to shield his eyes. "Do you understand what I'm saying, Lace? I don't want to fumble things. I want this to be good for you."

"Daniel." She touched his jaw, the side of his throat, and reveled in the warmth of his flesh. "I know you're uncertain. But it'll be okay. I promise."

"You don't mind...instructing me?"

His voice dropped, low and husky and aroused, and Lace

wondered at his reaction. Was he really so nervous at the prospect of making love to her? Her heart softened.

No! Not her heart. She would not get emotionally involved with Daniel Sawyers. Their worlds were too different for them to ever harmonize for any length of time. She would not be drawn in by him, by his vulnerability and need. He was just a man, as flawed as any man. As a therapist, she could help him, and take her own pleasure in the bargain, but she wouldn't let him confuse the issues.

"Daniel, do you think you can accept a brief affair with me?"

He stiffened, and Lace thought he might balk. He hesitated, the intensity of his gaze boring into hers. After a long, nerve-stretching moment, he leaned down and kissed her. Another brief, unsatisfying kiss. But she intended to change all that very soon.

"I don't want an involvement any more than you do, Lace."

She swallowed her hurt, insisting to herself that it was exactly the reply she'd wanted. "Good. Then we're agreed."

Daniel touched the tip of her nose. "There's just one thing. As your doctor, I insist you wait awhile before embarking on any amorous adventures. No, don't frown at me. I know what I'm saying. You need to let yourself heal, Lace, to let the stitches do their work."

"And until then? Do we just go on as usual, baiting and sniping at each other?"

"No. I'm not sure I could, in any case. You'll take it easy, I'll check on you occasionally, and you'll come to my house for Christmas. It'll give us both a chance to get used to the idea of being together."

Lace didn't need to get used to the idea, but she supposed Daniel might. This was all new to him. Not that she was the experienced expert he thought. She'd no more hopped in and out of beds than a tadpole hopped from lily pad to lily pad. But that was her own business, not Daniel's. And in the way of understanding sexual drives and urges, she certainly was the expert.

She stuck out her hand and waited for him to take it. "So, we have a deal?"

Daniel shook her hand. "Deal."

Lace wrapped her arms around his neck and pulled his mouth down to her own. "I think we should seal this particular bargain with a kiss." This time she didn't give Daniel the chance to pull away. She took her time and exploited every trick she knew to make him crazy with need.

When she finally released him, his glasses were fogged and his face was dark with lust.

"You're an evil woman, Lace."

She accepted the insult with a grin, then patted his cheek. "Don't worry, Danny. When the time comes, I'll be gentle with you."

His eyes flashed, and he said in a whisper, "I can hardly wait."

LACE WAS SERIOUSLY CONSIDERING writing a book on extended verbal foreplay. Her experiences with Daniel would serve as the perfect data.

It had been a week since the conception of their plan, and Daniel had utilized his time well. He'd managed to insinuate himself so deeply into her thoughts, not a moment passed that he didn't in some way interrupt her work or her routine. She'd find herself smiling for the most absurd reasons, but try as she might, she couldn't banish him from her brain.

She remembered when he'd stopped by to check up on her because she'd refused to let him remove her stitches. He'd complained endlessly about her defection to another physician. That same day, she'd found him looking through her collection of books. Not fiction for entertainment, but what she considered her texts, books on sexuality, on various other cultures and condoned behaviors.

She'd thought to tease him. "Find one with a lot of pictures, did you?"

He'd looked down at her, his eyes warm with desire, and shown her the book. "Yes, this picture." She'd blushed at the intriguing position of the couple and felt Daniel's gaze on her, watchful. "I'd like to try this with you, Lace."

She shook, just imagining such a thing. And then he'd whispered, "I bet you taste so damn good…"

Lace had refrained from teasing him further.

Now she was tired, having worn herself out with her first full day out of the apartment. Daniel had gotten the day off work and chauffeured her around, and she hadn't bothered to deny him. She liked being with him too much, and she still wasn't comfortable enough to drive herself.

"You look exhausted. Let's call it quits."

"Not yet. One more stop, okay?" They'd been to the radio studio, where she'd checked to make certain everything was ready for her next show. She presented her producer with the letters she'd share on the air and the topic she wanted to cover, and they went over the format. Daniel had watched, looking uncomfortable.

Next they'd had lunch in the mall and Lace had managed to get some of her Christmas shopping done with Daniel's help. She found it wasn't nearly the chore she'd anticipated, in fact, it was almost fun. She bought Guy several ridiculously expensive fishing lures that Daniel swore he'd love. For Max, she bought the newest jazz CD. When Daniel asked how she knew Max liked jazz, Lace only winked at him, earning a scowl.

She even bought her mother a gift, a beautiful crystal vase, though they hadn't even acknowledged a holiday in too many years to count. Daniel stayed by her side, teasing and suggesting the most outrageous things. But when she bought a very sexy teddy for Annie, he'd stomped away, telling her he'd meet her at the food court. Lace used the private moment to buy Daniel's gifts, then fretted the rest of the afternoon over whether or not he'd like them.

"I need to stop at the post office. It's on the way to my place."

Daniel slanted her a quick glance. "I thought we'd go back to my place for a while."

It wasn't what he said, but how he said it, that caused her weariness to vanish, replaced by acute interest. She swallowed, then turned her head on the headrest to stare at him. "Oh? And what do we need to go there for?"

His hands flexed on the wheel, tightening, and she could see the movement of his jaw, the subtle way he shifted in his seat. "You're almost healed. Another few days and you'll be…fine."

Even though the snow continued to fall and the temperature was in the twenties, Lace felt too warm. She opened her dark cape and concentrated on breathing.

Daniel glanced at her again, and then continued. "I thought we could use today to…practice a little."

"To prepare for our nefarious plan?"

He reached across the seat and took her hand. "It's not nefarious. It's… Hell, I don't know what it is. I'm only a man, Lace. I can't take much more of this."

"Well, I'm a woman, and it hasn't exactly been easy on me."

"No?"

She shook her head. "I think about you all the time."

"When you're trying to work?"

She nodded and he said, "Me, too. When you're eating?"

"Yes."

His fingers tightened on hers. "When you're in bed?"

Her heart pounded, shaking her. "Especially then."

"Good. I'm glad."

"Misery loves company?"

"I haven't been miserable. I've been on pins and needles and grouchy and not at all myself. And to top it all off, the nurses at the hospital are acting so damn strange. Suddenly they're coming on to me in force. I can't go into the dining room without practically getting attacked. It's bizarre."

Uh-oh. Lace remembered prodding the nurse in the emergency room to be more aggressive in her pursuit. Thinking of it now, she realized what a petty, childish thing she had done. Not that she'd admit it to Daniel. "Hmm. Maybe your new sexuality is showing through, inspiring them all to greater daring."

"What are you talking about?"

"You've been friendlier with me, easier to be around."

He laughed. "Yeah, but you're the only one I ever wasn't friendly to."

"Gosh, that makes me feel so special."

His laughter stopped. He pulled her hand to his thigh and pressed his own over it. "You are special, Lace. I think that's why I had such a hard time understanding you. I've never met anyone like you before."

"You mean someone so brazen and unashamed?"

To her surprise, he seemed to seriously consider her words. "I'm afraid you'll take this the wrong way, so please let me finish." He paused, and she could see him visibly gather his thoughts. "You are brazen, but not in a bad way. You believe in what you say, in the work you do. I think that probably makes you more effective. And I know you're stronger than anyone I know, male or female. I've enjoyed helping you out while you were recuperating, but I have no doubt you'd have managed just as well on your own. Even without family or a hoard of friends."

She'd never in her life heard so many compliments, not aimed at herself. He was wrong, of course. She wasn't strong, and her brazenness hid an insecurity, a fear of never finding love, of going through her entire life alone. Of being like her mother.

She didn't rely on friends because she'd never been comfortable enough with the natural intrusion of friends. People got close, and they wanted to share your life, invade your thoughts and dreams. His sister Annie, in her open, careless, honest way, had wheedled her way into her heart. She loved Annie as she'd love a sister if she had one. If she wasn't careful, she might begin to love the whole family.

"What are you thinking? You're so quiet."

Lace quickly censored her thoughts, and decided which ones were safe to share. "I was remembering how Annie and I met."

"At Annie's bookstore?"

"Yes." Lace smiled, thinking of the quaint, conservative little bookstore Annie owned. It was located in a very exclusive neighborhood, on the same strip with several other specialty shops. "She'd ordered a shipment of my last book. She saw in my bio that I lived in the area, so she wrote to my publisher, and they forwarded her letter." Lace grinned, giving Daniel's thigh a squeeze. "She was most impressed with my prose."

Daniel didn't take the bait. "She's still young and impressionable."

"She's in love."

He almost drove the car off the road. "What the hell are you talking about?"

"You didn't know? You haven't seen the signs? What do you do? Walk around with blinders on?"

They still tended to insult each other with great regularity, but neither one took the verbal assaults seriously. Not anymore. "Annie is only stretching her wings. She's not in love." He scoffed at the mere idea.

"Yes, she is. And that's why she wrote me. She read my book, and knew I'd understand her predicament."

"What predicament?"

"Being sandwiched between a serious older brother who pretends she's still a child, and an aggressive middle brother who growls if men even look her way."

"Max does that?"

"Max is as protective as you are, only in a different way. He's determined to browbeat any suitors away. And if that doesn't work, he'll just get physical."

Daniel narrowed his eyes. "I hadn't realized. About Max,

I mean. Though I can picture him doing just that." He flashed her an unreadable look. "I still don't think Annie's in love."

"Think what you like. Doesn't matter to me."

"Okay, smartie. So, who's she in love with?"

Lace grinned. "I can't tell. It's a secret."

"Ha. You just don't have a name."

Caressing his thigh just enough to distract him, Lace leaned close and whispered, "Wait and see. I imagine the truth will come out soon enough."

As she'd hoped, he ignored her words and concentrated on her touch. "Will you come home with me, Lace?"

"What will you do to me?"

His jaw clenched and he shook. "Whatever you want me to."

She closed her eyes against the impact of his words. "What if I want to do things to you?"

He took his eyes off the road long enough to pull her up close and kiss her hard. Then he gently pushed her back to her own seat. "We can iron out the particulars when we get there. But in the meantime, do me a huge favor and withhold all further provocation. It's not necessary, believe me, and I have no idea how to perform CPR on myself. Much more of this and I'll expire with a heart attack."

Lace kept her words to herself. But her thoughts drifted, and before they reached his house, she felt certain she was in as bad a shape as Daniel. Maybe worse.

Chapter Seven

DANIEL WATCHED AS LACE slowly pulled herself from the car. He was rushing things, pushing her too fast. She still needed time to heal, and today, with all the running around, she looked especially tired. Beautiful, but tired. He held her arm to make certain she wouldn't slip on the icy ground and looked down at her.

"This was a bad idea."

Lace reached up and smoothed her fingertips over his mouth. "Nonsense. It's an excellent idea. Don't be nervous."

His eyes widened. Lace thought he feared the idea of being intimate? What he feared was the depth of his feelings for her. It wasn't something he'd bargained for. Knowing she'd gone to another doctor to have her wound checked, then later to have the stitches removed, had outraged his possessive instincts. He didn't trust anyone else to care for her—and he didn't want anyone else looking at her body. Ridiculous, being that he was a doctor himself and understood the level of detachment between physician and patient.

Somehow it just didn't matter with Lace.

"You look ready to fall on your face. Have you taken a pain pill today?"

She scoffed. "I don't need them anymore. Honestly, Daniel, I'm fine. Quit clucking like a mother hen, take a deep breath and invite me in."

He succumbed to her suggestion. Of course, being that he was male and she was more beautiful and desirable than any woman he'd ever known, she might have stood silent and he'd have given in. He wanted her too much to wait.

A huge wreath decorated his front door, drawing Lace's attention. "You enjoy decorating for the holidays, don't you?"

He unlocked the door and pushed it open. "It's a tradition. My mother always had a wreath on every door, mistletoe in every doorway, and lights strung over everything that didn't move. Annie and Max can barely remember, but I do."

He held her hand as they stepped inside, then he kissed her, a light, teasing kiss that made her smile. He pointed toward the ceiling. "Mistletoe," he said.

Lace kicked the door closed with her small boot, took him by the collar of his coat, and pulled his mouth down to her own. "A real kiss," she whispered against his mouth.

Damn, but she could make his hair curl when she put her mind to it. Daniel tried to keep his hands at his sides, tried to moderate his breathing. But then her tongue touched his and he lost control. He pulled her gently closer, meshing their bodies together, instinctively pressing his groin into her soft belly. He ate at her mouth, loving the taste of her, and she moaned in approval.

"Lace..."

"Let's get out of our coats." He watched as she shrugged off her cape, letting it slip to the floor behind her. Dressed in her requisite black, she looked stunning. A black, hip-length cashmere sweater, black leggings, and black ankle boots made the paleness of her hair and the deep green of her eyes more pronounced.

She looked at him expectantly and he slipped his own coat off, draping it over an arm. He wanted to get out of everything, wanted her naked and open and anxious, but he had to play shy and timid. That took a lot of thought, so he used the time it took him to put their coats away to ponder the problem.

"Would you like some coffee?" Even as the words left his mouth, he winced. He sounded like a damned inane fool.

She blinked at him in lazy confusion. "Above all things, coffee was what I wanted."

He started to laugh, but turned it into a cough. Impatient little witch. "You can look around at the house if you like, while I get the coffee going."

To his surprise, she headed down the hall to the bedrooms. Daniel leaned around the corner and watched her.

"Which room is yours?"

His brain immediately conjured vivid images of her stripping naked, reposing herself on top of his patchwork quilt, arranging herself for his perusal. He shook his head. "The door at the very end of the hall. Along the way is the hall bath, my study and a spare room, in that order."

"Thanks." She disappeared into his bedroom, and curiosity got the better of him. He followed.

"What are you doing, Lace?"

"Just looking around, as you suggested. You've seen my bedroom, inspected my drawers and my underthings. It only seems fair that I have a peek, too."

"You intend to check out my briefs?"

"Hmm. Later, when you undress." Her eyes shown brightly with a mixture of nervousness and excitement. "But for now, I just wanted to see your house, to see if I come away as surprised as you did."

He barely registered her words; his brain had quit functioning when she mentioned watching him strip. "Lace, aren't you going a bit fast?"

She looked under his high, antique bed. Why, he had no idea. Did she think he hid girlie magazines there? Or maybe a girlie? Next, she peered into his closet.

"I'm only trying to catch up, Daniel." Her hands trembled as she rifled through his clothes. "Don't worry. I'm not rushing you."

"I wasn't worried."

She flashed him a quick, nervous smile. "Good. I want you to relax, to think of this as a natural thing."

"'This'?"

"Us being together. There's nothing to fear, you know. I'm not going to be judging your performance." Her cheeks pinkened and she cleared her throat. "As you said, we'll just get better acquainted with each other."

Crossing his arms behind his back, he leaned against the wall. He needed the physical support to remain upright. "I sort of figured we'd start in the living room, have a little conversation, maybe neck a little."

"I imagine we'll neck a lot." She tilted her head toward him. "You do like kissing, don't you? Even though you need some practice?"

"I like kissing."

"Excellent." She perched on the edge of his bed and bounced lightly, testing his mattress, he supposed. His vision fogged. "Soft enough. That's good."

He started to ask, *Soft enough for what?* but couldn't seem to force the words from his mouth, not with Lace leaning down to tug off her boots. Then he noticed the slight frown of pain her movements caused her, and he went to her.

"Let me do that."

Kneeling, he took her small foot onto his lap and pulled off her boot. Lace took his actions in stride, leaning back onto her elbows on his bed and watching him with an interested gaze. After he'd pulled off the second boot, he stood. "Comfy?"

"I'm getting there."

Her voice had dropped a little and the pink flush staining her cheeks spread to her throat. Arousal. His knees nearly buckled. He wanted to step between her legs and lower his body onto hers, to press his hard frame into her soft one. He wanted to ride her gently until she cried out, then ride her hard until they were both insensate. Instead, he sat beside her on the mattress and tried to look uncertain. The effort sorely taxed him.

"Are you sure you don't want any coffee?"

She took several fast, shallow breaths, then shook her head. "I want you."

His eyes closed and he swallowed. If he moved, he'd blow everything. He hadn't counted on the effect of her words, of her desire. He couldn't do this, couldn't pretend a distance he didn't feel, not when every muscle in his body strained for her, not when he felt harder than he ever had in his entire life.

The bed dipped as Lace sat up. He felt his glasses slide off as she removed them, then the cool, soft touch of her mouth on each eyelid. Evidently she'd taken his hesitation for reserve and was determined to encourage him.

"Number one, Daniel. There's nothing to be embarrassed about." Her voice was soft, breathy. "Anything we do to-gether, anything we find mutually satisfying, is good."

His fingers knotted in the quilt to keep from touching her. He kept his eyes closed. Lace leaned across him to put his glasses on the nightstand, then caught the hem of his sweater and worked it up his body.

"I love how you look, Daniel." He obediently raised his arms when she nudged him, and the sweater skimmed over his head. Lace tossed it aside and then smoothed his hair back into place, petting him, but not where he'd like, not where he desperately wanted her touch.

Her knuckles brushed his belly when she began working on his belt and he groaned, a ragged, hoarse sound. His body shook with the restraint put on it, and matched the nervous shaking of her hands.

With her lips touching his ear, Lace whispered, "Lean back."

When he didn't do so quickly enough to suit her, she pressed her hands to his shoulders and urged him backward. He went, but she went with him, landing on his chest with a soft sigh. He felt her hair sweep down to tickle his cheekbones as she touched her mouth to his. Her hands coasted over his shoulders, then his chest, lightly striking over his nipples. He pressed his head back into the mattress and tried to think of other things, of the hospital, the snow outside. Lace kissed his throat.

"You're so tight. Relax a little."

His rough laugh showed her how ludicrous he thought that suggestion to be.

Then she went back to his belt.

Out of sheer preservation, Daniel caught her hands. "Lace, wait." He didn't recognize his own voice.

"Shh. It's all right. I won't hurt you."

That bit of inanity nearly pushed him over the edge. Enough was enough. If she didn't slow down, he wouldn't last, wouldn't be able to give her pleasure, and more than anything, more than his own need, he wanted to see Lace McGee in the throes of a climax.

He carried each of her small fists to his mouth and kissed them. "Don't you have some catching up to do?"

When she lifted a brow, he touched the edge of her sweater, then saw her cheeks darken with color as understanding dawned.

"You...you want me to take my clothes off?"

Her nervous response was endearing, especially in light of how hard she'd been working to relax him, to put him at ease. "Don't you want to?" he asked, managing to inject just enough insecurity into his question to prompt her to action.

"Sure. All right." If anything, she looked even more uncertain, and he wondered at it. Perhaps she had a special way of doing things, a certain organization to her seduction. Maybe disrobing was supposed to come later, but he needed to have access to her now, to touch and taste her so that they'd both be in the same boat, so to speak. When he drowned, he wanted her with him.

Lace turned her back and wiggled out of her sweater, taking her time about it. Daniel admired the smooth line of her back, the dip of her waist, the flare of her hips. She had one tiny mole on the top of her right shoulder blade, and he leaned forward to kiss it. Lace froze.

Warily looking over her shoulder at him, she asked, "Well? Shouldn't you be getting your shoes off?"

He didn't understand her rush. To Daniel, most of the pleasure in lovemaking was taking his time, enjoying a woman's body, playing with her, teasing. Letting the tension build until they were both crazy with need. Lace seemed to be moving at Mach speed for some reason. He wondered if his supposed inexperience made her nervous, or if she assumed he was the one in a hurry.

Maybe she even thought he'd back down if she didn't race through things.

He smiled at her. "If that's what you want. You're the one in charge here, remember."

She unhooked the front closure of her bra—a snowy white, lacy affair that surprised him as much as it pleased him. She held the cups to her chest and kept her back turned to him. Despite his building urgency, he shrugged, willing to let her call the shots.

When he leaned over to yank off his shoes and socks, Lace draped herself across his back and hugged him. The shock of feeling her soft, full breasts against his skin made him shudder. He started to turn to her, but she held him tight. "Shh. Relax, Daniel."

He wished she'd quit telling him that. Relaxation at this point was as beyond him as the moon.

Smoothing her palms up and down his skin, she let her nipples graze his back again and again until he knew he'd explode if she didn't stop. It would all be over with, and Lace would be assured of his inept abilities. He grit his teeth and forced her to release him as he turned.

Her gaze moved away as he looked at her. She was so

damned sexy, so beautiful. It was his turn to press her back onto the mattress, and she allowed it, closing her eyes and biting her lips. Daniel stripped her leggings off her with one long tug, taking her matching white bikini panties at the same time. Lace turned her face away, until her nose almost touched the mattress. But since his attention wasn't centered on her nose, he dismissed her actions and took in the beauty of her body.

She wasn't perfect, as he'd always thought, but the narrowness of her hips excited him, as did the slight swell of her belly. Beneath her breasts he could see her ribs and he thought she needed to gain some weight, but her legs, long and lightly muscled and smooth, made it impossible to draw a deep breath.

The curly tangle of hair between her thighs was pale and silky, and he smiled. A true blonde.

Belatedly remembering his plan, he whispered, "I want to kiss you, Lace."

Her eyes shot open, caught the direction of his gaze, and she gasped. "Where?"

Everywhere. "Wherever you'd like."

She licked her lips and a frown of concentration puckered her brow. Finally, after an undue amount of thought and an audible swallow, she touched her breast. "Here."

Daniel laid his hand gently on her breast, then watched her belly hollow out as she sucked in her breath. Slowly, letting her anticipate his touch, he circled her nipple with one fingertip. Her nipple puckered, and the pale pink turned rosier. Lightly, he pinched, and she twisted, curling in on a low sound of pleasure.

Never had he been so aroused over so little, but seeing Lace's free response nearly broke his restraint. He leaned down and licked her, one slow stroke of his tongue. "Here?"

Her breathing turned raspy, and she nodded.

He kissed her, a small, lighter-than-air touch, then asked, "You're certain?"

"Yes!" She gripped his head and pressed him closer.

Smiling, he took her deep into his mouth and sucked tenderly. Lace tangled her fingers in his hair and held him tight, one of her long legs snagging his hips and pulling his body close. She groaned and whimpered, and her reaction fueled his own.

He kissed her other breast, then jerked free to shove off his pants. Lace watched him through wide, glazed eyes. He lowered himself back to her side and cupped her mound, tangling his fingers in her soft, curly hair. She arched against him, breathless, trembling. "Daniel, please."

"Tell me what to do." No longer playing the novice, he asked out of a sense of seduction, knowing the question would arouse her further, would allow her to keep that impression of control.

"Touch me." The words were said on a moan, and Daniel complied.

His fingers pressed, parted. The soft sounds coming from deep in her throat encouraged him.

"Open your legs a little, sweetheart."

The second her thighs parted, he slipped his finger in, not deep, just teasing, testing her readiness. To his surprise and immense pleasure, she was wet, hot, swelled. And incredibly tight. He groaned with her.

They each seemed to have forgotten their roles, and Daniel had no intention of reminding her. He could barely think, barely breathe; he sure as hell couldn't act!

Lace's hips lifted in tandem with the movements of his hand and suddenly it was too much. He turned away to retrieve a condom from the nightstand, and he no sooner had it on, than Lace was reaching for him, her fingers digging deep into the muscles of his shoulders, urging him to haste.

A single second of clarity righted in his mind, and he clasped Lace's hips, remembering her injury. "Onto your side, sweetheart."

She froze, then stared at him.

"I don't want to hurt you, Lace." His words were hushed, hurried. "It'll be easier on you this way. I can control things better."

She frowned, her eyes momentarily darkening in suspicion, but he didn't give her a chance to think about this evidence of his experience. He turned her to face him, then brought her uninjured leg over his hip.

Lace stared at him wide-eyed, confused, anxious, curious. He wanted to bury himself in her, make her a part of him, but he'd noticed the still pink scar on her bottom, an angry reminder of her delicate condition. Daniel touched it lightly with his fingertips, soothing her, then summoned the last of nearly lost reserve and entered her gently, measuring her, clenching his jaw at the tightness of her, the natural resistance of her body. He saw Lace squeeze her eyes closed, saw her soft lips part as she drew in a long shuddering breath. Her shoulders grew taut, her back arched as she pushed her hips toward him.

By small degrees, he went deeper, trying to moderate his movements, trying to protect her from the violence of his lust. He moved one hand to her belly and caressed her, smiling at her small cry of excitement.

Her feminine muscles squeezed him, holding him so tight. *Too tight,* as if she'd never been touched this way before. And in the space of a heartbeat, realization hit and he lost his breath in one loud whoosh.

"Lace?" He stared at her flushed face and waited for the world to right itself.

Her arms slid up to tighten around his neck and she pressed her cheek into his throat. "This…" She swallowed, and he could feel the slight movements of her body, the way she tried to remain still but couldn't. "This is a…a *bad* time for talking, Daniel."

"But you're a *virgin?*" He tried to dip his head, to see her face, but she kept her expression hidden. A virgin? His mind couldn't simulate the consequences of such an occurrence. He stared at her tumbled hair, at her trembling shoulders, and he felt something strange, something warm and insistent and deep invade his soul. It curled in his chest, squeezing him, making his vision cloud with emotion, making his heart ache.

"Yes, Daniel, I'm aware of that." She sounded ragged, her voice trembling. "It would be a difficult thing for me to miss."

Damn difficult for him to miss, too. Why hadn't she told him? Various reasons presented themselves, but he couldn't seem to grasp a single one. "Lace..."

"Not *now*, Daniel!"

She moved, pressing back against him, demanding his attention—*as if she didn't already have it.* And he groaned, rational thought completely beyond him, his wits successfully scattered by the tight, rhythmic clasp of her body. He held her hips and thrust himself completely into her, reveling in her groans, her awkward attempts to counter his movements.

No man had ever held her this way. No man had ever touched her as he had.

The truth pounded through his brain, through his heart. His body seemed to pulse with physical and emotional sensations, combining to destroy his strength and thought. On some subconscious level, he remained aware of her recent hurts and moderated his thrusts, careful not to add to her injury. She cried out, first in low groans, then increasing, each sound, each small whimper, driving him higher until he knew he wouldn't last, until he was lost and there was no hope for it, no pulling back.

He covered her breasts with his palms, lightly bit her shoulder and muffled his hoarse shout against her soft, fragrant skin as he shuddered out his release.

After a moment his weight caused her to collapse. Daniel rolled onto his back, his arms wide, his legs numb, his body still pulsing in pleasurable throbs of aftershock.

He became aware of Lace moving beside him, of her watching him curiously. "You're not going to do something stupid like fall asleep, are you?"

Grinning was a feat requiring more strength than he presently owned. "No. Rest."

Lace smacked his shoulder. "Why did you quit?"

He cocked one eye open and found her looming over him. "I was done." He meant *done for,* shot, incapable of breathing, much less moving, but she didn't take it that way.

She leaned down until her nose almost touched his. "Well, I wasn't done!"

"I know. Sorry." He closed his eyes, fighting the urge to laugh. "Let me catch my breath and I'll show the...depth of my atonement for leaving you."

"Humph!"

She started to leave the bed, but he caught her arm and tugged her back down. "Don't be angry, Lace. I said I'll make it up to you."

"How?"

"Don't look at me as if I have evil intents on your fair person." Now he did chuckle. The absurd humor of the situation did much to revive him. She scowled, started to speak, and he kissed her. A real kiss, using all his expertise, intent on showing her just how good they could be together.

And Lace, unfulfilled, her body still warm and trembling, melted like an ice cube in the August sun.

Daniel kissed her until she clutched at him, until her nails dug into his flesh, until her body moved against his in need. He slid down her body, to her breasts and her still rosy, puckered nipples. He nipped and licked and praised her for her deep, throaty moans, given without artifice, without holding back. His tongue flicked over the tip of her nipple and she cried out, pulling him closer. He suckled her until her hips jerked upward, seeking him, her need as strong as his own.

"You're so beautiful, Lace."

This time she didn't tease him about the compliment. She

whimpered, her body damp with a fine sheen of sweat. He kissed her belly and she writhed beneath him as he moved lower, lower. When he parted her with his thumbs and covered her with his mouth, she returned his praise in breathless words and seductive sounds, begging for more, and he gave it to her.

Without hesitation, in halting gasps, she told him what she liked, and in the middle of a muttered, nearly incoherent sentence of unnecessary instruction, she reached her peak, gasping, her body taut and her scent strong. She gave a muffled scream, and he loved it, thrilled with her response, and his obvious success. Daniel held her steady and continued to kiss and lick and stroke her until she went limp and her moans faded to soft, satisfied sighs.

He'd never taken so much pleasure in his ability to make love. He felt like crowing, like writing his own damn book—which could sit beside Lace's on the shelf. He gathered her close and stroked her back, her injured bottom. He felt the edge of the scar there, and wanted to kiss it. He kissed her open mouth instead, and smiled when she didn't so much as pucker. Breathing seemed to require all her concentration.

He was almost asleep, his brain finally at rest since the first time he'd met her, his body appeased, when suddenly Lace leaned up and her small fist thumped hard against his chest.

Here we go again, he thought, and opened his eyes in question.

"You miserable fraud! You rotten cretin! You know exactly what you're about, don't you?"

His chest swelled with pride; he felt like the Cheshire cat, his grin was so huge. "Actually, yes, I have been known to gain a compliment or two."

Her eyes narrowed to mere slits and she started to hit him again, but he caught her wrist. "Stop that. You'll hurt yourself."

Her eyes nearly crossed in her rage. "Dammit, Daniel—"

He interrupted, energy surging back into his body. "What about you, Lace? A damned *virgin?* I almost had heart failure!"

"So why didn't you?"

She didn't mean it, he thought, feeling his own annoyance grow. "If you want to know, I was too busy listening to you beg me to—"

She slapped her hand over his mouth. "I never begged."

He grinned, removing her hand. "Yeah, you did. And I enjoyed every word."

She jerked away from him. "Don't change the subject, Daniel. You lied to me."

True enough, but as far as he was concerned, the point was moot at this stage. He didn't want to fight. "Lace, we've both been less than honest, don't you think?"

"I never lied to you! You drew your own ridiculous conclusions. But you deliberately deceived me."

Leaning up on one elbow, he growled, "My conclusions weren't that ridiculous based on how you behaved around me. You came on to me constantly, Lace, with no show of discretion, despite the fact you knew I didn't want you."

"Ha! You wanted me all right. At least be honest about that."

He couldn't very well deny it, given that even now, he was getting hard again. They were on top of the quilt, both naked, and his renewed interest was more than obvious if the woman bothered to look down. He shrugged. "Yeah, but I did my best to hide it."

"Now that's a fact I know all too well." She looked at him with distaste. "You spend so much time hiding, from yourself and everyone else, it's a wonder your patients can ever find you."

"At least I own an ounce or two of propriety."

"Which translated, means I do not? Well, let me tell you something, *Danny.* I may have encouraged your stupid assumptions, but only because you made me so mad, always acting like you were better than me."

Quietly, his guilt strong, he said, "I never said that."

"But you thought it. It scares you to death that Annie and I are friends."

He felt lost, no sensible argument coming to his aid. Going on the defensive seemed his only recourse, and he did, summoning up his best show of umbrage. "Lace, how can you possibly be a virgin?"

"Simple." She curled her lip in a credible sneer and glared at him. "All I've ever met are jerks like you."

"So why did you sleep with me, Lace?" As he spoke, he trailed his fingertips down her arm and watched goose bumps rise in the wake. Ha! Regardless of what the woman would like him to believe, she wasn't immune to him. Not by a long shot.

That fact filled him with intense male satisfaction.

Lace scooted off the bed, then pulled back the coverlet and climbed beneath, pulling it up to her chin. Daniel enjoyed her antics, consoling himself over the loss of her nudity by the fact that she hadn't left the room or even the bed. She'd only grown tired of his overly interested gaze.

Sighing, he came to his feet beside the bed. He felt Lace watching him, her gaze warm and full of curiosity. He was still half hard, but he supposed they had to talk before they could proceed further.

The late afternoon light barely shone through his frost-covered window. Outside, a tree branch heavy with snow scraped the side of the house, moved by the winter wind. And in his bed, huddled under his covers with an adorable show of belated modesty, was the most appealing, most complex and intriguing woman he'd ever met. He stood by the side of the bed and slipped on his glasses; he wanted to see her clearly, to make certain he didn't miss a single thing about this very special moment in time. Then he propped his hands on his naked hips.

Lace's gaze skittered away, then back again. She licked her lips. "Why don't you put something on?"

"Answer my question, Lace."

Tightening her grip on the quilt, she glared up at him in

defiance. "Why shouldn't I have slept with you?" She waved a dismissive hand at his body. "You're available, attractive and even you had to have noticed the sexual chemistry between us."

"I'm not buying it, sweetheart."

"Don't call me that."

"You didn't complain earlier."

Heat blossomed in her cheeks. "I wasn't myself then."

Laughing, he sat on the edge of the bed and flicked the tip of her nose. "Whoever you were, I liked you. Hell, I still like you. Don't you like me just a bit?"

"No."

"Tsk, tsk. You shouldn't lie, Lace. A few hours ago I might have believed you. But not now. Now I know just how discriminating you've been all your life. And I know a little thing like sexual chemistry wouldn't have changed anything if you'd truly despised me."

"Well, there's where you're wrong. I'd never felt it before, so how could I help but respond to it?"

He wondered if she had any idea how her words affected him, how territorial they made him feel. He moved closer to her, propping his back on the headboard and tugging her close despite her resistance. "Just let me hold you, Lace. That is what men and women do after sex, you know." He paused, struck by his words. "Come to think of it, you wouldn't know, would you? But it's true. They hold each other."

"Not always." She tried to wiggle away, but when he held on, she relented and plopped back against him. "I know more about sex than you ever will, Daniel. I've been studying it my entire adult life. And what you say isn't at all true. Sometimes, after sex, the man just gets up and walks away."

"Or the woman."

She shrugged, a nonverbal agreement.

Daniel enjoyed the feel of her at his side, the plump softness of her breast pressed into his ribs, the silkiness of her hair against his chin. He kissed her crown and breathed in her scent.

He was aware of her thinking, considering everything that had happened. He didn't know what conclusions she'd drawn, and it bothered him. "Lace?"

Her sigh was one of disgust. "Honesty forces me to admit that there are a few select times when I suppose I like you a little."

He burst out laughing. "So fulsome with your compliments." She leaned her cheek against his chest and his arms tightened. "Well? When do you like me? Or is the situation so rare, you can't even remember anymore?"

"I remember." Her voice had turned soft, gentle. "When you're with Annie. You're so careful with her and it's obvious how much you care for her, how close the two of you are. It's a wonderful thing to witness. And Max, how you deal with him, though sometimes you are so blind I want to smack you. But other times, I can see how Max respects you, and he's a good man, mostly because of you."

He felt touched to his soul by her praise.

"Sometimes when I'm at the hospital with my own work, or meeting Annie there, I see you with a patient, and you have that intense, concentrated look on your face because you care so much."

Here she was, waxing eloquent on his sterling character, and he thought of all the times he'd put her down, judged her harshly. He'd been an idiot, a complete fool.

And he'd dug himself into a hole so deep, it would take him a while to work his way out.

His hand smoothed over her hip, toward her bottom. "I didn't hurt you, did I?"

Her nose bumped his nipple as she shook her head. "No. I'm fine."

"Lace?" He wanted her again, right now, this time with no games between them. He cupped her chin and started to tilt her face up. But she slipped away.

"Oh, no, you don't. I'm still mad at you, Dr. Sawyers. What you did was reprehensible. Will you take me home, or should I call a cab?"

Chapter Eight

"DO YOU SEE SANTA CLAUS out there, or are you just avoiding Daniel?"

Lace turned, smiling at Guy Donovan as he stepped up beside her at the dark window. She'd been staring out, daydreaming, feeling vaguely discontent. She welcomed the interruption to her thoughts. "It's a beautiful sight, with all the snow on the trees and the twinkling lights everywhere. I love Daniel's house, especially how it's situated here among all the trees."

Daniel's house had a homey, lived-in look, for a bachelor. The furniture, though dark and heavy, was comfortable and functional. And he'd hung prints on all the walls and set photos of his family everywhere. The house was one floor with a large basement and a spacious yard that abutted the woods in back and a narrow creek on one side; it was a house meant for a family, for kids.

Resting his long lanky body against the wall, Guy crossed his arms over his chest and studied her. "This house is fine. But Daniel should have kept his family home after his father moved out, instead of me living there. But the memories are too tough for him to deal with."

"I know." Daniel had already explained to her that Guy agreed to live in the family home, since Annie and Max had both taken apartments, and Daniel didn't want it. And like Daniel, his father avoided the house and the memories. All too often, it seemed, he avoided his children as well. Any reminder of his wife, especially at the holidays, was more than he wanted to deal with. Lace understood that, and how difficult it was for Daniel. "Daniel remembers his mother better than Max or Annie do."

"I remember her, too," Guy said. "She was a fantastic lady. Unlike Daniel, I like the reminders, seeing little things every day that bring back the memories. They're good memories. I practically grew up in that house, and I think it's important to keep it around, for Annie's and Max's sake."

"You and Daniel have been friends a long time."

A smile spread over Guy's face, and for the first time Lace noticed how handsome he was. With his ruthlessly short hair, rangy walk and sloppy attire, he'd always seemed inconspicuous enough.

Even now, at Daniel's Christmas get-together, Guy was dressed in a loose flannel shirt over a faded gray T-shirt with jeans that had seen better days. And his hair, short as it was, still managed to stick out at odd angles.

He ran his hand over that hair, demonstrating for Lace how such a style was possible, then nodded. "We've known each other since grade school. He's like a brother to me." His gaze scanned the room beyond them, and as Annie came into sight, her snug red dress hugging the curves of her body, Lace saw Guy stiffen and scowl.

Distracted, keeping his gaze on Annie, he muttered, "The Sawyers are like family, Max and Annie included."

Annie laughed at something Max said, swatted at her brother and moved out of view.

Guy gave his attention back to Lace. "I'm glad you came today. Annie enjoys your company and she needs more friends, to get out more often. She's been kind of strange lately."

Despite her resolve to forget Daniel's perfidy, Lace asked, "You're not worried about me corrupting her?"

"Annie? Ha! She has a will of iron and more stubbornness than her two brothers combined. Even as a baby, she could get her way on any and every little thing. No, Annie will always do exactly as she pleases, and she couldn't possibly be influenced by anyone to be other than what she wants to be. Usually a pain in the neck."

Lace looked back out the window. Snow on Christmas Day was supposed to be a magical thing. She felt anything but magical. Since that ill-fated day when she and Daniel had made love, she hadn't been able to think straight. She wanted to stay away from him, because she knew he was dangerous, both to her heart and her beliefs.

But he'd made her feel things she'd never imagined, and she wanted to feel them again. Even now, being in his home and hearing the music, the laughter and easy, casual conversation, made her crave things she had never wanted before. She wondered where her mother was, what she was doing and who she was with. She wondered if her mother had liked the vase, or if she'd even gotten the gift yet.

Lace swallowed and took another sip of her punch. Without her mind's permission, the words came out. "Daniel doesn't want me anywhere around his sister. He doesn't even want me around Max."

Guy tilted his head, considering that. "He's always been overprotective of Annie. He lost his mother, and he's afraid of losing her, too. Plus, he doesn't think any man is good enough for her, and he can't quite reconcile himself to the fact that Annie has grown up, that she's a woman now, and men might want her. It's easier to blame you than to accept that things are changing. As far as Max is concerned, he's just jealous."

Lace nearly dropped her cup of punch. "Jealous? Why in heaven's name would he be jealous of Max?"

"Lace." Guy shook his head, looking down at her with a

chastising frown. "You're not naive. You have to know Daniel wants you. But he thinks Max wants you, too. Hell, he thinks every man wants you, and it makes him nuts. That's the main reason he's so rude, you know. Not because he doesn't like you, but because he doesn't want every other man liking you."

Lace thought about the possibility of what he said. Obviously Guy had no idea that she and Daniel had already gotten past the hostility, however brief their truce had been. How could he know? Since that day, they'd hardly spoken without bickering. Daniel was irritated that she wouldn't see the reasoning behind his deception—even though he hadn't given her a good reason. And Lace simply wanted to avoid losing herself to a man who disdained her very existence, who was ashamed to admit he wanted her.

"Come on. Brooding over here in the corner isn't going to prove anything. And Annie is starting to give us worried glances. Besides, if you hide over here too long, Max will join you and try to steal a kiss, which will provoke Daniel just as Max hopes it will, and they'll start arguing. Christmas will be ruined."

Lace laughed. "So I have the power to single-handedly ruin a holiday for the entire family? I don't think so."

"I know so." Guy took her arm and herded her back to the living room. Lace felt like a shrimp beside him, he was so tall, a good three or four inches taller than Daniel and Max, who shared a similar height of six feet.

Daniel called everyone to dinner and Guy played the gallant, seating her next to him. Annie sat across from Guy, and Daniel and Max took opposite seats at the head and foot of the table.

They were still serving themselves when Max said, "Heard your show last night, Lace."

She scooped up a serving of mashed potatoes and passed on the bowl. Without looking up, she said, "That was a fun one, wasn't it?"

"I thought so." Then Max added, "And damned sexy."

"I wanted to do something a little more lighthearted for the holidays."

Guy handed her the platter of ham, then joined in. "I heard it, too. I loved the fellow who told how he'd met his wife in the back of a taxi they'd shared on Christmas Eve, both of them rushing to get a last-minute gift."

Annie leaned forward. "I heard that! It was so funny. Imagine practically making love to a stranger in a taxi!"

The sound of a chair scraping back drew everyone's attention. Daniel stood there, glaring at Lace. "Excuse me."

He walked out of the room, stiff-legged and stone-faced. Lace threw down her napkin, muttering to herself.

Max burst out laughing. "God, he's got it bad. I wish I could get him to listen to one of your shows, Lace. Imagine his reaction."

Lace turned her narrowed gaze on him. "He's never even listened?"

Annie reached across the table to pat her hand. "Now, Lace. You know how he is. Don't let it bother you."

Guy just pursed his mouth and looked thoughtful.

"I should probably go. Daniel obviously doesn't feel comfortable and I feel like an intruder."

Vehement rebuttals followed her statement until Daniel reentered and calmly set a bowl on the table. He scanned the group, his eyes finally landing on Lace, his expression once more composed. "I forgot the sweet potatoes."

Max chuckled. "Can't have Christmas dinner without sweet potatoes."

Other than the music in the background, silence reigned while everyone finished serving themselves and began to eat. Guy endeared himself to Lace for all time when he reopened the conversation.

"I've listened to quite a few of your shows, Lace, and I think you do a fantastic job. It always amazes me how many people call in, and how open you are about things, making them comfortable, giving them someone to talk to when they have no one else."

Annie glanced at her brother, then lifted her chin. "She does a great service. Even the show last night, though it didn't concentrate on problems, gave people a chance to remember how they'd felt when they fell in love for the first time. One man said he and his wife had been arguing about how expensive the holidays have gotten and how much she'd spent, when your show came on. Then he got to thinking, remembering when they'd met and all they'd been through, and instead of arguing, they...well..." Annie blushed, her gaze going to Guy. "You know."

Lace sighed. "They made love. I know. Too often people forget what is important and get wrapped up in the little things that annoy. It's all too easy to forget your priorities."

Max nodded, trying to look serious. "Like making love."

Exasperated, Daniel threw a spoon at him. "Will you knock it off?" But it was obvious he wasn't really angry because he chuckled. "You're such a damned reprobate, Max."

"It's my most redeeming quality."

They all laughed and after that, conversation resumed at a normal level. Lace stayed quiet, wishing herself elsewhere, anywhere other than in the midst of this family camaraderie. She felt out of place, and very uncomfortable. Fearing she might start another squabble, she simply stayed quiet and ate. Several times she felt Daniel watching her, but she refrained from looking at him, giving all her attention to the removal of the walnuts from her fruit salad.

When they all returned to the living room to open gifts, Lace tried to sidle off to a corner alone, but somehow she ended up sandwiched on the couch between Annie and Max. Guy sat on the floor across from them and Daniel passed out presents.

Max was incorrigible, shaking every gift, making wild

guesses about what might be inside. Annie and Guy ridiculed him, saying he'd be lucky to get more than a lump of coal.

After all the presents were dispersed, Daniel held up an arm, gave them all a huge smile, then dropped his hand as if signaling a race. The unwrapping began, and Lace, who'd had visions of a very dignified display, laughed hysterically at the frenzied ripping of silver paper and colorful ribbons.

Annie "oohed" over her teddy, then held it up to show the others. Max cursed, Guy's ears turned red and Daniel cast a frown at Lace.

Lace waited, on edge as the others opened presents. But her fears were unfounded. Max cheered over his jazz CD and Guy launched a sermon on the type of fish to be won with his new lures. Lace was relieved by their apparent satisfaction of her gifts and her insecurity was put to rest.

She sat there smiling, pleased with herself, until Max nudged her to open her own gifts. Tentative, Lace opened her gift from Max. Inside a sturdy box, nestled in tissue paper, she found a sculpted kitten of colorful carnival glass. The kitten frolicked, rolling itself playfully around a shiny ball. Lace bit her lip and thought of the perfect place to put the treasure, in the window over her kitchen sink where the sunlight would pour through it.

"It's beautiful, Max. Thank you."

Max grinned at her, looking almost bashful, and for the first time, she gave him a kiss. He pretended to swoon, much to Daniel's disgust.

"Now mine." Guy prodded his present toward her. She hadn't realized that everyone else had finished with their gifts, their enthusiasm making the process speedy in comparison with her restraint. She pulled the ribbon aside and carefully unfolded the paper. She found a beautiful selection of pastel-colored stationery bordered with flowers, her initials embossed on the top in bright, elegant script.

She ran her fingers over the lettering and then smiled. "Oh, Guy, it's perfect."

"So glad you like it. I know you do a lot of correspondence."

She accepted Guy's hug and did her best to ignore the way Daniel scrutinized her reactions. She didn't want anyone to know how emotionally touched she was by the gifts. She didn't want them to know how needy she suddenly felt.

Annie dropped a package in her lap. "Mine next. Come on, Lace, you're so slow."

Lace laughed, wiped at her eyes and, to please Annie, ripped the paper away. She eased her gift from the box, and it unfolded into an incredible mobile of crystal birds in every color. Fifteen birds hung suspended from gold chains at various levels. "Oh, Annie." Almost breathless, Lace searched for words. "It's…it's…" She bit her lip and shook her head.

Annie laughed at her surprise, and they hugged each other, laughing and crying, oblivious to the indulgent male smiles surrounding them.

"My turn." Daniel picked up a large flat package, two feet by three feet. Annie scrambled to get the other presents from Lace and pile them together. When Daniel set the package in her lap, Lace blinked at the weight of it.

"Careful. It's fragile."

Lace couldn't begin to imagine what it might be and she hesitated, looking at Daniel and feeling shocked at the tenderness in his eyes. She licked her lips and Max nudged her.

"Don't leave us in suspense. Get the thing open."

Teasing herself, Lace pulled away a corner of the paper, peeked inside, then covered it again. Her hand went to her throat and she blinked at all of them.

"What is it?" Annie asked.

Guy leaned forward. "Yeah, what did he get you?"

"It's too much."

Daniel shook his head. "I thought it was suitable."

"Oh, it is. But Daniel, it's…"

"Open the damn thing," Max complained.

Daniel nodded, encouraging her, watching closely to see her reaction, and Lace took a deep breath. She peeled back the paper and a beautiful, oak-framed stained glass appeared. The colorful glass was arranged in an exquisite profusion of spring flowers, delicately crafted, so many colors intertwined and complementing each other that even Guy and Max stared in wonder. Lace's black sweater and slacks made a dramatic backdrop for the brightness of the glass as she held it balanced on her lap.

Lace knew it was an artist's piece, not a factory product. She could barely breathe, it was so beautiful, and so perfect. Already, she wanted to see it with the sunshine glowing through it, over it. She imagined it hanging in her bedroom, the many colors floating across her rainbow bed in the morning, brightening her day. She laid it flat on her lap.

Burying her face in her hands, she burst into tears.

She wasn't sure how it happened, but suddenly there was a lot of shuffling and murmuring and she was alone in the room with Daniel and he was lifting the glass carefully away from her. His arms went around her and he hushed her with whispered words. "It's all right, Lace."

She shook her head. She felt like an idiot, started to say so and hiccuped instead. "How did they all know?"

"That you like color?"

She nodded.

"I don't think they're all as stupid as I am. They know you, Lace. They care about you."

That made her cry harder. She didn't want them to care about her. Did she?

Daniel handed her his hankie. "I hope these are tears of happiness, that you're not considering breaking the glass over my hard head."

"And ruin my gift? No, I wouldn't do that."

"I'm glad." He rubbed her back. "You know, you scared poor Annie to death."

"I'm sorry." Lace buried her face in his shoulder and refused to surface. She felt shamed to her very bones at her ridiculous display and didn't want to face anyone, much less Daniel.

"No reason to be sorry. Annie shuffled everyone into the kitchen to help with coffee. Max and Guy probably think it's your time of the month or something."

Lace slugged him in the stomach for that male-inspired observation, and he grunted, then grabbed her fist and flattened it on his thigh. "Be fair, Lace. To the average man, that's a thing of mystery. Men feel safe accounting all excessive female displays on a woman being womanly."

"The average man? I take it you're excluding yourself from that category?"

"I'm a doctor. Of course I'm exempt."

"I love my gift, Daniel. Thank you."

He cupped the back of her head and tilted her face up. When she allowed it, he wiped at the tears on her cheeks. "It feels so damn good to hold you again, Lace. You've made me miserable these past few days."

"Good."

A smile tilted his mouth. "You like it that I was unhappy?"

"I like it that I wasn't the only one feeling horrible."

He kissed her, but when they heard the conversation in the kitchen, he broke away.

"Does your family know we're...involved?"

Stroking her cheek with his thumb, he smoothed away a new tear and smiled. "Nah. They figured I was the most qualified to deal with your hysteria, so they ran like the cowards they are and left me to fend for myself."

Mortification had her hiding her face again. "This is awful. I'm so embarrassed."

"I'm sorry. I shouldn't tease you." He kissed her temple and then set her away from him. "They know you well enough,

Lace, to know you're usually alone on the holidays. And they know how emotional this time of the year is for everyone. No one thinks anything of it."

Running her fingers through her hair in an attempt to straighten it, Lace considered what to do next. She couldn't quite bring herself to look at Daniel.

"Would you like to help me pick up all this paper, then we can join everyone else?"

"Do you think they really liked my gifts? I wasn't sure..."

"Yes, *they* did. Very much"

Hearing the emphasis on "they," Lace grinned. She'd deliberately held his gift back, not wanting him to open it in front of everyone. "I have something for you, Daniel. But you have to wait until later."

His gaze darkened and he looked at her mouth with interest. "I hope it's what I'm thinking."

She laughed. "Well, it's not, so stop thinking it."

"Go away with me, Lace."

Her heart skipped a beat. "What?"

"Go away with me." He took her hands and held them close. "I know you have some time off now. Annie told me you're on vacation until after the first of the year. I am, too. Go away with me."

She stared at him, her body already heating in anticipation and her stomach growing tight. She carefully considered her response. "Go away, where?"

"I have a cabin. We could go there."

"I've never heard anything about a cabin."

"That's because I've told very few people about it."

"Wait a minute." A horrible suspicion began to gnaw on her brain and she glowered. "Why would you be secretive about the cabin?"

He looked away, then back again. "It just seemed appropriate, Lace."

Her eyes narrowed. "Is this some secret bachelor's cabin

where you conduct your little liaisons? Is this where you gained all that damned experience you used against me?"

He frowned. "Lower your voice. And I didn't use anything against you, dammit. I gave you pleasure."

"Ha! Answer my question. Is this where you take women you have affairs with so that your reputation won't get tarnished?"

His face reddened and to Lace, that was as good as an admission of guilt. She started to stand and he grabbed her. "Wait a minute. It's not like that at all. I've always tried to be discreet, something readily agreed on by the ladies involved, and this was the easiest way. But I haven't been there since I first met you and I only ask now so that we can be alone together, uninterrupted."

"You don't want anyone to know we're sleeping together!"

He pulled off his glasses and rubbed his face. "Lace, I'm not ashamed of being with you, if that's what you think. But I think we need time alone together to sort things out."

"What's there to sort? We wanted each other. It's as simple as that."

"Nothing about it was simple and you know it."

"It was for me."

He shook his head. "Okay, then. You say you slept with me because you wanted to. So what's changed? And don't tell me you don't want me anymore, because I won't believe you."

She didn't have a ready answer. And despite her arguments and indignation, she desperately wanted to go with him. "I'll have to think about it."

He made a sound of disgust and stood. "You do that."

Lace watched him begin snatching up tattered paper from the floor with excess energy. He wadded it into tight balls and hurled it all into the fireplace, where the paper burst into colorful flames. Lace stood to help him, her thoughts whirling.

As she tossed her own wad of paper into the fire, Lace shook her head. Daniel would someday get over his ridiculous conclusions that love was harmful and too powerful.

Then he'd marry some prim and proper little lady, probably a doctor's daughter or some such, and he'd live happily ever after in esteemed propriety.

And, like her mother, she'd miss him forever.

Lace squeezed her eyes shut and tried to push that troubling thought away, but it had rooted itself deeply and she felt buried beneath it. A wad of paper hit her in the rump and she turned. Max grinned at her.

"Sorry. You're blocking the fireplace."

With an evil smile and a sigh of relief to be distracted, Lace wadded another ball. Max went running. He caught Guy, who'd just started to wander in, and used him as a shield. Unfortunately, Lace had already let the wadded paper ball fly and it hit Guy square in the chest. He went stock-still and stared.

Lace took a step back, trying to stifle her laughter, but the expression on Guy's face proved to be too much and she giggled.

"Okay, then." Guy advanced, slowly, keeping Lace in his sights. Lace held out her hands, trying to ward him off even as she laughed some more. Just as he was ready to pounce, Annie slipped up behind him and slapped a huge red bow to the top of his head, where it clung to his short hair. Guy whirled on her and they both went running. Max watched them go, then hustled around the room gathering up new paper bombs, preparing for their return. He loaded up his arms and crept off after them.

Daniel slipped his arm around Lace. "They're all nuts, aren't they?"

She smiled. "Wonderfully so. You don't mind that they're racing through your house?"

"Why should I?"

Since she couldn't think of a single reason, she shrugged. They heard squealing from the guest bedroom and Max came tearing out, Guy right behind him, pelting him repeatedly in the back of the head with the paper bombs. They flashed past into the kitchen where a loud crash followed. Annie, her feet now missing her sexy high-heeled shoes, came through with her own arsenal, in hot pursuit.

"While we have a moment alone, tell me you'll go to the cabin with me." He tipped up her face, kissed her lightly and whispered, "I need you, Lace."

Her lungs squeezed tight and her heart expanded. There was really no reason to fight it, she decided, gladly giving up her resistance. "Yes, I'll go with you."

His eyes turned hot and she felt it clear to the bottom of her stomach. "You won't regret it, Lace. I promise."

Oh, that tone of voice, the meaning behind the words. She leaned toward him, and Max shouted, "We're going outside to build a snowman. Want to come along?"

Guilty, they jumped apart. When Lace looked at Max, he didn't taunt her. He kept his brows raised in a mildly curious expression.

"Mmm, how about I help Daniel clean up, then I'll make some hot chocolate for when you come back in?"

Max shrugged. "If you're sure you won't join us?" His gaze traveled from Lace to Daniel and back again. They both shook their heads.

He narrowed his gaze. "All right, then. But you two behave yourselves in here. Don't do anything I wouldn't do."

Laughing, Lace pointed a finger at him. "There isn't anything you wouldn't do!"

"Oh, yeah. In that case, have at it." He gave Daniel a salute and seconds later he and Guy trudged outside.

Annie ran past to the guest bedroom, and when she reappeared she wore jeans as tattered as Guy's, with scuffed boots, one of Daniel's old sweatshirts and his coat. She waved on her way out.

"My sister, the tomboy. What a relief. For a minute there, when she showed up in that damn killer dress, I thought I'd lost her forever."

Lace took in the affectionate smile on his face and felt compelled to warn him. "You'll never lose her, Daniel, but the woman in the red dress is as much a part of Annie now as the tomboy. Just as you've saved her old clothes, you now have to accept the new. And even you have to admit she looked terrific."

Instead of admitting anything, Daniel looped his arms around her and kissed her long and deep. His hands cupped her bottom and he urged her closer. "What I noticed is how good you look." He stared at her mouth, speaking through small nipping kisses. "You're beautiful."

Embarrassed, she pulled away and forced a laugh. "I imagine I look wrecked after crying and making a fool of myself."

"No one thought you were a fool, least of all me." He studied her face. "Tell me how you've been this past week. You didn't overdo it, did you?"

"With my friendly neighbors dropping in to help, not to mention Annie and Max? No, I didn't overdo."

Daniel stepped closer, looming over her. She knew that look, the one he employed when irritated, and she braced herself. "Your neighbor? The guy with all the gold chains and the killer dog?"

"The dog is being trained and already shows much better manners. The neighbor is full of gratitude because I was so understanding. He offered to pick up my mail and paper since you weren't there to intimidate him." She lifted her chin. "I declined his offer."

Daniel relaxed and she rolled her eyes. "For heaven's sake, you couldn't really be worried about him."

"Not worried. I just don't like him."

"Why?"

He muttered something, then threw out his arms in exasperation. "His damn dog tried to have you for breakfast. That's reason enough, isn't it? Now tell me when we can leave."

Wondering if Guy had been right, if Daniel could possibly

be jealous, she decided to let it drop. "Instead, why don't I give you your present?"

His brows lifted. "I wait with bated breath."

Lace went to a bag she'd set in the entry hall and carried it back to where Daniel stood by the tree. He hadn't moved. She handed him the first gift from the bag. He turned it this way and that, shook it, squeezed it.

"Oh, for heaven's sake, will you just open it?"

"All right." He tore the package open and removed a pair of lemon yellow silk briefs. Lace bit her lip to hold back the laughter while Daniel examined his gift from every possible angle. Finally he said, "The color will do wonders for my eyes."

Lace coughed, which turned into a snicker, and finally a robust laugh. When she started to quiet, she took one look at Daniel, and lost it again.

"Brat."

"I'm sorry." She took deep breaths to gain control. "Does this mean you don't like your gift?"

"I like it fine, as long as you don't expect me to wear it."

"Oh, but I do." She bobbed her eyebrows as she said it. "I can already picture it."

"Well, don't."

"I have one more thing for you."

"More underwear?"

She chuckled again, but shook her head. "No. Something else."

This package was smaller and she warned him not to shake it.

It was wrapped in a way that the lid came off without tearing the gold foil paper and Daniel treated it gently, setting the lid aside. He pushed back the tissue paper and then stared. "A pocket watch."

Lace licked her lips, overcome with nervousness. "Annie told me you didn't wear a wristwatch because it bothered you. I thought this way you could drop it into your pocket."

He lifted the watch out carefully, as if it were made of fine crystal. Lace practically bounced beside him, hoping he'd like it, afraid he wouldn't. He studied the watch, hefted it in his palm.

Lace swallowed, then summoned every ounce of her courage. "I had it engraved on the back."

His gaze flicked to her face and then back to the watch. He turned it over in his palm and read the inscription. "Dr. Daniel Sawyers—brother, friend, physician." His eyes met hers. "I don't understand."

It was impossible to stay still, and she shifted again. "That's what you are," she explained with a small shrug. "All those things. You understand what it means to be family, to have responsibilities. And you take those responsibilities to Max and Annie very seriously. And you're the very best doctor I've ever known and an incredibly good friend to Guy. I didn't know how to say it…how to put into words how much I admire you for that."

He touched her cheek and she rambled even more. "I know we argue a lot and I sometimes insult you."

"Sometimes."

"So I wanted you to know how I really feel, that I'm glad to know you and that I think you're an incredibly good man."

He stepped close, crowding her, the watch now gripped in his fist. He wouldn't let her look away, wouldn't let her hide from the admission of her words.

"Do…do you like it okay?"

"I like the watch very much. I like the inscription even better." He kissed her, and there was so much in that kiss, things she couldn't begin to comprehend, but she felt them all the same.

She blinked up at him and he smiled. "Thank you, Lace."

"Well." Lace felt at a loss for further words. The way he watched her made her feel vulnerable and she didn't like it. With a false laugh, she stepped away and clasped her hands together. "I'm glad this is working out. Maybe this little trip you have planned to the cabin will clear the air, get rid of some of the sexual tension between us, and we'll actually be able to be friends instead of adversaries. What do you think, Daniel?"

When she looked up, Daniel again looked remote. He turned the watch over in his palm, shook his head and stuck it in his pocket. "With you, Lace, I never know what the hell to expect. I think I'll just wait and be surprised."

Chapter Nine

DANIEL WATCHED HER WALK AROUND, pretending to familiarize herself with the cabin. She looked ready to jump out of her skin. He smiled to himself and slipped up behind her. "Are you nervous?"

She jerked, then turned to face him. "Nervous? No. Why would I be nervous, for heaven's sake?"

Her gaze darted around, studying every inch of the cabin. She looked at the fireplace, where he'd already started a fire, and then to the candles he'd lit to provide added muted light, to help set the mood.

Looping his arms around her, he anchored her to him and nuzzled her neck. "Maybe you're nervous because you're not as worldly as you like to pretend. Because being with a man, and making love, is new to you."

"Ha!" She pushed against his chest, putting space between them. "We've already done…" She waved at the bed. "This."

"Not really." Daniel slipped her cape off her shoulders and draped it over a chair. If she had any inkling of the things he wanted to do to her, that he planned to do to her, he had no doubt she'd be twice as skittish.

The cabin was small, with a king-size bed in the only bedroom, visible through the open door. A plush furniture grouping sat to one side of the living room, forming a conversation pit that faced a large stone fireplace. A state-of-the-art entertainment center occupied one entire wall. Scented candles were situated everywhere, even, she had noted, in the bathroom, which was equipped with a Jacuzzi tub.

The cabin was a place of seduction, a retreat meant to indulge the senses. It was obvious he intended to indulge Lace very thoroughly. And himself in the bargain.

"Lace, it's okay to be a little unsure of yourself. Talking about sex and making love are two different things."

She stiffened and turned to glare at him. "Are you suggesting I don't know what I'm talking about?"

At the moment every word she said, every action, delighted him. She was so womanly, and she was his. No man had been with her except him, and she was here with him now. He felt exuberant, alive and nothing could damage his mood.

"Sweetheart, I'm only suggesting that you might be a little unsure of yourself. After all, despite all your vocalizing on the subject, you have very little hands-on practice."

"That doesn't mean I don't understand—"

Daniel kissed her. He didn't want to waste another single second debating the issue. Finesse was the last thing on his mind, and he kissed her with all the hunger, greed and urgency he felt. He pushed his tongue into her mouth, then groaned when she touched her own to his.

"Damn, Lace…"

He kissed her again. She cuddled close, pressing her body into his, trying to get closer. Their clothes were in the way and he wanted her naked, now, but he pulled back. She went on tiptoe to try to kiss him again, and he had to hold her back.

"Just a minute, Lace. Let me catch my breath."

"Why?"

He hugged her tight, charmed by her innocence. "Lace, what we did the last time, that wasn't even close to what it should be. I goofed, mostly because I wanted you too much and I rushed things."

"It felt right to me."

"Which only goes to show that what I said is true. You need more experience. With me."

She looked around the cabin again and scowled. "It certainly seems you've had enough practice. I can't believe you have this place, that you sneak here for your little rendezvous."

"I don't sneak, I'm only discreet. How many times do I have to tell you that?"

"Who else knows about this place?"

He sighed. When Lace wanted a fight, she was like a bulldog with a meaty bone. "My father knows. And Guy and Max."

With her hands on her slim hips and the most evil expression he'd ever seen in her eyes, she stalked up to him until they were nose to nose. "I see. All the men know. But not poor little innocent Annie."

"There's no reason for Annie to know…"

"Have Guy and Max used this place?"

He felt like squirming, but resisted the inclination. "It's not my place to say what other men have…"

"Ha! In other words, they have. So this is the 'guys' place,' is that it? This is where the men hang out when they want to do lascivious things?"

With his teeth gnashing together, Daniel agreed. "It allots a certain amount of privacy, yes."

"So. What if Annie had wanted to indulge in some lascivious pursuits? You prefer she does her rendezvousing out in the open? You would keep this palace of private seduction from her?"

He removed his glasses and rubbed his eyes. "All right. I'm a male chauvinist pig. Feel better? I wallow in the double standard and I probably always will, at least where my little sister is concerned." He sighed and gave her a questioning look. "How the hell did I go from apologizing for my feeble performance to discussing my lack of understanding on the feminine sexual revolution?"

She grinned at him and shrugged. "I'm sorry. But it just rankles that you have this place."

"Why? I thought you believed in mature, adult relationships. You know how I feel...*felt,* about getting involved." Lace didn't notice his correction, and Daniel decided not to rush his fences. Especially with her being so prickly. "I'm a man, Lace. I have the same urges as any other."

"Not toward me, you didn't. At least, not until you found out I was a virgin. Now I'm suddenly good enough to grace your little cabin?"

Okay, so my good humor isn't endless. Daniel twisted his jaw, trying to hold the words back, but Lace tapped her foot on the hardwood floor and he lost the struggle.

"Dammit, can I help how I feel, Lace? I can't deny that I'm...flattered to be the only man you've been with. But I swear, if you hadn't been a virgin, I'd still have asked you here. Long before we made love, I knew I was fighting a losing battle. And I might be a fraud, but I'm not a total hypocrite. I don't expect all women to be virginal."

Lace plopped down on the couch and put her hands on her knees. "I suppose I can understand. Most people do tend to feel territorial in these situations."

He bit his upper lip, not overly thrilled with his feelings being termed a *situation.* She started to articulate on her latest theory, but Daniel held up his hands. "I concede to your professional assessment. In fact," he lied with a convincing air, determined to get things back on his designated track, "I was hoping you'd give me a demonstration of all your assembled knowledge."

She didn't look insulted by his suggestion. She looked intrigued.

He held out his arms like a sacrifice. "I'm waiting to benefit from your wealth of scientific edification."

"Is that so?" She pushed herself up from the couch and

came to stand in front of him. He dropped his arms and smiled. "Anxious to get started, are you?"

He traced her collarbone with one finger and watched her shiver. "Very anxious. Will you enlighten me with your accumulated wisdom? Will you instruct me?"

She bit her lip, then looked at him suspiciously. He saw comprehension in her gaze, and then stubborn determination. She blushed, but she stared him in the eye. His groin tightened when he realized what that look meant.

"Certainly, Daniel. I'll instruct you. If you're sure you want me to."

His lungs constricted, but he managed to croak, "Absolutely." Hell, he'd had fantasies about it. "You just tell me what to do, and I'll do it."

She nodded, resolute. "Okay. First off, I think you're right. We rushed things the last time. Not that it wasn't wonderful, but...we should try to get to know each other's preferences a little more."

He preferred her naked, moaning his name while he watched her climax, but he kept the thought to himself.

"Fine. What would you like to know?"

"Let's get comfortable, shall we?"

She took his hand and led him to the couch in front of the fireplace. He sat and she half sprawled beside him, her long legs stretched out, her arm on the couch behind him. She toyed with his shirt collar, her breasts pressed into his shoulder. The witch.

"Now, Daniel, tell me what turns you on."

He swallowed. All right, if she wanted to play games, he could hold his own. "You turn me on."

"No, no, no. More specific. What is it a woman does that you like?"

His gaze narrowed and he considered his replies. She was right when she said he'd been more conventional in his activities. He'd certainly never spoken so openly about his preferences with a woman. But with Lace, he felt challenged.

"I like it when a woman isn't restrained. When she moans to let me know how she feels—the way you did."

Lace blushed. He smiled and expounded on his confession. "You moan very nicely, honey. Deep and raw and real."

She cleared her throat and slipped her hand inside his shirt. "Anything else?"

"Yes. The way you moved. I touched you and you pushed against my fingers, my mouth." He was hard, aching. His blood rushed through his veins. "And I like the way you smell. All soft and female and sweet."

"Daniel…"

He cupped her breast and found her nipple stiff and beckoning. He toyed with it and Lace closed her eyes, a soft moan escaping her lips. "Just like that, Lace. You like it when I touch you here, don't you?"

She pierced him with a look so intent, so hot, he almost gasped. "I like it better when it's your mouth."

He stripped her shirt over her head and tugged down her bra. At the last second he caught himself. He licked her, letting his tongue flick and hearing her small anxious breaths.

Without hesitation, she said, "I want you to suck me, Daniel."

His control shot to hell, he did as she asked, moaning with her as he drew her into the heat of his mouth. He left her nipple wet and blew on it, his breath causing it to pucker even more. Then he switched to her other breast.

Lace reached for his shirt and began tugging it off, her movements no longer calculated, but frenzied. "Don't you want to hear all the things I like, Daniel?"

"Absolutely," he mumbled while helping her remove his shirt, at the same time continuing to kiss her soft flesh.

"I like your chest." She pulled away enough to run her fingers through the hair there. "When I first saw you sleeping at my apartment and I saw your chest, it made me feel funny."

"Funny how?" His voice was breathless, almost as breathless as hers.

"All tingly and warm. I'd never really wanted anyone before, I don't think." She shook her head. "No, that's a lie. I'd wanted you before that, too. Just not quite that badly."

"You should have told me."

"Mmm." She let her fingers trail down to his slacks. "I should have had my wicked way with you, knowing what you think of me?"

He kicked off his shoes as she tackled his belt. "I don't think you're wicked."

She chuckled. "I know. Now you mistakenly think I'm some innocent little maid." She licked his chin, and then his chest. "But I am wicked. Very wicked."

"I never said..."

"Take off your clothes, Daniel, and let's go to bed."

He shouldn't have been surprised. Lace was out to prove a point, and he knew, whatever the point might be, he'd enjoy it. He grinned, daring her with a look. "I will if you will."

A smile twitched on her mouth, then she stood and very casually stripped in front of him. He could barely breathe; every muscle in his body turned rock-hard. As she removed each article of clothing, she watched him—and lectured.

"A lot of women are terribly shy about being naked. Did you know that, Daniel?"

He nodded dumbly, his mouth dry at the sight of her.

"They think their bodies are inferior because they try to compare themselves to all the nude models in men's magazines. It's hard to convince them that men don't expect perfection, that no two bodies are alike and that's a good thing. Breasts are different, different sizes, shapes. Nipples can be pink or mauve or—"

"Lace."

"Some men like petite women, but a lot of them like a woman with a few extra pounds."

He leaned forward and kissed her belly, his hands going to her bottom, cuddling her, touching her. She tangled her fingers in his hair and he said, "Your body is perfect."

She laughed. "I'm far from perfect, but I'm glad you approve, because I'm not ashamed of my body."

Slipping his hands into her panties, he felt the softness of her bottom, her plump flesh, before skimming them down her legs. She stepped out of them and moved back. "Your turn, Daniel."

He stood and undid his slacks. When he started to push them down his hips, Lace knelt in front of him and took over the task. He locked his knees to remain standing.

"Do you know what you're doing to me?" She'd positioned herself as a sexual supplicant, and his male brain became frantic at the sight.

"Of course I do." She peeked up at him. "And I know what I'm *going* to do to you."

He groaned, causing her to laugh. "I haven't done it yet, Daniel."

"It doesn't matter." He trembled like a virgin himself when she wrapped her small hands around his hardened arousal. He squeezed his eyes shut and clenched his jaw. "My imagination is going wild here, Lace."

"In all my studies, there was one particular thing that intrigued me, that stirred my curiosity."

"Lace…"

"Do you know what that one thing is, Daniel?"

He groaned.

"I suppose I should just show you."

The warning given, she leaned forward and he felt her mouth close around him. He yelled, and Lace paused. "I've never done this, but I like it. Are you okay? Am I doing this wrong?" She stroked him lightly, then replaced her fingers with her tongue. "Or this?"

He couldn't get air into his constricted lungs, so he couldn't very well talk. He shook his head.

"You'll tell me if you want me to do something different?"

He nodded, and his hand tangled in her hair, urging her back to her seduction.

It was the most exquisite, most sensually exciting thing a woman had ever done with him. And since it certainly wasn't his first time, he decided it had to be Lace. She was different from every other woman he knew, so being with her, making love with her, was different. Not just unique, but better, more intense, thrilling.

When he knew he couldn't take it anymore, he pulled away. She looked dazed and warm and very aroused. Her breasts, flushed with excitement, rose and fell with her rapid breathing. The fact that what she'd been doing had excited her, too, made him full with emotion.

He scooped her up into his arms and carried her to the bed. "It's my turn, sweetheart," he said between warm, gentling kisses. He felt ready to burst with some vague, heavy sense of perfection and he couldn't quit touching her, kissing her.

Lace wound her arms around his neck. "That was your turn."

"No. My turn is getting to watch you as you climax."

Her lashes lowered over her eyes. "Daniel."

He smiled at her pink cheeks and laid her carefully in the middle of the bed. "You like it." Keeping his gaze on her, he opened the closet and located a box of condoms. He set them on the nightstand. "You like the way I talk to you. It excites you."

Lace widened her eyes at the box, then admitted, "Actually, it does. But then, everything about you excites me."

His heart skipped a beat. "Is that a fact?" He stretched out beside her. "I could just look at you and be happy."

"But I might not like it."

Her muscles tightened when he laid a hand on her belly. "Do you like this?"

"Hmm." Her lips parted.

"And this?"

"Daniel…" She breathed his name.

His hand slid between her thighs, light and teasing. He stroked. "Do you know what I'm going to do to you, Lace?"

With her eyes closed and her body taut, she whispered, "What?"

He leaned over and whispered in her ear, and she moaned, pressing her head back, offering herself to him. He kissed her breasts and her belly and when he moved between her thighs she groaned in heightened anticipation of his promise.

Daniel loved every sound she made, every movement. She was so open, so free and honest and *real*. He kissed her deeply, heady with the taste and scent of her body. He brought her to an explosive climax, loving the way she screamed and clutched at him and praised him. And before the small convulsions had ended, he thrust into her. Once again, she shuddered and cried out his name, this time taking him with her as she came, and beyond his release, he realized something else.

He loved Lace McGee.

LACE WAS THE MOST UNINHIBITED lover he'd ever known, ever imagined. She had no modesty once she got used to being nude with him. In fact, in the four days they'd been at the cabin, they'd seldom bothered with clothes, and she'd quit blushing after the first day.

She was also the most talented, demanding lover he'd ever known. Lace could make him lose his control with just a look. When she talked sexy to him, he went wild. And when she touched him, quickly learning through her openness and honesty what pleased him most, he couldn't hold back.

Lace was a very quick learner.

Daniel thought it could take him a lifetime to get used to

her. Only he didn't have a lifetime. Lace would only grant him a short interlude of intimacy. She'd been very specific that their affair had a limited time period. He could understand her reasoning. They were from different worlds. His, staid and conservative and stifling. Lace would smother in his extended company, and he'd sooner give her up than ever make her unhappy.

She slept beside him on her stomach and he admired the smooth line of her back and rounded bottom. She'd healed nicely, he noticed with a professional eye, her scar only a thin pink line. In another month, it would barely be noticeable. He traced it with his fingertip and she stretched awake.

Turning her head on the pillow to look at him, she smiled. "Good morning."

He continued touching special places on her body, lightly, teasingly. Behind her knees, the small of her back. Down the length of her spine and beyond.

"Mmm-hmm." She purred, smiling. "I like that."

Without meaning to, he asked, "Do you like me?"

She rolled onto her back and faced him, her green eyes slumberous, her pale hair spread out on the pillow. "I think you're the finest of men."

"Lace." Lying back down beside her, he propped his head on a fist and made a big production of stroking her belly. "I'm being serious."

"Of course I like you. Do you think I'd sleep with a man I didn't like?" When he didn't answer, she sighed and sat up, cross-legged, unselfconscious in her nudity. "Daniel, just because we're so different doesn't mean I can't understand who you are. I've always been free to do as I please, responsible only for myself. But you, you've always been out to save the world."

He smiled, though he felt unreasonably sad. "Not the whole world. Just my small part of it."

She smoothed his hair. "Have I ever told you how sexy I think your glasses are?"

Laughing, he wondered how she could come up with such inane things to say at the most improbable times.

"You look so intellectual, so serious and professional."

"You look like a vamp, sitting there like that, seducing me. And here I was hoping to have a serious, professional conversation."

Lace pulled a pillow in front of her. It barely covered the high points of interest. "There. Behold a modest woman."

Unable to resist a moment more, he kissed her, but they both ended up laughing. That was another thing he loved about Lace. She could make everything fun. She lightened his life with her teasing insults and her absurd taunts. She'd forced him to drop his cloak of propriety, and he'd honestly enjoyed every moment.

He'd also learned to trust her instincts.

"You don't have a modest bone in your body, but I've decided you are very astute when it comes to my sister."

She stilled, all teasing gone. "Is that so?"

"Yes. I thought about it, and I watched her. You're right, she is in love. I'm not sure who it is, and—" he looked at her over the rim of his glasses "—don't suppose you'll tell me?"

Lace shook her head. "I can't. I promised."

He accepted that. Lace would never break a promise, and he wouldn't ask her to. "The problem is, I'm afraid she's going to get hurt."

Lace took a deep breath. "I'm afraid of the same thing. I've tried to warn her, to..."

"To tell her love doesn't exist?"

She looked away. "No. That's not my place to say. I've never tried to discourage people from seeking love. But I want Annie to be prepared. Even the examples of supposed love I've seen have been unrewarding, unhappy experiences most of the time. People end up hurt. Annie's so free with herself. She doesn't know to protect her heart."

He wondered if that's what Lace was doing: protecting her

heart. But he seriously doubted her heart was involved with him. She'd made it clear, way too many times, how different they both were. He remembered her accusing him of hiding, and knew it to be true. Even now, he hid, because the truth would be too bitter, too painful, to deal with.

"You've been a good friend to her, Lace. She should have been able to come to me, but I was too busy trying to force her to stay the same. I see that now."

Lace put her arms around him. "Be happy for her, Daniel, even if things don't work out. She's a wonderful person, a beautiful, caring woman, and you're the reason why. You've done an incredible job with her."

"You give me too much credit," he said, but he liked hearing it. He liked knowing there were things about him that Lace admired. He took her shielding pillow and tossed it across the floor, then pulled her naked body against his own as he fell back on the bed. "Make love to me, Lace."

She cupped his face and kissed him while she straddled his hips. He raised his palms to her breasts and watched her head fall back, her eyes close.

Someday Lace would find a man as forthright and uninhibited as herself. Then she'd give up her ridiculous notions that love didn't exist and she'd marry him, living her life independently of society's strictures. Being free in a way he never could be.

The thought filled him with rage and remorse, but he tamped it down. He didn't want her love, didn't want to tie himself to a woman the way his father had. As Lace had pointed out, a lot of people depended on him and he couldn't let them down, couldn't take chances with their happiness.

Which meant he couldn't take a chance with Lace.

She didn't believe in love, and that made her the worst possible risk. And although she claimed to like him, liking wouldn't be enough, not between them. He and Lace had no future together, and he'd known it from the start.

All he could do was take the time he had with her, and then let her go.

He caught Lace and pulled her beneath him. She blinked up at him in surprise. "I thought you wanted me to make love to you?"

"I changed my mind. I want us to make love to each other." He stared at her, trying to find something he knew didn't exist. Lace closed her eyes against his probing gaze.

He cupped her jaw, almost roughly, regaining her attention. He saw confusion and distress, and he couldn't bear it. He kissed her hard, his tongue thrusting, his mouth eating at hers, devouring, and for a long time, he couldn't stop kissing her. When he finally did, they were both numb with pleasure.

Later that day his beeper signaled the end to their idyll.

Chapter Ten

JANUARY WAS A MISERABLE MONTH of sleet and cold. It seemed he'd no sooner stopped seeing Lace than the sun stopped shining and winter lost its appeal.

Everyone appeared to be in the doldrums, his family included. They'd been hanging around lately, watching football games or playing cards and generally making nuisances of themselves, Guy especially.

"I've had it. I'm going to head home." Guy, sitting on the opposite end of the sofa and eating popcorn, yawned hugely.

Daniel pulled out his pocket watch, fingered the engraving on the back as he always did, and checked the time. "It's only ten o'clock. What's your rush?"

"You. You're miserable company."

As much as he wanted to deny it, he knew it was true. "Like you're so choosy?" Daniel flicked off the sports channel they'd both been ignoring and tossed the remote on the table.

"I know when to get away from a bear."

Max, doing sit-ups on the floor at their feet, grunted a muffled, "Amen," to Guy's comment.

Daniel nudged him in the ribs with the toe of his shoe. "Not a word out of you."

Guy stared at Max. "What's with him, anyway? Why all the exercise all of a sudden?"

Daniel shrugged. His brother's peculiarities always eluded him. "You planning on entering a body-building contest, Max?"

"Nope." He huffed between counting. "Ninety-nine, one hundred." He fell back on the floor, breathing deeply. After a minute he pushed himself to a sitting position. "Just staying in shape. I was thinking of taking another trip."

"Where to this time?" Daniel hated it when Max traveled, but his brother had a bad case of wanderlust and there was no curtailing his interest. He wondered what Lace would say about Max's tendency to run off for long stretches.

He no sooner thought it than he shook his head. He and Lace were history, and unlike his father, he was determined not to mope.

"What?" Max stared at his brother in confusion. "You're shaking your head at me and frowning and I haven't even said anything yet."

Guy laughed. "He was probably thinking of a certain blonde bombshell who shall remain nameless."

"Who? Lace?"

Guy tossed a pillow at Max. "Don't throttle him, Dan. Lace is the only blond bombshell we know at present."

Max snorted. "Not me. I could name a dozen."

Daniel held up his hands. "Enough, all right?"

Guy stood, then stepped over Max. "It's not enough. You miss her. Hell, we all do, except Annie. She still sees her." He pointed a finger at Daniel. "Your little sister has been especially weird lately. You should keep an eye on her."

Daniel waved away his concern. "Be patient with her. She's in love."

Both Guy and Max gawked at him. "What!"

"You guys should pay better attention." Daniel didn't add

that it had taken Lace's prodding for him to notice and be convinced.

Guy slowly sat back in his seat. "She's in love? With who?"

"Hell if I know. I wish I did because the jerk is making her unhappy."

Guy stared at him. "She won't tell you?"

"No." Then Daniel looked struck. "You should talk to her, Guy. She feels funny talking to me because I'm her brother and she's afraid I'll disapprove."

Max stood and put his hands on his hips. "If the guy is making her sad, then you can bet I disapprove! I'll find out who he is and—"

"No, don't interfere, Max. Annie's all grown up and she has to handle things on her own."

Guy shook his head. "I'll talk to her." He looked galvanized with new purpose. "I'll stop by and talk to her tonight."

Daniel stared at him. "Uh, Guy, not a good idea. It's getting late and you know Annie has to be up early to open the bookstore. Just stop in and see her tomorrow at work."

"Right. Tomorrow. I'll do that." Guy stuck his hat on his head, picked up his coat and walked out without another word.

Max chortled. "I think you're both pathetic." Then to Daniel, "Why don't you just call Lace? Tell her how you feel?"

For the first time that he could really remember, Daniel wanted to talk to his brother about his problems. He didn't want to burden him, but he needed his advice, and Max knew more about women than most three men put together.

He looked at Max and said, "I wish I could, but I'm afraid to."

Max blinked at the outpouring of brotherly confidence, started to say something, changed his mind and pulled up a chair. "What do you mean, you're afraid? You don't think she'll be glad to hear from you?"

"I have no idea. You probably don't know this, but—"

"You and Lace were involved? Of course I knew it. I probably knew before you did that you were hung up on her. That's why I chased her in front of you."

"To annoy me?"

"To get you going before she got away." Max gave him a wide grin and Daniel laughed. "She cares about you, too."

Daniel's smile froze. "You can tell?"

"Lace is a very open person. She's easy to read."

"Damn." Daniel slumped back in his seat and rubbed the back of his neck. "The thing is, she likes me okay, I think. And we're...compatible in some ways."

Max gave a sage nod of understanding. "Uh-huh."

"But I don't know if she loves me. And if she doesn't, and I pursue this, I could end up like Dad."

Max whistled. "You really have been stewing on this, haven't you?"

"I don't ever want to be like that. I don't ever want to forget the people around me and end up living in a void."

Max let his hands dangle between his spread knees and considered things. After a moment he looked up and stared at Daniel. "I hate to be overly blunt, but you're being an idiot."

"Gee, I'm glad you decided to soften that for me."

"You're nothing like our father, Daniel. He's flighty and irresponsible and even though we know he cares, he's not the type of person you could ever depend on."

Though he tried to hide it, Daniel was shocked. Max had seldom mentioned their father's vagaries, and never with such vehemence. But now Daniel realized just how much Max had observed. Trying to make excuses for their father, Daniel said, "He misses Mom."

"Bull. I'll bet he was that way his entire life. Just as you've been a rock for as long as I can remember. I've always known you were there for me. So has Annie. I don't for a second believe you'd ever forget either of us, so don't use that lame excuse as a reason not to call Lace."

"But…"

Max waved him to silence. "You're miserable now, but you haven't abandoned anyone. And you never will."

Put that way, it did seem pretty absurd. Daniel couldn't really imagine not caring about his brother or sister, even Guy and his father. Or Lace.

"Give it up, Dan. You're as rock-solid stable as they come and nothing and no one is going to change that."

"That could be a problem, too, you know. I mean, Lace is so different from me. She probably finds me boring."

Max puffed up his chest like an affronted turkey. "If you've bored her, then you're an insult to the Sawyers machismo and I'm disowning you as a brother."

"I don't mean I…" Daniel floundered, then shook his head. "What I mean is, we're very different people."

"Opposites attract. Not a problem."

Daniel chewed that over, and then shook his head. "I don't know."

"Look at it this way. If you're miserable—and believe me, you are—imagine how Lace must feel. You haven't called her in a damned month."

Daniel felt a pain in his heart at the thought of Lace being unhappy. "Why do you think she's been miserable?"

"Because I for one listen to her show. And I've been by to see her. She and Annie have taken to crying in their colas together at that same bar where Annie got picked up by the police. Which by the way, wasn't Lace's fault."

"I know. It was just another example of Annie's stubbornness."

"There are a lot of men at those bars."

Daniel halted his dejected study of his shoes and shot Max a glare. "Your point being?"

"Lace is a very sexy woman. She gets hit on all the time. She and Annie both do."

Anger propelled him from his seat and carried him to within an inch of Max. "And you just sit there and allow it, I suppose?"

"Nope. That's why I've been hanging out there with them. So I can scare off all the prospects. Though I doubt it was necessary. Not once has Lace or Annie acted interested in anyone."

That was something at least. "Oh, hell, what radio station is she on?"

Max laughed the entire time he tuned in the station for Daniel, then he bowed. "I have to go. I'll let you sit here and suffer alone awhile. It'll be good for your character."

Max was just through the door when Daniel shook himself out of his stupor and jogged after him. "Max, wait."

"What?"

"You said you're thinking of taking another trip."

"So?"

Daniel crossed his arms over his chest, trying to block some of the cold. "You're not leaving anytime soon, are you?"

Max looked wary. "I don't know. Why?"

With a weary sigh and a smile, Daniel slapped him on the shoulder. "Last time you left without telling me. This time I'd like to know first. And if it's at all possible, I'd like you to hang around for a little while longer. I might need more advice."

Max studied him, uncertainty written on his face, then he nodded. "All right. Sure." He started to turn away, and then added, "If I decide to go, I'll let you know beforehand."

"I appreciate it. And Max?"

"Yeah?"

"Thanks. For everything."

Again Max studied him, then nodded. Seconds later he disappeared down the walk.

Daniel went back into the house, rubbing his arms to warm himself after being outside, clapping his hands against his body. It was damned cold out, but colder still inside himself. He'd done Lace a terrible wrong, treated her abominably, worse than he'd ever considered himself capable of treating a woman.

He loved her, missed her. He wanted to make love to her right now, this very minute, to talk with her and discuss his family and all their foibles. He wanted to argue with her until he was blue in the face and until she lost her temper and then he'd make love to her some more and let her wear him out. He'd convince her—somehow—that all her reasoning on love, and his reasoning, as well, was pure nonsense. They were intelligent people, even though his intelligence hadn't been much in evidence of late. They would....

His ears suddenly prickled with the sound of Lace speaking on the radio. Damn, he'd been so busy allowing his mind to meander, ruminating on all the ways he intended to fix things between them, he'd missed a good portion of her show. He pulled up a chair and permitted himself to be soothed by her gentle, concerned tone.

"You can't sit back and wait for things to right themselves on their own, Ally. If you love him, you have to take charge of the situation and tell him."

The woman, a young woman judging by the sound of things, spoke uncertainly. "I'm not sure how he feels, and now he says he's being transferred and he didn't exactly ask me to come with him..."

"So?" Lace's voice, so sweet and sure and caring, stroked over Daniel, warming him from the inside out. A gnawing ache started in his gut and swelled until he wanted to howl. He wanted to be with her, right this instant, but she continued talking, and he continued to listen.

"Love is always worth taking a chance on. And that means honesty, from both of you. It's a myth that men are always confident and brazen. Perhaps he loves you, but he's feeling as vulnerable and unsure of the entire situation as you are. You'll never know unless you ask. And isn't it worth the risk of a little heartache, a modicum of embarrassment, to find out? If you just let him leave, you'll never know, and surely that will hurt worse than the truth, whatever the truth might be."

The girl's voice quavered, then finally she said, "You're right. He did…did look at me funny, kind of watchful, when he told me he'd been transferred. Maybe he was waiting for me to say something."

"Maybe he was waiting for a declaration of your feelings." Lace's tone gentled, became thoughtful, when she continued. "There's no guarantees in life. It's so easy to find love and lose it, to mistake love for the wrong emotions. Trying to guard your heart could cause you to lose the one you want. And any good relationship, any lasting relationship, should begin with total honesty. Tell him how you feel, then demand that he do the same."

With new resolution, the woman said, "I will! Right now. And thank you. Thank you for everything."

Daniel could hear the smile in Lace's voice, in her words. "Thank you, Ally. I hope things work out, but if they don't and you want to talk, you know how to reach me."

"I do. But you're right about one thing. Knowing will be better than not knowing. If he doesn't care, I'll handle it, but at least I'll be certain I didn't throw anything important away."

"You know, Ally, you're a very smart young woman. I have a feeling you'll be just fine."

Both women laughed softly, and then the radio station broke for a commercial. Daniel surged to his feet, innervated with new purpose. He'd heard enough, more than enough. Damn her, how could she say all those things and not believe in love! It was past time the woman began to heed her own words, and he intended to insist that she start right now. He grabbed up his coat, not his warmest but the closest to hand,

and went through the house to the garage. If he hurried, he'd catch her at the station. He shivered with the cold as he pulled out of the driveway, then smiled with anticipation.

He had her own words to use against her. She'd argue him into the ground, but the woman wouldn't dare argue with herself.

LACE GRABBED UP HER CAPE and whipped it on. Tonight's show had brought her to her senses. She was filled with renewed reason, refreshing anger. How dare Daniel walk away from her—allow *her* to walk away—without letting her tell him how she felt? Didn't he want to know?

The thought that until just moments before, she hadn't even known how she felt flitted in her mind, but she pushed it aside. Her actions were her own, and she was accountable for them, but he had to be accountable for his, as well. She intended to go to him now, tonight. He'd hear how much she loved him if she had to hit him on the head to make him listen. And she'd demand to know if he'd missed her at all, if he wanted to spend more time with her.

All her adult life she'd spoken openly of the pleasure to be found from sexual involvement, but she'd been a fool. Yes, there was pleasure, but it went beyond what she'd thought possible. She loved Daniel, and that made his every touch, even his every look, something special, something that affected her and filled her and became a part of her. She hoped he felt just a little of the same. She suspected he did, and she hoped he wouldn't rally against it just because of who she was and what she did. She couldn't change, wouldn't change, not for him or anyone else. She was proud of herself and her accomplishments, but she wanted him to be proud, too.

If it was at all possible, she intended to find out.

The night was cold and black, the moon hidden behind thick clouds. Lace said good-night to the guard at the front door of the station and headed outside, only to be pulled up short on the front step by a familiar form, a cherished voice.

Daniel stepped out of the darkness and gripped her arms. "I have to talk to you, Lace. Tonight. And don't argue with me."

She threw back her head. The wind tossed her cape and she shivered but ignored the discomfort of the cold. "Why not? I enjoy arguing with you. I'd love to argue with you until I'm too old to manage it anymore."

She waited to see what he would say, what he would do. He stepped closer and the warmth of his body touched her; she could smell his wonderful unique scent, mixed with the smell of the brisk cold and the dampness that hung in the air. It filled her, swirling in her belly and making her ache. She added without thinking, "God, I've missed your scent. And your nearness. And you."

She wrapped her arms around him and pulled him close, pressing her nose into his throat, opening her mouth against his chilled skin, tasting him, suddenly wanting to eat him alive.

Daniel shook. "Lace..." He didn't say anything more. He cupped her face, almost roughly, and pulled her mouth up to his. He kissed her until her body felt weak and she laughed.

"I never thought that was true, never thought it could happen."

He kissed her face, the bridge of her nose, her ear. "What?"

"I thought it was a silly romantic cliché that a woman's knees would go weak. But mine have."

"Mine, too." He kissed her again, his tongue thrusting deep and his hands sliding down to cuddle her bottom, to pull her closer still and support her. "Everything in me feels weak when I'm with you. But strong, too. Like I could take on the world."

"Daniel..."

Suddenly he stepped back and his hands were on her arms again. To her surprise, he shook her, and his voice was enraged. "You're not a hypocrite, Lace. You're intelligent and honest and I insist you stop being so damned stupid!"

"I'm intelligent but stupid?"

"You know what I'm talking about." He shook her again, and because she was so enthralled by his uncharacteristic display, she allowed it. "You told that woman on the radio tonight to be honest. You told her all about love. You have to believe in love or else you're lying not only to yourself, but to your audience, to all those people who rely on you."

Lace stared up at him, bemused, barely able to make out his features in the darkness. "I believe in love."

His hands tightened and he started to shake her again, then he paused. "What did you say?"

"If you weren't so busy trying to rattle my brains, you'd have heard me the first time. I love you, Daniel."

She threw it out there, attached negligently to her other words, hoping the flow of all the words together would make her declaration less conspicuous. She waited, breathless, for his reaction.

His reaction came swiftly, and was somewhat expected. He kissed her, hard, his mouth moving over hers, devouring. He squeezed her tight against him. "I love you, too. Don't ever do this to me again."

Lace shoved back from him. "I didn't do anything to you! You're the one who played games and pretended and…"

He kissed her again, stopping only to laugh when she lightly punched him in the stomach. "I'm going to kiss you every time you try to pull away from me. You might as well give up. You said you love me and there's no going back. I won't let you go back. You're mine now and I'm going to do with you as I see fit—"

"Ha! From the very beginning, you've always done as you saw fit! That's part of…"

His mouth smothered her words and she ended up laughing too. "I'd cry *uncle*, but I approve of your methods. Will you marry me, Daniel?"

It had worked the first time, tossing out her thoughts in the progression of other thoughts. This time proved just as successful. Daniel picked her up off her feet and swung her around.

She expected a fulsome agreement from him, given his physical display, but to her surprise, and worry, he set her down and bent low to look her in the eye. The brisk wind ruffled his dark hair and chafed his cheeks. His glasses were dotted with melting snowflakes. "There will be problems, Lace."

Her stomach twisted, but she was determined to face the facts, to take her own advice and be brutally honest. "I know it. And I can't promise to change, Daniel. I won't change. My mother did everything she could to suit her husband, and it left her lost. She wasn't herself anymore, but she didn't know who she should be without him."

His smile was tender and pained. "You're not your mother, honey, and I don't want you to change. Ever. I love the woman you are. Don't you know that yet?"

Her heartbeat slowed, her pulse became sluggish. "You don't mind what I do?"

"I listened tonight. And I felt proud. And thrilled, because I knew I had you, I knew you couldn't lie to that woman and tell her all about love unless you believed it yourself. You've just been…skittish because of your mother."

Lace went on tiptoe. "Don't start analyzing me again."

"How about I analyze myself instead, then?"

She waved a hand at him, indicating he should continue.

"I've been scared to death of you, Lace. My father fell apart after my mother died, and it was like living with a shell of a man, no life in him, no laughter or caring for anyone but his own grief. He's still not the same, though he pretends to be. I saw how it had destroyed him, and I didn't ever want it to be that way with me. I could always keep a distance with women, could put on a show of being social, but I held back so much. Then you showed up and you argued with me about everything and stirred me until I was blind with lust, and still, even though I thought I didn't like you, I couldn't put you out of my mind. You obsessed my brain and all my male parts and I hated it."

"Did you hate me?"

"I was too busy fantasizing over what I'd do with you to hate you. And then you got hurt and it was like taking a sucker punch in the stomach. I got to know you, and everything changed and I realized I didn't have to worry about falling for you because I didn't think you'd ever fall for me."

"You were wrong."

"I know." He grinned. "You love me. Max explained it all to me."

"Oh, to have been a fly on the wall when that conversation took place."

Daniel laughed, his breath gusting out in front of him in a white cloud. The wind whistled and Lace huddled deeper into her cape. She was cold, but she wouldn't pull her booted feet from the snow until she'd heard it all. This was more than she'd ever hoped for—and she wanted to commit every word to memory.

"Max can tell you all about it later. But for now, will you come home with me?"

"I have my car here."

"We can get it tomorrow. Tonight I need you." His tone dropped, grew husky and seductive. "It's been a lifetime."

More like two lifetimes, she thought, those words enough to satisfy her. She turned to go back inside. She told the night guard that her car would be left in the lot, so no one would worry, and walked back out to Daniel. They made it to his home in record time. And minutes after that, they were in bed together, their clothes scattered, their bodies straining together.

Daniel moved over her gently, rhythmically, holding himself in check, watching her face. "Tell me again."

Lace, swamped in pleasurable sensation, struggled to pull her thoughts together enough to form coherent words. "I love you." Her voice rasped and she threw her head back, her body arching up high against his.

Daniel kissed her throat. "That's it, Lace. That's it."

She sank her fingertips deep into his shoulders. When the pleasure finally abated, she forced her eyes open and stared up at him. "Why didn't you join me?"

"I'm having fun just watching for now." He pulled her legs higher around his waist and rested. "I can't believe you love me."

"It defies logic, I know, but it's true."

"Witch." He thrust, a slow, even stroke, and Lace gasped, giving Daniel reason to smile in satisfaction. "When can we get married?"

"I'd marry you now, Daniel, if you could manage it. I love you. Believe me, nothing will change that. You're the most incredible man I've ever known."

"You don't think I'm too conservative and boring?"

"I think you're too sexy for rational womankind, and intelligent beyond measure, and so caring and loving and good—"

"Stop!" His laughter gave her pleasure and she tightened herself all around him. "Next thing I know, you'll be trying to canonize me."

"No, I want you alive and healthy and hearty," she said, moving beneath him, watching his expression shift, his gaze grow hotter, "so you can finish what you've started."

"You always did present a convincing argument."

A few minutes later Lace grumbled a complaint when she couldn't find a blanket on the bed. They were all on the floor and she was getting cold now that they weren't quite so active. Daniel, mostly dead to the world and any problems in it, pulled her close and threw one leg over hers. Lace snuggled up to his side.

Lace thought he was asleep until his low voice filled her ear. "Will you use me as data for the next book?"

She snorted, then smoothed her hand over his hairy chest. "Maybe, but not in the way you hope."

"You plan to ignore my awesome lovemaking techniques? Wasn't that you who swore I was the greatest lover alive, who touted my every move, who—"

"Stop bragging, Daniel. I intend to be the sole beneficiary of your expertise." She levered herself up on an elbow and stared down at him. "But I do think I've learned a great deal about love. I understand now that it comes in various disguises, and that love can't be second-guessed."

He eyed her serious expression. "Because I feared it and you didn't believe it existed?"

"Exactly." It still unnerved her just a bit to discuss it, to realize how close she'd come to losing Daniel out of sheer stubbornness. "We both believed love, in whatever context, was to be avoided. But no matter how hard we both tried, we fell in love anyway."

"I didn't stand a chance. You berated me and wore me down and flaunted your charms until I lay helpless and unable to defend myself." He began toying with her breast, his expression enthralled. "I think of all those wicked things you did to me at the cabin, and I…"

Lace tightened her fingers in his chest hair, challenged him with a look, and waited.

Daniel took the precautionary method of holding her wrist and then kissed her nose. "And I fell in love."

Lace laughed. "A smart man always knows when to quit."

His arms went around her waist. "Ah. But an even smarter man always knows when to begin again." So saying, Daniel flipped her onto her back and grinned down at her. "Now, where were we?"

Lace touched his face, his shoulders. She loved him so much, she knew there couldn't be anything threatening in her feelings, only happiness and contentment. She kissed his grinning mouth and whispered, "We were about to begin the rest of our lives."

"Hmm. Then we should definitely start things off right."

Lace found out exactly what he meant, and she had to applaud his decision. Making love with Daniel, holding him close and hearing his whispers of love was the very best beginning she ever could have imagined.

ANNIE, GET YOUR GUY

To Barb Hicks, a wonderful friend
and dedicated reader. I can't thank you enough for
all your support! You give me my daily smile, Barb.
Thank you for that.

Chapter One

ANNIE SAWYERS felt her jaw drop at the impressive pile of magazines, articles and books her friend had just carried in. She'd had no idea the topic could be so...extensive. "Good grief. Are all these on sex?"

Lace huffed as she dropped the large stack onto the floor. "Every single one."

"But...I thought sex was...you know, pretty clear-cut and basic."

Lace chuckled. "Variety is the spice of life. And believe me, they make fascinating reading."

"You've read them all?"

"These, and dozens more." Lace was a well-known sex therapist and Annie's best female friend to boot. Just recently, she'd married Annie's older brother—to the shock of the rest of the family. Not because they didn't adore Lace, but because Daniel was such a stuffed shirt. The two of them complemented each other perfectly.

Lace straightened and gave Annie a smile. "If you're not inspired after this, I give up."

Annie didn't say it, but inspiration wasn't her problem. It was feminine confidence, and lack of male response, that had her hesitant. "I don't know, Lace. I mean, I don't think Guy particularly wants me sexually inspired."

"No doubt about that! Which is why you're going to seduce him."

Annie's eyes widened. "But I've never seduced anyone in my life. Last time I tried that with Guy, he thought I was challenging him to arm wrestle. And he let me win! Do you know how humiliating that was?"

After three blinks, Lace asked, "How in the world did he confuse—"

"Maybe I should have taken off my clothes first? Do you think it'd help if I got—"

"No! No, don't do that." Lace gave her a wan smile. "I'll help you. Your seduction techniques will be unparalleled. Irresistible. Provocative. I promise, he won't stand a chance."

"I dunno." Annie felt the tiniest bit queasy. "What if I do this, take my best shot, give it all I got…"

"Annie."

"…and he laughs at my technique and pats me on the head? That's what he usually does, you know." Annie frowned, hating her own hesitation on this particular subject, but still very aware of her irrefutable shortcomings. She was a wonderful businesswoman, strong, independent, capable, but she wasn't beautiful and sexy like Lace. She wasn't feminine.

She had no siren's call.

For the most part, Guy thought of her as a tomboy and a little sister. She loved him beyond distraction, more so every day it seemed, while he was content to give her brotherly advice, and the occasional stern lecture on propriety. He didn't seem to realize that her efforts at looking more appealing, more womanly, weren't meant for the general male masses, but rather his very individualized notice. All he cared about was protecting her—the same as her two overbearing brothers. It was more than any mortal woman should have to bear, and was behind her request for help from Lace.

Lace gave her a patient look. "Annie, Guy might not even realize you're interested. He's been with your family for a long time, now. And with you being the only female in a house-hold full of males, he's naturally adopted the same attitude as your brothers and father. It could be he just needs a bit of…encouragement."

Annie sighed. Guy was her very best friend, her confidant, and he knew her in ways her family didn't. She'd been in love with him forever. Still, what Lace said did make a bit of sense.

"I suppose that could be it." Guy had been living in the Sawyers household since his early high school days. He and Daniel were sophomores when Guy's father had to take an early retirement due to health problems. Guy's mother and fa-ther had moved to Florida, but Guy and Daniel had been friends forever, played sports together, hung out together. They were both popular, and they'd had their futures mapped out. It only made sense that Guy would want to finish school in his hometown. So he'd been welcomed into the Sawyers household.

Lace nodded. "Guy has pretty much adopted your family as his own. And now that I'm in the family, too, I see how they tend to put you on a very high, pastel-pink padded pedestal. They don't want to think about you leaping off the damn pe-destal in search of debauched entertainments."

Lace laughed. She'd always been amused at the way Annie was pampered by the men in her family. "I imagine Guy feels no one is allowed to have sexual thoughts about you." Then, with a prissy voice, she added, "You're too pure."

"But I don't want to be pure!" To Annie, that word had al-most become an insult.

"Pure is rather boring, isn't it?" Lace agreed. "But you haven't helped that image by turning interested men away, you know. You've got 'sweet and innocent' stamped all over you, and it's my guess the men in your family like it just fine that way. I know Daniel does. He's fighting the image of you as a grown, mature woman with all his might, despite my en-couragement to the opposite."

Annie's groan was long and frustrated. If even Lace, whom

Daniel adored beyond all reason, couldn't turn Daniel around, how could she ever reach Guy?

"Of course I turned men away," Annie muttered. "The only man I want is Guy. I fell hopelessly in love with him when I was eighteen."

Lace sat down and crossed her long legs, her expression rapt. "Details if you please."

Annie stared at Lace, debating. The memories of that long ago day were precious to her, and she'd never had anyone to share them with. She hadn't dared tell any of her female friends, not when they were all actively lusting after Guy themselves. And she could just imagine what would have happened if she'd tried talking to Max or Daniel about it. Her brothers gave new meaning to the term "overprotective."

She sighed, then opened up to Lace. "Guy had caught me crying in the backyard. It was Mother's Day, and I was upset, though why I don't know. I don't even remember my mother, she died when I was so young. But it seemed so lonely that day. Dad always took off then, during every holiday, really, like he couldn't bear the memories after losing Mom, but I know Mother's Day was especially hard on him. And Daniel was studying, Max was probably off getting into trouble some-where." She glanced away. "And I just felt so...alone."

"I understand."

As always, Lace's tone was gentle and commiserating. Annie really appreciated having a sister-in-law that she could confide in. It was a unique thing, and very nice. "Guy started out by sitting on the porch swing with me and patting my back in that awkward way men have when they don't know what to do with a female. It really bothered him whenever I cried, I guess because I didn't do it much. Being raised with all boys has a way of toughening a girl up."

Lace made a face. "I know they treated you more like a lit-tle brother than a sister."

"They did their best, especially since Dad was so withdrawn. And for the most part it was fun. I got to do all the things they did, fishing, swimming in the lake, playing baseball. They always included me. Well, except that one time when I caught them playing spin the bottle with a bunch of neighborhood girls. I thought Daniel would box my ears for spying."

"The hypocrite."

Annie laughed. "It made them very uneasy if I acted at all feminine. The first time I wore panty hose, or when I got my ears pierced, they harassed me for days. And I remember when I had to ask Max to go to the store for me to buy tampons. He actually said, *what for,* and when I just glared at him, his ears turned red!"

"Did he go to the store and get them?"

"Oh sure. Max would do anything for me, but he didn't like it. After that, he made Daniel do all my shopping." She laughed again. "When Max first noticed I'd matured, he accused me of 'sprouting breasts' as if I'd done it on purpose just to nettle him. He went out and bought me a bunch of vests. When I refused to wear them, he got into the habit of walking in front of me, so no one would notice."

Lace had to bite her lip to keep from laughing. "Max is a rascal."

Annie shook her head. "As if anyone would notice such an unnoticeable attribute." She stared down at her modest bustline. Puberty had come and gone a long time ago, so she supposed it was time to give up hope.

Lace made a disgusted sound at Annie's distraction, then prompted, "So you were in the backyard, crying, and Guy was trying to console you...?"

Just the memory made Annie warm inside. "He patted my shoulder, then hugged me, asking me not to cry. He kissed my cheek, like he'd done a dozen times. I turned toward him, he drew a big shaky breath, and the next thing I knew, he was holding my face and giving me this killer kiss and it was *incredible.*"

"You mean—"

"Yeah—" Annie nodded enthusiastically "—tongues and all."

Lace struggled with a smile. "I was going to ask if that was your first kiss, Annie, not the actual particulars of it."

"Oh." Annie frowned in thought before answering. "No, it wasn't my first kiss, but it was definitely my first lust."

"Ah-ha. Got to you, did it?"

"Boy did it." The kiss had been a hungry, *I-want-you-bad kiss*. It had startled her a little at the time because it was the first time she'd felt a man's tongue, the first time she'd really understood lust, or wanting a man so much. She'd been hugged up to Guy's muscled chest many times in the past, but that time it was different because he didn't feel like a friend— he felt like a man, hard and hot and so sexy.

She'd belonged to Guy ever since. She still wanted to curl up and savor the memory whenever Guy failed to see her as a grown woman. For at least that one moment, on that one day, he'd wanted her. Almost as much as she wanted him.

Lace's look was thoughtful. "What did you do when he kissed you?"

"I'm not really sure. I know I stared at him and I kind of froze. Guy started apologizing, stammering all over himself, backing away as if he thought I might leap at him. Then he suddenly just walked off and he never mentioned it again. Since then, it's almost like he's avoided me. Except when he wants to lecture me on something."

Lace snorted. "He and Daniel are a lot alike."

"Like brothers."

"So Guy's never kissed you other than that one time?"

It was difficult trying to explain the way their relationship had gone over the past few years. Annie was twenty-five now, but Guy treated her almost as if she were still eighteen and off-limits. She understood his reservations when she had been young and inexperienced.

But now? Well, she was still inexperienced, but he couldn't know that for sure. And at twenty-five, she sure wasn't too young. But whenever she got too close, he started putting up barriers and she hated it.

"Once," Annie said, dredging up the wonderful memories, "on New Year's Eve two years ago, I took him by surprise. We were in the basement looking for more folding chairs because the party got a little bigger than expected. When the clock suddenly chimed and we heard all the shouts, Guy laughed because he knew everyone was kissing. I didn't give him a chance to think about it. I…well, I sort of jumped him."

"And?"

Frustrated, Annie muttered, "And he let me kiss him for all of about thirty seconds. Then he stumbled back like I'd slugged him. He accused me of being drunk even though he knew I hadn't had a drop. He hustled me back up the steps, keeping me at arm's length—and Guy has incredibly long arms. He spent the rest of the night glued to his date while watching me like I was a molester of innocents."

"That's it?"

"No. There's been a handful of times, but it's usually only because I'm able to take him by surprise. Like when I turned twenty-one and he gave me my necklace." Instinctively, her fingers curled over the small, glossy black pearl on the delicate silver chain that she never removed. It felt warm to the touch. "I threw myself against him that time and tried kissing him. He laughed, but only until I caught his mouth. Then he kissed me back."

"Ahh. Progress."

"For about three seconds."

"Let me guess. He ran again?"

"Yep. Like someone had scorched his very sexy backside."

"Men can be so difficult."

Since Lace was not only a sex therapist, but married to

Annie's brother Daniel, Annie figured she knew all about difficult men.

"He's not like that with other women, you know."

"He's thirty-five, Annie. Surely you don't expect him to be a monk."

"No. I've heard plenty of women talk! According to them, he's a fabulous lover, but I can't even get a second look out of him."

Annie picked up the book on top of the stack and flopped back onto the couch. "I'm dying here. All my sexuality is going to atrophy if Guy doesn't take notice soon."

"I have a feeling he'll come around."

"And I'll turn into an old dried-up loaf of whole wheat while I'm waiting." Annie opened the book, surveyed a few pictures, then tilted the book for a better angle. "Good grief!"

"Looks interesting, doesn't it?"

Actually, it looked more than interesting. It looked downright seductive. And enticing. "Is that even possible?" She turned the book, trying to figure out what body part belonged to which person.

"Trust me, it's possible."

"It doesn't look very comfortable."

Lace peered over her shoulder, then shrugged. "It's…creative, I agree."

"Guy will never go for it."

Lace burst out laughing. "He'll go. Trust me."

Annie desperately wanted to be convinced. Not a day went by that she didn't imagine what it would be like to be married to Guy, to sleep with him every night, to have the right to touch him however and whenever she wanted.

The thought of however and whenever had kept her awake many a night.

She wanted them to share a life, to share everything. "You're the therapist."

"Only a sex therapist, Annie. And since you haven't gotten to the sex part yet, I have to admit I can't predict people's reactions about situations. I'm only going on good old female intuition when I tell you Guy must be somewhat interested. If he really thought of you as a little sister, as he claims, none of those hot kisses ever would have happened. Even you have to realize that."

"Do you really think so?"

"Yes, but honey, wanting and loving are worlds apart. Do you think you can handle it if Guy makes love to you, but isn't *in* love with you?"

This was where it got tricky. Unlike Annie, Guy had no problem dating—frequently. He had his pick of women and most of them were more like Lace—sophisticated, sexy businesswomen with a style all their own and lush bodies and self-confidence oozing out of every feminine pore.

Annie's body wasn't something to brag about. She was built okay, and she wasn't ashamed of her body, but it certainly hadn't driven Guy into a lustful frenzy yet. And though her small bookstore was a source of pride for her—something she loved dearly—it was far from a glamorous job.

It seemed to her that if Guy was going to fall in love with her, he'd have done it by now. But she couldn't simply give up. And at the moment, she only wanted to concentrate on one thing at a time.

"The truth is, Lace, when I imagine going my whole life without ever getting to be with him, I feel miserable. I want *something*, even if it doesn't last. And who knows? Maybe if we do make love, and he doesn't want me after that, I'll finally be over him. It could be a sort of exorcism. But I have to at least try." Then she winced. "If you really think he'll want me, that is. I don't relish the idea of making a complete fool of myself."

Lace lifted her brows. "Men are pretty basic in some things, Annie. Guy's already shown a physical interest, and even though you're always denying it, you're a real cutie. I'm guessing—but it is only a guess—that he'll want you once you give him a proper nudge in the right direction."

"Maybe," Annie allowed. She was used to emulating the men in her life, going after what she wanted with full force, unwilling to let incidentals discourage her.

She said aloud, "But...*seduction.* I don't know anything about seduction." The idea tempted her, getting to explore the long length of Guy's lean body, getting to touch him and kiss him to her heart's content.

It would take forever.

But there were drawbacks. If she bumbled it and lost Guy's respect, on top of everything else, she didn't think she could bear it.

Lace reached out and patted her arm. "That's my field of expertise. So with my help, and the books, you'll ace it. I promise, most unattached, interested men are not too difficult to seduce. The only problem now is going to be picking the time and place."

Annie had her mouth open to offer a suggestion—such as the sooner the better—when the doorbell rang. She looked at Lace, her brows raised. She didn't want any interruptions now, not when they were just getting to the best part. She scowled at the door. "Sorry. Let me see who it is."

The second she opened the door, her brother Daniel burst inside in a very uncharacteristic way. "Listen up quick. Guy is right behind me. He'll be here any minute. Don't tell him I just got here, but I had to talk to you before he did. I knew he was coming here, so I raced to beat him."

Annie stared owl-eyed. "What in the world is the matter?" Daniel, her levelheaded, oldest brother was definitely in a dither about something.

He drew a deep breath. "Guy's getting married."

That blurted comment had Annie groping blindly for a chair as the world seemed to tilt beneath her. *"What?"*

Obviously frazzled, Daniel roughly ran a hand through his hair. "He said he plans to ask Melissa to marry him." Before Annie could find a response to that, Daniel raised his hands in immense frustration. "I know. I know. She's all *wrong* for him. I tried to tell him that, but he's not listening to me. So this is where you come in, sis. You're close to Guy, in some ways more so than I am. Make him think it over, Annie. Reason with him. Try to get him to take some time…"

Daniel suddenly stopped talking, as if only then realizing how quiet she was. "What's the matter? You look ready to faint."

Annie tried to answer him, she really did. Her mouth moved, but nothing came out. Marriage? All her plans were disintegrating before she could even try them out. Her soon-to-be-learned excellent seduction skills would never find fruition?

Thank goodness for Lace, who stepped into the breach. "Your delivery needs work, Daniel."

"Lace!" He eyed his bride with ill-disguised suspicion and just a hint of lust. "I thought you were out shopping today."

"I was. I bought a couple of up-to-date books that your little sister's conservative bookstore doesn't carry." She flashed her patented wicked grin, guaranteed to make him wary.

Daniel's eyes narrowed. "Books on what?"

Annie loved her brother dearly, and she knew he loved Lace. But to him, Lace was everything Annie wasn't, sexy and seductive and mature and totally female from the top of her platinum blond head to the bottom of her long sexy legs. When they'd first met, Lace had thrown Daniel for a loop, driven him crazy, then to Annie's relief, she'd returned Daniel's love. The two of them were perfect together, but Daniel was still skeptical about Lace assisting in Annie's transformation from tomboy to femme fatale.

He didn't want her to transform.

Lace shrugged her shoulders. "Books on sex, of course."

"*What?*"

With a taunting grin that had Daniel's glasses fogging, Lace said, "We're gathering modern info on seduction, sweetheart." Then she leaned close to him to whisper, "Annie's seduction as a matter of fact."

Into the quiet that followed that statement, Guy suddenly appeared in the open doorway. "Who the hell is trying to seduce Annie?"

Not a blessed soul, Annie wanted to scream, but she was temporarily sidetracked by her one true love.

The wind outside had played havoc with his ruthlessly short, light brown hair. It stuck up in odd, spiky angles, making his hair look like an animal's natural defense.

His ears and his lean cheeks were ruddy from the cold and his endlessly long, leanly muscled jean-covered legs were slightly damp from the freezing rain. He had the collar to his bomber jacket turned up and Annie could see a wrinkled flannel shirt beneath. It didn't look as though he had shaved today, and his brown eyes were red rimmed, giving the impression he hadn't slept much the night before.

He looked tall and lanky and tired—and so sexy she wanted to take his hand, grab a book and head for the nearest bedroom.

Annie slowly stood while devouring him with her hungry gaze. "No one is trying to seduce me."

Lace smiled, examined a fingernail, and announced, "Annie's going to do the seducing."

Both Guy and Daniel turned to stone. *"What?"*

Annie sent Lace a reproving glance, which she ignored. That was the problem with having a friend who was just a bit zany, with too much intelligence and imagination for her own good. Annie held no fear that Lace would actually give her away. In fact, she probably thought she was helping by whetting Guy's curiosity. But Guy didn't look whetted, he looked appalled. And to mention it in front of Daniel? Her brother was not a man taken to frivolity, despite Lace's constant assurances to the contrary.

"I'm twenty-five years old," Annie explained, trying to calm the two men staring at her with the same morbid fascination they might give to a train wreck. "I think my sex life should be my own business."

Guy shoved the door shut behind him then crossed his long

arms over his chest. Somehow he managed to look even taller. "What sex life?"

A good question.

Again, Lace spoke up. "You certainly didn't expect her to remain a virgin forever, did you?"

"It was a nice thought," Guy muttered.

Daniel rounded on Lace, his face still red. "This is all your doing, isn't it?"

"I certainly didn't arouse her, if that's what you're talking about."

Daniel sputtered while Guy's eyes widened. "Annie is aroused?"

He sounded horrified, and then to her discomfort, he looked her over as if checking for signs. Annie squirmed.

Lace shrugged, her grin in place, looking a bit smug. "It's been known to happen."

Guy noticed the books and magazines then and stalked forward. "My God. You've got a literary arsenal here." He picked up the copy of *Kama Sutra* and flipped through it, his eyes growing darker by the moment. His gaze cut to Annie. "How many men were you planning on seducing? A baker's dozen?"

She could feel her face turn hot. She hadn't figured on anything as outrageous as a group confrontation, for crying out loud.

With few choices, she tried to bluster past her embarrassment. "If need be."

"Why?" Guy demanded, at the same time Daniel said, "The hell you will!"

She glared at each man in turn. "I don't need to explain myself to either one of you."

Daniel brushed past Lace and picked up *The Year's Most Popular Erotica.* He skimmed the titles inside, then gawked at Annie. "Good grief, Annie. What are you doing with this stuff?"

Since Annie wasn't quite certain what she was doing, she lifted one shoulder and grimaced a smile. Lace went on tiptoe to peer over Daniel's shoulder. "Ahh. Erotica. I brought that one so Annie could compare. You know, most women think their fantasies are odd or different or even weird. I wanted Annie to have an idea of what some of the most popular fantasies are, so she wouldn't suffer that insecurity."

Daniel scowled at Lace. Guy looked positively apoplectic.

Lace remained supremely unaffected by their silent condemnation. "She does have fantasies, you know."

Twin masculine stares turned Annie's way. She cringed, wishing she could find a hole to hide in, or else a big piece of tape to slap over her friend's uncensored mouth. "Uh, Lace…"

"I also brought the first and second issue of *The Joy of Sex*. Great text, and the illustrations are superb—and very inspiring."

Since Lace's course of action had effectively silenced both men, Annie felt a bit braver, and decided to join in. She picked up a slim volume and pretended to be familiar with it. "This one is on the male…uh, orgasm. How to make it better." She almost choked as she said it—then immediately imagined Guy in the throes of passion. She stared at him, unblinking.

"Actually," Lace commented, "it's how to make it better than great." She waved a hand. "Not that most men need any help in that area. But I couldn't find that many books on helping women increase their own pleasure. I brought some articles though. They ought to ensure that things go satisfactorily for you."

Guy wheezed as if he'd gotten sucker punched in the gut.

Daniel huffed and stomped over to first one wall then another. His dark gaze bounced off Lace several times while he paced. Lace just smiled her serene smile at him. She knew Daniel could never stay angry at her for long. And Annie knew, deep down, he loved Lace's free-spirited, natural way. She only wished she could be so cavalier.

Guy finally caught his breath, then looked slightly ill, but he refrained from glaring. Guy seldom got really angry, and when he did, only those who knew him well were aware of it.

He wasn't so much mad now, as confused and obviously irritated. Confused because, after all, Annie was "pure," and irritated because she didn't want to be.

Seeing Guy like this was pretty intriguing. Generally, he got along fine with everyone, even with their middle brother Max, who had a hard time getting along with himself, much less anyone else. But Max liked Guy. Everyone liked Guy. He was an unofficial member of their family. Except to Annie.

She wanted more, so very much more.

Unlike her family, she wanted to thoroughly debauch Guy, and have him debauch her in return.

In a lethal, almost predatory tone she'd seldom heard from him, Guy asked, "Who are you planning to seduce, Annie?"

Lace chuckled and leaned toward Guy with a wicked gleam in her eyes and a conspiratorial stage whisper. "The guy's a real dope. Can you believe he hasn't even noticed her, and she's sending out all the signals? Annie's getting desperate." Then Lace's gaze settled on Annie, and she said, "I have a feeling the guy's getting desperate, too, if you know what I mean. He's thinking of taking some pretty desperate measures himself."

Annie felt her heartbeat pick up. Surely Lace wasn't suggesting Guy would marry another woman just to set himself apart from her? That seemed to be stretching it just a bit. Or was it? *Oh please, don't let him be in love with another woman.*

"It's not that Perry fellow, is it?" Guy growled. "He's not at all right for you, Annie. We talked about that, remember?"

Perry Baines was a nice enough person. He worked with Guy at the company as an advertising executive, and he had been persistent in his pursuit. But Annie wasn't interested. She'd only gone out with him as a friend. *And to make Guy jealous,* a small voice prompted. But since it hadn't worked, since Guy had only warned Annie that Perry was a wimp, without a single sign of jealousy, she ignored the small voice.

"Perry is...nice," she said, unwilling to admit she had no prospects at all.

Guy whirled around and said to Lace, "You know I love you to death, Lace, and I think you're the best thing that ever happened to Daniel—"

"Gee, thanks, Guy." Daniel's tone was wry.

"—but is it really necessary for you to encourage Annie in this ridiculous business?"

It was Daniel who answered. "Lace finds it impossible to keep her nose out of anything. She's been working on fixing Max up, too."

Annie winced. Now that was a dead-end endeavor. Max would never settle down with one woman. He had wanderlust in the worst way.

Annie made the attempt to regain control. "Both of you just leave Lace alone. She's certainly being more helpful than you two would have been."

There was a general enthusiastic grunting of concordance from the men on that point, since their idea of help would have been to dissuade her—or lock her in a closet.

Suddenly Guy frowned at Daniel. "What are you doing here?"

"Ahh…"

"He was just leaving with me," Lace said, saving Daniel from a lie. "He promised me a ride home." She latched onto Daniel's arm, hugging it to her breasts, and at the same time scooped up her black wool cape. Everything Lace wore was dark.

Since Daniel was caught, he didn't refute Lace's claim, but neither did he look happy about it. He pulled Annie close for a hug with his free arm, then whispered, "Talk some sense into him, sis. Make him think about what he's doing."

Annie nodded. "I'll try." *Boy, would she try.*

Daniel resisted as Lace attempted to drag him out the door. He caught Annie's hand. "And for Pete's sake, don't seduce anyone!"

Lace gave a theatrical groan. "Big brothers are surely a nuisance. I'm glad now I didn't have any." And with that, she led Daniel away, leaving Annie and Guy alone. Annie bit her lip.

Silence filled the small apartment after the door closed, then Annie turned to face Guy. He watched her closely, which sent her heart into a tailspin. She tried to swallow her nervousness.

Damn, why hadn't Lace given her a few basic instructions before taking off? She didn't think there was any way she could wing it on her own.

His eyes narrowed speculatively, and in a low voice, he asked, "Well, Annie? You want to tell me what this—" his hand swept the pile of books "—is really all about?"

Chapter Two

NOT ON A BET, Annie thought, wary of the way Guy watched her now. She stiffened her shoulders and refused to look away from his probing gaze. He probably thought he was intimidating her.

In truth, she was getting a little turned on.

Having all of Guy's undivided attention made her warm inside, and a little giddy.

"What I do, and who I do it with," she said with what she hoped was a decisive tone, "is my own business, Guy Donovan."

As she spoke, she began gathering up the books. He was right, there was enough reading material to keep her busy for a month.

One thin book fell open to a particularly graphic image of a couple intimately, happily entwined. The woman, positioned mostly on the top, wore a lecherous grin and little else. Somehow Annie couldn't quite picture herself propped up on Guy that way.

But the lecherous grin, oh, she could easily give in to that right now!

Annie quickly scooped the book into the stack. She peeked at Guy, and knew that he had seen the picture, too. A strained expression replaced his frown.

Annie cleared her throat. "Why are you here?"

Guy shook his head as if to clear it. "We can talk about that later."

"We can talk about it now. All other discussions are over." Planning to be a seducer was difficult enough. Talking about it with the seducee would be impossible. She needed time to formulate her plans without Guy's verbal assistance.

Guy tilted his head, then closed his large hands over her shoulders as she started past. Her knees almost turned to pudding.

He was so big her head barely reached his chin, but she loved every single inch of him. All her life, she'd known she was loved by her family. But her father had always either hidden away, too overcome with his grief from losing his wife, or too involved with his skiing equipment business, to pay much attention to his children.

Daniel had filled in as best as he could, so he was as much a parent figure as a big brother, which gave him a double-whammy impact. But Daniel had always been studious and very serious about his education. He'd seemed a bit overwhelming to a little sister who made B's with an effort and was shy to boot. And Max...well, her brother, who also happened to be the epitome of a middle child, was just plain difficult and always had been. She never doubted his love, but he was more likely to tease her than hug her. That's when he was even around. Max was traveling more often than he was at home.

Guy gently shook her out of her reverie. "Promise me something, honey. Before you actually decide to do anything, talk to me about it. Okay?"

Since she suspected at least a little discussion would be necessary before she could seduce him, Annie nodded agreement. Anything to put this subject to an end. Then she remembered that Guy was supposedly marrying Melissa, and there wouldn't be a chance for her to do any seducing at all.

Her heart punched against her ribs with the heavy throb

of panic. Damn him, why was he so blind and stubborn where she was concerned?

Guy watched her with a concerned expression. "You okay, honey? You want to talk about it?"

Guy was almost always there for her when she needed him—just not in the way she needed him now.

"Sometimes talking doesn't do any good."

He obviously didn't like hearing that. "You know I'll help you out any way I can."

"Really?" Maybe if she just told him she wanted to sate herself on his body...but no. She wanted so much more than that. She wanted sexual satisfaction, but she also wanted his love.

She wanted everything.

Sadly, she shook her head. Guy stepped forward and hugged her close and Annie found her nose pressed to the lower portion of his hard chest. She drew a deep breath and sighed. Man oh man, he smelled so good.

"I have needs," she said, her words muffled by his flannel.

Guy froze. She could feel the accelerated thumping of his heartbeat. "Uh...money?" he asked hopefully. "Business advice? Because you know I'd gladly—"

"Personal needs." Then she said more boldly, *"Intimate needs."*

Guy turned her loose like she'd caught on fire. "What the hell do you mean, talking like that?"

Innocently, she asked, "Like what?"

His big hands flapping in the air, Guy said, "About...*needs* and all that."

Annie realized she was botching it in a big way, but darn it all, she was tired of pretending she wasn't a woman. In the past, Guy had always just seemed to know when she felt alone or lonely or sad. Even before he'd come to live with them, he never appeared to mind when she hung around, which meant a great deal to a young girl who didn't make friends easily.

Being with Daniel Sawyers and Guy Donovan had given her

instant popularity in school, especially with the girls who vied for the older boys' attention. Both Daniel and Guy had always been well known in the community, and sought after as eligible bachelors from the time they'd graduated high school. But they each had planned their futures, so while they dated, they didn't get serious with any one female. And they had always allowed her to tag along.

Through it all, Annie had fallen hopelessly, irrevocably in love.

This was the first instance that she could remember where Guy wanted distance between them. She hated it. Summoning up a skimpy smile, she asked, "Don't we always discuss things, Guy?"

His gaze moved over her face, as if searching, then he spoke very slowly. "Yeah. Most times we do. I wouldn't have it any other way, Annie."

"Then you should know that, despite how you see me, I'm a woman. I'm not sexless."

His face colored and he sputtered, "I never said—"

"And I *do* have fantasies."

"Good God!" He took the books from her hands and set them aside. "Listen to me—"

"Do you want to hear my fantasies, Guy?"

He swallowed hard. He cleared his throat. "Okay. Yeah. We can...uh, we can talk about that." He led her to the couch and dragged her into a seat. "Now the thing is, fantasies are fine. I just don't think you're ready to actually seduce anyone. Definitely not that ass, Perry. See what I mean?"

Annie's eyes narrowed. "You don't think I can do it."

"I never said that, dammit!"

"You think I don't have what it takes. You think I'm not sexy enough."

"I think you're plenty sexy!"

"Really?" Annie scooted a little closer to him, beyond

pleased that he'd made such an admission. Progress, she thought, whether he realized it or not.

Guy stared into her eyes, then at her mouth, before he growled and leaped away from the couch. He stalked around her small living room, grousing as he stepped over and around the variety of sex books, and finally stopped in front of her with his hands on his hips. Looking far too resigned and determined, he said, "Not to change the subject—"

"Ha!"

"But I came here to tell you something."

"This sounds serious." She felt herself shaking inside, with dread and heartache.

"I suppose it is. Not bad, really. But...well, I'm going to ask Melissa to marry me."

Even though she already knew it, Annie flinched. Hearing it from his own mouth was worse than when Daniel had said it. "Is that so?"

"I know it's kind of unexpected, but she'll be the perfect wife for me. Even your father thinks so."

"Dad?" Now how did her father get into this? It was true he valued Guy very highly. After all, neither of his sons had followed in his footsteps to help run the prized family business. Only Guy had done that, and done it very well, so well that Dan Sawyers seldom set foot in the offices anymore.

Guy had also taken over the family home, given that they'd each gotten apartments. Guy's presence there had changed Annie's memories of the house, and made them all pleasant. He'd insisted that their family home should be preserved, and if Annie ever wanted it, it would be waiting for her.

She wanted to share it with Guy, but now he was talking about marriage to Melissa.

Annie considered the possibility of hitting him over the head with one of the sex books, since that might be the only use the book got. But he was so much taller than her, that would be difficult.

"Your father let me know," Guy said, "in very blatant terms, that it was time I had a wife. He's changed a lot since Daniel's marriage. He looks at things differently now."

Her father *had* changed. Used to be, she seldom saw him at all. His grief had sealed him away to the point he avoided most reminders of the love he'd lost, including his family. His feelings for his wife had been so all encompassing, nothing else had mattered. Only very special events had warranted her father's attention.

When her mother died, Annie had only been two years old. She didn't really remember her mother, but years later she'd overheard Daniel saying to Guy that he'd lost both parents on that awful day. Now that Annie was older, she realized what a godsend Guy had been for Daniel. Guy had been there for him as he tried to bear the brunt of the familial burdens.

Guy interrupted her melancholy thoughts. "Your father suggested she be someone smart, savvy, independent, a woman who could make a man comfortable—"

Standing to face him, Annie said, "There you go. He obviously wasn't talking about *Melissa.*"

He gave her a familiar chastising look. "Don't be sarcastic, Annie. Melissa understands the business. And she's the only woman I've been seeing lately, so of course that's who Dan meant. I doubt he expected me to grab some stranger off the street."

She swallowed hard, trying to get the melon-sized lump out of her throat. "But *Melissa?*"

Guy stifled a laugh and reached out to yank on her hair. "Listen up, brat. Just because you don't like her doesn't mean she's bereft of qualities that appeal to a man."

No no no! Annie did *not* want to hear this. She slapped a hand over Guy's mouth. He very gently pulled it away, then held on, rubbing her fingers between his own.

"It's not the end of the world, Annie, despite what your big brother thinks."

Annie chewed on her lips a moment, trying to gain composure. It wasn't easy with Guy touching her. "And what does Daniel think?"

"He says I'm allowing myself to be seduced by the idea of marriage, not by the bride. Marriage isn't something to enter into lightly. There should, at the very least, be strong emotions involved."

Guy sounded just like Daniel as he said it, even to the point of mimicking Daniel's somber voice.

"Well, he's right," Annie said, quick to defend her brother. Especially since they seemed to be on the same side for a change. "Daniel should know, what with just getting married and everything."

"The way he floundered with Lace hardly makes him an expert. He almost lost her before he realized he was madly in love."

"Do you...that is..." Annie couldn't quite force the words out of her mouth, not at all certain she wanted to know.

"Are you trying to ask me if I love her?"

Annie could have guessed, given the way he said those words, that Daniel had already been over this question many times, too. Though they had ended up in vastly different careers, Daniel and Guy were still very close.

Annie looked up at him, and her heart squeezed painfully tight. "Do you, Guy?"

He looked so incredibly, impossibly masculine standing there staring down at her with such intensity. It didn't matter that Guy had originated the "grunge" look long before it became popular. It didn't matter that his short hair was always going in odd directions, or that he often skipped shaving in the mornings, which left him with a faintly appealing beard shadow.

Guy was kind and generous, strong and proud. He worked hard for her father, and had nearly doubled the company since assuming the position as the "heir to the throne." He valued his friendships and was loyal to those he loved. He never tolerated injustice or bullies and he went out of his way to help others.

He was tall. He was gorgeous.

And he smelled so good.

She loved him.

Guy jerked off his coat and tossed it to the couch. His well-worn jeans hugged his thighs and his faded flannel shirt hung loose over a snug gray T-shirt that clung to his flat abdomen. His very large, booted feet were braced apart, and his frown was fierce enough to make most people quail in apprehension.

People who didn't know him well.

"Do you?" Annie asked again.

"No." He sounded disgusted, with himself and with her for asking. "Not the romantic, mushy heartsick love that you're talking about. But I suppose I respect her—"

"You suppose?"

"Dammit, Annie. You're as stubborn as your brother."

And doubly motivated.

"I think we'll make a good marriage, all right? I'm almost thirty-five, and it's time I started a family. The last thing I want to do is wait until I'm old, then end up with an only child, like my parents did."

Annie knew how much he had resented being alone all his life, and how much he had gravitated to her busy family. Guy's father had been somewhat ill for a long time before he retired, and between work and the restrictions of his illness, he hadn't been able to do the things with his son that most men did. Her father had filled a huge void in Guy's life, at least some of the time.

Annie softened. "That was difficult for you, wasn't it?" She wanted to understand why a man like Guy would want to marry a woman he didn't love.

"It wasn't that big of a deal," Guy denied. Then he continued, "But it's time I settled down, and since I haven't found any one particular *perfect* woman, it might as well be Melissa. We get along well. And God knows, she fawns all over me."

"She fawns over the business." Melissa had made no secret of the fact that she wanted to work with Guy.

Guy grinned. "She's not immune to my physique either, brat."

Annie considered hitting him.

"But you're right. Since she's involved with her own company, I can talk to her about the business without confusing her. We have similar interests—"

At that little bit of idiocy, Annie promptly choked. Everyone knew Melissa was a woman out to make the most of her life, be it fun, men, or money. Guy was just the opposite. He genuinely cared for people, and would give a man the shirt off his back if he needed it.

Guy gave her a mocking glare. "I should think you would be happy for me."

"I should be happy that you're planning to—" *Marry the wrong woman.* "—make the biggest mistake of your life?"

"Actually, I'm trying to avoid a few mistakes."

Annie had no idea what that meant, and Guy didn't look willing to explain. She drew a deep breath. "What you need, Guy, is some isolated, quiet time to think things over, to really decide what it is you want."

"That's Daniel's speed, Annie. Not mine. I'm the mover and shaker. Remember?"

Annie tossed up her hands. "Those are Dad's words, and you know how ridiculous they are. It's insane that Dad's still disappointed just because his son refused the family business and became a very respected doctor instead. Good grief, you'd think Daniel was a derelict the way Dad goes on."

Guy laughed. That was one of the things Annie loved most about him. He always had a ready smile or a friendly laugh, even when he was frustrated. "Dan's as proud as any father could be, even of Max, and heaven knows that proves he's a proud papa for certain since Max *is* a derelict."

Annie shook her head, trying to conceal her own smile. "Max is just trying to find himself." At least, that was what Lace had claimed.

"In the wilds of Canada? All alone?"

Annie shrugged. "So Max is a little different. That's no reason for Dad to complain."

"Your dad enjoys complaining and you know it. That's why he grumbled so much when you bought the bookstore and went into business for yourself. He likes to grouse." Guy glanced around her newest selection of reading material and shook his head. "Heaven knows he'd have a conniption if he saw what you've gotten into now."

"Evidently," Annie said, ignoring his reference to her seduction plans, "he enjoys playing matchmaker, too."

"He only made the suggestion, Annie. But he was right."

Annie was of the opinion he couldn't be more wrong. She desperately needed to convince Guy of that. "You know my dad isn't the most astute of men. That's why you're running his business for him."

Guy shrugged. "He needed help. Daniel wanted to be a doctor, you wanted to be independent of the family, and we're still trying to figure out what the hell Max wants to be, other than a pain in the ass. Dan needed someone."

"So you felt obligated to be there for him?"

"Not obligated," Guy quickly denied, but Annie could see the lie in his expression. "Dan would never put pressure on me, you know that."

"He's pressuring you to get married!"

"No he's not. He just…suggested it."

"And you feel obligated to do as he asks."

"Will you stop putting words in my mouth? The fact is, I respect Dan. A lot. He made it possible for my father to retire early. And he did take me in and treat me like one of the family."

Which, since Dan tended to hide from life, wasn't really saying that much, at least in Annie's opinion. She wished Guy's mom and dad were here now. They were wonderful people who had worked for her father for years. They were friends as much as employees, and Annie knew her dad wanted only what was best for them.

They were also very reasonable, and would probably be able to talk some sense into their only son. "Have you told them about Melissa yet?"

Guy shook his head. "After I propose and Melissa says yes, I'll call them. Or maybe fly down to see them." Then he added with a touch of enthusiasm, "You could go with me. Mom would love to see you again."

And Annie would love to see her. Mary Donovan had done her best to mother Annie until they'd moved to Florida. "Just me, you and Melissa on a honeymoon trip, huh? Yeah, I can see what a fun trio we'd be."

Guy frowned, then turned away. "Yeah. Maybe not."

Annie reached out and touched his forearm, bared below his rolled-up sleeves. The warm, smooth muscles bunched beneath her fingers and turned rock-hard. The impersonal touch she'd intended was forgotten as she got lost in the feel of him. Guy looked at her over his shoulder, one brow raised in question.

Annie dropped her hand and cleared her throat. "You haven't mentioned marriage to Melissa, yet?"

"I was waiting for the right moment. I will soon, though."

Annie felt renewed hope. There was still a chance to steer him around. Melissa would never make him happy. Guy might not be willing to admit it, but she knew he wanted a family of his own. Melissa wanted to get ahead without any encumbrances, especially encumbrances that required diapers and midnight feedings. She'd never love him, never make him and their marriage a priority.

In a way, Annie would be saving Guy by forcing him to see the huge mistake he'd be making.

She could save him by seducing him.

Annie pondered her own forced justification of what she planned, but found no real drawbacks. Feeling lighthearted again, and just a bit anxious, Annie asked, "You feel like pizza? I'll treat, sort of a we-hope-you-come-to-your-senses celebration."

With a wry smile, Guy said, "That can go both ways, you know. Maybe with a little time you'll get over this dumb idea of jumping some guy's bones."

"Well," Annie said, looking at him through her lashes, "I had hoped to be a little more subtle than that, but if you think jumping his bones might be more successful—"

"No!"

Annie grinned and he added, "Bone jumping is not the way to go."

Advice from Guy? It'd be a perfect addition to her plan. "Okay, so why don't you stick around and you can give me some pointers on what is—or isn't—the way to go?"

His face once again a mottled red, Guy snarled, "Now how could I refuse such a wonderful opportunity?"

She wouldn't try to make a move on him tonight, she decided. After all, she hadn't even read the books yet. And since Guy was the only man she could ever remember wanting, she knew nil about turning a man on. But she could test the waters, so to speak. And if she could get him to open up just a little, maybe she'd be able to find out specifically what it was *he* liked—and then she could use it to her advantage.

A few months ago, when she'd confided in Lace that she wanted Guy, Lace had given her several suggestions on how to find out if Guy was indeed interested in her or not. And true to Lace's predictions, he hated it if she flirted with other men, if she went to a singles' bar, even when she dressed in clothes that showed her more feminine side.

But then, so did both her brothers, so that really hadn't told her a thing.

Maybe now was as good a time as any to try another experiment. Her heart raced with nervousness—and anticipation.

She gave Guy a fat grin. "Call and order the pizza, then make yourself comfortable. I have a few quick things I have to do."

He nodded, his gaze wary now as he focused on her bright smile. Annie wondered just how he'd look at her when she finished getting ready. One thing was certain. Before he tied himself permanently to someone else, he would see her, actually *see* her, as a woman, and not just the younger sister he never had.

And then he could make his choice.

Chapter Three

GUY LET OUT the breath he'd been holding as the bedroom door closed behind Annie. He felt tense from his toes to the roots of his hair, and that was saying something since his hair was so short, roots were about all he had.

His present mood had nothing to do with this wedding business, though he was half-dreading that already, too. No, it had to do with Annie. It was all her fault.

Seduction? What the hell did his sweet little Annie know about carnal seduction? Guy snorted to himself. Nothing. She knew absolutely nothing about it, he was sure of that. Why, she'd seldom even dated, and never seriously! Not that she couldn't if she chose to.

Most times she seemed unaware of it, but Annie was a real looker. Though she might be a petite little thing, her gentle curves were in all the right places, perfectly symmetrical, perfectly balanced. *Perfect.*

Good God, now she had him thinking about her curves.

He swiped a hand over his face and paced to the couch. The phone sat on an end table and he called the familiar number of their favorite pizza place. After he replaced the receiver, he looked around, trying to find something to occupy his mind other than Annie's body.

Or her plans for seduction.

Or her selection of reading material.

The books were impossible to ignore, given that they were scattered everywhere, the titles fairly screaming up at him. Sex, sex, sex. In Annie's apartment, where sex didn't belong.

He didn't want to, but he picked up *The Joy of Sex* and skimmed through it. He got hot under the collar and hot in his pants, at the same time. His brain felt confused and bruised as he imagined Annie looking through the same book, planning on incorporating what she saw with some faceless, nameless man. *Dammit.*

Guy paced some more. Whoever the guy was, he wasn't good enough for her. Not if Annie had to resort to seducing him. Was the guy a blind fool?

Women like Annie were rare. She was kind and gentle and smart and she knew how to take care of herself, though her brothers spent the better part of their lives trying to do that for her. Guy supposed he was guilty as well, only to a lesser degree. But she was such a tiny thing, with such an enormous capacity for compassion, it would be easy for someone to take advantage of her.

The thought of someone breaking her heart filled him with a killing—and jealous—rage.

He knew what he had to do then. Once he resigned himself to his fate, he actually felt a bit better. Guy sprawled on the couch and put his feet up on the square glass coffee table. While he formulated his plans to save Annie from her own curiosity, he idly flipped through the books. They weren't without their appeal, he had to admit. In fact, they were downright sexy as sin. And Lace had been right; the pictures were exquisite.

Annie definitely needed his protection. A sweet little thing like her could easily be swept away by the sexual promises the books described. It would be a great injustice for Annie to waste her innocence on a jerk who didn't really want her, who might not appreciate her. *A guy she had to seduce.*

An image of that damned Perry fellow came to mind, the

way he looked at Annie, with the familiar sign of lust in his eyes. Guy's palms started to sweat. He definitely would not let Perry touch her.

He wiped his hands on his jeans, then decided he'd just have to help her, whether she realized she needed help or not.

It wouldn't even be that difficult. There was an easy camaraderie between them. Guy had felt it from the first time he'd met Annie, when she'd been no more than elbow high to him. With ten years separating them, he'd always considered her something of a baby. She'd been all big blue eyes and wild dark hair then, with skinny little legs and a shy smile. But she'd trusted him. And he'd liked her. Whenever Daniel had been too busy studying, or Dan had been working, or Max had been harassing, she'd come to him. Her faith in him, her friendship, was something he'd always hold dear, something he valued more than anything else in life.

Their relationship had been strained on occasion as Annie matured; there were times when his riotous hormones possessed his mind and his body, blocking out all rational thought. He'd forgotten that she was his best friend's baby sister, and done things then he shouldn't have done.

Like kiss her.

And touch her.

And want her.

But for the most part, he suppressed those urges. *For the most part.*

There were still nights when his subconscious took over and he woke up from a dream of loving her and suffered immense disappointment. What he needed, he'd decided— thanks to Dan's less than subtle hinting—was his own woman. Then he wouldn't use Annie to fill all the gaps in his life. It wasn't fair to her to make her a surrogate mate just because he couldn't find a woman he wanted to get serious with. It was a lamentable breach of friendship to use her that way.

And maintaining his friendship with Annie was definitely

a priority. He was close to Daniel, but the male-based friendship had restrictions, rules that couldn't be ignored. With Annie, he didn't have to worry about being one of the guys, about maintaining his macho image. He loved Daniel—and even Max—like brothers. But it was Annie he was totally at ease with.

Because they were so damn close, it was easy to let his thoughts go wandering into taboo directions. But it shouldn't be that way. And as soon as he married, it wouldn't be. There would be someone else to fill the void.

Before he got engaged, though, and everything changed between them, he'd take care of this one small problem for her. That's what friends were for, and Annie was still his best friend. She always would be. She deserved a guy who'd chase her, not the other way around.

After coming up with a course of action, Guy immediately felt more relaxed. Hell, if he was home and in his own bed now, he might even be able to sleep. God knew he hadn't gotten a wink of rest last night, he'd been so keyed up with thoughts of his future.

He was busy reading a small book on sensitive parts of the female body, nodding in recognition of most and raising a brow over those he doubted, when Annie walked in. He looked up, and the book fell from his hand, landing with a thump on the carpeted floor.

Every male-inspired cell in his body sprang into full alert, shooting his relaxed state straight to hell.

He gulped twice, tried to speak, and decided the effort was beyond him. He shook his head instead, trying to gather his frayed senses. Annie gave him a slow, sleepy smile, and glided—*he'd never seen her glide before*—on bare feet over to the couch.

"I thought about what you said, Guy." Her voice was low, throaty. Seductive! Guy gripped the sides of the couch to keep himself from joining the damn book on the floor. "And

I decided I should talk to you. Who better to tell me what I'm doing wrong around the...uh, man I want to seduce?"

Guy eyed the slinky little outfit she had on with grave misgivings. This was definitely not a good thing. Oh, it looked good enough. Real good. Perfect in fact. And that was the crux of the problem.

Very, very slowly, he came to his feet. "Uh, Annie..."

"Do you think this dress would turn him on? I have high heels to wear when I'm actually going to seduce him. That way, we'll be on more even ground." She gave him a sly look. "He's a lot taller than me."

His eye sockets felt singed. "Everybody's a lot taller than you." He spoke deliberately, trying to give his mind time to catch up with his tongue, which suddenly felt clumsy. And that was probably because his tongue had thought of much better things to do than talk.

The dress, a beige, sweater-type material, literally clung to her small body, outlining her soft breasts, displaying her flat belly and rounded thighs. The damn thing landed well above her knees and perfectly matched the color of her pale, smooth skin.

When he finally managed to lift his gaze to her face, he saw she was blushing and watching him very intently. She was probably waiting for a compliment—damned if he'd give her one! He'd take no part in encouraging her to wear such a provocative dress out in public.

He'd take no part in her seduction.

He felt his brows pull down in a vicious frown. He jutted his chin toward her, knowing he was about to hurt her feelings, but not seeing any other way. "You look more naked than not."

She didn't even blink an eye at his harsh tone. "You've never seen me naked, so how would you know?"

His blood seemed to pump hotly through his veins. Moving closer so that he towered over her, he said in a low, drawl, "I've seen you. Don't tell me you've forgotten?"

He hoped to embarrass her just a bit, and then she'd go and change back into her requisite jeans and loose top.

Only she didn't do that.

Annie immediately averted her gaze while scuffing her bare pink toes on the carpet. "I was only seventeen then—and a very late bloomer. It wasn't like there was much to look at."

Tenderness swelled inside him, almost obliterating his shock at seeing her appear so sexy. He could remember that day as if it had just happened. Hell, he'd go to his grave remembering.

"The way you carried on," he said, his tone low and gruff, "I was afraid the whole neighborhood would know what had happened."

"I was mortified," she admitted with a shrug. "When Marcy and Kim convinced me we could skinny-dip without getting caught, I stupidly believed them. But of all the people to catch us…"

He couldn't help but smile at the memory of their combined high-pitched girlish wails. He'd had a headache for an hour afterward. "I'm not sure who was stunned more. Me or you three girls."

"Marcy and Kim both swore they were in love with you after that."

He'd barely noticed them that day. All his attention had been on Annie. "Marcy and Kim were both trouble. I should have told their parents instead of just walking away."

"Walking?" She peeked at him, then quickly away again. "As I remember it, you stomped off cursing and even your ears were bright red. *After* you gawked for a good five seconds or so."

Chuckling now, he touched her chin to tip her face up. "I was set to strangle you when you got home. Here you were, all ready to hide for the rest of your life, and I wanted to wring your neck. Neither of those two girls would leave me alone after that. They both thought I'd be overcome with lust for their adolescent bodies after seeing them in the raw."

"Actually," she said, now smiling too, "I believe they were counting on it."

Embarrassed as he'd been, Guy had known he had to talk to Annie right away, or she'd be avoiding him forever. He was older, mature, a grown man despite how the sight of her had affected him, so he knew it was up to him to relieve her embarrassment.

He'd pretended outrage, both to help her through the awkwardness of it, and to hide his own unaccountable discomfort with the situation.

She might not have considered herself physically ripe, but his reaction to her was staggering. He'd felt like a lecher because he'd even noticed her, much less that he couldn't get the image out of his mind. It was the first time he'd ever really thought of Annie being female, of being someone other than Daniel's little sister, or a cute kid who he liked as a friend. She'd stood shivering in the shallow water, one hand over her very small breasts, the other splayed over the notch of her thin thighs, and his knees had damn near buckled. He'd had to limp away like a man with two broken legs.

He still felt guilty when he remembered it—and he remembered it more often than he should.

At ten years her senior, he was far too old then, and too trusted by the Sawyers clan, to be thinking the things he'd thought. At the time, he hadn't even known there were such vivid, carnal things to think about. He certainly never had in the past. Not that he was a prude. Hell no. But females had come and gone in his life without a lot of notice from him. He'd taken pleasure in them, enjoyed them, and then gotten on with his plans.

Annie, well, she had inspired him to new depths of lust.

And he'd been fighting himself ever since because no matter what he told himself, no matter how much he loved her as a friend, his gonads insisted she was uncommonly sexual and appealing. He and his gonads had been on very bad terms ever since then.

Guy groaned and walked away from her. He'd felt so damned disgusted with himself then, as if he'd done something obscene to her when, in fact, he hadn't even looked for more than the few seconds it took for her nudity to register. And as much as he hated himself, he'd carried that picture in his mind ever since as a teasing reminder of Annie's shy, innocent femininity.

She wasn't acting so shy now.

"Guy?"

Her tone made his spine stiffen. He kept his back to her, thinking that might be safer than actually looking at her, so soft and sweet and curious. "You can't really be thinking of wearing that thing in public?" he grumbled.

"Of course not."

His knees turned to butter. *Thank goodness!* He was just managing to regulate his heart rate when she said, "It's for private viewing only. Maybe at his apartment. Or mine."

Before he could think better of it, Guy whirled to face her again. "Who the hell is this jerk you want so badly? If it is Perry, I swear I'll—"

Annie crossed her arms under her breasts and he realized she wasn't wearing a bra. He started to shake.

"Oh, no you don't," she said, sounding annoyed, oblivious to his struggle for control. "You'll try to intimidate him into staying away from me, won't you?"

That was exactly what he intended to do. He was beginning to feel just a bit desperate. "Honey, any guy who doesn't want you, isn't worth all this trouble."

As she turned to pace away, Guy got a tempting view of her backside in the dress.

To hell with the pizza. He had to leave.

He started to reach for his jacket, but Annie forestalled him.

In a very small voice, she asked, "What if he has good reason for staying away from me? What then?"

"Don't be ridiculous." He didn't mean to sound so harsh, but she was torturing him by slow degrees. "What possible reason could he have? No, the guy's just an idiot, and you don't really want to bed down with an idiot, now do you?"

Staring at him in what appeared to be humble exasperation, she muttered, "Unfortunately, I believe I do."

He drew a long breath. "Annie, honey, let me explain something to you about sex."

Her brows lifted, her expression intense and fixed.

Guy faltered, then forced himself to go on. "Sex isn't all romantic."

"It isn't?"

He shook his head. "No, it's hot and sweaty and sometimes crude and…"

Her eyes darkened, her lips parted, her cheeks flushed. "You make it sound wonderful," she breathed.

Guy had absolutely no idea how to reply to that.

The doorbell rang.

Annie took a deep, shuddering breath, then started toward it.

Guy grabbed her arm. *"Don't even think it."* He knew he sounded panicked, but there was no way in the world he'd let her go to the door in that dress.

"What's the matter with you?" she asked, and damn if she didn't sound amused.

Guy pulled her toward the hallway and out of sight. "The poor pizza kid would likely have a heart attack. He's young and vulnerable, and probably horny enough as it is without you flaunting yourself in front of him. Here, stay out of sight while I get rid of him."

Annie grinned, but thankfully, she didn't fight him.

After he'd accepted and paid for the pizza, then closed the

door, Annie came up to stand very close to him. "So you think my dress looks good enough to turn on the pizza deliverer?"

"He's nineteen. A strong wind would turn him on."

Surprise replaced her expression of anticipation. "Really?"

Guy moved away from her, needing the distance from her barely veiled body. "I think your body looks good. The dress isn't even noticeable."

"You mean it?" Annie skipped next to him to keep up with his long-legged, agitated stride. She stared up at him anxiously with those big blue eyes. "You honestly think I have an adequate body?"

Adequate? Guy thunked the pizza onto the counter in the kitchen and turned to glare down at her. Was she yanking his chain, or did she really have no notion of how sexy she was? Right now, in her bare feet, she probably stood five-two. Her hair, a rich shiny shade very close to black, but softer in color, fell past the middle of her back and made a man wonder what it would feel like drifting over his chest, his abdomen.

Other places.

Her blue eyes were huge, thickly lashed, staring up at him while she awaited his reply.

He didn't want to, but his gaze dropped down her body again. Everything suddenly seemed warmer, slower, closer. He could hear her small unsteady breaths, smell her soft, clean scent—a fragrance unique to Annie and guaranteed to drive him crazy.

His stomach muscles clenched when he saw that her nipples were tight against the soft fabric of the dress. She had her hands laced together over her middle, her knees pressed close together, her toes curled.

Evidently he was no stronger than the pizza kid.

He gave up with a groan, leaning down in slow motion, giving her plenty of time to move away, even hoping she would because he felt beyond control.

Instead, she moved into him, lifting her face, her lips

parted, her breath now coming faster. He was a fool, an idiot...
Oh damn, she tasted good.

His mouth ate at hers, carefully, thoroughly. Every time he
kissed her, it was better than the time before. He gave a small
suction and captured her soft tongue, then gave her his own.
He heard her weak moan. Her lips were damp and clinging
and tasted incredibly hot and sweet.

But he didn't touch her otherwise. He kept his hands resolutely at his sides, though it almost killed him, especially
with her pressing so close, letting him feel her rounded breasts
against his rib cage, her stiff little nipples burning him. He
wanted to lift her to the counter, to part her slim thighs, to...

Her small hot hand opened on the left side of his butt, and
she copped a feel.

Guy jerked back, panting, disillusioned, turned on.

Eyes dreamy, Annie sighed. Her smile was content—her
hand squeezing. The world shifted a little, then righted itself
and everything became clear.

She was practicing on him!

The first curse word out of his mouth made her jump. The
second had her scowling darkly and removing her hand from
his backside. The third...well, he didn't know what the third
did because he didn't wait around to see.

It was time to leave. Past time to leave. Damned if he'd let
her hone her skills on him while planning to seduce some
other fool.

Halfway out of the room, he realized he couldn't leave
things this way, not with the plans she had in mind. He'd
never get to sleep wondering if and when she was following
through on those damned idiotic plans.

He turned back—and Annie, rapidly dogging his heels,
slammed into him. He clutched her shoulders to keep her
from falling, then gave her a slight shake. "Don't seduce anyone! Do you hear me?"

"Everyone on the block likely heard you!"

He gave her another small shake. "If the man needs to be persuaded, then there's something wrong with him. Trust me on this, Annie."

"No." She still looked a bit dreamy, her eyes softened and her mouth swollen. The hand that had clutched his bum was now cradled protectively to her chest. "There's nothing wrong with him. He's perfect."

Guy roared in frustration. "You," he said, lifting her to her tiptoes, "obviously don't know a thing about men. I'm telling you, the guy's dense."

With a placating tone, she said, "Okay, okay. He's dense." She struggled to catch her breath, staring up at him with round, hopeful eyes. "So…what you're saying is that I'm enticement enough? He'll actually want me *without* this planned seduction?"

Guy's eyes widened; he didn't know what he was saying, but it sure as hell wouldn't be an admission like that!

He gently shook her again—it seemed his safest course. "You told me to think about proposing. All right. I'll make you a deal. You think about this seduction business, and I'll think about proposing. We'll both give it a lot of thought. All right?"

To his surprise, she immediately agreed. She stuck out the hand she'd used to grope him and said, "Done."

Cautiously, Guy enclosed her slender fingers in his own. "Annie…?"

"You can't back out now, Guy." She pumped his hand hard twice, then released it. With her fists on her hips and her chin tilted up so she could stare at him eye to eye, she said, "Before either of us makes a move on our new intentions, we'll discuss it. We'll hash it out completely. We'll make totally certain we know exactly what we're doing, what we're letting ourselves in for. We'll have no doubts before we—"

Guy put a finger over her lips. "Enough, Annie." He moved his hand quickly enough when he felt how damp and swollen her mouth still felt from his kiss. *He had to leave.* "I'll call you tomorrow. And in the meantime, try to think about why you'd even want to sleep with this jerk."

She smiled at him and then sighed. "I already know why."

Her voice was so soft, so heated, he felt it lick right down to his abdomen. And it hurt, a kind of hurt he didn't even want to acknowledge, much less think about. Stepping back, he cleared his throat and tried to come up with a logical reason for leaving so soon.

Annie didn't give him a chance. She flapped her hand in the air. "I know, I know. You're leaving." Then she grinned. "Do you know, you do that every time you kiss me."

He carefully inched his way toward the couch where he'd thrown his coat. "What?"

"Kiss me and run. Why is that?"

How could she stand there in that lethal dress and question him so innocently? It was a mystery set for greater minds than his own. Especially when he could barely concentrate on what she was saying. "I, ah, didn't mean to kiss you."

She sighed again, more dramatically this time. "Oh, Guy. It sure felt like you meant it."

"Annie," he said, feeling desperate, "you know I think of you as—"

"I am not your little sister, Guy!"

Didn't he know it. He cleared his throat. "Maybe not, not literally anyway. But I've watched you grow up, seen you turn independent. And you are Daniel's little sister. He trusts me. Dan trusts me. Hell, even Max trusts me, and that's saying a lot because from what I can tell, Max doesn't trust anyone."

She looked confused. "What does trust have to do with this?"

Everything, he wanted to shout. Her family depended on him to look after her just as they did. They depended on him to view her in the same light.

Her father had said plenty of times that Annie needed someone special, someone who was just right for her. And Daniel often worried that she'd get taken in by a man playing on her sensitivity, her vulnerability. Max wanted to wrap her in cotton and tuck her away someplace safe. He'd gladly pound anyone who hurt his sister—they all would. Annie was so sweet, she just didn't have what it took to shield herself from the many users of the world.

Because he was male, Guy knew exactly how base men could be. He knew what they had uppermost on their minds. From a pizza delivery boy to a corporate wheeler-dealer—they all wanted the same things. Annie just hadn't realized it yet.

He owed the Sawyers family, more than Daniel or Annie or Max knew. Hell, even he hadn't known the extent of Dan Sawyers's generosity until a few years ago. It had been more than enough that Dan had let him move in, that he'd forced himself out of his self-imposed isolation to attend some of Guy's high school awards ceremonies, that he'd attended his college graduation. He'd treated Guy like a son, and taken great pride in his educational accomplishments.

But Dan had gone one further. He'd paid for that damn education while letting everyone think a scholarship had been provided. He'd known there was no way Guy's own parents could foot the bill, and rather than make it difficult on Guy, he'd silently, and very privately, taken care of everything.

Somehow, someway, Guy vowed he'd manage to pay the man back, not only the money, but all the support. The Sawyers clan had accepted him, made him one of their own. They believed in him even when he didn't believe in himself. He owed them all a lot, whether they knew it or not.

He couldn't very well repay them by getting involved with Annie. Not when all the men in her family were so overprotective. They wanted the best for her, and as a hanger-on, an outsider, a damn charity case, Guy was far from the best.

His chest hurt with the reality of that, but he refused to dwell on it too long.

When he didn't reply, Annie gave him a challenging look. "I'm not wearing any underwear, Guy Donnovan. None at all."

All the breath in his lungs wheezed out of him in a loud gasp, as if he'd just taken a sucker punch. At the same time, his body tightened in acute arousal. *"What?"*

She dared to laugh, the little witch, shaking her head and sending her hair drifting over her shoulders so that one long curl fell forward to frame a tight nipple. She smacked his shoulder, gave him a brief distracted caress, then said, "I was just making certain you were still with me. You took so long to answer my question."

What question? It was difficult to remember after her little bombshell.

He sternly instructed his eyes to stay on her face, not to go wandering down that luscious little body again, trying to see things that he'd be better off not seeing. His eyes nearly crossed with the effort.

"Guy, I was only teasing. I have my panties on."

Even hearing her say the word "panties," making a reference to her intimate apparel, had him in a frenzy of lust. He was pathetic, beyond the ragged edge. He considered gagging her before she killed him.

Annie laughed again at his blank-brained expression. "Relax, Guy. I only said that because Lace told me it was a big turn-on for men. You know, telling them you were naked beneath your dress." She waited two heartbeats, then asked, "Is it?"

"Is it what?" He felt like an idiot, but he wanted very much to see if she was telling the truth. For some reason, every male hormone in his body screamed that she really was naked beneath that not-quite-there dress. He had to curl his hand into a fist to keep it from sliding up her thigh, seeking warm feminine parts, discovering the truth on his own. If she wasn't wearing panties, he'd feel her soft, silky skin, her damp flesh, her...

His body reacted accordingly to the mental provocation. He

closed his eyes and said a quick prayer she wouldn't notice his blatant erection.

"Is it a turn-on," she patiently repeated, "for men to think a lady is naked beneath her clothes?"

He snatched up his coat and pulled it on with more force than grace. Within seconds, he was on his way out the door, his pace determined, his head down in concentration.

"Guy?" She hung half out the door, watching his hurried and desperate retreat.

"Yes," he shouted back, "it is. And stop listening to Lace."

"Why?"

Now that there were a few feet separating them, he slowed and walked backward, watching her watch him, and he said, "Because young ladies shouldn't do or say things like that. And," he added when she started to take umbrage, "it's very bad for my general health."

Annie laughed in undiluted delight. "Too much stress?"

Too much temptation. "Get back inside your apartment before someone sees you." After that frowning order, he gave a quick wave of his hand, then raced down the steps and headed outside.

Thank God it was still raining. He could use the freezing shower to cool off his mind and his body. He had to get a grip. Annie was not for him and she never would be, despite the fact she seemed to want to experiment with him—probably because she did trust him so much, which was all the more reason to resist. She was a friend, a valuable friend that he didn't want to lose.

And if he lost Annie, he'd lose Daniel and Dan and Max, too. They were family to him. Very close family. He loved his mom and dad, but he'd been an only child, born late in life, and they were so far away now. He saw them three or four times a year at best, and spoke to them only monthly.

Dan had been able to do all the things with him that his own father couldn't do. He'd taught Guy things, took him under his wing and showed him how to run the family business. And Guy and Daniel were every bit as close as brothers could be. *They were his family.*

So what the hell was wrong with him?

His hair was soaked by the time he got into his car, and his hands were shaking, as much from his turbulent thoughts as from the cold. He was still slightly unsure about marrying Melissa, but he was dead certain he had to do something. He couldn't screw everything up by doing things with Annie he had no business doing.

And oh, the things he wanted to do.

Erotic things. Carnal things. Hot, wonderfully debauched things. Her brothers would kill him if they could read his thoughts right now.

He'd noticed the small, black pearl necklace he gave her years ago, nestling between her breasts still. The necklace had been a gift of friendship then; tonight it had turned him on painfully to see it against her skin, to know she wore it always.

Even when she slept, or showered. When she was naked.

He didn't want to lose her. He didn't want to lose her family. He felt nearly overwhelmed with conflicting emotions when he pulled out into the early evening traffic. His mind churned over several possible ways to solve his dilemma, but his thoughts kept coming back to her damned seduction, and how *he'd* like to teach her anything and everything she ever wanted to know.

He was busy cursing the fates that had thrown two female problems in his lap at once, when a traffic light turned green and he started forward. Unfortunately, the oncoming semi tried to stop for the light, but when he put on his brakes, the icy rain made the task impossible.

Guy watched, seeing it all in slow motion as the truck skidded and slid sideways, and then, with a horrifying crunch, rammed into the side of his car.

He barely had time to think, much less react. And then it didn't matter. His car crumbled in around him, and his head hit something solid. Everything went black.

Chapter Four

WHEN THE PHONE rang, Annie jumped a good foot. She'd been lying in the bed for hours, perusing one of the many magazine articles Lace had given her and daydreaming about seduction techniques and how to apply them to Guy Donovan. He'd been on the ragged edge tonight, of that she was certain. He wanted her.

At least in that dress, he did.

She felt guilty for the wicked thoughts she'd been conjuring, almost as if the caller could read her mind. She actually blushed as she answered the phone on the third ring. She tried to sound sleepy, rather than excited. After all, it was past midnight.

"Hello?"

"Are you awake, Annie?"

Daniel. Something must be wrong for him to call so late. "What is it? What's happened?" At first, she feared Guy had done something stupid like elope, and her stomach knotted in dread.

But it was even worse.

"He's okay now. Really. But Guy had an accident after he left your place. He's here at the hospital."

The words barely registered before she was out of the bed, the phone caught between her shoulder and ear, and she was scurrying to find jeans to pull on. "What happened? What's wrong with him?"

She could hear the panic in her own tone, but didn't think Daniel noticed. "He damaged his knee a bit, enough to keep him from jogging for a while. And he's got some pretty ugly contusions, especially around his ribs."

Her vision blurred. "Oh God. *Contusions.*"

"Bruises, Annie. Just very colorful bruises. He also hurt his head."

His beautiful head! She began shaking, feeling as if she might split apart. "How..." She had to gulp. "How bad?"

"He's awake, and he's going to be okay. But he's a bit antsy and unmanageable." There was a pause, then, "Honey, can you come to the hospital?"

As if she'd stay home? "I'll be there in just a few minutes."

"No! You'll be here in about an hour. It's a long drive for you and the roads are a mess. The freezing rain turned to snow and plows are out everywhere. Just take it easy and drive careful, all right? I don't want both of you in here with me."

"I'll be careful," she promised, then hung up before he could caution her more. It was just like Daniel to be overly concerned with her driving at a time like this. He would hurry, but he didn't trust her to do so.

She was out the door in two minutes flat, her hair still ratty and uncombed, her clothes hastily donned, her shoes pulled on without socks. Daniel was right, she soon discovered. The roads were awful, and recognizing that fact only made her more anxious. How badly had Guy been hurt in this horrid weather? Daniel's reassurances didn't relieve her one bit. He was capable of softening the truth, to keep her from rushing. Guilt swelled inside her until she thought she'd choke on it.

Her awesome seduction technique had driven him away! He'd literally raced from her apartment and it was all her fault.

It took her half the time Daniel had predicted to reach the hospital, despite the road conditions. She rushed through the emergency room door and then skidded to a halt when Lace came forward to meet her.

"Lace? What in the world are you doing here? Did Daniel call you, too?" Had he called the whole family? Was Guy even worse off than she'd first suspected?

Lace gave her a generous smile. "I was here visiting Daniel when they brought Guy in. Come on, I'll show you where they're keeping him."

Though she hurried forward, Annie felt her own misgivings. "Is he really okay, Lace?"

Lace gave Annie's hand a squeeze. "He's going to be fine, but he's a little dopey at the moment. Ah, here's Daniel, and Annie, you know what an excellent doctor your brother is."

Annie did know; Daniel was one of the very best. But at the moment that fact didn't ease her anxiety one bit.

"Daniel? Tell me what's wrong with Guy. Why is he still here if he's okay? And where is he? I want to see him." She would only feel secure that he was truly okay after she'd scanned the length of his magnificent body herself.

Daniel clasped her shoulders to stop her from pushing forward and gave her a brotherly squeeze. "Just hold on, sis. I need to talk to you before you go in."

"Oh God."

"Now, Annie, you have to get a grip. It's not as bad as it looks. Guy has a lot of colorful contusions, but we've cleared his cervical spine. There were no neck injuries, no trauma to his head."

"You promise?"

"Honey, you know what a hard head Guy has." Daniel smiled at her.

"But he doesn't have much hair to cushion it."

"I promise, other than a few bruises, his head is fine." Daniel patted her back in his brotherly manner. "He does have some pretty severe, and I'm sure painful, scrapes and bruises to his right shoulder and ribs, and his right knee might need some orthopedic care. Right now we can't determine the extent of the injury to his knee because of the swelling. In a few days he can go to a specialist and see about the possibility of surgery, though I doubt it will be necessary. For the time being we've put an external, removable knee immobilizer on him, and he'll need pain medication for a spell. He'll have to use crutches to get around, and I'd recommend as much bed rest, with his knee elevated, as possible for the next few days."

Annie covered her mouth with a hand while tears welled in her eyes. And Daniel claimed it wasn't too bad? It sounded worse than awful.

It sounded like her attempts at seduction had almost killed him!

"Now Annie," Lace said, coming to stand by Daniel, then leaning against his side. Daniel slipped his arm around her, taking comfort from her nearness. "You can't go in and talk to Guy if you're falling apart. He really is going to be okay, you know. Your brother wouldn't lie to you."

"Of course not," Daniel said, doing his best to soothe Annie, but looking relieved to have Lace's help. "Nothing is broken or seriously injured, but bruises can hurt almost as bad as a break, so he's going to need some care."

"I'll do it," Annie blurted before she could temper her reaction.

Daniel sighed. "That's what I assumed. You two were always closer than most brothers and sisters."

Lace rolled her eyes, but at Annie's pleading look, said nothing.

"Can I see him now?"

"All right." Daniel reluctantly eased away from Lace, then took Annie's hand to lead the way. "The thing is, honey, he's a little screwy and disoriented at the moment. Considering his body size and his injuries, I gave him a whopper of a painkiller. But I think I may have overdone it." Daniel laughed. "At least now I know why he never drinks."

Just as they rounded a corner of the emergency room, Annie could hear someone singing. It was an old *Mary Poppins* tune, shouted out in a flat, wavering baritone that had all the nurses holding their ears.

Daniel merely chuckled. "He's right through there. You can just follow the noise. But watch yourself. He tried to hug me—and nearly tossed me to the ground."

"I had to save him," Lace said with a grin, sidling up to Daniel again. "We all three almost toppled."

Annie wavered forward, her steps tentative.

Guy rested on his back in a narrow metal bed, a thin blanket pulled up to his waist. His hard, hairy chest was bare and decorated with numerous bruises. His short hair jutted out every which way, his eyes were squeezed closed, but his mouth was wide open.

He started in wailing, "Ohhhh, su-per-cal-la-frag—"

And Annie whispered, "Guy?"

He grew instantly silent, then cocked one eye open. "Ahh, another little lady friend. Come to inflict more torture on my poor male person, have you?"

He was grinning, but she flinched at his words. "Of course not. How do you feel?"

"Like I fought with a semi and lost. And yourself?"

A semi? Thank God he wasn't killed. She approached his side slowly, her feet dragging, her heart pounding. "You look like you lost. You've got bruises on top of your bruises."

"You look like you're ready to cry." He studied her face with blurry, pain-filled eyes, then said softly, "I'd really rather you didn't."

"I won't."

"Did you like *Mary Poppins* when you were little?" Before she could answer, he laughed. "What am I saying? You're still little. I meant when you were younger."

She nodded, pulling a chair up to the bed and sitting beside him before her knees gave out.

Very carefully, she reached through the bed railing and closed her cold fingers around his large hand. "You used to watch it with me when no one else would."

"Impossible. I hated that damn movie. Still do. Maybe not the first dozen times I saw it, but after that…"

She felt her bottom lip begin to quiver. Even though he'd hated it, he'd still watched it with her? "Guy, I lo—"

"Are you wearing your panties?"

Her declaration died in her throat. *"What?"*

"Tell me the truth now, Annie. And no more of your teasing." He eyed her body from head to toe, but since she wore her usual of jeans and a sweatshirt, he couldn't see a thing. "Well? Are you or not?"

His brow was puckered with a suspicious frown, and Annie had to draw a deep breath to calm herself. Good grief, she'd almost blurted out that she loved him. Not that he would have thought that much of it. Her family was loving, and it wasn't uncommon to show it, to say it, to make it known. But she wouldn't have meant it the way he'd want to take it.

She was trying to find an answer for him when Daniel walked in. "So, how are we doing?"

"Daniel." Guy suddenly had a sappy grin on his face. "Do you know you're the best doctor in the whole damn world? I mean it, man. You saved me." Then to prove Annie's earlier point, he said, "I love you like a brother, Daniel."

Daniel shook his head. "I love you, too, Guy." To Annie, he said, "That's about the twelfth declaration of undying love I've gotten from him since the pain medication kicked in."

Annie stifled a watery grin.

"And I mean it, too. It was my only spot of luck this dark night, that you were on duty." Guy groaned, his eyes squeezing shut again. "Damn but I wish my head didn't hurt so bad."

"As long as you insist on yodeling, your head is going to continue to hurt like hell. You need to rest *quietly.*" Daniel grinned as he said it, apparently amused despite his suggestions. "Annie, why don't you step out here a minute. The nurse needs to check Guy's vitals again and I want to talk to you."

Guy jerked his eyes open and his gaze landed on Annie. "Are you leaving?"

He sounded almost desperate, and the dreaded tears threatened again. She pitched her voice low in a soothing tone, in deference to his aching head. "No, of course not. I'll be right back."

"Promise?"

"I promise."

Guy grimaced, then shouted loud enough for the fourth floor to hear, "Daniel, make damn sure she's got all her underwear on!"

Daniel started in surprise. "For crying out loud, Guy!"

"She's a tricky one, I tell you." He winced as he lifted his arm to point an accusing finger in her direction. "You best keep an eye on her."

Daniel pursed his mouth shut, and Annie gasped. She quickly escaped out the door, towing Daniel behind her. Two nurses began to chuckle.

The second they were out the door, Daniel laughed out loud. "I told you he was juiced. Never seen anyone quite so high on legitimate pain medicine before. So far he's confessed to loving me, the X-ray technician and the nurse who took his blood."

"Has he mentioned me?"

"Nope, sorry honey, but he hasn't said a word about you. He may be upset with you about this foolish scheme of yours to experiment."

Annie stiffened. "It's not foolishness."

"Yeah, well, whatever nonsense it is, do you think you can put it on hold awhile?"

"Why?"

"Because I've thought of a way to save Guy from himself."

Lace sauntered up in time to say, "This ought to be good."

Daniel looked over the rim of his glasses at her. "I'm glad you're still here, sweetheart. I think we can use your help."

"Oh goody."

Daniel had to force his gaze away from his wife, then he stated, "I want you to kidnap Guy."

It took a moment for Annie to realize that he was done. He wasn't going to expound on that small instruction. She cleared her throat, tried to erase the sound of her burgeoning excitement, and inquired with a feigned calm, "Oh?"

Lace looked at the ceiling and whistled. Daniel ignored her.

"If you nurse him, and keep everyone else away from him, he'll have nothing to do but think about how asinine it is to propose to Melissa. He'll probably be laid up for a few days, maybe even a week before he starts feeling whole again. I could give you complete instructions to follow on how to care for him, how to medicate him—"

"How to soothe his savage breast?" Lace asked innocently.

Daniel shrugged. "If need be. It would be the perfect time for him to reflect on what he's doing and why he shouldn't do it."

"How, exactly," Annie asked, intrigued despite her worries, "do you propose I do this? Guy is actually a whole lot bigger than me, so it's not like I can bully him."

"He's not up to a fight right now," Daniel explained. "And with the medication, I think he'll be more agreeable than not."

"He'll want to check in at work, you know that."

"He can't get around well enough for that. It's important that he stays off his feet."

"By phone then."

"I don't mind phone calls," Daniel told her, "but he'll need to take it easy, relaxing and recuperating until the swelling in his knee goes down. If anyone attempts to visit him—"

"Like Melissa?"

"Especially Melissa," Daniel agreed. "But all things considered, she should understand that he's not up to visitors."

Annie was beginning to take to the idea. Alone and isolated with Guy? It had possibilities. If he couldn't run off, if he was grounded, mostly in bed—*a perfect position*—then his life wouldn't be threatened by her seduction techniques, now would it?

"That's it?" she asked carefully, wanting to make sure she understood. "You want me to keep Melissa away from him?"

"It's a start."

Annie certainly loved the idea, but it had its drawbacks. "I'm not sure I can bar people from his home, Daniel. I mean, bedridden or not, Guy will have something to say about that, I'm sure."

Daniel cleared his throat. "I wasn't exactly talking about his home. I think you should take him away from here."

"Take him away?"

"From this area. Annie, you know he could use the time to reflect on this marriage business and to take a break from work. I'll talk to Dad. He can certainly fill in, or find a replacement for Guy for a while."

Annie blinked at Daniel. "But...where would I take him?"

Daniel removed his glasses and began polishing them on the hem of his white coat. "Well, now I had an idea about that. We have this, ah, cabin of sorts."

"A cabin?" Annie eyed the smile on Lace's face and the way Daniel wouldn't look at her. "You and Lace bought a cabin? When?"

"Well...actually..." Daniel slanted a look at Lace, then stiffened his spine. "I bought the cabin before I met Lace."

"You did?" Her brother seemed very edgy all of a sudden, making Annie frown in contemplation. "How long have you had it?"

"For a while now. It's a nice place, but a little rustic." He tried to distract her by changing the subject. "I'd take Guy there myself and force him to listen to reason, but I can't manage time away from the hospital right now."

Annie was amazed—and not the least bit diverted. "You own a cabin and you've never told me? Do Dad and Max know?"

Daniel wasn't one to lie, but Annie could see he was considering doing just that. Then he nodded and looked resigned. "Dad and Max, and even Guy have all been there. It's a bachelor's cabin, Annie, and that's why you didn't know."

Lace hooted with laughter. "Now that really hurt, didn't it? I mean, admitting to your sweet little innocent sister that you're a normal man." She turned to Annie, still grinning. "Since our marriage, however, Daniel has only been to the cabin with me."

"Actually," Daniel said, his expression stern, "Lace and I were there *before* we were married."

Rather than being embarrassed by this divulgence, Lace seemed more amused.

In a conspiratorial tone, she whispered to Annie, "All macho men need a place to indulge their baser instincts, a place to be human, without tarnishing their poor little innocent sisters with the lusty knowledge of it." She leaned against Daniel's shoulder and grinned widely. "That's right, isn't it, Doctor?"

Fascinated, Annie watched Daniel turn his very stiff back on Lace, almost causing her to fall. "Everything you need can be delivered there before you arrive. I'll call first thing in the morning and have a couple loads of wood dropped off so you'll be able to stay nice and warm. The fireplace has a blower, so it pretty much heats the whole cabin. And I'll have some food put in the fridge. The freezer is already stocked."

"You have electricity for appliances, but no heat?" Annie had a hard time taking it all in.

It was Lace who explained. "Think about it, Annie. Isn't a warm, cozy fireplace more of an inducement to romance than a furnace? There's even a store of wine and soft music aplenty, isn't there, Doc?"

Daniel didn't answer her, but he did flex his fingers. Annie wondered if he was thinking of strangling his wife. "I wouldn't suggest giving Guy any wine. Between his low tolerance and the pain medicine, who knows how he'd react to it."

Annie shook her head, still dumbfounded. "Max has been there. And Guy? And *Dad?*" It was bad enough imagining Guy taking a woman to a secluded cabin in the woods for sensual purposes. But her father?

Again, Lace answered. "It's as I keep telling you, Annie. No normal, healthy person lives as a monk. Responsible, mature sex is a vital part of life."

Daniel turned on her. "That's enough out of you."

In a gentle tone, Lace asked, "What's the matter, Daniel? Afraid little sister might find out how human you are? Or are you afraid she might find out how human *she* is?"

Daniel seethed in silence for a moment, and Annie thought what a ferocious sight he was. It was the first time she'd ever thought of her oldest brother that way, he was generally so…so…*placid.*

Daniel visibly calmed himself. "I'm not as dense as you think I am, sweetheart."

Lace lifted both brows. "No?"

"No." Then Daniel took Annie's arm and dragged her three feet away from Lace.

"I seriously doubt Guy would give up work and go to the cabin willingly. You know how devoted he is to the job. So we're going to have to outmaneuver him."

Lace rejoined them as if she'd been invited. "You know, I'm all for Annie doing this. But tell me, what did this Melissa do that was really so bad?"

"Nothing. She's just not right for Guy."

"Why?" Now Lace sounded suspicious. "You aren't intimately acquainted with her, are you?"

Daniel gave Lace the most evil grin Annie had ever seen on his handsome face. "Jealous, sweetheart?"

Lace's eyes narrowed and she started to turn away, but

Daniel caught her arm and whipped her back around to face him. Before Annie could blink, or give them a moment's privacy—not that she really would have—Daniel treated Lace to a scorching kiss. Annie felt her cheeks heat.

Who needed books when her own brother carried on so right in front of her? And contrary to Guy's reaction, Lace seemed to wallow in Daniel's technique. It was beyond fascinating.

"I love you, Lace."

"Hmm. I know." She patted his chest and smiled. "But that doesn't answer my question."

"Melissa is a businesswoman through and through. She isn't the type to inspire thoughts of hearth and home. At least, I didn't think she was. But now with Guy... I just can't believe such a mess. The whole idea of marriage is ludicrous." He tilted his head. "Does that answer your question?"

"Fortunately for you—yes."

Daniel went back to the business of the cabin, keeping one arm possessively over Lace's shoulders. "You'll be isolated enough, so Guy will have nothing to do but recuperate and think on how ridiculous this marriage plan is."

Annie nodded.

"And you," he added, "can think about this crazy seduction farce."

Lace smiled widely. "Oh, I'm sure she will. After all—" she winked at Annie "—the cabin is set up for seduction. How could she *not* think about it?"

And better yet, Annie thought, how could Guy not think about it? The setting would give her the perfect opportunity to try her hand again, only this time Guy would be at her mercy. He wouldn't be able to run away from her.

"But what if something happens to him?" Annie glanced toward the room Guy was in. She could still hear him singing, and a gaggle of nurses hovered, peeking in at him, giggling and flirting.

Shameless hussies.

What good woman took advantage of a downed man?

Annie frowned, realizing she intended to do just that! "What if he starts hurting worse, or he needs a different medicine?"

"I can make sure you have all his prescriptions before you leave, which should be sometime tomorrow morning. I want him to stay tonight just so we can keep an eye on him, but he'll be fit enough to go tomorrow—with the right care. In fact, if I know Guy, he'll probably be insisting on leaving."

"You make this sound pretty easy."

Daniel nodded. "It will be. I'll write out all the instructions for you. But to be on the safe side, you can take my cell phone with you. Just be sure to hide it from him. If Guy knows you have it, he'll call for a cab and race on home to propose." Daniel gave Annie an understanding look. "And we don't want that to happen, do we?"

"No." She most definitely didn't want him offering himself up to Melissa.

Another nurse started into Guy's room, and Annie heard Guy greet her with a whistle. The painkillers had put him in a strange mood, and she wasn't willing to let another woman— not even a nurse—take advantage of his sudden vulnerability. "I'm spending the night with him," she announced, then waited for someone to argue.

Instead, Daniel merely nodded and Lace said, "Do you want me to run home and get anything for you?"

"Thanks, Lace, but I'll be fine." She just wanted to get back to Guy, to see him and be with him—and keep other women away.

Lace held out her hand. "Give me your keys. I'm willing to bet you didn't park your car for the night."

"No, it's in the emergency zone." She dug in her pocket and extracted her bulky set of apartment and car keys. "Thanks."

"You're very welcome." Lace decided to call it a night after she moved Annie's car, and kissed both Annie and Daniel goodbye. Daniel promised to be home soon. His shift had ended hours ago, just as Guy had been brought in. Annie knew he had to be exhausted.

Daniel turned at a loud growl from Guy's room. He muttered a curse. "I think our patient is acting up just a bit. It shouldn't surprise me, I suppose. Men generally make the worst sort of patients. Come on, the nurse can probably use our help."

Annie followed quickly, anxious over the cursing complaints that echoed out of Guy's room. When they stepped through the doorway, Guy was struggling with a flustered nurse while she tried to remove his blanket.

"Get your hands off me, woman!"

"I need to check your ribs, Mr. Donovan."

"You're not getting me buck naked!"

Daniel rushed forward with a sigh. "That's okay, Ms. Dryer. I'll take care of it."

Guy focused on Daniel's face, his own expression indignant. "I've been harassed by pushy women one too many times today."

Though Annie felt the heat pulse in her cheeks at the charge, Daniel didn't seem to notice. And he certainly didn't understand Guy's meaning.

Daniel tried to placate Guy. "I do understand. But the fact is, if you want to be released in the morning, I have to make a final check on your hulking body. Big as you are, you aren't invincible. Especially up against a semi. So shut your trap and let me do my job."

"You're a damn good friend to me, Daniel, you know that? Damn good."

Daniel slanted a look at Annie that clearly said, here we go again. Daniel lowered the sheet, barely maintaining Guy's modesty, and Annie got an eye-opening view of his solid midsection. His abdomen was ridged with muscle, even in his relaxed state. And lower down, his hipbones appeared lighter than the rest of his skin, dipping in toward delectable male territory.

The same hair that lightly furred his chest ran in a silky trail down to circle his navel, then further down to...

Guy looked up and caught sight of Annie watching with rapt interest. He snatched the sheet back up to his stubbled chin while looking at her as if she were a pervert.

Daniel glanced over his shoulder at Annie, and his face softened in an understanding smile. He tipped his head toward the door. Gently, he said, "Give us a minute, sis, will you? Guy's feeling unduly shy all of a sudden."

She didn't want to leave.

She wanted to stay and see more of Guy's powerful body. She wanted to pull that sheet just a tad lower. Maybe more than a tad—to his knees would be nice.

She wanted to inspect every single bruise and scrape and hurt on his entire body, and she wanted to kiss them all better. It didn't matter that he was badly battered, he still had the most beautiful male body she'd ever seen, all long muscles and hair-dusted skin. She loved him.

Hopefully, once she had him at her mercy, she'd be able to view a bit more of him. Like maybe, all of him. In great detail. She smiled with the thought, then left the room reluctantly.

She busied herself by arranging for her assistant at the bookstore to work full shifts until further notice. She gave the woman both Daniel's and Lace's numbers, and received a promise that everything would be looked after properly.

It was another fifteen minutes before Daniel came out again. He went directly to where Annie anxiously waited. "He's fallen asleep. I figured the medicine would take him out sooner or later. Come on. I'll get you something to eat and we can talk about the cabin."

"I don't want to leave him."

"He's out cold, Annie. He won't know if you're there or not and I've given instructions for the nurses to page me if he wakes."

"I'm not hungry, Daniel. Can't I just sit beside him?"

Daniel gave her a speculative look, then finally nodded. "All right. I'll have an orderly bring you up a more comfortable chair. Would you like a pillow, too, just in case you get a chance to doze?"

"Thank you." Annie would have agreed to anything just to get it settled. More than anything, she simply wanted to be by Guy's side, holding his hand and assuring herself he was truly okay.

Above her guilt, which was extreme, she felt the driving determination to give a relationship with Guy every opportunity. If that meant throwing herself at him, taking advantage of him, acting like a trollop, then she would.

And if her heart got broken in the bargain, she'd just deal with it.

Daniel gave her one more lengthy look, then drew her close for a hug. "I have to get out of here. Guy should pretty much sleep through the night, but if there's any problem, you can call me at home. Dr. Morton will be here the rest of the night, and he's good, but I'd still want to know—"

"I understand. I love him, too." Annie smiled up at her brother, fighting off her tears. "And I promise to call you if there's any reason."

Daniel kissed her on the forehead. "Don't wear yourself out. Try to get some sleep. Guy's going to need a lot of attention in the next couple of days, and you'll have to be up to par. Especially given how he reacts to those painkillers."

After Daniel left to order the reclining chair and pillow, Annie slipped into Guy's room. Standing by the bed, she lifted his large hand and cradled it between her own. She watched his chest rise and fall as he breathed deeply in sleep. She inspected the swelling bruise on his temple, the ugly scrape on his shoulder. She didn't realize she was crying until a tear landed on their entwined hands.

She *would* do what was best for him. If that meant whisking him away to someplace private where he'd have to listen to her reasonable arguments, then so be it.

She'd do whatever was necessary to keep Guy from marrying the wrong woman. And if while they were at the cabin, he convinced her he truly only loved her as a sister, that Melissa was the right woman for him, then she'd give him up without a hassle. She wanted him to be happy.

But first he'd have a choice. He'd know how much she loved him, that everything could be wonderful between them if he'd only give them a chance. And then he could decide.

The chair was delivered and situated close to Guy's bed. Annie sank into it, but she didn't sleep. Instead, she stayed awake all night and planned Guy's seduction. She intended to give this her very best shot. Guy was more than worth the effort.

Chapter Five

"HE WOKE UP off and on all night," Annie told Daniel first thing the following morning. "Part of the time he wanted to sing, and part of the time he was groaning. The nurse gave him pain medicine twice, though he didn't really come right out and ask for it."

"He wouldn't. He's a stubborn ass, and you know it."

Calling Guy stubborn was a gross understatement. Throughout the night, Guy had been downright impossible. He'd hurt, but he resisted admitting it. "He still looks exhausted."

"Don't fret, Annie. I think his exhaustion has more to do with what was on his mind before the accident than the accident itself. My guess is, he's suffering conflicting feelings about his intention to propose to Melissa."

"You don't think he really wants to get married?"

Daniel lifted a brow. "I think he wants marriage a lot. It's Melissa I'm not really sure he wants. He likes her fine, and she's a very attractive woman, not to mention smart."

Lace poked him in the ribs. "You're on thin ice."

"Lace! When did you get here?"

"I left the house shortly after you did."

"I thought you had to be at the radio station this morning."

"Not for a couple more hours." She turned to Annie. "I hope you don't mind, but since I had your keys, I went by your apartment and packed a bag for you. This way you can stay here with Guy until it's time to leave for the cabin."

Annie hadn't even thought about packing a bag. "Thanks. How did I ever get along without you?"

Daniel, with a gentle smile, said, "I've often wondered the same thing."

Lace grinned at both of them. "It's too early for drama, so both of you can just knock it off." She leaned into her husband, who put his arm around her. "Annie, I put the bag in the back of your car already. And don't worry, I packed everything you could possibly need."

"Uh...thanks." Annie briefly wondered at the impish gleam in her friend's eyes, but she figured that could be as much from the fact her husband was caressing her hip as anything else.

Annie had been given a toothbrush from the hospital staff and she'd washed up in a private bathroom. Her clothes were a wrinkled mess, but she didn't care enough to change them. Her hair—she'd almost groaned when she'd seen how ratty it was. She untangled it the best she could, then put it in a long braid. Lace had once told her she had beautiful, sexy hair so she should wear it loose.

There was nothing sexy about it now. It was such a hassle keeping it tangle free.

They were on their way back from the cafeteria where Daniel had insisted that she eat some fruit with her coffee. The food sat like a lump in her belly. In minutes, she'd be stealing away her one true love and with any luck, she might get the chance to apply some of her new lascivious lessons to his person.

Daniel thought she was going to nurse Guy back to health.

Instead, she intended to molest him.

She knew, were Guy not loopy from the drugs, he'd never agree to letting her steal him away.

Daniel handed her a couple of pieces of paper. "Here, I've written out directions on how to get to the cabin. You shouldn't have any problems, but keep my cell phone handy just in case. And here's a list of things you'll need to know, like who to call if you need more supplies or anything. There's a local woman who keeps the place clean and does the linens and keeps the cabinets stocked. And there's instructions on how to work the controls on the hot tub—"

Annie drew to a halt. "The hot tub?"

Daniel kept walking, ignoring her interruption and not looking at her as he said, "Soaking in the hot tub might be the perfect therapy for Guy if he's up to it. But he'll definitely need help getting in and out."

Guy wet and warm from frothing water...

Daniel hid a smile and nodded to the list. "Everything is pretty easy, but I don't want you to have any trouble getting settled."

"What if the ride makes Guy uncomfortable?"

Daniel checked his watch. "Given the timing on his last pain pill, he shouldn't feel a thing for a few more hours. But often the next day after an accident is the worst. You're more aware of all your aches and pains then. If he's resistant to the pain pills, you might try—" Daniel coughed "—giving him a, er, massage. That ought to...set him straight."

Annie wanted to rub her hands together in glee. "I'll take care of him, Daniel. Don't worry."

Daniel nodded, and Annie realized just how tired he looked. "When was the last time you slept?"

He gave her a crooked smile. "I was on my way home when Guy came in last night. All things considered, I didn't rest easy when I did finally get in bed."

Lace made a sound of mock outrage. "That was your fault! I was nearly asleep when you started—"

Daniel again covered her mouth. Grinning, he pulled her close and kissed her. "Why don't you go out and start Annie's car so it can warm up while we get Guy ready to go."

Lace looked a little dazed and disgruntled. Finally, she just agreed and went out. Daniel watched her go, that silly little grin still on his mouth.

Annie said, "I had no idea you were so insatiable."

Rather than looking embarrassed this time, he shrugged. "I didn't, either. But Lace…well, she distracts me mightily. And last night I needed a distraction."

Annie hoped Guy would feel the same. She was ready and able—eager—to distract him in any way necessary. Most especially in the way she assumed Lace had distracted Daniel. "You know, marriage appears to agree with you."

"Having Lace close, loving her—that's what agrees with me. I'd recommend it to anyone. Including you." Daniel flicked the end of her nose. "When you find someone who's good enough for you, that is."

"And just who would be good enough, Daniel? Answer me that, will you?"

Daniel drew up blank, his expression bemused. Just then a nurse interrupted to tell Daniel that she'd found some newer scrubs for Guy to wear home.

Lace pulled the car right up to the emergency room entrance. Daniel helped maneuver Guy into a wheelchair for his ride outside and even supplied him with a few blankets. Guy's long body overflowed the chair in every direction, and his injured leg, jutting out straight with the support apparatus around his knee, preceded them out the door. Daniel carried a pair of brand new crutches for him, then stowed them in the back seat.

They barely managed to get him situated in the front passenger seat of her small car with a seat belt around him before Guy started snoring again, his head dropped back against the seat. Annie tried to smooth his hair, which immediately popped back up into small spikes. She covered his legs to keep them warm, then put the car in gear. Daniel stood to the side, Lace beside him, both of them waving her on.

Guy toppled over, his breath leaving him in a whoosh as the impact caused him renewed pain. Annie waited for him to awaken, but he didn't. She adjusted her position so that his head was in her lap, and when Guy looped an arm around her thigh one broad palm beneath his head, it took all her concentration to keep them safely on the road. His fingers were so close to where she'd often imagined them being. Of course, now, he was all but unconscious. And still it gave her a thrill.

She was a pervert, she decided, and didn't care.

An hour long ride?

With Guy so close, it would probably seem twice as long, but she thought of the possibilities when they finally arrived, and she started to hum. Fate was on her side this time. She would read her books, she'd study hard and Guy, bless his wounded heart, wouldn't stand a chance.

The next time she had him this close, he'd be wide awake and fully aware. With any luck at all, he'd even be willing.

ANNIE TURNED OFF the engine and gently shook Guy's shoulder. Other than wincing every now and then, he hadn't moved during the entire ride. The last sleepless night, and those before it, were taking their toll. She knew he had to be sore, so she was careful when she tried to wake him.

He slept on.

"Guy?" She shook him a little harder this time and he stirred the tiniest bit. His large hand squeezed her thigh more firmly and he turned his face inward, nuzzling against her in a most scandalizing way.

In a most thrilling way.

Annie froze. *"Ohmigosh."* Surely it was depraved to enjoy the attentions of a sleeping man.

"Shh." Guy, evidently not quite sound asleep, yet not quite awake, kissed her leg, his fingers now cuddling. "Not so loud, sweetheart."

Never in her life had she heard that tone of voice from Guy.

His fingers…good grief. They were sliding higher and he was so hot she felt burned. She could barely breathe. "Uh…"

"Just relax," he murmured in a low, sleepy, persuasive tone. A seductive tone.

Did he even know who he was touching? If he called her by another name, she'd…

Annie gripped his shoulder again. "Guy Donovan! You wake up this instant!" If they were going to do this, Annie was just scrupulous enough to insist the man at least be fully conscious.

Guy went still, then yawned hugely and started to stretch. He ended that quickly with a grimace.

Bleary-eyed and not quite focused, he struggled into a more or less upright position and looked around. He saw the cabin, tilted his head, and yawned again. Without a word, he started to leave the car.

"Guy wait!" Annie hustled out and around the car. Guy cursed and groaned as he managed to crawl out of the car. He swayed on his feet when Annie handed him the crutches and grabbed his side. Luckily, someone had salted the gravel drive so there were no apparent slick spots, but it was still uneven and rocky.

"Don't move," Annie told him, aware of the cold cutting through her, the wind whistling, "until I get the door unlocked. Do you understand me?" He was still entirely too dopey for Annie to trust him. But he seemed to be holding himself steady, and she knew she had to get him inside.

Guy propped himself against the car and gave her a cocky grin.

Annie had no idea what to make of that. She watched him closely, constantly looking back at him with a frown as she made her way to the front door. There were two locks, and she'd gotten them both open and had started to turn when Guy muttered a low complaint right behind her.

She whipped around and nearly ran into him. Luckily she stopped herself in time because she really didn't think there was any way she could control his weight if he started to topple. "I told you to stay put!"

He used only one crutch, letting it take some of the weight off his right leg as he hobbled past her. "I need to lie down."

Annie hovered. She wasn't quite sure what to do. He seemed to be managing okay, so she hated to touch him and maybe put him off balance. But Guy still seemed more asleep than awake, moving by rote toward the bedroom.

She followed along behind him like a shadow. She'd never seen the cabin before, and wasn't getting much of a chance to look at it now as she rushed behind Guy, so she figured he knew where he was going better than she did.

She noticed a warm fire crackling in the fireplace behind a glass screen, a huge entertainment center, and a lot of open space as Guy led her along. An enormous seating arrangement—she thought it might be called a pit—was strategically positioned in front of the fireplace.

When Guy safely reached the bed and sat down on the edge, she breathed a sigh of relief.

Cold air blew in through the open front door, and Annie was just about to go close it when Guy started struggling with his coat. Annie rushed to help him. He kept giving her sappy grins and thanking her as she tugged the bomber jacket off his wide shoulders. Annie smiled at him. He was so silly with the effects of the drugs.

Then he pulled his shirt off over his head, and her smile fell away. Even with the bruises, he looked too gorgeous for words. She was standing there watching him in appreciation, his coat clutched to her chest, when he stood, balanced on one leg, and untied the drawstring at the waistband of the scrubs.

Before she could draw a deep breath, the loose bottoms dropped to his ankles.

He had nothing on underneath.

Without so much as a blush of modesty, Guy sat back down on the bed and clumsily worked his shoes and socks off. Annie didn't think to help him. The man was naked; looking at him was a delight. Getting close to him would have been too much temptation to resist.

She just knew she'd want to touch something. Maybe everything, but a few things specifically...

Once his shoes and socks were off, he gingerly lifted his injured leg onto the mattress, then fell back with a long hearty sigh.

Annie was so enraptured by the up close and personal view of his nude body, it took her a couple of minutes to realize he was snoring again. He was on top of the quilts, stretched out in beautiful bruised perfection, wearing nothing more than a stabilizer on his injured knee.

Annie licked her lips. Well, well, well.

Who'd have thought the man would be *this* accommodating!

She realized he apparently associated the cabin with nakedness, and that took away her smile. As she continued to survey him from collarbone to knees, she wondered at the myriad of things he'd done with the women he brought here. Just how lascivious and lewd were the cabin interludes?

Wind carried a dusting of snow in through the open front door and drew Annie out of her voyeurism. She forced herself to back away from Guy.

When she reached the warm fireplace she turned and hurried outside. The sooner she got the car unloaded, the sooner she could go back and feast her eyes on him some more. Who cared if it was unethical? An opportunity like this might never come along again.

Annie grinned as she thought of his reaction when his head finally cleared. Guy obviously had no idea what he was doing, and that gave her an absolutely splendid idea.

She could barely wait.

GUY WINCED AS he got one eye open and tried to focus on the source of his irritation. The setting sun, in vivid shades of orange and crimson, sent a slanted beam of light through the narrow opening in the drapes directly into his eyes. His mouth tasted like cat litter and his body ached from one end to the other. When he started to sit up, a flash of intense pain radiated from his knee to every other muscle in his body.

He groaned out a quiet curse.

It dawned on him slowly that he wasn't at the hospital anymore, nor was he at home. However, the room, even the bed, were familiar. *The cabin.*

Guy looked around at the nightstand and saw by the handset clock that it was nearly six-thirty. The last thing he remembered clearly was Daniel waking him at the hospital, shoving him into scrubs and telling him it was time to go. That damn medicine the nurse kept forcing on him made him groggy. When he took it, he felt like he was dreaming and awake at the same time.

And in those odd dreams, Annie was always there. Touching him. Smiling at him.

Letting him touch her.

He looked down at his throbbing leg and saw it was stiff as a morning erection, sticking straight out thanks to the wraparound brace cushioning his knee.

Besides desperately needing a drink of water, a shower, and something to eat, Mother Nature called. Rather loudly.

Guy threw off the quilt and carefully scooted to the edge of the mattress. Crutches were propped by the padded swivel chair and he reached for them, using them to haul himself to his feet.

Thank goodness the cabin wasn't large, so the bathroom wasn't too far away. Otherwise, he doubted his ability to make it.

The bedroom was right next to the bathroom. Naked, he hobbled the short distance, awkwardly using the crutches to try to take the pressure off his knee. His shoulder hurt like the devil, too, but he ignored it. When he stubbed his toe, he swore crudely.

"What in the world are you doing out of bed?"

Guy jumped and almost fell off his crutches.

Annie!

She stood there before him, looking like the woman he'd always known, and the woman he couldn't help dreaming about.

He quickly scanned the cabin, but he didn't see anyone else. All he noticed were dozens of opened books and magazines, scattered around everywhere.

Good God, she'd been studying!

Undeniably alarmed, Guy stared at her. Her dark hair fell loose to her waist. She had brushed it into soft waves and it reflected the crimson and gold glow from the crackling fireplace. She wore some type of lust-inducing skintight leggings that fit her like a second skin, and his own flannel shirt, unbuttoned far too low.

She looked tempting as hell to his foggy brain and abused body.

Guy shuddered as he tried to figure out what to do. He was naked, after all, and there was no place to hide. Hobbled as he was by the crutches and the knee wrap, trying to run would be ludicrous. Not that he intended to do so anyway. The only thing worse than being caught in the raw with Annie as a spectator, would be to put on a bigger show by fleeing.

With no other options left, he crisscrossed the crutches in front of his lap—hardly adequate coverage, but it was the best he could do under the circumstances—while balancing on one leg. "What the hell are you doing here?" he barked.

Annie wasn't the least bit hurt by his tone. She frowned and shook what appeared to be a cooking spoon at him. Dear God, please don't let her be cooking. He could likely survive anything but that.

She advanced despite his frantic warnings for her to stay away. "You should be in bed."

He answered that by asking, "Where's Daniel?"

"At home, I suppose." She shrugged one narrow shoulder,

causing his shirt to shift lower on one side. He could see the swell of her right breast. "He was heading that way right after he saw us off."

Guy squeezed his eyes shut and concentrated on not shouting. No. It couldn't be. Daniel wouldn't leave him here alone with Annie.

"Uh, Guy, do you realize you're naked?"

Guy stared at her like she'd suddenly gone blond. "Of course I realize it! It'd be a little hard to miss, especially with the way you're staring!"

Annie didn't answer, and she didn't avert her gaze. He felt her appreciation like a hot stroke smoothing his chilled skin. "Look at my face, dammit!"

She did, but she took her time about doing so. "Well how was I to know?"

"How were you to know what?"

"That you realized you were naked? You didn't realize it earlier. Or at least if you did realize it, you sure didn't care. Not that I'm complaining, you understand."

Guy shook his head, trying to make sense of what she said. He was naked, he was unsteady on his feet, and though he hated to admit it, he was mortified. Plenty of women had seen him naked. Plenty of women weren't Annie.

"What do you mean—"

She lifted her dark brows high and smiled at him. "I mean you stripped naked right there before me, grinning the whole time. You pretty much flaunted yourself, and I found it very…educational."

Horrified, he shook his head and said, "I didn't."

Annie nodded. "You did."

She looked pleased with that fact, and waved her spoon at his abdomen and the crossed crutches, which only managed to hide the really essential stuff. "All this belated modesty…well, you might as well not bother. I've seen everything you own. In fact, I studied it real close, too."

Worse and worse. "You didn't."

She nodded again, vigorously. "I did. And I don't mind telling you, it's all rather strange."

Guy choked and she took another step closer. "Oh, I didn't mean *you* looked strange! No. Of course not. In fact just the opposite! You're so...well..."

She'd gotten breathless, and her gaze ventured south once again.

"Annie."

"Okay, never mind that." A slight blush colored her cheeks, but Guy had no idea if it was embarrassment or excitement. "I was talking about how it'd work. For sex. You didn't really seem...*capable*—"

Masculine outrage washed over him. "I was asleep! And drugged!" He was beginning to sound hysterical. Not good. He definitely needed to remain in control.

Guy cleared his throat. He couldn't deny that he felt affronted at her criticism of his male parts. But he shouldn't. It didn't matter...

"Dammit, Annie, this is ridiculous. Now please turn your head. Or better yet. Leave the room completely."

"Why?"

"Because," Guy said, gritting his teeth, "I have to use the bathroom and the situation is getting critical."

"Oh!" Annie took another step toward him. At this close range, the crutches did him no good at all. "I can help."

"Not in this lifetime!"

With the spoon clutched in one fist, she propped her hands on her hips and scowled. "Daniel said I was to help you."

Pain, embarrassment and annoyance caused his eyes to narrow. "Daniel won't be able to say anything else when I get through with him."

"Now don't be like that. You're the one who asked to come here."

"I did not!"

"Sure you did." She sounded positive on that point. "You said you needed time to think and to recuperate, and so you wanted me to bring you here. Daniel agreed and told me all about the cabin." She gave him a severe look. "I can't believe you all kept this from me."

He had no idea how to defend their deception on the cabin. In truth, having Annie here was a specific fantasy for him, one he'd never thought to find in reality.

He gave up trying to think of excuses and explanations when Annie reached for his crutches. She was so determined to help, she left him the option of either falling on his face—which he had no intention of doing, especially not bare-assed—or letting her have her way.

She had her way.

Annie repositioned the crutches under his arms and then rushed into the bathroom ahead of him. "I took up the throw rug from the floor so you wouldn't slip. Do you want me to stay and help?"

She sounded far too hopeful. *"Hell no."*

"Spoilsport." She started backing out, her gaze cataloguing every small part of his physique. He couldn't recall ever feeling quite so vulnerable. He didn't like it.

"Let me know when you're done," she said, once again sounding breathless, "so I can help you back to bed."

Using his crutch, Guy shoved the door closed behind her. He squeezed his eyes shut and tried to convince himself this was only a dream. A bad dream. A damn nightmare.

But when he opened his eyes again, the tile floor still felt cold beneath his feet and his knee still throbbed in discomfort.

How the hell did he end up in this situation? He'd just have to put an end to it immediately. As soon as he cleaned up a bit, he'd have Annie take him home where he could suffer in silence. And he would suffer, but not because of his injuries. His home was Annie's home.

The house she'd grown up in, the house that had sheltered

all three Sawyers siblings and one hanger-on, would have been sold long ago if Guy hadn't taken it, preserving it, waiting for Annie to want it for herself. So far she'd refused the house with all its less-than-perfect memories. To Guy, the memories were wonderful.

Daniel, now that he was married, was starting to come around. He even talked about his mother more, and he and his dad were beginning a new relationship.

Annie would come around, too, eventually. He'd always figured that some day she would marry and want the house. He'd accepted that as a fact. But he'd never thought about her getting sexual with a man. Now she wanted to experiment and it was eating him up inside.

He couldn't stay here alone with her.

After he splashed his face and brushed his teeth, he was done for. He hurt in places he hadn't even known about. Just getting back to bed would be a triumph, much less facing the cold and the long drive home. But he'd find the energy somewhere.

Guy limped to the door and opened it a crack. He peeked out, and caught Annie peeking in.

They both jumped.

"Are you okay?" Annie asked, at the same time Guy demanded, "What are you doing?"

Annie sighed. "You're awfully surly. Do you need another pain pill?"

His entire body throbbed, his shoulder almost more so than his knee, with his ribs running a close third. He did his best to ignore it all. "No, I don't want any more pills."

"Afraid you'll do something even more outrageous than stripping down to your sexy hide?"

Guy ground his teeth together. The last thing he wanted was for Annie to think his hide was sexy. *Liar.* "No."

"No what?"

It was his turn to sigh. Through the closed door, he yelled, "No, I'm not afraid I'll do something else outrageous." What could be more outrageous than flaunting himself to her? *Don't even think it.* "And no I don't want any damn pain pills. What I do want is something to wear."

Guy waited, but when Annie didn't answer, he peeked out the door again. She was still there. And she was still peeking. "Well?" he asked.

"I'm thinking about it."

He grumbled, and she quickly said, "If you get dressed, it might make you more uncomfortable. I mean, you're only going to be in bed under the quilts anyway. At least, I hope this time you get under the quilts. Last time you flopped—" She hesitated, then said, "Well, flopped isn't a very pretty word is it?"

Heat rushed up his neck. "Annie," he growled with very real menace.

"What I meant was," she rushed to explain, "you *sprawled* on top of the quilts and I had to work for almost twenty minutes to get one free from under you." And in an undertone she added, "You weigh a ton."

"I weigh two twenty-five and you should have left the room, not played around with the quilts!"

"It wasn't the quilts I wanted to play with."

"Annie!"

"As to that, I couldn't quite make myself leave the room, either. Everything of interest was in there." In a softer voice, she added, "I love the differences in your skin texture. Did you know the skin on your hips is smooth and you're so hard and—"

Guy tried for a measure of patience. "Go—get me—something—to put on. *Right now.*"

"You are so stubborn!"

He could hear her moving away and gave a sigh of relief. The paneled wall felt icy against his bare back as he leaned against it, keeping his injured leg straight out. He'd noticed in the mirror that he had so many bruises, he looked like a beat-up tomcat. At the moment, he felt more like something the cat had dragged in.

"Here you go."

Annie started to come in, but Guy held the door firm, only letting it open enough to get his hand out. "I can manage."

"I wouldn't mind helping."

He'd never survive her help; the conversation alone was about to kill him. "I've been dressing myself since I was two. I think I can get along without your assistance."

"But now you're injured."

"This conversation is hurting me a lot more than any damn injury! Go...cook something."

Dear God, he couldn't believe he said that. It was a true indication of his discomfort that he'd make such a horrid suggestion.

For good measure, he not only closed the door firmly, he locked it. Annie was in a very strange mood, and though his head was now finally clearer, he still felt very confused about some of the things she'd said.

In no way did he recall asking her to bring him to the cabin. Hell, he didn't even remember the drive or climbing into bed. And he sure as certain had no memory of strutting his nakedness—or *flopping*—in front of her. Just the thought nearly sent him into spasms.

But she had looked.

The image formed in his mind: Annie looming over his bared body, studying him in minute detail. Her long hair had probably touched him in ways he'd only dreamed about.

She'd said his hide was sexy.

Guy shook off that damning fact. Annie was in a curious frame of mind these days, and so he assumed a certain amount of that curiosity extended to him. He supposed it was natural, even if it did make things a little sticky for him. She was now interested in the more sexual side of men, and he was a man she trusted.

He'd treat this incident just as he had the one at the pond, when she'd been so young. He'd ignore her embarrassment— even though she hadn't really exhibited any.

Chapter Six

GETTING THE SCRUB bottoms on were harder than he'd figured. Thankfully they were soft and loose, and that helped,
but the bathroom wasn't exactly spacious. He sat on the edge
of the wide square Jacuzzi tub, which took up the majority of
the room, and sort of bent sideways at the waist until he could
hook the pants around his foot on his injured leg. After he'd
gotten them pulled halfway up, he stuck his other foot in. Hop-
ping around on one leg, which jarred his aching head and
made his ribs and shoulder hurt worse, he managed to get the
pants to his waist.

That was all she'd brought him. No shirt. Not that he should
care. Annie had seen him without a shirt before, but now that
she'd seen him without his pants, too… It just seemed different. More intimate.

He opened the door and Annie, who'd been leaning on it,
nearly fell inside. Guy managed to hold on to his crutch with
one hand and catch her with the other. Given the fact that she
was so slight, it wasn't difficult.

She smiled up him and her hot little hands flattened on his
pecs. He noticed right off that her nipples were hard.

Now his were, too.

Forcing his gaze to her face, he gave her a stern look then
stepped around her. "Where are the rest of my clothes?"

Annie hustled along behind him as if waiting to catch him in case he fell. Ha! He'd flatten her if he did. He was way taller and over a hundred pounds heavier.

"Why do you want more clothes?" she asked.

"Because we're leaving."

"Leave! But we can't."

"We most certainly can."

"No."

"Yes." Why the hell was she being so difficult? She probably had no idea what torture it was to be this close to her, but determined not to touch her.

"I've hid the keys to my car."

Little witch. He wouldn't look at her. "I have no idea why you're doing this...."

"I'm trying to force you to think about a few things."

"I can think better at home."

"You're not going home."

He'd almost reached the bedroom. "You don't want to drive me, fine. I'll call a cab."

"We don't have a phone."

He glared at her over his shoulder. "Try again, Annie. There's no way Daniel sent you up here without a phone. I know him too well for that."

She looked deflated. "If you go home, Melissa will just convince you to marry her."

He took another awkward step toward the bedroom. "Is that what this is all about?"

"No." A moment of silence, and then, "You promised to tutor me."

Guy halted in mid hobbling step. Very slowly, he pivoted on his one good leg to face her. "I did what?"

Annie crossed her arms under her breasts. It was blatantly obvious she wasn't wearing a bra, which led his beleaguered brain to wonder if she'd foregone her panties, too.

He concentrated hard on keeping his gaze on her face, trying to sound unaffected. Failing, he asked, "Have you forgotten your underwear again?"

She shrugged. "Lace packed for me, but she didn't include any underthings. In fact, she didn't really pack me too much in the way of clothes at all."

His breath caught in his lungs. "Lace needs a good swat on her backside."

Annie's eyes widened, darkened. She stared at him intently. "I read about that. Some men like it." Her gaze studied him, searching. "Some women, too."

Damn, he was putting ideas in her head. *He was putting ideas in his own head.*

"Do you?"

Guy sucked in a long breath. "We're not going to discuss this."

"You do!" She looked equal parts scandalized and excited. "It's okay," she rushed to assure him. "I thought it sounded…interesting." Then she frowned. "I prefer that you don't think about Lace's bottom, though."

Guy flexed his fingers on the rail of the crutch. "I don't—"

"You promised," she smoothly interrupted, "to tutor me. You said you wanted to come here so you'd have time to think and heal and because you didn't want me seducing someone else. When I argued with you, you promised me that you'd teach me everything I needed to know."

Guy stared. His body was as still as he could make it, but he felt himself thickening, extending. In the loose cotton pants, there'd be no way to hide his erection.

Tutor Annie? The thought was almost too erotic to bear. Had he really made such a promise?

His brain actively tried to recall even a smidgen of what she claimed. Finally he shook his head in denial, even while his heart pounded with need.

Annie grinned. "You said I could ask you anything and you'd answer it honestly."

His lungs deflated. She meant tutor her, as in verbal explanations.

Disappointment warred with relief.

"I can do that," he said, quick to reassure her that words were fine, while trying to make sure he didn't accidentally promise anything more. "We can talk about anything, you know that."

"You also told me you'd explain things. Everything." Her lashes lowered, her cheeks warmed. "And that if I was so curious you'd even be willing to demonstrate—"

Annie stopped in the middle of her sentence. "Guy? Are you all right?"

His knees were back to feeling like butter, even the hurt one which only moments before had been vying with other male parts to be the stiffest. His leg had been losing.

"C'mon," Annie said, grabbing his arm and practically dragging him to the bed. "You look feverish. I think you need to lie down. Daniel said you should stay off your leg as much as possible for a few days."

Guy gratefully dropped to the side of the mattress, glad for the excuse to collapse.

Annie placed her wooden spoon on the nightstand, then put her small hands on his bare shoulders and gently pushed him flat. Her soft breasts moved beneath the flannel, teasing him, cramping his muscles. The black pearl rested in her cleavage, and he knew it would be warm to the touch, just as Annie was warm to the touch.

It was bad enough that she was so near, so determined. But then she crawled right into the king-size bed with him to fluff the pillow behind his head and put another pillow beneath his leg.

She didn't cover him.

Guy snatched the quilt over his lap, and it too tented over his erection. He doubted a layer of lead could hide his present state of arousal.

Annie didn't appear to have noticed. Yet. "Are you comfortable now?"

He was in bed with her, never mind that he was all but incapacitated—his imagination was working just fine. Of course he wasn't comfortable.

He firmed his resolve and grumbled, "I have a damn headache." He hoped she'd take the hint and leave him alone in his misery.

Her small cool palm cupped his jaw. "Would you like a pain pill?"

"No!" If he did anything at all to blunt the edge of his control, he'd end up with Annie naked in the bed with him. He groaned at the image.

She gave him a coy look. "You don't trust my motives, do you?"

He didn't trust his own, especially when he was drugged.

Her smile told him she knew exactly what he was thinking. "You know what would help?"

She continued to stroke his face until he caught her wrist and pulled her hand down. "Some aspirin," he suggested, anxious to give her something to do besides taunting him. "They're in the medicine cabinet in the bathroom."

Annie shook her head. "I was reading some of the things Lace packed for me—"

"Not those damn sex manuals?"

"Well, yeah. Some of them." She looked at his mouth. "The best ones actually. I guess that's why she couldn't pack me more clothes. The books took up a lot of room."

"Lace has no business—"

"She's being more helpful than you!"

"I doubt she would be if you were coming on to her!"

Choked laughter filled the bedroom. Annie wiped her eyes as she tried to subdue her humor. "Bet that'd even take Lace off guard, huh?"

"Nothing takes Lace off guard."

"Do you really think I'm coming on to you?"

Guy refused to answer.

"Is it working?"

He pinched his mouth shut.

"You know, myths and jokes aside, an orgasm gets rid of headaches."

Guy strangled on an indrawn breath. While he wheezed and sputtered, Annie patted his chest and continued her discourse. "According to what I've read, an orgasm helps to dilate the blood vessels in your brain, which relieves a headache."

Was she offering him an alternative to the aspirin? He finally caught his breath enough to utter, "That's pure nonsense."

"It's documented data, in a book."

"You shouldn't be reading those books."

"We could try an experiment." As she said it, she looked at his lap, then blinked.

Guy groaned, knowing exactly what she'd seen. Though his reaction was all too common to being in bed with a beautiful woman, Annie wasn't just any woman. She was his best friend. She was Daniel's little sister.

His body didn't seem to care. And there was nothing he could do about it now except brazen it out.

"You have an erection."

She said that with the same enthusiasm as if he'd just solved world peace. She looked overjoyed. "Is that for me?"

It took all his control not to cover himself with his hands. He'd never before been embarrassed about his body's reactions in front of a woman. But then, he'd never had to fight this hard to resist a woman.

"Annie, this conversation has gotten way out of hand. In case it's escaped your notice, I'm kind of banged up."

"That's why I'm trying to help! Did you know sexual fantasies can increase your tolerance to pain?" At his skeptical look, she said, "It's true! In a study, people who indulged sexual fantasies were able to tolerate discomfort three times longer."

"Good grief."

She touched his leg, low on his thigh. "You're not wincing anymore."

Bemused, Guy realized she was right. Not only had his leg stopped throbbing, he'd forgotten he even had legs. All his awareness was centered on what was between them.

Now, with her hand petting his thigh through the quilts, he was only too aware of his body parts. All of them. Sexual fantasies suddenly dominated his mind.

"And another thing. An orgasm can—"

"I know, I know." Even hearing her say it made his skin heat. It was the strangest, most arousing conversational topic he'd ever indulged in. "It supposedly gets rid of a headache." Guy wondered why no one had ever told him that before. He wondered if Daniel and Max knew. Max probably did. Max knew everything about women inside and out. He was such a Romeo.

And Max would probably kill Guy if he knew he was in bed with his sister thinking things he shouldn't think.

"Yes," Annie agreed, "but it can also relieve muscle strain and help you sleep, and—"

"Cure the common cold?" Maybe he could joke his way out of this. Maybe Annie wouldn't notice how rough his voice had gotten, or how his hands shook.

"Actually," she said, her own voice a little raspy, "it does help to relieve the symptoms of a cold. It can clear up your sinuses and temporarily get rid of your stuffy head."

Guy covered his face with an arm, wishing for oblivion. Annie began to massage his leg.

"Stop that!"

"I want to make you feel better." She stretched out next to him on the bed, keeping her head propped on one hand. In a sexy whisper, she said, "Let me help you, Guy."

His leg didn't ache, but everything else on him did. "Annie, this is insane." She was so close he could smell her and it made him want her even closer. It made him want to nuzzle between her breasts, between her legs.

Of its own volition, his arm circled her, his hand opening on her waist.

"Because we're friends?"

"Of course." His words were low and rough and he struggled to regulate his breathing. "And besides that, I'm in no shape to...to..."

"Have an orgasm?"

His stomach clenched. "I was going to say have sex."

She licked her lips and it was all Guy could do not to lick them, too. Annie had one of the sexiest mouths going. Full, pink.

"In one of the books," she whispered, "there's this whole chapter on handwork. I could—"

Guy covered her delectable mouth. If he didn't shut her up, he was likely to explode. "Don't even say it, dammit."

She tried to nod and speak at the same time, but her words were muffled under his hand.

"Annie, you want your first time to be special, don't you?"

Her blue eyes looked very soft, almost caressing his face as she nodded.

He gulped, refusing to interpret that look. "Then you need to wait."

Her eyes darkened and her brows drew down, indicating she had something to say. Cautiously, Guy uncovered her mouth.

"You're a hypocrite."

Guy sighed. "I'm just trying to protect you."

"Ha. How many women have you been here with?" As she spoke, she sat up and Guy could see that his rejection had hurt her feelings.

"Annie." He tried to catch her hand, but she bounded off the bed.

"You come here for your lascivious little rendezvous with other women, then tell me I need to wait."

"I come here for privacy, that's all." He scowled at her—

until the left side of the over-large flannel dropped down her shoulder and she didn't bother to pull it back up. She was too busy pacing, but Guy was on pins and needles thinking it might dip further any second and then he'd see her breast.

And her nipple.

He held his breath and tried not to stare.

"I guess that's what I'll do, too."

Guy reared up in the bed. He'd totally lost track of the topic, what with her teasing him with the possibility of a peek show. "What the hell does that mean?"

"It means since this is a family cabin, I can have my own sordid little affairs here. I'm sure Perry won't be as unwilling as you are."

Before he could respond to that she marched out of the room.

"Annie!" Guy was just about to climb out of the bed and go after her when she returned with a glass of water and the aspirin bottle.

"Here's your miserable pills." They hit his chest with a plip, plip. The water sloshed over the side when she shoved the glass into his hand. "I doubt they're half as much fun as what I suggested. Of course I can't say for sure since you refuse to cooperate."

Guy sputtered at her audacity. "You make it sound like I turned you down for a loan! Sex is more intimate than that. It's not something you can jump into lightly."

She leaned down until she was nearly nose to nose with him. The neckline of the flannel gaped, testing his honor not to peek. The necklace swung free, glinting in the lamplight.

In a growl that spoke of frustration and anger, she said, "I don't intend to jump lightly. When I jump, it's going to be whole hog, hot and sweaty and with no holds barred."

Guy scowled at her as he tried to ignore the throbbing in his groin. "You don't know what you're saying."

"Shocked you, huh?"

Actually she was turning him on. "Yes."

"Well aren't you the discerning one?"

His eyes narrowed. She was verbally doing him in and he didn't like it. "I try."

She stuck her nose in the air. "For the record, I didn't even ask you for sex. I offered to service you."

"Oh, for the love of…" He sounded horrified, but he couldn't help that. The image was now firmly rooted in his brain and his gonads more than liked the idea. Every nerve in his body, especially those in his more sensitized regions, screamed for him to say yes.

He shook his head no.

Annie snatched up her spoon, shook it at him, then turned on her heel to storm out again. Guy shouted, "Where are you going?"

She looked at him over her shoulder. "Now I have a headache, too, but I'll be damned if I'll settle for aspirin."

She closed the door behind her.

Guy sat there in the bed, utterly speechless. His body pulsed, his mind ached. He had a raging hard-on.

Surely she didn't mean to insinuate she was…that she'd… *Did she have that chapter on handwork with her?*

He held his breath and listened as hard as he could, but he didn't hear a sound. Of course, he had no idea how much noise she might make. All women were different and…

Every pain on his body had magically disappeared, overwhelmed by sensual awareness. It dawned on him that Annie was right, that his fantasies had obliterated the hurt from his injuries.

Even a semi couldn't compete with Annie bent on seduction.

Hell, she'd yelled him into arousal.

But now he had a new pain, the ache of acute sexual frustration. He'd take a throbbing knee any day.

ANNIE STIRRED THE contents of the pot as it came to a boil, then turned it on low and stuck a lid on top.

What was Guy thinking right now? She was caught between amusement at the last alarmed look on his face, and righteous indignation that he had turned down her offer flat. Lace had been wrong; Guy needed more than a little encouragement.

Annie had just settled onto the couch with another book, hoping to find a way past his defenses, when the bedroom door opened.

Guy stood there, his face flushed darkly, his chest straining with interesting muscles as he used the crutches to support himself. He filled the doorway.

Annie closed the book and came to her feet. "You should stay in bed!"

He looked her over slowly, as if checking for signs of sexual satisfaction. Annie flushed. Had he really thought she'd be out here cavorting all alone? The image that came to mind, what *he* must have been imagining, scalded her cheeks.

Tentatively, trying to cover her new embarrassment, she said, "You must be getting hungry. I'll have food ready soon."

Guy didn't answer her, and her nervousness increased. "Did the aspirins help?"

His eyes narrowed. He looked...hotly aroused. Annie checked the book in her hand to reaffirm her suspicions. *Straining muscles, flushed skin, dilated eyes.* Yep, Guy had all that. And as she looked at his chest she saw his small brown nipples were drawn tight, visible beneath his springy chest hair. Her breath caught.

"What have you been doing, Annie?"

The gravelly edge to his tone made her experience every single one of the symptoms she'd just catalogued on Guy. She cleared her throat. "Making soup?"

He looked toward the kitchen, as if he didn't quite believe her.

"It's just chicken noodle. You know I'm not a very good cook. But it should be ready soon. I know how often you usually eat, and so I thought..."

She knew she was rambling and drew to a halt. Oh, he looked hungry all right. "Would…would you like to rest here on the couch instead of in the bed? Maybe we could watch a movie."

His nostrils flared, and without a word he made his way to the couch. Annie shoved aside her pile of books.

The seating arrangement was actually as wide as a bed and formed an open square. "Careful now. Let me go get you a couple of pillows."

Guy groaned as he lowered himself, but the sound was quickly cut off. Annie knew he wanted to hide his discomfort from her.

She also knew she'd added to that discomfort.

Shame at being so self-centered in her goals bit into her determination.

But he had been hard, she reminded herself. So she knew he wasn't totally immune.

She rushed into the bedroom and grabbed the pillows off the bed. She also saw the aspirin still sitting on the nightstand and got caught with a grin.

Guy had his eyes closed when she approached him. Softly, she touched his shoulder. "Lean forward for me."

He did as she asked and Annie slipped the pillow behind him, then carefully lifted his leg to wedge another pillow under there. "Daniel said to keep your leg elevated. Here." She handed him the aspirin and the water, then admonished, "Take them this time."

He didn't argue. After he'd swallowed the pills, he asked, "Did you oversalt the soup?"

"Nope, not this time."

"Did you throw in any weird ingredients?" He kept his eyes closed, holding himself away from her.

"I didn't season it at all because I was afraid I'd ruin it."

Annie sat on a cushion beside him. It was very difficult, but she managed to keep her hands to herself. "In fact, I'm not sure I'd even call it soup, really. I just boiled some chicken until it was tender, then threw in noodles. I was going to make a salad to go with it."

"How much longer do you think?"

He was being cautiously polite, and that broke Annie's heart. Since he'd slept the better part of the day away, she knew he had to be hungry. Now for food as well as satisfaction.

"I can get you some now if you like." She stood, but before she could walk away, Guy caught her hand.

"Annie."

She squeezed his fingers. "It's okay. I shouldn't have pushed you like that." She pulled away, not wanting him to say more, unwilling to hear his explanations and excuses for turning her down.

From the kitchen, she asked, "Do you want milk or water or tea?"

"Milk. Thank you." He hesitated before saying, "It doesn't feel right to just sit here and be waited on."

"I want to do this, Guy. You'd do the same for me."

"Damn right I would. But that's different."

"Why?" Annie loaded up a plate.

"Because you're female. And small."

"And you care about me?"

A slight hesitation, then: "Yes."

She could feel him watching her, the heat of his gaze. "I care about you, too, even though you're big and male." *Especially because you're big and male.*

"And you trust me?"

I love you. "Yes."

"That's good. Because I want to talk to you."

Outside, the wind rustled branches against the roof and ice pellets drubbed the windows. It seemed a new storm was brewing, though inside they were warm and cozy. The fireplace burned hotly, and there was plenty of dry wood on the hearth and on the covered porch. She'd called Daniel while

Guy slept earlier. Everything was set. He could talk all he wanted, but she wouldn't take him home.

Guy appeared content enough sitting up on the seating group with his leg cushioned. Annie placed a tray in his lap with the chicken and noodles, a small salad, milk and the salt and pepper shakers. She got her own plate of food and sat across from him.

After Guy had salted and peppered his food, he tasted it, then gave a nod of approval. "Good."

Annie grinned. "Had you worried, didn't I? But there's no need. Daniel knows I'm not the best cook around so he made sure there was simple stuff to fix. We won't starve."

His brown eyes smiled at her. "I remember those chocolate cookies you baked for us." Gradually, Annie could see him relaxing. "You'd used unsweetened chocolate."

"I didn't know there was a difference."

"Max ate them with his beer. Said they were better than salted nuts."

They both chuckled, and for the next hour they joked and teased and generally carried on in their normal mode of camaraderie.

When Guy was done eating, after three refills, he patted his flat abdomen and sighed. "Delicious. I probably just put on a few pounds, but it was worth it."

Annie carried the dishes to the kitchen. She wished she'd thought of some kind of indulgent dessert, but she hadn't. Cautiously, she said, "You know a good way to lose weight?"

His groan turned into a laugh. "Don't tell me. Sex."

"You already knew that one?" She resettled herself in the seating area with him.

"Annie, honey, you've got sex on the brain."

It was more than her brain clamoring for attention right now.

"It's a fact!" she assured him. "Why, you can burn off a lot of calories in vigorous sexual activity. Not that I really know the difference between the vigorous and the lazy stuff, but I thought it was interesting."

Guy twisted to face her. His expression was still somewhat strained, but also accepting. "Sweetheart, sex is not a cure-all for everything that ails you."

Annie stretched to reach a specific book, and then flipped to a dog-eared page. "Sex," she said, reading out loud, "can lower your cholesterol and tip the good cholesterol/bad cholesterol ratio. It kicks your respiratory system into overdrive which makes you breathe deep and adds oxygen to your blood, which nourishes all your organs and tissues. And sex releases endorphins, which are effective painkillers."

Guy rolled his shoulders, as if easing tense muscles.

Annie flipped to another page. "Accelerated blood flow to the…uh—" she nodded at his lap "—that area, takes pressure off the brain which helps you relax and eases tension in your neck and back."

She frowned at him. "Guy, you *do* look tense."

He burst out laughing, which wasn't quite the reaction she'd been going for, but at least he wasn't pushing her away again. Deliberately, Annie shrugged one shoulder and let the flannel droop again. She'd noticed his preoccupation with the shirt earlier, how it had affected him each time the material had slipped down her shoulder.

This time was no different.

His laughter stopped abruptly.

"I'm surprised," she said, adding an edge to her tone on purpose, "that you don't already know this stuff. I mean, here you have this little love nest and you don't even know what you're doing."

His jaw firmed. "I know exactly what I'm doing."

"You couldn't prove it by me."

"Honey, I don't want to prove it to you."

"Okay, so you don't want me. Tell me what you do with other—" she nearly choked, but managed to finish "—women."

LORI FOSTER

Guy came up on one elbow to frown down on her. His brown eyes were intense, as hot as the flames in the fireplace. "I have sex. Is that what you want to know?"

Her heart thundered in jealousy, but she tamped it down. "I want details. Do you strip for them like you stripped for me? Do you let them examine you?"

The look on his face was comical. "I feel violated."

Annie snorted. "I'm not buying that for a minute. I'll tell you it surprises me, though. Being that this is a little love nest, I figured I'd find some neat stuff. You know, like mirrors on the ceiling, or sex toys hidden away. I guess the Jacuzzi tub counts, but I'm not quite sure how it'd work."

Guy groaned.

"You could at least take this seriously," she said, watching him closely to catch his reaction, "so when I approach Perry I won't embarrass myself with my ignorance."

His short hair stood on end. "You really want to get involved with Perry?" His voice rose to a near shout.

"Not involved. I mean, I don't want a relationship with him." She shuddered even as she assured him of that fact. Perry didn't turn her on. No man turned her on, except Guy. "But so far he's the only one willing. You're certainly not."

Guy dropped flat to the couch and covered his face with his arm. He muttered, but Annie couldn't hear what he said, except for the key words of "torture" and "intolerable" and "witch."

"As I just pointed out, Guy, sex is necessary for my general health and well-being." She saw his chest rising and falling with labored breaths. "You do want me to stay healthy, don't you?"

Guy didn't respond to that, except to give another groan. Annie said, "I guess you don't need all the props, huh? That, or else you don't know what to do with them. Is that it? No experience with the kinky stuff?"

"I'm not discussing my personal...experiences with you, Annie."

She shrugged, and the flannel slipped just a little bit more. She waited and when he finally looked at her, she shrugged again for good measure.

Guy's hands curled into fists, held at his sides on the couch. "I don't want you going to Perry."

Her heart pounded, making her breathless, making her body tremble. "You don't want me, period."

He looked away and Annie could practically hear his turbulent thoughts.

Finally, very softly as if the words were forced out, he said, "Yes I do."

Annie's mouth opened, then snapped closed. Cautiously, hope building to the boiling point, she asked, "You do?"

Guy scooted up on the couch until he was sitting upright with his leg stretched out before him. He took up a lot of room, and looked sexy doing so.

His eyes glittered at her, unwavering. "My erection is for you."

"It is?" She felt like a damn parrot, but he'd done such a quick turnaround, she wasn't sure what to think.

She hadn't known brown eyes could look so burning. Guy reached for her, caught her arm, and pulled her up to his chest. "It is. And now I'm going to start your instruction."

Chapter Seven

GUY HELD HER close, feeling her nervousness and glad of it. "You're too brazen, sweetheart. You need to learn some subtlety."

"Do I scare you?"

What she was really asking, was would she scare that other man, the man she wanted to seduce. It enraged him. "No. But you can push a guy right over the edge, when what you want is a man who's in control."

Her dark lashes swept down to hide her eyes. He wasn't fooled for a second.

"Look at me, Annie."

She did, and her expression was so hungry, so anxious, he almost lost it.

"What are you going to do?" she asked. She looked at his mouth, his throat, then met his gaze.

Control, Guy reminded himself. He had to stay in control. "Anything you want me to."

Her indrawn breath was sexy and sweet at the same time. "I want you to...have sex with me."

She had started to say make love, he was sure of it. But she didn't want him to love her. She just wanted sex. She wanted to experiment.

Guy understood that, but everything in him rebelled

against it. Annie was a healthy, attractive, energetic woman, and it was only natural that she wanted to experience more of the sensual side of things. The wonder of it was that she'd stayed innocent so long. Of course, she'd been so protected by her brothers when she was younger, any male would have had a hard time inching close. And then she'd stayed busy getting her bookstore opened up and off to a good start. For the most part, she had never seemed all that interested in sex.

Now he knew better.

Because he understood, and because he cared about her, he'd show her a few things, and still hold on to what honor he could. Anything would be preferable to her going to Perry; the mere thought made him nuts.

"Lie down here beside me."

Annie bit her lip. "Should…should I take my clothes off first?"

Muzzling her became a real possibility. It might be necessary to save his sanity.

"No. Quit pushing. From here on out, let me tell you what you need to do, okay?"

Her lips parted. "Is this a fetish of yours?" Obviously that idea appealed to her. "I mean, you being dominant and everything? Because I've read a whole chapter on fetishes and…"

His hand covered her mouth. "I'm not…dammit, Annie, will you just do as I tell you?" His control was nearly nonexistent.

She laid down. Stiffly. Staring up at the ceiling. The audacious woman demanding satisfaction was now hidden behind a mask of uncertainty.

Guy rested his hand on her belly. He felt the heat of her and his own body burned. She was so soft, so slight.

She was holding her breath.

"Annie, are you nervous?" Gently, he caressed her and watched her face color with desire. That, or she was suffocating.

She gasped for air. "I'm…worried."

Guy leaned down and kissed her temple, a featherlight touch, teasing, brushing. In her ear, he whispered, "About what?" In the back of his mind he thought perhaps now that he'd called her bluff, she'd back off.

In his heart, he prayed she wouldn't.

"Orgasm face."

His hand, his heartbeat, stilled. "What?"

"I'm worried about orgasm face. I read this article that said some people look really dumb when they climax. They make funny sounds and jerk and jump and roll their eyes and I'm afraid I'm going to look really bad because I've had very little practice."

Every pulse beat of his heart made him more rigid. He couldn't quite seem to form a coherent sentence.

Annie, still stiff beside him, turned her head to see his face. "You could go first." She sounded inordinately enthusiastic about that idea. In her new eagerness, she forgot she was nervous and reared up over him, bracing one hand on his bare, bruised shoulder, the other tucked close to his side. He could feel her breath on his nose. "If you went first, I could see how you look and then I wouldn't be so worried how I'd look."

"No."

Her eyes crossed, trying to see him so closely. She frowned. "Why not?"

Guy didn't tell her he had no intention of taking his own release.

He felt pressured into assuring her first experience was a good one—a good one not with Perry—and that was his plan. But he wouldn't actually make love to her. He wouldn't share intercourse because that would cross too many boundaries.

And once he crossed them, he wasn't sure he'd ever be able to find his way back.

When he didn't answer her right away, her face softened into lines of understanding. "You're a grunter, aren't you? Do you scrunch all up, too? I won't mind, I promise. If we both look dumb, then I guess we could just close our eyes, right?"

Ignoring her ridiculous words, especially since he had no idea what the hell he looked like when he came, Guy caught the back of her head and pulled her down until he could kiss her throat. Another series of light, tempting kisses.

Annie groaned. "I like that."

He kissed her collarbone.

"And that."

He opened his mouth against her skin.

"And that!"

He sighed. "Annie, I don't need a blow-by-blow report."

Her chest heaved and her fingers dug into his shoulder. The pain was nothing compared to the pressure building in his groin.

Panting, she said, "I read in one book that you should tell your partner what pleases you."

"I know what pleases you."

"You do?" She pushed back to see his face again. "How?"

Guy turned the smallest bit and kissed her wrist. Her fingernails had left small indentations in his bruised skin. "By this. By the way you react."

"Ohmigod! Am I hurting you?" She looked appalled by her own actions and would have pulled away if he hadn't caught her to him. Her squirming not only hurt his aching body, but it further incited his lust.

Muscles clenched, Guy asked, "Do you feel how close you are to me? You're pushed up against my hip. I can feel your heat there. And where our chests touch, I can feel your heartbeat pounding." He smoothed his hand over her back. "Why don't you just forget the damn books, okay?"

She tucked her face into his throat. "I don't want to hurt you."

He smiled—until she reared up and said sincerely, "I'll be gentle with you, I promise."

The laugh took him by surprise, and annoyed Annie.

"I don't want you to laugh at me, either."

"I'm sorry." He smoothed her thick, silky hair. "But I think you're adorable."

She peered down at him, considering his words, before nudging her face into his throat again. "What if I have a silly orgasm face?"

As she spoke, her lips brushed his skin, burning him, driving him nuts. "All women look different—"

Her arms stiffened, lifting her away. "How many female orgasm faces have you seen?"

Ferociously, she stared down at him. Guy bit back his grin. He hadn't expected this, hadn't expected to laugh with her, to have fun with her now. He'd been all set to be a martyr, but Annie wasn't letting him.

"Every orgasm face I've seen has been female. I sure as hell haven't been watching any men."

"That's not what I mean and you know it." Then she blinked. "Have you…you know. Ever seen yourself?"

Despite her resistance, Guy pulled her down to rest against his chest. "Rule number one. You never discuss other partners when in bed."

She tried to stiffen her arms again. "But—"

"Rule number two." He crushed her close so she couldn't wiggle. "You don't ask the guy you're with embarrassing questions."

"Why should you be embarrassed? I bet you look great when you're straining and groaning—"

"*Rule number three,*" he said, deliberately drowning out her words. "Never argue with a man who's trying to give you pleasure."

She slumped against him. One second she was docile, limp, the next she clung to him so tightly his shoulder and ribs screamed in protest. "I don't mean to argue with you. I'm sorry."

"Shh." He could feel the tremors in her body and knew she was excited. Just because he had to suffer unrequited lust, didn't mean she should. Hopefully, what he intended would be enough. She couldn't go to Perry. She deserved so much more than that slobbering fool could offer her.

Since he couldn't think of a single alternate to Perry, he had to sacrifice himself. *Sacrifice! Ha!*

"I'm going to kiss you, Annie." At least that would give her mouth something to do beside bombard him with outrageous comments.

"Hallelujah."

"Don't be a smartass," he warned. "Now just relax, okay?"

"I have been kissed before, you know."

A growl rumbled in his chest. "I don't want to know."

"Why?"

Guy covered her mouth with his own. It was a simple kiss, easy, as teasing as the kisses he'd put on her throat. Annie pressed closer; her lips parted. Lightly, he slipped his tongue in, then back out again.

She gasped. Their lips were still touching when she said, "Can you do that again?"

He did. And again and again.

She tried to follow him, tried to deepen the kiss, but that would have interfered with his plans.

Her small fist connecting with the center of his chest took him by surprise.

"Stop teasing me!"

Guy smothered a laugh while he rubbed away the new ache. "And you accused me of trying to be dominant."

Before the words had finished leaving his mouth, Annie had clamped her hands on either side of his head and held him immobile for a killer kiss. What she lacked in finesse she made up for with verve.

He wanted her. More than he'd ever wanted any woman. He struggled to distance himself from the effect of her warm damp mouth on his, her slim body along his side, her hands, gentle and warm and so damn small and female. He knew he'd lose his head entirely if he didn't break the kiss.

He did that by the expedient manner of grasping her behind.

Annie lurched up with a moan. Her eyes, heavy and soft, stared at his face in wonder. "Do I look like you?" she asked on a husky whisper.

Her thick lashes were at half mast, her blue eyes vivid with heat, her rounded cheeks flushed to a rosy glow. She was beautiful. "Hell no."

She touched his jaw. "Your face is flushed," she murmured low, "and your eyes look...hungry."

His abdomen pulled tight; his erection throbbed. "Then yes, in that way you look like me."

"Is it always like this?"

He cuddled her behind a little closer, wanting to distract her, wishing she wouldn't keep analyzing things. "No. Usually the woman is too involved to be so chatty."

"Oh."

"Kiss me again. I like it."

"I thought you weren't supposed to tell me what you liked—"

Guy took control. He kissed her, stroking his tongue deep, slanting his mouth over hers, amazed by the perfect fit.

"Give me your tongue, too, sweetheart."

She did, shyly at first, then hungrily. Her hands coasted over his chest and stopped at his nipples.

"Annie." She gasped as he took her wrists and tried to move her hands away. "Don't do that."

"Why?"

He shifted to the side to face her more fully. His knee smarted and he winced until he'd gotten it properly situated. He kissed her palm and said, "There are better places to touch me." Like on his back, where it didn't matter as much.

"I read that men are as sensitive there as women."

"Let's find out." He covered her breast through the flannel. Soft and delicate. He wanted her naked, but wasn't sure he could take the sight of her nudity.

Her heartbeat slammed against his palm. Her eyes closed, her back arched.

"Such a reaction," he whispered, using his thumb to taunt her nipple into a stiff peak.

"I—"

"I know. You like this."

With her eyes squeezed shut, she bobbed her head.

He didn't mean to, but he heard himself ask, "Have you ever lain like this with another man?"

"No."

He watched her face, gauging her reaction to his touch. "Has any other man touched you here?"

"*No.*"

His blood rushed through his veins. "Then no other man has done this either." He caught her nipple between his finger and thumb and tugged gently.

Her moan was loud and very satisfying.

Guy kissed her chin, the bridge of her nose, her closed eyelids while he continued to tug and tease and roll. Her breaths turned loud and harsh.

"Guy!"

"What about this?" Easily lifting her slight weight, he levered her upward until he could reach her breast. He took her flannel covered nipple into his mouth.

His teeth nipped, causing her to jump. His lips plucked, and she moaned in response. He suckled, and her entire body stiffened, bowed. The shirt, once his but now scented by her body, grew quickly damp.

Annie's hands tunneled through his hair and held him tight. Her leg came over his, bumping his knee but barely noticeable other than the fact her body was perfectly aligned with his, the notch of her thighs pressed tight to his groin. He covered her bottom and drew her closer still. His hands were large enough to completely cover her rounded tush.

Suddenly she pushed him away and before he could ask, she started fumbling with the buttons on the flannel.

"Annie, wait." He caught her hands and tried to still them. If she stripped, he'd lose his fragile grasp on control. "Let's go slowly here, honey."

"No." Buttons went flying when she gave the shirt a frustrated jerk. Eyes wide, she looked at him, chagrined.

"Well." Guy cocked a brow and tried to ignore the sight of her partially bared breasts, her cleavage, the edge of one firm nipple. He cleared his throat. "That's the first time a woman's ever ripped her own clothes off for me."

Annie's chin lifted. "You're hurt. I was trying to give you a hand." Then she looked uncertain. "Would you rather I rip your pants off?"

Tenderness overwhelmed him. He'd known this woman since she was a shy little girl. He'd watched her grow up in the shadow of her older brothers, one a serious, somber over-achiever, and one so charismatic, everyone loved him, male and female alike.

Her father had ignored her, her brothers only wanted to protect her. And Guy...he just wanted to love her.

He did love her.

Curving his hand around her thigh, he urged her to lift her leg completely over his waist.

"Guy?"

"I want to get a good look at you, Annie. You're so damn beautiful." He nudged and shifted until he had her sitting on his abdomen.

Her face was pink, her gaze wary. "I'm not beautiful," she said, trying to scoff. But at his scorching look, she asked, "You think I'm beautiful?"

Slowly, Guy parted the shirt until it slipped down her arms. He had a hard time swallowing past the lump of affection and lust and love choking him.

"I think," he rasped, cuddling each small breast in his large hands, "that you're sexy and sweet and undeniably beautiful."

"Oh Guy."

"Lean down here."

Her thighs tightened on his hips. "Lean…?"

"Down here." He glanced up and caught her breathless anticipation. "I want to kiss you some more."

Her chest rose and fell. "My mouth?"

"Your nipples."

"Ohmigod."

Guy paused. She was aroused, but also wary. And he knew without a doubt that she was a virgin. The last thing he should do was to rush her. "You're shaking."

"It's…well, we're…" She frowned at him, gloriously naked from the waist up, her hair steaming down to her behind. "Shouldn't we be in the bed?"

Guy wondered if she was changing her mind, if she was stalling. "Why does it matter?"

"Because I want you naked, too, and it'd be easier to work these bottoms off you in the bed. There's really not enough room here."

Now he was shaking. "Here is fine."

Annie gave him a speculative look for a good five seconds, then slipped off his body before he could stop her. A nice bounce in her breasts distracted him as she stood beside him by the couch.

"I want my first time to be in a bed." She made it a demanding statement.

"Honey, it doesn't matter." Except in his mind. Getting in bed with her would definitely be a mistake. He just knew it.

"I want us both naked and ready, not just me."

He leaned up to look at his lap. His erection tented the scrub bottoms. "Uh, Annie, I'm as ready as I'm going to get." Beyond ready. Desperate actually. Not that he needed to be ready for what he planned.

"But it's getting late," she pointed out. "I didn't sleep much last night."

The way her mind worked never failed to amaze him. "Why not?"

"Because I watched you sleep." She seemed unaware or unconcerned with his scrutiny of her breasts. "Those damn nurses kept creeping in and trying to look you over. They're shameless."

Guy ignored her comments on the nurses. There was a husky catch to his voice when he asked, "You stayed all night at the hospital with me?"

"Of course."

She was so matter-of-fact, as if any other choice would have been incomprehensible. His heart softened even more.

"And since I know we're both tired," she added, "and already well fed, I figured we'd do...*this*, now that you're being more reasonable. Then we'd turn in."

He desperately tried to put her off. "You make *this* sound like baking bread."

"Oh, no." She looked down the length of his body. "I expect this to be loads of fun and very exciting."

"Not that you want to put any pressure on me, huh?"

Annie scowled at his dry tone. "I'm willing to make allowances for your injury." She glanced at his leg. "Will you be able to do this with your injured knee? We can refer back to the books for some different positions if it'll help to keep from hurting you."

He didn't want her nose back in those damn books. "You're not going to cause me any pain," he assured her. *No more than the pain of a terminal hard-on.*

"Still, it'll be better on the bed where we can maneuver. I realize sex requires some mobility."

"For the love of...we're not going to be doing acrobatics." At least he didn't think so. Perhaps she'd read a chapter on *that*, too! And ridiculously, the thought of Annie being "mobile" made his stomach clench and his muscles tighten with sexual expectation.

Annie shrugged. "I read that men just want to sleep afterward. So we might as well be in the bed so you won't have to move again."

With every breath, she managed to insult him. "Only a total pig falls asleep right afterward!"

"A pig, huh?"

She looked so skeptical, he figured the books had convinced her otherwise. Then he added, "Perry would probably fall asleep."

"You think so?" With her upper body naked, she sauntered to the fireplace and banked the fire until only mellow glowing embers remained. She closed the glass screen securely.

Guy watched in appreciation, every small turn and twist of her slender body. The shadows in the room emphasized all the curves and hollows of her perfect body.

With a smile, she returned to him and picked up his crutch, then began tugging on his arm. "C'mon. I'll help you to the bed. Then you can just doze off afterward."

Gritting his teeth, Guy insisted, "I will *not* doze off."

Determination shone in every line of her face. Giving up, Guy hauled himself painfully to his feet. He didn't tell her that he knew he wouldn't fall asleep because for him, there'd be no afterward. Just Annie's pleasure, her response, her awakening.

He swallowed hard.

He'd ease her into things. He was the experienced one, the one in control. He'd overwhelm her sexually and she wouldn't even realize that he wasn't completely involved, that he'd held himself back.

He'd use his hands, his mouth and his tongue, to make certain she enjoyed herself. Once he'd given her a climax—and he fully intended to watch every nuance of her orgasm face— he'd cuddle her close and, given what she'd just told him about being up all night, *she'd* be the one falling fast asleep.

In *his* arms.

It would have to be enough for him.

Guy stopped by the side of the bed and propped the crutches against the footboard. The air was chilled, the bed wide and comfortable. The small lamp on the nightstand was on, lending dim illumination to the room.

He drew a slow, deep breath and tried to gentle his voice, to stop the trembling in his hands. He'd be careful with her. He'd be tender and understanding.

He'd go very, very slow.

Before he could turn and face her, Annie reached around him and pulled open the drawstring on his bottoms. They dropped to his knees.

"Annie."

"Indulge me," she whispered, unrepentant. "I really do like looking at you."

He gasped, but then her arms were around him, both her small warm palms cuddling his painful erection, her soft breasts pressing into his back, and all he could do was feel.

His moan was a harsh sound in the otherwise silent room.

Against his shoulder blade, he felt Annie's open mouth, damp and delicate. "Does this bruise hurt?"

"No." His voice was a croak.

"This one?"

He shook his head. Her inquisitive hands measured his length, his width.

"It's amazing how you feel," she said with awe. "Silky soft over such rigid hardness."

"Oh God."

"I wanted so badly to touch you this afternoon. I should be sainted for resisting your irresistible body. I hope you appreciate my consideration." Her hand squeezed with just the right amount of force. "Another woman wouldn't have shown you such regard, you know. But I respect you."

He wondered what the hell that was all about. "No other

woman," he rasped, pointing out an irrefutable fact, "has taken advantage of me in a drugged state."

"No other woman has *had* you when you were drugged. I think, under the circumstances, I've shown exemplary behavior."

With her small hands stroking, cuddling him, he could barely follow her words, much less offer up an argument. "Annie." He tried to reach down for the scrubs, intending to cover himself before it was too late.

"Don't be shy, Guy. I'll be careful with you."

He growled. Their hands did battle for control of the bottoms, and Annie won. But then, his heart wasn't in the struggle. Not really.

"You feel wonderful," she breathed. "But you have so many bruises. I'm so, so sorry you were hurt."

She began kissing him every place that he was marked and it was the most exotic, the most erotic thing he'd ever experienced.

Thank God she stayed on his back. If she'd moved to the front with her hot little mouth, he'd be a goner.

Just thinking it nearly did him in.

Guy clenched his fists, hoping to regain his sanity, knowing it was futile.

Her hand squeezed. "I read about this in the books, too. How a man likes to be held tightly, more roughly than a woman."

She'd read about it, Guy thought, in anticipation of doing this to Perry.

That dark thought infuriated him and he jerked around to face her. The abrupt movement caused pain to shoot up his leg, and he didn't quite manage to hide his wince or his low grunt.

"Lie down."

Annie, breasts flushed and rosy nipples tight, pressed against his shoulders even as her eyes drank him in. The way she looked at him was better than how most women touched. And it made lying down a necessity.

After shoving a pillow beneath his knee and admonishing him not to move, Annie stretched out beside him. But she didn't stay there. Her hands were everywhere, stroking, exploring, exciting.

Guy attempted to slow her down, but she kissed him, his shoulder first then his collarbone, then his ribs.

Her southerly path had his mind rioting with ideas. "Annie," he gasped, "stop."

"Shh. I want to make you feel better." She squirreled around until her delectable backside faced him, and she could give all her attention to his groin.

And she showed no reservations at all.

He was supposed to be initiating *her!*

Guy started to tell her so, but her tongue touched a bruise on his upper thigh and stole his voice. His body lurched.

"Easy," she whispered, seducing him, setting him on fire, stealing away all his hesitation. He was beginning to feel like a virgin on prom night.

"I studied up on this all day while you were sleeping," Annie told him. "I'm pretty sure I know what I'm doing."

"You're not supposed to be doing anything," he reasoned. "You're a damn virgin."

She peered over her shoulder at him, and gave him a pitying look. "Virginity and stupidity are not synonymous."

"Virginity and timidity should be!"

"Oh good grief." She climbed off the side of the bed and started shucking off her leggings. Guy could only gape.

And breathe hard in anticipation.

And feel his body react.

Too late to close his eyes now.

"I know I'm not perfect," Annie explained, "but Lace assures me it won't matter."

She straightened slowly, her bottoms on the floor, her face bright red but her gaze direct.

She hadn't worn panties.

Guy thought he might come from just looking at her.

Not perfect? She was the most perfect woman he'd ever seen. Her body, her smile, her blush. The brazen way she'd seduced him so thoroughly, her strength and her determination. Her caring. They all combined to make her irresistible to him.

Guy took a deep breath and held out his hand. "C'mere."

Two seconds later Annie was in the bed with him, her skin silky and hot against his own, and he knew he was a goner.

The battle had just been won.

Chapter Eight

"IT'S KIND OF cold in here, isn't it? Are you chilled? I don't want you to get sick on top of everything else."

Guy could hear the concern—and the slight nervousness—in Annie's tone as he pulled her on top of him. She tried to keep her legs closed, and he clasped her thighs and opened them over his. His injured knee got bumped, but the pain was a dull ache compared to his pounding lust.

Annie tucked her face in close to his throat and her fingers bit into his upper arms. Now that they were all situated, now that he'd quit fighting her, her bravado had melted away.

He hadn't done a very good job of seducing her, overwhelming her, making her forget herself. She was all too aware of the uniqueness of being with him, and that wouldn't do.

He wanted her mindless with wanting, and set about getting her there.

"It's hot as hell," he told her, stroking her shoulder, the small of her back, over her firm, silky bottom. "You make me hot."

"That's—" she gasped as his hand slid between her thighs from behind "—*good.*"

She'd nearly screeched, in mingled surprise and excitement. He didn't need to ask if any other man had touched her this way. Her reaction was telling enough for him to know this was a new experience.

Stroking his fingers over her, he found her wet, ready, despite her nervousness. He touched her gently, opened her, then carefully pushed one finger inside.

Her muscles clenched, her body tightened, and he whispered, "Shh. Easy now."

She was deathly silent.

Guy kissed her shoulder, her throat, loving the taste of her warm flesh, inhaling her scent. With his free hand he rubbed her nape, then brought her mouth to his.

He took her gasping breath and gave her his own as he continued to stroke deep inside her.

His mouth still against hers, their lips wet, he whispered, "You're so tight."

"I'm sorry." She wiggled, trying to accommodate his finger, the unfamiliar intimacy, and the movement tantalized his swollen erection.

"Don't be sorry. I love it." *I love you.* The words burned in his throat, but Annie didn't deserve his emotional trap. He'd give her what she wanted, but he refused to burden her with the rest.

"I...I want to touch you, too."

He couldn't give her that. "Not right now."

"Guy—"

"I'd lose it, sweetheart. I'm too close to the edge already." An understatement if ever there was one. In truth, he'd fallen off the cliff the second she'd popped the buttons on her flannel shirt. He'd been teetering there for months anyway. Maybe even years.

Marrying Melissa was out of the question.

Hell, he couldn't marry anyone, not when it was Annie he loved.

Yet she was just experimenting, and this was only one step in all the new experiences she wanted, *deserved*, to have.

"Do you know how soft you feel, Annie?"

Gasping, her narrow back arched, she asked, "Am as I soft as you are hard?"

"Yes." He kissed her again. He wanted to imprint himself on her, to force the same memories on her that he knew would stay with him forever.

With one arm tight around her waist, he brought her higher so that the warm notch of her thighs rested on his bare abdomen and he could attend to her breasts.

Annie helped by stiffening her arms, raising her breasts over his mouth. To his distraction, the movement also caused her mound to press more firmly against him, making him nearly incoherent with need.

Keeping his hips still, holding back the savage urge to take her, was the hardest thing he'd ever done.

She made no sound as he drew one taut nipple into his mouth. Other than the grasp of her feminine muscles, she was immobile. He drew on her for long minutes, stroked her with his fingers until they were both shaking and on the verge of coming.

"Annie?" She didn't answer and when he looked at her, he saw her face was utterly still, drawn tight, her eyes squeezed shut, her teeth sunk into her bottom lip.

Guy smoothed her backside as he studied her. "Sweetheart, I need to know if you like what I'm doing."

Her head bobbed, sending her hair to play over his chest, his shoulders.

"Tell me."

Her eyes snapped open; her breath left her in a loud rush. "You told me not to," she rasped, accusing. "You told me to be quiet."

Her nipples were wet, stiff. He plucked at them with his fingertips. "I told you I didn't need a blow-by-blow report. I never told you to hold your breath, to be so quiet I wasn't sure if you were still alive."

Her lashes lifted until her eyes were round. He could practically feel the groan bubbling up inside her before it burst out, loud, heartfelt.

"I *love* what you're doing to me! I feel like I'm melting on the inside and coming apart on the outside and I never want it to end, but I want to find the end if that makes any sense and—"

Guy kissed her, smiling, damned pleased with her enthusiasm. "And this?" he asked, still teasing her mouth with his as he moved his fingers out of her, higher, finding a spot that made her entire body shudder.

"Yes!"

Watching her face while he carefully stroked her, he judged her response, and he saw the moment she was near climax. He wanted it with her. He wanted to see her scream, to see her face contort. Orgasm face. He smiled painfully, biting back his own cresting need to come.

Annie lurched off him. Panting, she moved out of reach before he could stop her.

"What is it?" Was she afraid of what she felt? Ha. Not his Annie.

"I want you with me." Her breasts rose and fell rapidly, shimmering, her nipples flushed dark and pointed. She swallowed hard, still breathing in pants. "I want you inside me my first time."

The words alone were almost enough to send him into oblivion. Summoning herculean control, he lied, "I don't have any protection."

"I do."

His conscience slumped in regret while his body did a robust cheer.

Then all he could do was gaze in mute surprise as Annie pulled a shoebox out from beneath the bed. It overflowed with a variety of rubbers in every color of the rainbow, every size, some French ticklers, some haltingly plain.

"Where in the world...?"

"Lace sent them. She included a note telling me not to show them to you until the right time, because some of them might intimidate you."

Annie climbed over him, the box in hand and settled herself at his side. She stared at his erection, the box, then asked, "Large?"

Guy dropped his head back on the pillow and stared at the ceiling. He wasn't a saint. And no mere man was set up to resist the irresistible.

With a distinct lack of enthusiasm, he said, "Average will do."

"You're kidding?" Her voice rang with disbelief. "They come larger than *that?*"

He didn't open his eyes; he wasn't prepared for her speculation on the size of male parts, especially not his male part.

Actually, he wasn't prepared for any of this.

"Are you okay, Guy?"

"Yeah." Why not? Why not do this for her, and then suffer silently while she carried her newfound knowledge to that other lucky bastard?

This, he was certain, was one of those times when a man's two heads debated over the ideas of wisdom. And in this case, bigger was not better—not when the smaller of the two was winning.

"Blue? Red?"

His hands fisted in the sheet. Her voice was breathy, anxious, awed. He couldn't answer, then realized he didn't need to when he heard the rustling of plastic, and felt Annie's warm fingers fold around him.

"It's all right, Guy. I know you're probably nervous. I promise I'll be very, very careful. You'll barely notice me."

Barely notice her? She was naked and sitting beside him and had his average male part held securely in her hand! Every fiber of his being was noticing her in a big way.

Annie expertly slid the condom—plain, thank goodness—

onto his erection. He ground his teeth together, some small part of his honor still warring with his decision, and still losing.

"You did that awfully well," he half complained, thinking that a little fumbling on her part might have helped him to regain his senses.

"I've been practicing."

Guy lurched as damning pictures ran through his mind. His sudden tensing caused her hand to tighten on his erection.

When their gazes clashed, Annie soothed him by saying, "Not on men, at least not before now. The book said to practice on a broomstick. I nearly went through an entire box before I got it right."

He fell back in relief, right before her thighs encased his hips and her hands braced on his chest.

"I can't know why they suggested a broomstick, though. As far as I can tell, there's absolutely no resemblance."

"Annie." Guy stared at her, amazed by her initiative, her determination.

"Shh," she said, stroking one pectoral muscle which he'd just noticed was incredibly sensitive to her touch. "I'm not going to hurt you."

If he hadn't been so turned-on, he might have laughed at her cocky, clichéd assurances which, under normal circumstances, she should have been receiving, not giving.

Instead he gave up. Annie on the make was a heady experience. Too heady to temper.

"Scoot up a little."

She anxiously did as he asked.

"Just relax, Annie." His fingers were large, rough against her soft flesh, and she made a crooning sound as he opened her, his touch as gentle as he could make it.

He held himself ready for her, and with the other hand cupped her bottom as she carefully prepared to slide down his length. "Easy now."

She flinched as his erection began to stretch her. It tore at his heart, and at the same time made him feel like doing the tarzan yell.

Sweat broke out on his brow.

Not to be deterred, Annie continued her descent despite her discomfort. In a rasp, she asked, "Are you sure you're just average?"

Her innocence filled him with warmth. "I promise."

Using the tip of one callused finger, Guy stroked her slick female flesh, up and around her most sensitive nerve endings. Her stifled groan broke the silence.

Clamped against his sides, her thighs tightened even more. He stroked her soothingly, insistently, watching her lips part, her eyes close. She was wet, but still a virgin, and she needed his careful care, his restraint.

"Go as slow as you like—"

His words died on a shout as she abruptly forced herself down in one hard, fast movement, taking him deep inside her, enclosing him in snug wet heat.

Sweet hell! Her nails bit into his chest, her muscles grasped him tight, and she yelled, "Guy!"

Amazingly, he felt her contractions begin. His back arched, his body pulsed. Pain radiated from his knee, his shoulder, but he didn't care. Pleasure overrode the pain. The pleasure of Annie coming, her scent, her gasps, her hands clinging to him.

His body alternately went into spasms of intense sensation, explosive release, then blessed numbness. It was by far the most pleasure he'd ever had, more than he'd ever expected.

He sank into the bedding, Annie draped over him, her soft mouth touching his throat as she gulped for air. Her limbs were still shaking, her heartbeat still thumping in counter time to his.

Long minutes passed while he refused to think. And then he heard Annie whisper, her voice still shaky but soft, "See, that wasn't so bad."

His every nerve ending was still tingling and she

thought it wasn't *so bad?* He got his eyes open. She watched him, her elbows propped on his chest, one hand stroking his jaw.

Weariness dragged at him. He felt too lethargic, too sated, to stay alert.

"I love your orgasm face," she said, and he realized that rather than watching her, she'd watched him!

"Annie." Damn, choking back the words was near impossible. He'd done what he shouldn't have done, and gotten more than he'd ever counted on. Regret weighed him down; regret that they couldn't stay here forever, regret that he couldn't claim her as his own.

Regret that she intended this as the first experience of many—with another man, a man who didn't deserve her.

Knowing he shouldn't, but too tired to stop himself, he touched her face, her lips, and whispered, "I'm sorry, Annie. So damn sorry. This never should have happened."

Her face paled, but she didn't say anything, just lowered her head. Guy thought she was going to kiss him again, and he closed his eyes, waiting. But the kiss didn't come, and then it didn't matter—because like a pig, he fell asleep.

GUY CAME AWAKE with a start at an unfamiliar noise. He looked around the room, but he was alone. He didn't know what had disturbed him, but now that he was awake, he discovered that every bruise on his body held new complaints.

Annie had loved him thoroughly, that was for sure. And then, without any pillow talk, without any reassurances, he'd passed out.

Damn, he was worse than Perry!

He closed his eyes while considering what he'd done.

Making love with Annie had been the sweetest, most emotionally devastating thing he'd ever experienced. She was good. Better than good.

Maybe he should read a few of her books.

Guy smiled. He felt so replete, he almost chuckled. *Annie had made love to him.*

"Look at him!" a familiar voice said, intruding into his thoughts. "He's banged up from one end to the other and he's smiling like a sap even in his sleep."

Guy lurched half out of the bed and his eyes snapped open so fast that his head throbbed. Silhouetted by the sunlight streaming through the large front window, Daniel stood there in the bedroom doorway. He looked like an avenging angel, highlighted as he was.

Then the significance of his appearance registered.

Daniel!

Obviously, Daniel was responsible for disturbing his sleep, but his appearance at this precise moment didn't make any sense. "Uh…"

Daniel frowned. He looked over his shoulder at someone and asked, "Is he still drugged? No? Then I'd like to know what he's so happy about, all things considered."

He turned to Guy again, waiting.

"Uh…" What the hell could he say?

And where was Annie? Guy hated to think of her being a witness to her big brother's disapproval.

Although Daniel didn't look disapproving so much as curious.

With a guilty start, Guy realized that the sheet barely maintained his modesty. And it was obvious he'd been sleeping naked. It was an effort, but he forced himself into a sitting position and covered himself more thoroughly.

In an affected tone that he hoped sounded calm and reassuring, Guy asked, "What are you doing here, Daniel?"

"Melissa knows where you are," Daniel said without hesitation. "And she's on her way."

"What?" The very last thing he needed was for Melissa to show up. Having Daniel as an observer was more than enough to have to deal with.

"Dad told her you were here. With Annie. I can't believe he did, but he did." Daniel shrugged.

"But...where is Annie?" He tried to see around Daniel and couldn't. It dawned on him that the cabin suddenly felt...empty.

And so did his heart.

He moved to the edge of the bed to stand.

Daniel rushed to his side. "Hey, you should take it easy. Here, let me help you."

Panic edged away Guy's guilt and any pain he felt. "Where the hell is Annie?"

Daniel, looking faintly satisfied, said, "She said she was getting ready to leave."

"Leave?"

"Yeah." Daniel clasped Guy's arm and helped him to stand, then grinned when he saw Guy was naked. "You think you should get dressed before you start chasing my baby sister?"

Guy's face went blank. What the hell was he doing? *What was Annie doing?* He shook his head and hurriedly looked around for something to put on. Daniel again came to his rescue and produced the scrubs from where they'd been half kicked beneath the bed.

Guy felt color race back up his neck when he remembered the way Annie had stripped him. And now her brother was standing before him.

Raising one brow, Daniel asked, "Undressed in a hurry last night, did you?"

With a lot of groaning and wincing, Guy sat on the side of the bed and worked the bottoms on over the knee immobilizer. He ignored Daniel's question to ask one of his own. "Why is Annie leaving?"

After adjusting his glasses, Daniel said philosophically, "I guess she figured that with Melissa here, she might as well take off."

"*Is* Melissa here?"

"She should be any minute."

Seconds later Daniel's younger brother, Max Sawyers, daredevil, world wanderer and admitted woman addict, stuck his head around the door. "The virago has arrived."

Guy felt stunned at Max's appearance. The last he'd heard, Max was still in the wilds of Canada, wrestling bears and personal demons.

Daniel nodded at Guy and answered unasked questions. "Yep, he's back. And no worse for the wear of roughing it in total seclusion."

"I had a relaxing time," Max claimed, and as usual he omitted any details. "That is, until your lady friend insisted that I give her a ride here." Max made a face. "She's not a happy woman."

Melissa pushed her way past Max. "What," she demanded in a shrill yet cultured voice, "is going on here?"

Guy, still shocked at seeing Max after so long, had just gotten to his feet. At the sight of Melissa, he dropped back down to the bed.

The enormity of what he'd planned, how idiotic it had been, slapped him upside his head.

He'd already decided he wouldn't marry Melissa, but now he realized he had never really wanted her.

Certainly not in the uncontrollable way he wanted Annie.

She stood there in a calculated pose, her rose-colored sweater, trim skirt and knee high boots designed to look outdoorsy chic and ultimately feminine. Her hair, an enhanced blond, was twisted on top of her head in a becomingly loose swirl.

The sight of her left Guy cold.

His mind was filled with the image of Annie's face as she'd stood before him in his enormous flannel shirt, wielding a spoon and ogling his body.

From that moment, when acceptance of their isolated circumstances had invaded his brain, he'd known he would make love to her. He'd fought it, but not hard enough.

Max sauntered the rest of the way into the room, ignoring Melissa—which made her fume—and concentrated on Guy.

Looking Guy over, Max took in every bruise and scrape and bandage. "Damn, what did you do to yourself?"

Daniel lounged in the doorway. "He tangled with a semi. And lost." Then, his gaze directed at Melissa, he added, "Annie has been nursing him."

Max straightened abruptly at that. "That's what she was doing here? But I thought she'd just found us out."

"No." Daniel gave an unaffected shrug. "I told her."

Melissa arched a brow. "She's been alone here with Guy in this cabin?"

Daniel smiled. "Yep."

Max, his eyes darkening to near black, asked, "Just what the hell is going on here, anyway?"

When no one answered him, Max looked at his smiling brother, then at Guy's guilty expression. He whistled. "I see. Well, if Annie was here to *take care of you,* then why did she just hightail it out of here so fast?"

Guy shot off the bed, hobbling and limping and cursing. The others darted out of his way, but he made it only as far as the living room when he realized Annie was gone. And despite the crowd gathered behind him, the cabin was empty without her.

Through the front window, Guy could see the spot where Annie's small car had been parked, now empty, the snow crushed in the wake of her departing tires.

Nearly numb with self-disgust, he stumbled, then allowed Daniel to help him to the couch.

Frustration exploded inside his pounding head. He could still feel her, her heated, brazen touch, and he could hear her scream when she came, her ragged panting breaths. He felt again the way she'd squeezed him during her climax.

Annie turned him on, made him laugh, delighted him and amused him and made him whole. He loved her so much— but not as a sister. There was nothing familial in his feelings.

"Damn it all," he said, venting before he exploded, "you people have rotten timing!"

Melissa took umbrage at that. "You and I had some business to discuss, and then suddenly you left and no one—" here she glared at Daniel "—would tell me where you'd gone. What did you expect me to do? Just wait around for you to make a deal with someone else?"

Guy groaned. The very last thing he wanted to discuss with Melissa was business, of either a personal or professional nature. He wanted to go after Annie. He wanted to explain...*what?*

There was nothing to explain.

Nothing had changed.

He looked at Melissa, his eyes red. "What we have to talk about can wait."

"Oh no you don't. We either have a deal or we don't."

Daniel threw up his hands. "Marriage is not a damn business deal!"

"Who said anything about marriage?" she asked.

The men all quieted. Guy waved a hand at her, weary to his very bones, hurting all over, especially in his heart. "I was going to ask you to marry me. But I've changed my mind."

Melissa looked astounded when he mentioned marriage, then insulted that he wouldn't propose to her after all. "What do you mean you've changed your mind?"

The entire situation was so bizarre, Guy laughed. "Can you honestly say you wanted to marry me?"

She examined a nail, pursed her mouth, shrugged. "I don't know. I'd have to think about it."

Sizing up the situation in a heartbeat, Max said low, "It'd be a damn shame if you married him."

Eyes wide, Melissa looked at the brother they all called a Lothario. He hadn't gotten his reputation by mistake. "Why?"

Guy watched in fascination as Max transformed from weary traveler to man-on-the-make. His eyes grew darker, his smile taunting. He no longer looked tired, so much as fit and strong. *And able.*

"If you married Guy," Max explained, "then you'd be unavailable."

Equally amazing as Max's mood switch, was the blush on Melissa's face. It made her look younger, and far more vulnerable than Guy had ever witnessed. She actually dithered.

"I…well, I'm not marrying him, now am I?"

Max took a step closer to her. From every pore, he exuded raw masculinity and sexual appeal. Guy and Daniel shared a look of awe.

"Do you love him?"

Mute, Melissa shook her head.

"Do you particularly want to marry anyone?"

"Not for a long, long time."

Max grinned. "Why don't you go wait in my car for me? I'll be right out."

Melissa may have been susceptible to Max's charm, but she was still a businesswoman. "Not so fast." She rounded on Guy. "We discussed a joint venture that would benefit both our businesses. Is that still on?"

Guy closed his eyes and leaned his head back. Every ache he hadn't felt last night now roared for attention. He felt like someone had used the semi to pound him into the ground. "We can discuss the particulars on Monday."

Melissa brightened. "I'll hold you to that." She glanced at Max. "Don't keep me waiting."

"I wouldn't dream of it."

After Melissa had left, Daniel shook his head at his brother. "You're dangerous."

Max shrugged. "I could see Guy needed some help. Poor beat-up bastard. She'd have made mincemeat of him."

Guy didn't bother to open his eyes. "True."

"So." Max carefully stepped over Guy's injured leg and sat beside him. "You want to tell me what's happening here?"

Guy had no intention of telling him a damn thing.

Unfortunately Daniel didn't suffer the same reserve.

"Annie wants to seduce someone."

Max shot to his feet again. *"What?"*

Guy groaned and covered his face. From bad to worse.

Without an ounce of sympathy, Daniel explained, "Annie told me she was going to have sex, and that was that. Lace was helping her."

There was a long hesitation, then Max said, "Yeah. That's the part I want to hear."

Daniel slugged him in the arm. "Lace gave her all these damn idiotic books on sex. Annie was all revved up to give it a try and Goofus here was planning on asking Melissa to marry him, so I sent the two of them here together to work it all out."

"Work it out, how?"

Guy dropped his arms. "I'm waiting with bated breath for this little explanation myself."

With credible unconcern, Daniel lifted off his glasses, polished them on a sleeve, and admitted, "I thought maybe you'd have sex with her."

Guy's jaw should have dislocated, it dropped so hard and fast. Max nodded slowly, as if thinking it over—and deciding it made sense.

Not knowing if the look on his face would give him away, Guy wheezed, "You wanted me to... to...?"

Max plopped back down beside him. "Better you than some other yo-yo. At least we like you, and we know you're one of the good guys. Hell, I always kinda hoped you and Annie would tie the knot. Come to that, maybe this is a good step in that direction."

Daniel crossed his arms over his chest. "So how about it?"

Guy slowly sat upright. He felt defensive and hopeful and angry enough to take on both brothers, even with his body more battered than not. "How about what?"

"Did you and Annie—"

"That's none of your damn business!"

Max and Daniel shared a look, then broke out in enormous grins. "They did," Max guessed, and Daniel said, "Looks like."

Guy started to jerk to his feet, but Max caught his arm. His smile was gone. "So what are you planning now, Guy?"

"I'm not planning a damn thing." How could he make plans when Annie wanted to take what he'd shown her and apply it to some other nameless, faceless guy? The thought made him crazed. Was that why she'd lit out of the cabin the second someone else had shown up to take him home? Was she that anxious to try out her new knowledge?

His hands fisted until his arms trembled from the strain.

Max held up both hands. "Hey, don't bludgeon me. It was a simple question. I mean, considering Annie was near tears when she left here—"

Guy grabbed him by his shirt collar. "Annie was *crying?*"

"Close enough."

"Why?" Why would Annie run out on him and then get weepy over it? Or had Daniel yelled at her? But no, he hadn't heard any yelling. Besides, Annie could hold her own against her brothers.

Daniel patted Guy's shoulder. "Turn him loose, Guy. Or have you forgotten that Melissa's waiting out in the car for him? If you mess him up, you'll have to deal with her."

Disgruntled, confused, Guy let Max go with a shake of his head. "I wasn't going to hurt him."

Max laughed. "Damn, but you remind me of Daniel when Lace was tormenting him."

"She still torments me," Daniel clarified, "I just like it more now than I did then."

"You look haunted," Max told Guy. "But Daniel survived this love business, so I suppose you will, too."

This love business sucked, but Guy didn't bother denying how he felt. He was too busy thinking about Annie crying, and it made his insides twist. "You know I love her?"

Max snorted. "What am I? Blind?"

"Lace hinted," Daniel told him, "although she wouldn't give me any names."

"That's why she sent all the condoms," Guy said with sudden understanding, then wanted to bite his tongue off when both Max and Daniel scowled at him. "Uh, I mean…"

Daniel shoved his glasses back on. "I'm going to put that woman over my knee."

Chuckling, Max asked, "Want any pointers?"

Guy decided he'd had enough. He pushed painfully to his feet and faced both brothers. "I want her to marry me."

Daniel sighed in relief. "Good."

Max nodded. "You better."

"You're okay with that?" Guy felt like he'd had the wind knocked out of him. "I mean, you've always said how no one was good enough for Annie and—"

"We've said the same about you," Daniel told him.

"You have?"

Max laughed and headed for the door. "You and Annie will be perfect together. Now if you'll excuse me? I'm off to be the sacrificial lamb."

It seemed Max's departure galvanized Guy into action. He gimped his way into the bedroom to finish dressing, and regardless of how Daniel cajoled, he refused a pain pill. For what he had ahead of him, he needed his mind to be crystal clear.

He had to get to Annie.

Her days of experimenting were at an end.

But first he had to settle things with her father.

Chapter Nine

DAN SAWYERS, the founder and owner of the company that Guy ran, looked right at home behind the desk he seldom used anymore. At that moment, Guy wondered if he'd been an enabler, making it too easy for Dan to shy away from the world and live in self-imposed isolation with the memories of his wife's death.

Since Guy was making such a huge change in his life by admitting his love for Annie, he decided to go for broke, and also force Dan to start taking a more active role in his own company, and with his family. Daniel couldn't do it, because as Dan's son, the hierarchy had already been decided. Max didn't appear to care enough to try, and Annie was too kindhearted to force the issue.

Guy was the only one close enough, yet also detached enough, to see the situation from all angles.

"I have something serious to discuss with you, Dan."

"Guy!" At Guy's entrance, Dan laid aside his pen, closed a folder and came to his feet. After one good look at Guy, however, he drew up short. "Good God! You look even worse than Daniel led me to believe. Shouldn't you still be in bed or something?"

Guy felt worse than he looked. But he was also determined.

Against the dragging weight of physical bruises, regret that he'd inadvertently hurt Annie and concern that Dan might not understand, Guy straightened his shoulders.

"I love Annie."

Dan blinked at him. He circled his desk to lean one hip on the edge. With an undue amount of caution, he asked, "You do?"

"Yes." In an even firmer tone, Guy added, "I'm going to ask her to marry me."

A slow smile spread over Dan's face. He rubbed his hands together. "Was it Melissa showing up that did the trick? I worried about that, you know. If maybe I was sending her too early. But you understand, I couldn't let you dither around about my daughter any longer."

The words swirled around Guy, confusing him further before they started to make sense. "You knew I was in love with Annie?"

Dan started to clap him on the shoulder, saw the precarious way Guy balanced himself on his crutches, and changed his mind. "Are you kidding? You watch her the same way I used to watch her mother." A familiar, accepted sadness invaded Dan's eyes, and he shook his head. "That kind of love doesn't come along every day."

"But…you suggested I should marry Melissa."

Dan snapped to attention, shedding his melancholy as if it hadn't existed. "I did no such thing!" He went so far as to shudder. "She's a nice woman and all, and very astute when it comes to business. However, I don't think she's right for you."

Drowning in confusion once again, Guy asked, "When you were talking about marriage—"

"Why, I was talking about Annie, of course!"

Guy found it hard to believe he'd been so dense. But evi-

ssibly make us lose money, well you're wrong." He began acing around the office. "Here's what we'll do. We'll be partners, running it together." He speared Guy with a look. "*You* an't deny that running the company makes you happy, too. You're a natural."

Guy shrugged. He loved the business and always had. "I won't work sixty-hour weeks anymore."

"Neither will I. We'll split up the load. With the company growing, maybe there's a chance I'll even be able to talk Max into getting serious and joining us."

Guy snorted at that. Max wasn't settling down for anyone. Plenty of women had tried to get him to do just that. "We'll see."

Suddenly Dan looked at his watch. "Now that we've got all that settled—"

"Nothing is settled. I owe you—"

"Don't argue with me!"

Guy raised a brow at that tone. He'd never heard it from Dan before. In a way, it was nice to see him being passionate about something besides his grief.

Dan was still scowling as he said, "You're like a son to me. I care a great deal about you, and I owe you more than money could ever repay. So forget that nonsense."

"You have it backwards." Guy knew if anyone should be grateful, it was him. But when he started to say so, Dan interrupted him.

"If you want to catch Annie, you better be on your way."

"Catch her? Isn't she at the bookstore?"

"Nope." With great relish, Dan said, "She came in to see Perry. I believe they're in his office."

Guy staggered back two steps. Damn, but she was moving fast! She'd only left the cabin that morning, and lunchtime had barely come and gone. If she was orchestrating a little office rendezvous already, Guy would...what? He had to tell her how

dently everyone had known what he felt, in s   p
tempts to hide it.   I

Still… "There's another problem."   1

Dan smiled as he once again rested against the
desk. "Besides getting Annie to say yes, you mea

Guy didn't want to think of that. Annie had to say
find a way to convince her. Drawing a deep brea
blurted, "I'm not going to run the company anymore.

Dan straightened. "But of course you are! You'll
Annie, the company will become yours, and that wa
stay in the family!"

Guy resolutely shook his head. "No. I'm already livir
your house. I don't regret that," he added quickly, see
Dan ready to interrupt again, "because now, Annie will l
there, too."

"If you convince her to marry you."

Through his teeth, Guy said, "I'll convince her."

"All right, all right. I'll take your word on it."

"But there's also the money I owe you…."

Like a fresh-baked pasty, Dan puffed up. "Now you can
stop right there! You don't owe me a thing, dammit!"

"You paid for my education."

"And got a hell of a lot in return!" Dan's face turned red
with umbrage. "So don't even start on that."

Rubbing his aching head, Guy said, "I can't just let the
money go. I want to pay it back."

"Fine. Pay it back by staying on in the company."

Surprised that Dan had misunderstood, Guy explained, "I
wasn't going to leave the company. But I don't want to run it
anymore, either. You should be running it. I saw you there behind the desk, and you can deny it all you want, Dan, but you
were happy."

"True. But I've been out of the loop too long, and if you
think it'll make me happy to step in full-time and blunder and

he felt first, then see about the rest before he started doing the caveman routine.

He turned around so quickly he almost fell off his crutches. Dan hurried to open the office door for him. "I'd welcome you to the family," Dan said, restraining Guy with a hand on his arm, "but I've *always* thought of you as a son."

Guy softened in the midst of his turmoil. "Thanks, Dan."

A shaky smile in place, Dan said, "Go convince my daughter. And Guy, I'd lose that evil look in your eyes first."

ANNIE WAS JUST handing Perry the book on bird-watching that he'd ordered from her shop when the office door flew open and bounced against the wall. Startled, she jerked around to see Guy filling the doorway. Heaving.

He hadn't shaved yet.

The stubble on his chin was now almost as long as the hair on his head. Combined with his dark eyes and the grim set to his mouth, he looked enraged.

Gorgeous and sexy, but enraged.

"Guy." She turned to stare at him. "What in the world are you doing up and about?"

Even as Annie said it, she thanked her lucky stars that she'd thought to wear sunglasses. The last thing she wanted was for Guy to see that she'd been crying. She knew he'd feel responsible and start more of his brotherly nonsense. At the moment, she didn't think she could take it.

Perry took his book from her numb hand and backed up three steps until he was behind his desk.

Guy stared at Perry as he growled, "You ran out on me this morning."

Annie forced a shrug, but her heart was in her throat, choking her. How dare he force her to relive this now. "Melissa was there."

"I didn't want Melissa there." He glanced at her briefly, and that one quick look carried the impact of a heated embrace. "I wanted you there."

"Really?" But she wouldn't get suckered in again. He probably meant as a little sister. He probably wanted her there so he could lecture her some more on propriety and explain to her that what had happened couldn't ever happen again.

She made a face and looked at him over the rim of her sunglasses. "Why?"

"I had…questions, for you."

He was still staring at Perry and that infuriated her. She stepped into his line of vision. "Stop trying to intimidate my friend."

Oozing menace, Guy asked, "Is Perry a *friend?*"

Perry edged out from behind his desk and held up the book. With more bravery than she'd ever given him credit for, he frowned and said, "She brought me this. That's all. Annie told me weeks ago that she didn't want to be more than friends, and I've respected that decision."

Just that quickly, Guy deflated. "Weeks ago?"

"Yes. And since it's obvious the two of you have things to discuss, I think I'll give you some privacy."

Annie didn't try to change his mind, and Guy said only, "Close the door on your way out, Perry."

Giving Guy a wide berth, Perry made a hasty and not too dignified exit.

Once they were alone, Annie asked, "So what questions did you have for me?"

"Do you think I'm a pig?"

"What?" That wasn't at all what she'd been expecting.

Guy shrugged, then limped toward her and put his crutches against the desk. "I did fall asleep," he explained while gently lifting her sunglasses away. He looked at her red-rimmed eyes and sighed. "You've been crying. Why?"

Annie folded her arms across her middle and fought the new rush of tears. "I don't think you're a pig. I told you, the books say that a lot of men fall asleep—"

"I'm not a lot of men," Guy interrupted to say. "And if I hadn't just been run over, there's no way in hell I would have left you like that."

She searched his face. His eyes were darker than usual, hot. "You wouldn't have?"

"No." Very, very gently, he kissed the bridge of her nose. "So why were you crying?"

No longer so certain of herself, Annie looked down at her feet and lied, "I just felt foolish, that's all."

There was a heavy moment of silence, then: "Making love to me makes you feel foolish?"

Her face heated. "No, I didn't mean that."

Guy cupped her cheeks. "I love you, Annie."

Smiling wistfully, she met his gaze. "I know. I love you, too."

Guy paused, then shook his head. "No, I mean I love you, and I love making love with you, and I want to continue making love to you, only after I'm able to get around without the crutches."

Her pulse started racing. She wasn't a coward, but she was terrified of believing him, of having her heart ripped out again. "Why the sudden change?"

"It's not sudden."

Annie licked her lips. "Right…right afterward, you told me it was a mistake, that it shouldn't happen again."

His thumbs smoothed the corners of her mouth before he bent and kissed her. Against her lips, he said, "Have you ever seen Daniel looking for his glasses, and they're right there on top of his head? Or in his pocket?"

"Yes. So?"

"They're so familiar to him, so much a part of him, that

he overlooks their presence sometimes. That's what I did with you."

"I've never sat on top of your head."

"No, but you've been curled up in my heart for a long, long time. So long that I've just gotten used to you being there. I like having you there. Losing you would leave me with an empty heart."

The tears trickled down without her consent. "Then why did you keep pushing me away?"

Guy closed his eyes and rested his forehead on hers. "Please don't cry. I'd rather be run over again than see you cry."

She sniffed, and managed to get her tears slightly under control.

"Annie, I was so afraid of changing things, of messing up, of maybe losing you and your family."

"You can't lose family, Guy, unless you walk away."

He smiled. "I know that now." He kissed her again, this time with more intensity. "So what do you say, sweetheart? Will you put me out of my misery?"

Annie gulped down a laugh. It felt like happiness exploded inside her, making even her fingertips tingle. Shyly, she circled her arms around him and rested his palms on her hard backside. "Do...do we really have to wait until the crutches are gone?"

Guy stared at her, them slowly broke out in an enormous smile. "I'd like to take care of you next time."

"I didn't mind." Annie nuzzled against his chest. "Even getting rid of the condom was educational."

He groaned. "Damn, I hadn't even thought of that."

"Will you marry me, Guy?"

Laughing out loud, he asked, "Will you ever let me be the aggressor?"

Annie cuddled herself up to him, carefully hugging him close and laying her cheek against his hard chest. "That sounds like chapter four in my newest book. We'll need some ties, only you never wear any, so I don't know—"

Guy tipped up her chin and kissed her. "Yes, I'll marry you," he whispered against her lips, and in his mind, he made a mental note to be wearing a tie the next time he saw her.

MESSING AROUND WITH MAX

To Barbara O'Neill, an awesome online comrade.
Thank you for always sharing your thoughts on my
books, especially the wonderful Amazon reviews!
I appreciate it more than I can say.

Chapter One

RAIN AND HAIL hitting the door was one thing. A woman was another.

She ran into it at full speed, and Max stared, seeing long blond hair stick wetly to the glass panel, a small nose smooshed up hard, red and looking miserably cold. The rain came down in a curtain, muffling her grunt but not obliterating it entirely.

Cleo took an instant dislike to the intruder.

Hurrying around the counter of his sister's bookstore, Max opened the door. The small feminine bundle tumbled limply inside. At first Max thought she'd been shot or bludgeoned on the back of the head. In a fury he stepped over her and peered through the downpour, looking for another body, for any type of threat. There wasn't anyone there. Just the miserable rain.

Cleo continued to complain and snarl and as Max knelt down by the felled body, which now moaned loudly, he said, "Pipe down, you mean-tempered bitch."

The woman on the floor gasped, rolled over onto her back, and started to open her eyes. She moaned again instead.

"I'm wounded," she snarled, every bit as ferocious as Cleo. "I could certainly do without your abuse!"

"I wasn't..." Max stopped when she got one eye peeped

open. It was a startling, dark blue eye, fringed by dark brown lashes. It was just the one eye, not even both, but he felt the impact of her gaze like a kick.

Cleo snuffled closer, poking her wet nose against the woman's face while emitting a low growl.

"Where are you wounded," Max asked, still not sure why she'd thrown herself against the door, or why she was still on the floor.

"All over." That one eye regarded him steadily. "Even my teeth are rattled, so the least you can do is not insult me while I'm still down."

Max wondered if that meant he could insult her when she got up. *If* she got up. She didn't seem to be in any rush to do so.

"Cleo," he explained, more quietly this time, "is my dog. And she is mean-tempered, but not really ferocious. She won't hurt you."

"I'm not afraid of dogs." Even in her less than auspicious position, she managed to appear affronted by the very idea, then she turned her disgruntled one-eyed frown on Cleo, who whimpered in surprise. "I just don't want snout tracks on my cheek."

Max hid a grin. "C'mere, Cleo. Leave the lady alone." Cleo obeyed—a first as far as Max could recall. She came immediately to his side, but continued to grumble out of one side of her mouth, making her doggy lips vibrate, while keeping her watchful attention on the downed female.

A puddle had formed around the woman and since she continued to recline there on the tile floor, apparently at her leisure, Max looked for injuries. He found instead a rather attractive if petite bosom covered in a white T-shirt that read I Give Good Peach.

His brows rose. What the hell did that mean?

The shirt, now soaked through, was practically transparent and put on display a lacy pink bra beneath. Not that he was looking. Nope. He'd made a deal with Cleo, and he intended to keep to his word. He stroked his fingers through Cleo's ruff, just to reassure her.

The damn dog looked beyond dubious.

Maybe she knew him better than he knew himself.

"Are you okay?" Max asked the woman, in lieu of what he was really thinking, which had to do generally with her wet shirt and specifically with what it was molded to. He *would* distract himself. But it'd be easier if she'd just get up.

With what appeared to be a lot of undue effort, she got both eyes opened and stared at him. "I'm seeing two of you," she muttered in surprise, "and surely that's a fantasy, not reality."

"A fantasy, huh?" Maybe she was delirious. Maybe she was drunk.

Maybe she was fodder for his next advice column. No sooner than he thought it, Max discarded the idea. It was just a tad too far-fetched to be believed. Even for his eclectic audience, who so far seemed to believe anything he told them.

One small hand lifted to flap in his face, the gesture making Cleo positively livid. The female human ignored the female dog.

"Well, you *know* what you look like, I assume. Two of you would be...never mind." As if just realizing what she'd said, she cleared her throat. "Yes, I think I'm okay."

Max had never met a woman like her, and that was saying something since he'd known a lot of women. He was so knowledgeable on the subject of females, in fact, that his column was a rousing success—written anonymously, of course. Even his family had no idea that he wrote it.

They all thought he was jobless.

This woman was most definitely different. She was flirting, then withdrawing—all while stretched out in sodden disarray on the tile floor. "You're sure?"

"My pride is permanently damaged," she admitted, "but beyond that I believe I'll live." She pushed herself into a sitting position, long legs stretched out before her. Cleo again tried to sniff her, but when the woman turned that blue-eyed stare on her, Cleo whimpered, backed away, and from a safe distance, started snarling again.

Max could understand that. Her eyes were incredible. Not the color, the shape or the size. But the intensity.

"Where's Annie?" the woman asked, looking around the bookstore with an air of familiarity.

"You know my sister?"

"I've bought tons of books here," she explained, "to use in my work. Annie and I've gotten to know each other pretty well over the past year. Now we're friends." Then she asked, "Why was the door latched?"

Cleo, suddenly acting brave, inched one paw closer and the woman absently petted her. Outraged, Cleo yapped and howled, and the woman ignored her bluster while continuing to stroke the dog's too-small head.

Amazed, Max could do no more than stare. No one other than he had ever ignored Cleo's hostile swagger to give her affection. Max looked the woman over again, this time with a different type of interest. His heart beat just a little too fast.

He was on a bride hunt, and since his bride absolutely had to get along with his dog—he was marrying for the dog, after all, to give Cleo a stable home and the love and acceptance she'd never had—he couldn't help taking note of the somewhat tenuous friendship forming right before his eyes. It amazed him.

It warmed his cynical heart.

In a way, it even made him horny. But then, the rain had made him horny, too. Hell, he'd been so long without, a smack in the head would have turned him on. The only action he'd seen lately had been in the damn newspaper column, and that sure as hell wasn't enough to appease a man of his appetites.

The woman snapped her fingers in front of his face. "Where'd you go, big guy?"

Max laughed. "Sorry. My mind wandered."

"I could see that." She looked him over slowly, brazenly, then asked, "Why are you in here with the door latched?"

Max remembered that his sister had the habit of leaving the door cocked open, something both he and Daniel had grumbled about endlessly, which was probably why Annie continued to do it. She lived to irritate her brothers.

"Annie isn't here, and the storm kept whistling through the door, so I closed it. I hadn't figured on many people shopping today anyway. And of course, I hadn't counted on a woman throwing herself against it." More softly, because she had that effect on him, he said, "That must have hurt."

She sluiced water off her arms, and wrung out her hair. "I nearly knocked myself silly, but I'll survive."

Cleo, still looking ferocious so no one would realize her real intent, nudged the female's hand for another pet. Max nearly gawked. "What are you doing out in this storm?"

"I needed a book. I was running to keep from getting soaked, but obviously I hadn't planned on hitting a closed door." Suddenly she grinned, and it made her face go crooked, made her eyes squinch up. She looked adorable, even with her smeared makeup and rain dripping from the end of her red nose.

And she was still petting his dog.

And Cleo was still allowing it.

Max settled himself more comfortably on the floor, where it appeared their conversation would take place. The woman showed no signs of rising any time soon.

Doing his best to ignore her clinging T-shirt and the equally enticing long legs displayed by her tight rain-soaked jeans, Max asked, "Do you need a doctor?"

"Oh, no. Really, I'm fine." She continued to grin, then added, "I'm Maddie Montgomery." To Cleo's dismay, she stuck out a slim wet hand, now slightly coated with dog hair.

Max took it, felt how cold her fingers were and held on. "Max Sawyers. You're freezing."

"And you're Annie's most disreputable brother."

"Her brother, yes, the rest is debatable." Especially lately, Max added to himself. His life as a monk was not an acceptable one.

Maddie pulled her hand away and struggled to her feet. "You know, I've heard tales about you that could curl a woman's hair. You look different from how I'd imagined."

She'd imagined him? Max walked toward the back room where he could find a towel, deliberately removing himself from temptation. Sexual excitement, the thrill of the chase, the discovery, had already begun a heady beat in his heart. After so many years of indulging his basic nature, his actions were often instinctual. He'd find himself seducing a woman without even realizing it, as if he went on automatic pilot or something.

A woman commenting on his reputation just naturally left herself open to a firsthand display of that reputation. Only now he needed a bride, not merely a temporary bedmate. Which meant he had to move slower than he preferred.

But he couldn't stop himself from asking over his shoulder, "How did you expect me to look?" *And,* he added silently, needing the information if he hoped to succeed in his new altruistic plans, *whom did you hear it from?*

"I dunno." She followed on his heels, the squishing and squeaking of her sneakers echoed by the tapping of Cleo's nails. "I thought maybe you'd have long hair, like the guys who model for the women's magazines. Maybe gold necklaces. Something along the lines of the gigolo look."

Finding her description absurd, Max shook his head. He picked up a towel and turned to face her. "Here you go."

She swiped at her face and throat. "You're not offended, are you?"

"More like amused. And curious." No woman he'd ever been with would have described him as anything less than macho, virile...but never a gigolo.

Intrigued, he asked, "Who's been talking about me?"

"Your sister, mostly."

Max almost tripped over his own two feet. "Annie?" Well, hell, that wasn't in the least exciting.

"Yes. Your sister loves you dearly, and she's very proud of you. But she claims you're a reprobate."

"Annie told you I wear gold chains?"

Maddie laughed. It was a nice laugh—natural, warm. Cleo stared at her as if confused, her doggy lips rolling and shuddering as she gave a low growl. "No, that part I imagined all on my own. Annie just told me what a romancer you are, how women seem to find you irresistible."

Max nodded. As many women as men read his column. And they sent him letters of appreciation. He knew women, inside and out, body and soul.

Which was why his weekly column was so successful. He liked it that no one knew he wrote the thing. Anonymity was his friend, otherwise he could just imagine the women who'd be chasing him. It was bad enough that his reputation was so well known, but if women found out he was the weekly love expert...

"I've heard about you from some other women, too."

Her statement drew Max out of his reverie. "Is that right?"

Maddie blotted at her hair as she spoke, oblivious to the sexy display of her breasts beneath the transparent tee. For the most part, Max kept his gaze fixedly on her face. But he was human and male and that combination made it impossible to ignore her tightened nipples completely. He couldn't *not* look every now and then.

"You're the world traveler," Maddie claimed with fanfare, "the lover extraordinaire, the prize every woman wants to win."

Her candid banter charmed Max. He couldn't quite decide if she was coming on to him, or poking fun at him, but she did it in such a way that either was okay. It was a unique approach, one he was unfamiliar with.

He leaned in the doorway, Cleo by his side. "Every woman?"

That crooked grin appeared again. "Certainly. I feel ready to faint just being in your presence. The sexual vibes are all but knocking me over. Why do you think I spent so long on the floor?"

Biting back a grin, Max asked, "Because you'd nearly knocked yourself out?"

"*Au contraire.* Because I opened my eyes—"

"One eye."

"—and saw you and the world tilted. I was far too dizzy to sit up straight."

Those beautiful eyes—both of them for double the impact—twinkled at Max, keeping him from knowing how serious she might be.

She started to dry her shirt, looked down and gasped. "Good grief!" She shielded her breasts with the towel and glared at Max. "You could have said something!"

Purposely being obtuse, Max asked, "About what?"

"About…about… I'm showing through!"

He shrugged. "It didn't bother me."

Grumbling under her breath, Maddie turned her back on him and tied the towel around her upper body, knotting it at the side like a sarong. Cleo barked, the sound far from playful.

"There, you see?" Maddie said over her shoulder. "The dog agrees that despite your reputation, you should have been gentleman enough to let me know that more was showing than should have been."

"Actually," Max explained, "Cleo just hates people to turn their backs on her. She distrusts anyone who does."

"Oh." Maddie shifted slightly toward Cleo, tilted her head, and said with real sincerity, "Sorry girl. But Max was rude for not saying anything."

Apologizing to his dog?

Cleo snarled.

"Aha!" Maddie said. "She obviously agrees that you're lacking in manners."

"Because I didn't tell you that your breasts were showing?" Max watched her closely, waiting for her to blush. She was far too cocky to suit him.

Maddie nodded at him instead. "Exactly."

Her lack of embarrassment disappointed him.

"You should have told me. A gentleman always lets a lady know when her modesty is threatened. And being a gentleman doesn't detract from your reputation, I promise."

"Okay." Glancing down at her plump bottom in the snug jeans, Max said, "You've got a rip."

She blinked at him over her shoulder, not understanding. "I've got a…?"

"Rip. In the seat of your jeans. Your panties, which match your bra and are really quite pretty, by the way, are showing."

Max watched as she slapped her hands over her behind. It was a generous, well-rounded behind and her hands weren't adequate. He added, "Just being a gentleman."

Maddie back-stepped to a chair in the seating area of the bookstore and plopped down. "I don't suppose you have another towel?"

"Nope. Best I can do is offer my shirt."

She flashed that silly, endearing grin. "Now, I certainly couldn't turn that down. But not yet please. I need to keep my wits about me for a bit longer, at least until I've gotten what I came for."

"Which is?" Max pulled out his own chair and straddled it to face her. The storm still raged, rain lashing the front windows and lightning splitting the dark afternoon sky. Thunder belched and rolled.

The lights in the bookstore flickered once, and all three occupants looked up to see if they'd go out. When they stayed on, Cleo settled herself nervously at Max's side, her head on his foot.

Max absently patted the dog while watching Maddie. She really was cute, though he hadn't thought so at first. And he enjoyed chatting with her. The things she said took him by surprise—not that he'd ever admit it to her.

It was a cozy scene, comfortable, until Maddie said, "Annie told me about *Satisfying Alternatives to Intercourse*."

Max almost fell off his chair. He did jerk to his feet to tower over Maddie, disbelieving what she'd said, not about to hear this concerning his baby sister, never mind that Annie was getting married soon. His reaction startled Cleo who howled like a hungry wolf.

"Now I see where she gets it," Maddie muttered, eyeing Max's antagonistic stance.

Startled, Max wondered if she was right, but he didn't relax one bit.

Shaking her head, Maddie gave an aggrieved sigh. "Well. It's obvious you know nothing about it."

Max choked. "Ha! I know a great deal as a matter of fact!" If he hadn't sworn off casual sex, Max thought, he'd show her just how much he knew.

"No." Maddie shook her head, looking somewhat pitying and utterly positive over her conclusions. "You're clueless."

Heat rose up Max's neck. He felt his male consequence pricked, challenged. In a tone caught between menace and sultry promise, he said, "I can name any number of alternatives. As to how satisfying they are, I suppose that'd depend—"

She actually laughed at him. "Down boy."

Cleo sat.

Maddie laughed again. "At least the dog obeys."

Ready to strangle her, Max shook his head. "Only when she wants to, which isn't often." Then he added, "And never for women. Cleo hates women."

"She doesn't appear to hate me."

"I know. Strange."

Maddie leaned forward, teasing glints in her blue eyes and whispered, "It's a book, Max."

"What's a book?"

Her eyelashes were spiked from the rain, her collarbone still dewy, and she smelled nice. Like the fresh air outside and a sexy woman inside. His muscles tightened. She was teasing and bold and funny...and she liked Cleo.

He wanted her, dammit, but he had made that ridiculous vow to his contrary dog.

"I work at the women's shelter," Maddie said, "teaching classes and counseling various groups. One of our biggest problems used to be unplanned pregnancy, but with one of the groups I have now, there's more to it. I mentioned this to Annie, and she ordered me a book that she'd heard about."

So she was a counselor, Max thought with admiration, and decided her extra empathy and area of expertise had a lot to do with why she'd so easily understood Cleo, and gotten past the dog's bluster. An amazing woman.

And an amazing reaction for him. He could never recall having such an instant liking and respect for a female.

On the heels of that thought, comprehension dawned. Max resumed his seat. *"Satisfying Alternatives to Intercourse."*

"Yes, that's the title." Maddie bit her lips, and Max thought she was trying to keep from laughing at him again. He appreciated her restraint. Of course, he also enjoyed the sound of her laughter.

"Annie left me a message last week saying the book was in, but I haven't had a chance to pick it up until now."

Max continued to watch her, a variety of thoughts winging through his mind—most of them now centered around why an attractive, intelligent woman would need a damn book to tell her such things. She had to be, oh, maybe twenty-six or so. Old enough to have learned plenty of alternatives by now. Heck, he'd even invented a few, and that was while he was still a teen.

"So you're going to use this book for…research?"

"More as a reference. It's nice to be able to state documented facts to back me up when I give information or make recommendations. Also, what I learn in the book will help make me more credible in some situations. Despite my four-year degree, two years specialized and two years in the field, I still get teased for being a newbie."

Fascinated, Max asked, "Wouldn't women accept what is said more readily if it came from…experience?"

Max hoped she'd give a clue as to whether or not her brazenness was derived from experience or just plain old cockiness. With women you could never tell, and he'd long ago learned never to make an assumption about a lady.

But his question backfired on him in a big way.

"That's an excellent idea! It's so nice of you to volunteer!"

"But I never…" Max faltered. "Volunteer for what, exactly?"

"Why, to talk to the women, of course." Leaning forward, her damn towel gaping a bit, she elbowed him in a show of conspiracy. "I can imagine you'd hold their attention, at least."

Max leaned back in his chair in appalled denial. "Absolutely not."

"You're refusing?"

"Yes!"

Scrunching up her face with a dark frown, Maddie grumbled, "Then it was worthless advice."

Max glanced down at Cleo and they shared a look. Strangely enough, the dog was silent. Her tongue lolled out one side of her mouth, and there was a look of confusion on her furry face that mirrored Max's. He cleared his throat. "Uh, *you* could tell them."

She seemed to give that a lot of thought. "After you tell me?"

He supposed that answered his question about experience. Maybe. With this one he couldn't be certain. But his curiosity grew by leaps and bounds with every word she uttered. "I'll be glad to…discuss things with you."

"Hmm. I'll think on that. Now—" Maddie tilted her head "—do you happen to know where Annie might have put it?"

"It?"

She made a sound of exasperation. "You do have trouble following along, don't you?"

"Not usually, no." In fact, he was generally the one guiding the conversation. He wasn't sure if he liked this new development.

Maddie drummed her fingers on the chair arm. "The book? The reason I'm out in this miserable storm in the first place?"

"I'll look." In fact, he'd be glad of the opportunity to gather his wits and get his thoughts back in order. But just as he said it, another rumbling boom split the air with deafening force. The lights flickered and went out.

Max, slowly sinking back into his seat, said, "Then again, maybe I won't."

They weren't in total darkness. Though the sky was gray and threatening, it was still midafternoon and some light penetrated the thick, ominous clouds. Added to that was the continuous flash of lightning, strobing across the sky. But the sudden obliteration of every noise—no humming light fixtures, no air-conditioning, no buzz from the small refrigerator in the back room—left them in a cocoon of silence.

Cleo yowled and launched her rotund body into Max's lap. Since she wasn't exactly a small dog, and in fact bordered on fat, she was an armful. Fur went up his nose, into his eyes, and a wet snout snuggled frantically into his neck.

Max caught her close, but couldn't prevent his chair from tipping sideways and both man and dog went sprawling flat.

Over Cleo's panicked rumble, Max explained, "She's jittery in storms anyway, which is why I have her with me today, but she's especially afraid of the dark."

Max expected some criticism from the woman. But as he attempted to soothe Cleo, crooning to her and rubbing her ears, Maddie left her chair and knelt beside them. Her knee bumped Max's chin.

"Poor doggy. It's okay." Cleo whimpered and barked and snarled, but still Maddie stroked her.

Her understanding was seductive. And Max could smell her again, that fresh sexy smell of woman and rain. He cleared his throat, afraid he was fighting a losing battle.

Maddie straightened. "I'm going to go lock the door. It's never a good idea to leave your shop open in a blackout."

Since she'd evidently forgotten about the tear in her jeans, Max got to glimpse those satiny pink panties again as she rushed across the room to the door. She should have looked ridiculous, he thought, what with her hair wet and a towel tied around her breasts.

Instead, she looked oddly enticing. At her ease, obviously very familiar with the shop and his sister, with soothing fractious creatures, human and animal alike. Maddie flipped the many locks and turned the Closed sign around.

When she faced Max again, there was a funny expression on her shadowed face. A look of mixed anticipation, wariness and greed. Yes, it was definitely greed. *Strange.*

"I suppose," she whispered, her eyes never leaving his face, "we should both be heading out."

Max nodded and sat up, Cleo's quivering, lumpy body held protectively in his lap. "Yeah. I need to get her home. She'll be more comfortable there."

Maddie bit her bottom lip. "The thing is, I took the bus here. And now—"

"You don't relish sitting at the bus stop in this storm and with no lights."

She nodded. "And wearing a towel and with a rip in my pants. I don't suppose I could impose on you for a ride?"

That look was still in her eyes, driving Max beyond curiosity. No matter what he told himself, he simply couldn't let her walk away. Not yet. "I can take you home. No problem."

And maybe by taking her home he could learn a little more about her. If she'd be suitable as a wife, well then, he owed it to himself to find out.

Her smile was blinding in the dim room. "Thank you."

"About your book…"

"It'd be hard to find in this darkness, I'm sure. Unless you know exactly where Annie put it?"

"Nope. Afraid not." Doggy slobber ran down his neck and into his collar. Did Cleo have to drool when she was nervous? But then again, she was always nervous. Which was why Max felt compelled to give her a stable home, to show her the good side of life.

Max hugged her closer to his heart—and he saw a very discerning, sympathetic smile on Maddie's face.

"I can come back tomorrow and get it from Annie," she said in a soft voice that made his muscles clench.

"Annie may not be here." Readjusting his bundle, Max stood and faced her, trying to ignore the rushing of his pulse. "I'm minding the shop for her while she and Guy make wedding plans."

Maddie's frown reappeared before she forced a smile. "That's right, she's getting married, isn't she? That's, um, wonderful." In a stage whisper, she added, "Guy *is* a hunk."

Max scowled both at the compliment to another man, and the attitude she couldn't hide. "Annie's marrying him because they love each other."

"Of course."

Max glared at her. "You sound skeptical and you aren't even hiding it well."

Maddie lifted one shoulder in a negligent shrug and brightened her smile another watt. "I'm sure they'll be blissfully happy. I just don't happen to believe in matrimony."

Cursing under his breath, Max asked, "Care to tell me why?"

"Sure, why not? But let's do this on the ride to my house." She turned away, again forgetting about the rip in her jeans.

But Max noticed big time. He hoped she wasn't serious about not believing in marriage, because if she were, he'd have to stop noticing.

And he'd definitely have to put his lust on hold.

Chapter Two

HE HAS A DOG, Maddie thought with a wistful sigh. A fat, ugly, needy dog that he treated like a queen. Her heart thumped with unnamed emotions; suddenly, Max Sawyers no longer seemed like just a sexy body, but also a very compassionate and sensitive man. Those extra qualities only added to his appeal—but they also made him something of a risk. She didn't want to be drawn to him in any way but sexually!

Annie should have told her more about him. She'd said Max was good-looking, but she hadn't explained that he was devastatingly gorgeous. And she'd said he was cavalier about life, but cavalier men did not commit themselves to mutts.

Annie had claimed Max would be perfect—in that she was correct. Except that he was *too* perfect.

Maddie looked at his profile as he drove. The wipers worked double time clearing the windshield, but still the rain was blinding. Thunder rocked the truck.

Maddie felt oblivious to it all.

The man was too attractive for words. Just thinking of the things he knew, the things he could do to her, teach her... Her skin tingled into goose bumps that had nothing to do with the cold and everything to do with Max. She had expected to be attracted to him; she hadn't expected to like him so much right off the bat.

Despite her innate timidity, Maddie would have brazenly sat close to Max, and had intended to do just that. But when they'd dashed through the rain to his truck, Max had left her to fend for herself while he strapped Cleo into a doggy seat, located right between them. And anytime she tried to lean closer, to see him better, Cleo snarled. The dog was already so upset by the turbulent storm, Maddie couldn't bring herself to cause the poor creature more distress.

She understood Cleo on a gut level. The dog's defensive attitude was similar to those of the women she dealt with in her job, and her heart just naturally went out to the canine. Not that Cleo needed Maddie's understanding when she had Max fawning all over her.

Cleo watched her with a jaundiced eye, curling her lips every so often in what might have been a silent threat, though Maddie thought that was just the dog's way of mumbling, since she hadn't actually done anything vicious.

Cleo was about the ugliest dog Maddie had ever seen.

Yellowish fur with streaks of white and gray, a head far too small for such a corpulent body, and squat legs, made her look like some botched scientific experiment—something between a dog and a pigmy sow, maybe a furry ball with a head and feet.

The whiter fur circled the dog's tiny head, making it appear that her head had been morphed on in the wrong spot. Maddie thought the dog's tail was long, but because it stayed curled up between her hind legs and glued to her belly, it was impossible to tell for sure.

"Why is your dog so mean-tempered?" she asked cautiously, and watched Cleo show a few more pointed teeth.

Max glanced at her, but gave most of his attention to the road, which now resembled a large puddle with the rain water pooling on it. "Whoever had her before me didn't treat her well."

Maddie nodded in understanding. The dog tried to fend

off all friendly overtures, rather than trust anyone and risk more hurt, just as Max traveled the world, searching for meanings he couldn't find at home. When Annie had told her of Max's penchant for traveling, especially during the holidays, she'd naturally begun ruminating on his psyche.

Her specialized education and work experience made it easier for her to understand others.

Understanding herself hadn't been quite so easy. It had taken her friends to point out the obvious to her, that she was now determined to arm herself with specialized knowledge so no man could ever humiliate her or take advantage of her again, due to her naiveté.

Looking at Max now, seeing the tender way he smiled at Cleo, her heart thumped. Though she knew she was getting in over her head, she still insisted to herself that it was a good plan. "How long have you had her?"

"I found her in the middle of the road about a month ago. She was just lying there and I thought she was…" He dropped his voice to a whisper, and spelled, "D-E-A-D."

Horrified as she was by the picture he painted, Maddie bit back a smile. "I gather your dog doesn't spell?"

In all seriousness, Max said, "Just a little. There are some words I can't say, hint at, or spell without her going nuts on me."

"Like what?"

"Like another word for inoculation, if you get my drift. Or the professional who might give her that inoculation."

"Ah. She hates medical personnel?"

Cleo howled. Obviously, Maddie had used words she recognized.

"That's about it," Max confirmed.

"So how do you get her there?"

"I speak to her in French." He sent Maddie a devilish grin, and added, "All females are partial to having French softly crooned to them. Makes them mellow."

Maddie snorted. "I don't understand French, and if a guy was going to croon to me, I'd darn sure want to understand what he was saying."

Why that made Max laugh, Maddie wasn't sure. His reactions left her confused as to whether he found her to be laughably odd, or appealing.

"She used to hate baths, too," Max said around his chuckles, "but I changed all that."

At the word bath, the dog's pointed ears lifted off her skull and she barked. Max laughed and rubbed her head.

"Should I ask?"

His grin was pure wickedness, but all he said was, "She especially loves bubbles."

Another bark.

Maddie found herself grinning, too, charmed by Max and his eccentric dog. So what that things weren't working out quite as she had meticulously planned? Annie had said nothing about a dog being at the shop, but then maybe she hadn't known. Perhaps Max only brought the dog along, as he'd said, because of the storm.

The unplanned rip in her jeans and the unfortunate transparency of her T-shirt had certainly gotten his attention.

She cleared her throat as they neared her street and said, "I'd like to repay you by cooking you dinner."

Max skipped another look her way. His eyes were so dark, so intense, they made her shiver.

"Not tonight." He answered slowly, as if coming up with an excuse—or because he didn't really want to say no. Maddie wasn't sure which but she hoped it was the latter. "I need to get Cleo home and out of the storm so she can settle down."

"Exactly. My apartment is close and quiet," Maddie urged. "Why make Cleo ride farther when you can come in for a spell and relax, eat a little, and maybe by then the rain will have stopped."

Max looked undecided, so Maddie worked on Cleo. Leaning close to the dog, she asked, "Would you like to come in, girl?"

Cleo snarled at the invasion of her personal space. Her lips rolled and undulated, her teeth dripping as growled threats escaped.

"There, you see," Maddie said, not the least put off by the surly dog. Cleo's reaction this time was based on jealousy, Maddie was sure. She had things all worked out and there was no way a possessive pooch would thwart her. "She likes the idea."

Max chuckled. "You really aren't afraid of her, are you?"

Maddie shrugged. "I think I understand her. She doesn't dislike me so much as she's afraid to like me."

"It took me two weeks," Max admitted, "just to get her to trust me enough to let me pet her."

Hearing that, Maddie felt tears at the back of her throat. No wonder Cleo was possessive! On impulse Maddie threw her arms around the dog and hugged her tight. Both Max and Cleo looked stunned.

"Well," Maddie said in a slightly choked voice, ignoring them both as she pressed her nose into Cleo's soft, clean fur, "she certainly loves you now."

Had Cleo been abandoned and ignored, Maddie wondered, much like the ladies she worked with?

Max interrupted her thoughts. "So why are you set against marriage?"

Startled, Maddie blinked at him. "That was a quick change of topic."

"You looked ready to cry," he explained with a shrug. "I can't abide whimpering women."

"I never whimper." Maddie sniffed, wiped her eyes, and said, "I'm not exactly against marriage, not really. It's only that I'm in no rush to get tied down any time soon. I tried that and it was humiliating in the extreme."

Max perked up. "Humiliating? How so?"

"You really want to hear this?" She no sooner asked the question than she had to instruct him to turn onto her street. Within minutes she'd be in front of her apartment building. It was either gain his interest now, or possibly lose the opportunity.

Max turned the truck, then said, "Yeah, I want to hear it."

Drawing a deep breath and doing her best not to blush, Maddie confessed, "I came home early one day and found my fiancé tied spread-eagle and naked to my bed while a woman I'd never met tickled him with a feather."

Choking, Max said, "You're kidding?"

"Turn here. This is my apartment building." Maddie felt the heat in her face, the remembrance of deep humiliation, and lifted her chin. "Nope, I'm afraid there's no joke. The feather was a huge lemon-yellow one."

"So what did you do?"

Maddie smiled. If he was curious enough, perhaps she could use that against him. She'd already sensed that his male pride was a good lever as well. When she'd teased him about being clueless on the book, he'd all but vibrated with sensual menace. It had made her heart pound.

"Come inside," she offered slyly, "and I'll tell you."

"Said the spider to the fly?"

Maddie gave him a cocky grin. "Afraid of getting eaten?"

His eyes heated, grew even more intense. "A double entendre if ever I heard one."

"I'm surprised you realized it, after all your admitted confusion about things sexual."

His teeth locked with a snap. "That sounds like a challenge."

"So it is." Annie had sworn to Maddie that forced seduction worked quite well on men. It certainly had worked for Annie! Guy had been resisting her for years, but once Annie got him alone and she could have her way with him...

Maddie grinned at the thought of having her way with Max. After she got him in the door, she'd make her move.

Max pulled into her parking garage and turned off his truck. Cleo was none too happy with the situation at all, and her menace was aimed at Maddie. The thick fur around her miniscule head bristled and stood on end. Maddie patted it back down, knowing good and well how important styled hair was to a female, even a mean female dog.

Through the impromptu grooming, Maddie continued to grin. Or was a grin considered a leer when one had lascivious thoughts on her mind? And how could her thoughts be any other way when Max was sitting beside her? He smelled good, his hot scent detectable even over the heavier smell of wet dog. And he looked good, his dark hair clinging to the back of his neck, his damp shirt showing off an impressive array of chest and shoulder muscles.

He was surprisingly kind for a Lothario, strong and gentle and understanding with Cleo, patient with Maddie herself.

Max smiled at how silly Cleo looked with her fur parted in the middle and brushed to the sides. Then he sighed in resignation. "So tell me, Maddie. What are we having for dinner?"

Maddie thought about saying *beefcake*, but curbed herself in time. Her mind moving a mile a minute, she climbed out of the truck while Max unlatched the dog and hooked Cleo's leash onto her collar. "How about chicken? I can cook that pretty quick." And then they could get onto better things.

"Chicken is fine."

Cleo woofed, for once in agreement. Her vocabulary, Maddie thought, was surprisingly varied. "We'll have to debone yours, girl. I wouldn't want you to strangle on a bone."

Max paused with Cleo held high in his arms. "You intend to feed Cleo, too?"

Appalled that he would suggest otherwise, Maddie said, "I certainly wouldn't eat in front of her!"

"And you'll even debone her meat?"

Maddie shuddered. "Can you imagine how she'd look gagging on a chicken bone?" She shuddered. "Please Max, it's not a pretty picture."

Max smiled. Then his smile spread and the next thing Maddie knew he was laughing.

"What?" His laughter had a curious effect on her, warming her from the inside out, making her toes curl. She led the way through the parking garage to the building entrance, while Max continued to carry Cleo rather than let her walk. Cleo looked as if it were perfectly natural for him to cart her around in such a grand style.

"Maddie."

His voice was so soft, so compelling, Maddie froze, then shivered. If he could do so much with just a word, she could only imagine what he'd do with his hands, his mouth.

"Are you sure you're against marriage?"

Looking at Max over her shoulder, Maddie saw his teasing smile, the sexy twinkle in his dark eyes, and she waved off his comment. Everything his sister had told her proved Max was a confirmed bachelor who intended to remain that way.

According to Annie, women chased Max daily, beautiful women, young women, mature women, wealthy women and women of lesser means. He'd traveled the world and everywhere he went, women wanted him.

Yet Max was still single.

That said a lot. And it told her that if she wished to gain her education, she'd have to keep things casual.

"Oh, I imagine I'll make a fine wife *someday*. But not for a long, long time."

"So if you don't want marriage, what *do* you want?"

Keeping her back to him, Maddie said, "To understand the attraction of a feather. To understand the lure of sex." She took a deep breath. "To notch my bedpost."

There was a pause behind her, no footsteps, no breathing. Even Cleo was silent. In a rush, Max again caught up. He didn't say another word.

She reached her door on the second floor, well aware of the fact that Max had carried fat Cleo up the stairs and still he wasn't breathing hard. He was in such superb shape.

She could barely wait to get a bird's-eye view of his body.

"Here we are," she said, trying to sound cheerful instead of triumphant. She stepped inside and waited, ready to pounce the moment she had the door closed behind him, barring his escape.

But Max hesitated on her doorstep.

"It just occurred to me," he said, looking down at Cleo who stared back in unblinking worship. "I should let her take care of business first. I wouldn't want her messing your apartment."

Maddie nearly panicked. Was he trying to escape already? And she hadn't even tried anything yet! Maybe she had come on too strong, maybe she shouldn't have mentioned that part about notching…

But then Max said, "You should change out of those wet clothes. We'll be back in five minutes or so."

Some of the tension eased from her muscles. He sounded sincere enough. "All right. I'll leave the door unlocked for you."

His eyes narrowed. "As soon as I get back, you can start explaining."

He made it sound like a threat, but Maddie was just glad he'd promised to come back.

The second he was down the stairs, she ran into her bedroom and shuffled through her closet, wondering what to change into. Not another pair of ultra tight jeans, she decided, unwilling to take the risk of a new rip. Tearing her clothes had *not* been part of the plan.

Of course, slamming into a closed door hadn't been on the agenda either. Still, she was working with what she had.

For late April it could still get cool, so she decided against a sundress, and instead pulled out a snug, long sleeved dress of beige cotton. It fell to midcalf, but hugged her bottom and her breasts. Across the bodice was a colorful mauve rose and the words In Full Bloom. And on the back, Freshly Plucked.

She rushed to the mirror, then gasped at her bedraggled appearance. It was a toss up who looked worse—her or Cleo. She grabbed a comb and attempted to get the tangles out of her hair in record time.

She heard the front door open and close. "Maddie?"

"Be right there." Quickly, she creamed off her ruined makeup and opted not to bother with more. She'd heard sex, when done right, was a hot, sweaty business. Surely Max would do it right, so perhaps makeup would be useless anyway.

Trying to look sexy and tempting, she floated out of the bedroom toward where Max stood at her picture window overlooking the main street. Both he and the dog were now more wet than ever. Cleo saw her first and got so outraged at the sight of her that she began bouncing as well as barking.

Max turned and attempted to calm the dog. *"Cleo."* Then he caught sight of Maddie and whatever else he'd intended to say never came out. She was sure she saw him gulp.

Cleo subsided, but not without a lot of grumbling. Almost defiantly, she went to Maddie's old, floral couch and climbed up—with a lot of effort—to spread out full length on the cushions. Even as her eyes closed, she continued to snarl.

Max cleared his throat. "I'm sorry. I'll get her down…"

"She's fine."

"She's wet."

Maddie shrugged. "The cushion covers are washable." Maddie looked at the dog, so worn out from all her nastiness and her fright of the storm. Even in her exhaustion, with her eyes closed and her round body looking like a boneless pile of scruffy fur with a head, her teeth showed in a low warning growl.

Maddie's heart softened. Speaking softly so as not to disturb Cleo, Maddie asked, "Do you think she's cold? I could get her an old blanket."

Looking a little bemused, Max walked toward Maddie. "She's got plenty of fur to keep her warm." Max stopped about a foot in front of her, well within range, she decided. Doing her best to repress all her old inhibitions, Maddie thought of what she might learn tonight. Never again would a man take her by surprise with his sexual preferences—like yellow feathers. She looked at Max's mouth for added courage, took a couple of deep breaths, then launched herself at him.

Taken off guard, Max fell back a step with the impact of her body. "What the—"

Maddie clasped his face, held on tight and found his mouth with her own.

Not bad at all, Maddie thought, and scoffed at her initial hesitation. He tasted even better than she expected. He tasted of experience, of sin incarnate, of a man who knew what he was about. A man who loved women and his dog.

He tasted hot.

Maddie waited for raging lust to take control of Max's body. She waited for his sexual instincts to kick in. Her ex had always told her that men could only take so much provocation, which was why he'd been driven to cheat.

So she waited.

Then she felt Max's smile against her mouth.

Well heck! Maddie opened her eyes to look at him. Not only wasn't he overcome with lust, it appeared he was about to laugh.

MAX'S FIRST thought was that she knew next to nothing about kissing, and his second was how soft she felt. His third thought was that if Cleo woke up, there'd be hell to pay.

Cleo didn't like other females to touch him.

Of course, the fact that she had gone to sleep in a stranger's place showed she was somewhat at ease with the newly introduced woman, and that shocked the hell out of Max.

If only Maddie wasn't against marriage.

Max held still, a little surprised, a little amused, a little turned on. He didn't kiss Maddie back as she smooshed her mouth against his, but neither did he push her away. He smiled, thinking how determined she seemed.

Around panting breaths, Maddie asked, "What's wrong?"

The words brushed his lips, heated with excitement, touched with anxiety. It was a potent combination. Max clasped her shoulders and held her back enough that he could breathe. "Oh, did you require my participation?"

"Well..." She looked uncertain. "Yeah."

He couldn't stop himself from caressing her, feeling the smallness of her bones, her softness. For such a gutsy, outspoken woman she was amazingly lacking in knowledge. "I take it my sister has been filling your head with her astounding seduction tactics?"

Maddie nodded.

It was almost laughable, only he couldn't quite seem to get so much as a chuckle past the lump of lust in his throat. It was like the blind leading the blind. "Why, Maddie?"

"Why what?"

"Why are you attacking... I mean *seducing* me?"

She blinked uncertainly. "Because I want you?"

"You aren't sure?" Max struggled to ignore the feel of her soft body against his while he tried to figure out what was going on. Even as brazen as she behaved, Maddie didn't strike him as the type of woman to jump into bed with men she barely knew. Not that he knew her well. But he knew enough. She said she'd been engaged, and he'd already witnessed what a giving, understanding woman she was. She treated Cleo as gently as he did.

Max narrowed his eyes. He was beginning to think he'd been set up from the start.

"I'm positive." She nodded again for good measure. "I want you."

He felt compelled to tell her the obvious. "I know women really well, Maddie."

Her lips parted. "I'm counting on it."

She looked so damn ready, Max shook her. "I mean, you little schemer, that I know when they're conspiring. You, Maddie Montgomery, are up to something."

If a man had written to him in the column with this exact situation, his advice would be to run like hell. But then, Max was only good at giving advice; he'd never been any good at taking it.

Maddie shrugged. "As you said, seduction."

Max was still skeptical. "And that's all?"

She took him completely by surprise when she said, "Why else would I have been out on such a miserable day like today? I planned the whole thing. Well, not the *whole* thing. I hadn't figured on hitting a closed door and ending up at your feet, or having my clothes play peekaboo. I just thought, what with the rain and all, I'd be stranded and you could offer me a ride home...."

"And we'd end up exactly where we are?"

"Sorta. I had figured on having you naked and in my bed by now."

Max forced himself to laugh. A nice, hearty male laugh of superiority that hid his surge of lust. "Your plans went a tad awry, didn't they?"

"I wanted to meet you face to face. After all the wonderful stories Annie's told me about you, I already felt like I knew you. I definitely knew I wanted you. So I suppose I can't complain."

She just kept knocking him off guard, Max thought, disgruntled. "So you didn't really want the book at all?" He was almost relieved. The thought of any woman reading such a ridiculous text made him shudder.

"Of course I want the book. It sounds fascinating and I'm looking forward to every word."

Max groaned.

Hearing the sound of his frustration, Maddie leaned forward and touched his shoulder, her eyes earnest. "But I wanted to meet you more than I want the book."

Max rubbed a hand across his forehead. "So you could seduce me?"

"Yeah."

Plenty of women had come on to him, but none had thrown themselves against a door, gotten drenched in the rain or cozied up to his dog.

It was the last that was getting to him more than anything else.

It ate him up to see how loving she could be; she was just what Cleo needed—another person to care about her, to make her feel loved. Yet Maddie said she didn't want marriage. What a situation. A suitable woman was close at hand, begging for sex, loving his dog, and Max felt forced to reject her because she didn't want a lasting relationship. Talk about the vagaries of fate!

"It occurs to me," Max pointed out, "that you could have just about any man. You're attractive—"

"Why thank you."

"And nicely built."

She beamed at him.

"So why chase me?"

Maddie took another step closer to him. "Because you're not just any man, Max. You're a man of experience, a man with an awesome reputation. I've been good all my life and look what it got me. A guy who preferred kinky feathers to me. Now I want to know about feathers! I want to know...*everything*."

"I hate to break it to you, but feathers aren't really all that kinky."

"You didn't see where she was tickling him!"

Max coughed, then decided to let that one go. "So, you want to use me to notch your bedpost, huh?"

She bobbed her head, her look endearingly sincere.

The idea should have been appealing to just about any red-blooded male, so why did Max feel so offended?

"All because your idiot fiancé fooled around on you?"

"It was so humiliating. I just didn't have the experience to deal with it, so I stammered and stuttered and made an idiot of myself." She shuddered with the memory. "I wish I had just left him tied there."

Her grumbling tone made Max smile. "What *did* you do?"

She snorted. "I'm ashamed to say I just stood there, staring. I couldn't think of a single word to say, and then the woman screeched and grabbed her coat and ran off."

"Just like that?"

Maddie nodded. "She left the feather behind. Troy was, as I'm sure you'll understand, in a rather awkward position."

Now that was a picture Max could enjoy. It was no less than the dishonorable blockhead deserved. "How long did you make him suffer?"

Maddie blushed.

"Maddie?" Max bent to see her averted face. True, he hadn't known her long. But he had a gut feeling that despite her declaimed lack of experience with such situations, Maddie would have found a way of getting even. "C'mon. Give."

She cleared her throat. "I went out to dinner."

Max grinned, pleased by her creativity.

"And a movie," she added with a wince.

Laughing, Max asked, "What'd you see?"

"I don't remember. I barely paid any attention. I was just trying to decide how to get Troy out of my apartment." She peeked up at him, all big blue eyes and innocence. "I thought about calling a friend to untie him, but then I didn't think Guy would appreciate it if I asked Annie to get that close—"

"No! That would have been a bad idea."

"I know. You're protective of your sister. I think that's nice." She patted his chest absently in approval, then said, "I finally just decided that I had to be adult enough to deal with it. So I went back. Troy started cursing me and threatening me the second I walked in, so I went to the kitchen and got a big butcher knife."

"You didn't...?" Max saw her wicked smile and relaxed.

"Scare him to death? Sure. It was no more than he deserved. He went from cursing to pleading. But then when I cut his right hand free and he realized he was safe enough, he went right back to being obnoxious."

Max saw something in her eyes, something wounded. Of course her vanity had been crushed. Gently, he touched her chin. "What did he say to you?"

"Typical drivel coming from a man who's had to hold his bladder for four and a half hours. He blamed me for everything." She shrugged. "Not woman enough, not sexy enough, too naive, too prim, blah, blah, blah."

Max flexed his fists, wishing he could get alone with the jerk for just a few minutes. It was no wonder Maddie was out to prove her sexuality. "I hope you didn't give his words a second thought."

She shook her head. "He was scum and I told him so. It took a lot of nerve for him to try to fob the guilt off on me." Her face red, Maddie started to raise her voice, and Cleo yawned. She cast an affectionate glance at the dog and began whispering again. "I decided to look at the nasty scene—and the nasty man—as an omen."

Max was touched by her feminine strength. No doubt about it, Maddie Montgomery was one helluva woman. "An omen, huh? How so?"

"Troy's faux pas was nature's way of telling me that I need to expand my horizons before I think about settling down. Without experience, it's no wonder I made such a bad mate choice. I mean, it takes practice to figure out what you really want. And with more experience, I'll be better able to empa-thize on the job with the women I talk to, and better equipped to handle the men I might see in the future."

"I see." He didn't see at all, and he didn't like the idea of her with other men. "You want to start practicing with me?"

Looking pleased that he understood, Maddie smiled. "Yes! You'll be the first of my wild oats!"

A thought occurred to Max. "Will you tell your fiancé what you're doing?"

"No, why?" She appeared puzzled by the question. "And Troy's not my fiancé anymore. He's an ex. What I do or don't do isn't any of his business."

"Are you sure you aren't planning to make him jealous?" Not that he'd blame her, Max thought, but he hoped she was well and truly over the fool.

"Well, I'd certainly accomplish that! I mean, look at you." Her gaze drifted over Max from sternum to knees, like a sen-suous lick. She took a deep breath that mirrored his own. "You'd sure make any guy jealous."

"Uh, thank you."

Maddie shook herself. "But that's not what I'm going to do. Why should I? I'm not an idiot. Troy can indulge in all the feather tickling he wants, so long as he does it away from me. He's of no concern to me at all anymore."

Max accepted her sincerity.

"But," she added, "if you're worried about getting into a hostile confrontation with him, you don't need to be. I would never let him bother you, I promise."

Max immediately rebelled. "I wasn't worried about a con-frontation and I certainly don't need you to protect me." He probably weighed a hundred pounds more than Maddie, and he sure as hell wasn't concerned about some idiot who in-dulged a feather fetish.

Maddie patted his chest again, then caressed him, then sighed. "I understand. You're a lover, not a fighter." Her patting hand was now stroking, driving him to distraction. "But that's all I want you for anyway, so it's not a problem."

That was *all* she wanted him for? How insulting! He was good for more than just sex, dammit. Feeling more like his dog by the second, Max growled, "I am *not* afraid of a fight."

"Shh." She attempted to soothe him, her small hands gliding over his chest, lower...

Max caught her wrists. He was breathing hard, his muscles aching. She stirred him, aroused him and annoyed him. "Dammit, Maddie." How the hell did she affect him so easily?

There was no easy way to break it to her, except to be brutally honest. The sooner the better, before he lost his thin hold on control. "I'm sorry, sweetheart, but the simple fact of the matter is, I'm not interested."

She snorted. "Yeah right. Annie says you're always interested."

He would strangle Annie when next he saw her. "Maybe a month ago I would have been. But things have changed."

Maddie's face fell. "You don't want me."

He cupped her cheek, let his thumb brush the soft fullness of her lower lip. "Oh, I want you all right. You can be sure of that." Max felt her uncertainty all the way to his bones. Here he was, shaking with lust, and she doubted her allure.

She stared at him, not comprehending for a long moment, and then suddenly she smacked her head. "I understand now!"

He almost hated to ask. Her assumptions had been so far off the mark all along, he wasn't sure he wanted to hear her newest revelation concerning his character. Resigned, he asked, "What is it you think you understand this time?"

"When we were discussing the book! You were totally confused about the whole thing."

"I was not."

"Don't look so indignant." She gave him a pitying look. "I know how reputations can get blown all out of proportion. I should have realized that no man could be so awesomely adept. It's almost absurd."

Max was ready to defend his awesome adeptness, but Maddie wasn't done explaining things to him.

"You don't have to worry about my expectations, Max. If you don't know everything, that's okay. It's not like I'm going to keep a scorecard. Heck, I don't know much, either, so I doubt I'd even notice if you screw up."

For the first time in years, embarrassed heat ran up the back of his neck. "Why, you little—"

She waved away his umbrage. "I'm sure we'll muddle through." Then, as if getting a brainstorm, she added, "The book could probably help! Besides, I just want to experiment and you're gorgeous and there must be at least a little truth to your reputation, right? So I know I'll be inspired."

Max saw her through a red haze. He squeezed the words out of his tight throat. "You expect us to...muddle through?"

"If need be, you can just lie there. I won't expect you to perform."

Max stared at the ceiling while he counted to ten. And then to twenty. Oh, it was *so* damn tempting to show her everything he knew, methods of seduction he'd learned in foreign countries and at home, all the different ways he could make her body sing.

And all the ways he could make her beg.

Men who read his column wrote to him for advice, and got the very best. Then women sent him letters of gratitude.

And this woman expected him to *muddle through?*

He met her gaze again, outwardly calm while inside he seethed. "You're not even close, honey."

"Uh-huh."

His temper cracked, then crumbled. "Stop sounding so damn skeptical!"

She pursed her lips in a wasted attempt at obedience. Max wasn't sure if he wanted to kiss her or throttle her. Both choices seemed equally appealing. "I have valid reasons," he managed to say with a semblance of calm, "for not wanting to get into another purely sexual relationship, and not one of them has to do with lack of expertise or fear of a physical confrontation."

"Is that right?"

"Damn right."

"And those reasons are?"

Max opened his mouth twice, but nothing came out. What could he possibly tell her? That he wanted to settle down for his dog? That one mangy beat-up mutt—a mutt now snuffling and snoring loudly on the couch—had accomplished what no woman could?

Even to his own mind, it sounded ludicrous.

He stalled for time until his brain started functioning again, then said with laudable nonchalance, "I don't travel anymore."

That took the wind out of her sails. "Why ever not?"

"I've been just about everywhere, seen just about everything."

She looked fascinated, a sentiment that reflected his own when it came to exploring the world. "Annie says you sometimes stayed gone for months. How did you support yourself?"

Such a personal question, although he appreciated her candor, her honest interest. "I worked."

"In foreign countries?"

"And in the States." He shrugged as he explained, "There's always something to be done, new building efforts in war-torn or natural disaster areas, odd jobs here and there. I've signed on to fishing vessels and cargo ships and done excursions for tourist kayaking in Alaska. And I've been an interpreter at the Olympic Games in Japan."

Her eyes were so huge, so impressed, Max felt himself puffing up. The only thing he'd ever missed in all his traveling was someone to share it with. He wondered if Maddie knew how much money he'd saved over the years, that he thrived on traveling without luxuries, living off the land instead. It was a cheap way to go, and because of that, he had quite a healthy savings account.

"Recently I decided it was time to settle down. And," Max said, expounding on his explanation though he wasn't certain why, "I have new responsibilities that keep me closer to home."

Her mouth formed an O. "Annie said something about Guy needing you to take your rightful place in the family company, but she didn't think you ever would. I'm glad she was wrong. She said it really hurt your father that you didn't want any part of the business."

Poleaxed, Max went speechless. It was true that Guy had asked him to come to work in the company, but he'd repeatedly refused. What could he contribute that his father and Guy hadn't already given? Max would only be another warm body, and there were plenty of those to go around. He had nothing unique, nothing special that the company *needed* from him. In fact, he'd never felt needed there, and he refused to feel needed now just because Guy was marrying.

"Actually," he said, slightly annoyed, "it's not that I have no interest in the company. It's just that I already have a job."

"Doing what?"

Max ignored her. His column was personal, and anonymous. And it took up very little of his time, so it wouldn't be a good example anyway. "With each new development comes another. I'm no longer traveling, and I'm no longer looking for meaningless relationships."

She drew herself up. "I don't think I like being referred to as meaningless."

"I didn't mean…" Max knew if he lived to be a hundred, he'd never be this frustrated again. "Maddie, getting together just to notch bedposts would be meaningless."

"A relationship based on devastating sex would be very meaningful to me!"

Exasperated, Max said, "So now I'm supposed to make the sex devastating when seconds ago you promised me I could just lie there?"

She blinked in surprise, then shrugged. "So I lied. I was trying to convince you. Truth is, I want you mobile and participating."

"You want me to be devastating?"

"Could you?"

Max almost smiled at the sweet, polite way she asked that. Droll, now that he felt in better control, he said, "It'd be a tall order—not that I'm not up to it, you understand."

"I'm not sure what to understand! One minute you claim all this great prowess, and the next you're running shy and saying you're not interested in a sexy affair."

"To a man who's had his fill of them," Max explained with ruthless and entirely false candor, "it sounds boring." She started to speak again, so he reiterated, "I-am-not-interested."

"I don't believe you."

Stubbornness made her eyes darken to midnight blue. Max cursed because he found her expression oddly appealing. Would her eyes go that dark when she was in the throes of a climax? When he was buried deep inside her?

Would she be this talkative, this argumentative, in bed? Or would she be sweetly submissive when he gave her the awesome sex she'd requested?

Those thoughts caused him to overstep himself, to admit more than he'd intended. "Look, it's not like I said I was becoming a monk or something. It's just that I want to settle down, to find a wife—"

She slapped her hand over his mouth. "That's not funny!"

Max pried her hand away, noticing how slim and cool her fingers felt in his. "Not funny, but true. I want a wife."

"Then why aren't you married already? According to Annie, women throw themselves at you."

"I have very precise requirements."

Chapter Three

MAX CREPT UP behind her, determined to set her straight, to make her learn the error of taunting his testicularity, which he had in spades. Hell, he *oozed* testicularity, blast her—and the loyal followers of his column could swear to it.

She was still unaware of his approach when Max whispered near her ear, "You could hardly scare me off when you kiss like a nervous schoolgirl."

Maddie gasped, her shoulders stiffening.

It was his own form of attack, and though he'd only known her a few short hours, he already knew she had pride and gumption—which was why she was determined to win with him. Her fiancé had wounded her, and she wanted to reassure herself the only way she knew how.

It was a contradiction of sorts, but he was glad she'd chosen him rather than some other man. The thing to do now was to reel her in for more than a quick tussel.

"I never claimed to be overly experienced," she stated, then asked worriedly, "Was I really that bad?"

"You showed no subtlety, sweetheart. No finesse." Determined to hide the tenderness he felt, Max added, "I felt mauled."

She started to turn to face him, but Max caught her shoulders and held her still. "Don't berate me. You claimed I was

"Oh."

She looked crestfallen, but he had no idea why. "I'm sorry to disappoint you, sweetheart. I really am."

He started to tell her she'd have no problem finding someone else to play with, but the words stuck in his craw. She shouldn't be playing with anyone. She should be a man's wife so she could share all that fire, all that caring, for a lifetime, not just for the duration of an affair.

Maddie turned around and paced away. Max watched the slight sway and bounce of her rounded behind, the way her hips moved seductively, and called himself ten times a fool. The woman was delectable, no doubt about it.

He also reread the decorative letters on her back. *Freshly Plucked.*

Just what the hell did that mean?

"If you want to get married," she said, sounding strangled, "that's fine with me. Hey, more power to you. But why not have fun until you've found your paragon to wed? Unless of course—" She didn't turn to face him while she made her gibe "—I managed to scare you off?"

She waited, not looking at him, and even though Max knew it was a tactic meant to make him relent, he couldn't stand the challenge. She'd struck at the core of his manhood one time too many.

It was past time he got control not only of his raging libido, but little Maddie Montgomery as well.

running scared, but you know that's not true. In fact, I'd say you're the overly nervous one, given the awkward, rushed way you jumped my bones."

"They're such nice bones, Max, I couldn't resist."

With comments like that, *she* was the one who was hard to resist!

Hesitation lacing her voice, she said, "I promise I'll control myself in the future."

Max didn't really want her to control herself. No, he wanted to get to know her better, to talk to her—and *then* she could jump his bones.

He needed to find a way to make her feel as intrigued as he did. He needed her to want more from him than just his sexual techniques—stellar as he knew those to be.

Close to her ear, he whispered, "I'm not afraid of any woman putting her hands on me. That's not it at all. In fact, I already told you the reason—lack of interest in a brief fling." He could feel her tension, her excitement, vibrating all along his nerve endings.

He stroked her arm. "But now I feel challenged to set you straight on your assumptions."

He heard her swallow. Good. "Should I demonstrate my lack of reserve, Maddie?"

Expecting outrage at his taunt, she surprised him by saying, "Yes."

Laughing softly at her wholehearted agreement, anticipating his little lesson more than he should have, Max bent to press his mouth to the side of her throat in a barely there kiss. He was starting to realize that Maddie would always manage to take him by surprise. It wasn't an unpleasant realization.

"Always go slow," Max whispered. "It helps to heighten the expectation."

He kissed her again, this time letting his tongue slip over her madly racing pulse. Her need to reassert herself, to prove her appeal, was mixed with the sweetest vulnerability he'd ever witnessed. She was audacious but caring, honest and earthy. Her skin was warm and getting warmer by the second, and she tasted nice.

Maddie braced her hands, fingers spread wide, on the wall in front of her. Max saw that she was trembling and more than anything he wanted to simply hug her, to tell her that there was no real rush. But he gave her just a little of what she'd asked for instead. With any luck, she'd realize on her own that a little more time would only make things better.

He skimmed her ear, his tongue briefly touching just inside, teasing. He heard her breath catch.

"You put your tongue in my ear!"

Max hesitated. "Yes."

Her sigh was long and heartfelt. "That was…nice. I hadn't realized…"

Shaking his head at her ex-fiancé's apparent stupidity, Max licked her ear again. Goose bumps raised on her skin. "A smart man always knows to take his time. The more frenzied stuff," he breathed, "can come later."

"More frenzied stuff?"

Her voice was hopeful. Max peeked at her face and saw that her eyes were squeezed shut. He smiled, and loosened her right hand from the wall. Lacing his fingers with hers, he brought her hand up to his mouth. "Sexual tension should build and build, and yes, it often ends up frenzied. Didn't you and your fiancé…?"

"Ex-fiancé. Yes, we did, but it wasn't *frenzied.* More like…" She searched for a word, then settled on, "Mundane." Her voice was low, breathy. "I guess I liked it okay."

Max vowed she wouldn't be left in his bed *liking it okay.*

Her hand tightened on his. "The thing is, Annie swears to me—"

"Forget about my sister and whatever harebrained things she told you. Annie likely has even less experience than you." Under his breath, Max muttered, "Or at least she did before Guy succumbed."

"She's read a lot of books," Maddie pointed out.

"And has been suggesting them to you?"

"Yes, but I like the idea of firsthand experience much better."

I just bet you do, Max thought, then got started on his instruction again. "Never neglect the less obvious places."

"Okay, right." She looked at him over her shoulder. "What less obvious places?"

Biting back a chuckle, Max cuddled her closer to his body. He drifted his free hand up to cup just below the soft weight of her left breast. "Everyone knows that women's breasts are sensitive, right?"

"Yes."

Max could feel her heartbeat thumping, knew she was nervous because despite her bravado, she wasn't accustomed to throwing herself at men. If her fiancé hadn't done her wrong, she wouldn't be here now.

Slowly, tantalizingly, he coasted his fingers down to her belly. "And here." Damn, she felt wonderful. Soft and firm and her musky female scent was beginning to get to him. Her hair, still slightly damp, felt cool and silky against his jaw. Max was aware of her stomach muscles clenching, of her suspended breathing.

"And lower?" she rasped hopefully, bringing him out of his fog of sexual need.

"Definitely lower." His voice was too rough, too affected by her nearness. "But that comes much, much later." Like in a week or more, he thought, if he could last that long! "There are other places to visit first, places that can really excite, too."

"But not like lower." She tried to sound insistent and even went so far as to squirm against him.

She sorely tested his resolve. But Max could hear Cleo

snoring in the background, which helped to keep his purpose at the forefront of his mind. Cleo needed a stable home, and Maddie seemed perfect to assist in that. She was the only woman he'd ever met who'd understood the dog right off. She'd make a perfect mother for Cleo.

Max wanted to move slowly enough that Maddie would insist on seeing him again. And again, until she got over her determination to be footloose and fancy-free. Until she was ready to go one further and really get to know him.

Max smiled. "Let me show you something." He lifted her arm and slowly kissed her wrist, deliberately leaving it damp from his tongue.

"Okay," she gasped, "that's great. But—"

Before she could continue, he kissed her palm, gently stroking with the very tip of his tongue, again leaving her heated skin damp, letting his warm breath fan the spot.

She gave a humming response.

He wanted to show her how nice going slow could be, but he didn't want to get overly intimate doing it. Cautiously, deliciously, Max sucked her middle finger into his mouth.

Maddie nearly jumped out of his arms. *"Oh my."*

He wrapped his tongue around her finger and tugged. Kissing her, experiencing her unrehearsed response, was a distinct joy. He wanted more, of her body, her time. Her affection for his dog.

And he always got what he wanted, one way or another.

Shifting restlessly, Maddie pressed her bottom into his growing erection. "Max," she breathed.

Realizing he'd gone a little too far, that she'd been more susceptible to his brief seduction than he'd expected, Max released her and stepped back. He had to catch her so she wouldn't fall.

Stumbling around, Maddie faced him. "You *have* read the book," she accused. Her eyes were heavy, her face flushed. "You know exactly what you're doing."

Max caught her gaze and held it. "I don't need to read the damn book."

She didn't look convinced. "Whatever. It doesn't matter to me, as long as you agree to a fling with me."

One side of his mouth kicked up into a regretful grin. She was so persistent and so entertaining. And so sweet. He wanted to say yes. "I already explained that I can't."

Shoulders stiff, lips tight, she said, "You're a tease, Max Sawyers!" Her face flushed darkly and her eyes glittered. "They surely have a name for men like you."

"Yeah," Max said. "It's 'experienced.'" He refused to take all the blame when she'd more or less dared him. And besides, it had only been her finger he kissed, not all the places where he really wanted to put his mouth.

His heart kick-started with that thought.

While Max watched, that calculating look came into her eyes and they narrowed, the blue getting brighter, hotter. She was so easy to read.

Sort of.

"I believe you're more than up to it."

Max bowed his head, a man accepting female accolades. "Of course." Now all he needed was for her to agree to his terms.

"And it's obvious you're not immune to me as a woman." Her gaze dropped to his lap, a look that was nearly tactile and as hot as a live flame. "I mean, I don't think you're carrying a roll of dimes in your pocket, are you?"

Forget his terms! Max's growl of outrage sounded in the room. "A *roll of dimes?*"

She shrugged.

"More like a flashlight!"

"Size, I assume," she said with a sniff, "is in the eye of the beholder."

"And you haven't beheld a damn thing yet, so don't go calling a man's business 'small.'" With a low growl, Max considered showing her just how impressive his... No, bad thought. He was struggling to resist her, not give in to her.

Maddie stared at him hard, knowing she'd almost won. "Small, large, it doesn't matter when you continue to refuse my very nice offer."

It *was* a nice offer, Max conceded, and just a few months ago he'd have accepted without hesitation. "Why such a rush, Maddie?" he asked, buying himself time to think.

That endearing vulnerability flashed into her gaze again before she squelched it with a come-hither look. "I'm twenty-six. I've been good all my life and now all I've got to show for it is a broken engagement that I'd rather forget and a lot of time on my hands."

"So why pick me?" Max hoped to hear something complimentary, something meaningful.

He was doomed to disappointment.

"I know all about you! Annie has told me so much. Ever since I met her, I've been enthralled with the stories about you. You're everything I'm not."

That surprised him. "Like what?"

"Exciting, experienced, daring. I've lived my whole life being a Goody Two-Shoes, and in my profession, that isn't really a plus. Evidently it wasn't a plus in my personal life, either."

"Your broken engagement," Max said gently, "is a blessing, I'd say."

"And I agree! But now that I'm free, it only makes sense to gain my own experiences. As you suggested, I'll have a better perspective for the job, and I'll have fun, too." She lowered her lashes, her look now timid when she added, "Besides, I sort of feel like I know you, because of Annie. Being with you feels...safe."

Max suddenly realized he was taking the wrong tact with Maddie. She was reacting on the rebound, doing what she could to counteract the embarrassing feather episode. Her haste was probably due in part to the fact that she might chicken out if she didn't rush through things.

Perhaps Maddie would forget about the *brief* part of the fling if he showed her how sexually satisfying a real relationship would be.

That idea appealed a whole lot more than walking away did. He didn't want to walk away; he *did* want to make love to her.

Why not? Maddie suited his criteria. She did her best to nurture his dog, she wanted lots of sex, and she was cute to boot.

He'd be holding up his promise to Cleo, and satisfying himself in the bargain. What more could a guy ask for?

He needed more time to consider the possibility of roping Maddie into marriage, but he had a gut feeling that once she was roped, she'd be incredibly loyal and giving. And she'd love Cleo. Maybe she'd even learn to love him.

That thought was far too heavy for his peace of mind, so Max decided to just enjoy dinner, and see what happened. For sure, Maddie wouldn't bore him.

Then his gaze again drifted to Maddie's breasts, and he got blessedly distracted. "You know, I'm just dying for you to tell me what all these suggestive slogans mean. *In Full Bloom, Freshly Plucked.* And earlier, your shirt said *I Give Good Peach.*"

Since Max was already thinking in possessive terms, jealousy nudged him and he asked darkly, "Do you want to have an affair with *me,* or are you hoping to turn on the entire male population?"

MADDIE ATTEMPTED to calm the mad gallop of her heartbeat. But it wasn't easy because Max was staring at her breasts and even though he sounded unaccountably annoyed, his rough voice stroked over her sensitized nerve endings like a slow kiss.

The way he'd touched her... Her finger would never feel the same. Even now, she realized she was holding it out apart from the rest of her hand. It was still damp, still tingling.

It was just a damn finger.

Maddie cleared her throat, determined to be as cavalier as Max. "Bea, one of the women I work with at the clinic, creates slogans for clothes." Talking normally was difficult, but Maddie thought she managed credibly.

"This was one for a florist, and a big hit, I might add. It was used as a giveaway when you ordered a certain amount of flowers and it drew in a lot of the younger crowd. Wedding orders came in like crazy."

Dryly, Max said, "I can imagine."

"The other one was for an independent company that created specialty jams."

"Specialty, as in peach jam?"

"That's right. And passion fruit—the slogan for that one is awesome—and kiwi, and wild blackberry, too." Maddie looked down at the dress that she knew complimented her figure but hadn't been enough to win Max over. "I think the slogans are nice."

"I think they sound downright nasty."

Maddie laughed at that, then dredged up another taunt. With any luck, he'd decide to prove himself to her again. "To a man who's afraid to submit to his baser side, it makes sense that the slogans would intimidate you."

Far from appearing amorous, Max looked ready to strangle her. "I am not intimidated!"

Maddie sighed. She knew he wasn't. He also wasn't the unconscionable playboy she'd imagined. No, Max Sawyers was a gentle man who loved his dog and had an innate honor that caused him to turn her down repeatedly.

He wanted to go slow, but going slow meant getting to know him, and already she liked him far too much. The more time she spent with him, the more risk to her heart.

She didn't want to care about another man. Glancing at Cleo snoring on the couch, Maddie decided it was bad enough to care about a man's dog. If she let it go any further than that, she could end up with her pride butchered beyond repair.

No, she wouldn't allow herself to get roped in like that again. If Troy with his limited experience had played with feathers, there was no telling what a man like Max played with—other than women's hearts. Getting overly involved with him would be like jumping from the frying pan into a raging inferno.

She was just about to let Max off the hook, to concede defeat, when he asked belligerently, "Were you just kidding about dinner, or do you intend to feed me?"

Her spirits lifted. "Can you be bribed with food?"

"No."

Despite her disappointment, she laughed. His honesty delighted her; she knew without a doubt that Max would always be truthful with her; his sister was right about that. He might be a confirmed bachelor, but he was an honorable one. "I'll feed you. Would you like to help me in the kitchen?"

"Will you behave?"

"Heavens, no!" Maddie winked at him, enjoying the banter between them. Never had she carried on so before, and it was fun. Not as much fun as she was sure an affair would be, but still very enjoyable. "I had no idea that becoming a vamp would be so enjoyable."

"You're not a vamp yet, Maddie," Max said with a growl reminiscent of Cleo in a malcontent mood. Not that Cleo appeared to *have* any other moods.

Maddie patted his shoulder. "Come on. You can tell me about your travels while I cook, and we'll both, unfortunately, behave."

An hour later Maddie had dinner ready to be served. Max had surprised her by being more help than she'd expected. Not only wasn't he a shallow playboy with only personal gratification on his mind, but the man knew his way around a kitchen. One more thing to like about him, she thought, and frowned at the idea. Liking him was *not* part of the plan.

As she set the food on the table, Maddie heard a noise from the couch and saw Cleo's nose move first. Then her front left paw. Her stubby legs started jerking as if she were trying to run to the table, but her eyes were still closed.

Maddie laughed out loud. "She's so fat, and still so attuned to the smell of food."

Max grinned, too. Softly, so softly Maddie barely heard, he said, "Cleo," and the dog's small head jerked up, her too large ears rising to attention. "Food," was his only other word, and Cleo instantly lumbered off the couch and to Max's side, to sit next to his chair.

Rubbing the dog's scruff, Max explained, "She was near starved when I found her. Since then, she eats like a glutton."

Hearing that brought a glitter of tears to Maddie's eyes. With a wavering smile, she reprimanded Max. "She's like a little kid with too many treats. Sometimes overindulgence isn't the best way to prove love. Look at her. She needs more exercise and less food. Or at least buy her food that won't make her any heftier."

So saying, Maddie began cutting up some skinless chicken into bite-size pieces. Max watched her with a curious little grin on his face. "You should have a dog of your own, Maddie."

"I would if I could afford one," she assured him. For the longest time she'd wanted a dog and a cat and a house—and a husband and children of her own. Maddie shook her head—that plan had come and gone. She said negligently, hiding the remnant of longing, "My salary doesn't allow for a lot of extras. And I'd never get a dog if I couldn't take care of her properly."

Max said nothing to that, but he had a strange look on his face.

"C'mere girl," Maddie called, then set the plate on the floor. When Cleo growled and snarled her way over to her, Maddie smoothed down her fur. "I think the local pet shop sells special food for overweight dogs."

Max shook his head. "She doesn't like dog food."

"Then disguise it with some chicken or something she does like for a while. You know it's best for her."

His gaze locked on hers, Max said quietly, "I can't believe you're really worried about her."

"Who knows," Maddie said around a laugh, "maybe her disposition will improve when she feels healthier. Do you walk her every day?"

"In the park."

Giving her attention to her plate so Max wouldn't see her yearning, Maddie said offhandedly, "Maybe I could join you both sometime."

"Maybe."

Jerking her head up, Maddie stared at him. "You mean it?"

"Sure, why not? You, Maddie Montgomery, just keep amazing me."

Why that made her blush, Maddie didn't know. It probably had something to do with the way he said it, with a hint of admiration and a look of lust in his eyes. At least to her it looked like lust. Not that she was an expert, just very, very hopeful.

She also wasn't used to praise, and certainly not that kind of praise. So she amazed him, hmm? "Enough to give in? Enough to put me out of my misery, to want to be the first notch on my bedpost?"

To her amazement, he didn't immediately refuse. Instead, Max thoughtfully chewed a bite of chicken, then swallowed a drink of milk before finally saying, "It's possible."

Maddie's eyes widened until she thought they'd drop out of her head. *It's possible* was a whole lot more encouraging than *I'm not interested.* Progress, she decided, and throughout the rest of the meal, she barely tasted her food.

Once Cleo realized the food was all gone and the humans wouldn't be handing her any more scraps, she slunk off to sleep on the couch again. Maddie watched her go, noticing that she moved even slower now than she had before being fed. When she lay down, her body looked twice as wide, spread out on Maddie's couch. Cleo was one lazy dog.

"What are you thinking, Maddie?"

Red with guilt, Maddie turned to Max and admitted, "I was thinking of conniving a way to get Cleo on a diet."

Rather than being angry or insulted, he nodded. "Good luck. If you can find a way to get her to eat the good stuff, I'd be indebted. My vet mentioned a diet last time we were in—"

At the word "vet," Cleo jerked awake, then fell off the couch during a vehement snarling jag. She looked surprised and embarrassed to find herself sprawled on the floor.

Max just shook his head, but Maddie leaped from the table and ran to the distraught dog. Despite Cleo's furious barking, Maddie cuddled her close and hugged her. "Shh. It's all right."

Cleo, going quiet in a heartbeat, looked as flummoxed as Max. Maddie ignored them both. She hated to see anyone or anything afraid.

She pressed her face against Cleo's scruffy neck and said again, "It's all right."

Very slowly, as if half afraid to move, Cleo began crawling toward Max with her belly scraping the floor. She kept casting worried, suspicious glances at Maddie, and Maddie kept pace with her, scooting along on her knees until they were both at Max's feet.

Maddie released the dog and saw that Cleo was staring up at Max, her expression a request for aid. It was obvious Cleo had no idea how to deal with Maddie's affection, which reminded Maddie of the women she worked with, how they'd first behaved when meeting her.

Many of them had moved on with their lives, happier, more content. The few that Maddie still saw now loved her, as she loved them. She hoped the same outcome was possible with Cleo.

Max laughed out loud and Maddie sat back on her haunches, shaking her head at both dog and man. "She still doesn't trust me."

"I beg to differ. She doesn't know what to make of you at all." Max patted one knee. Maddie started to move, but Cleo beat her to it, and lumbered up onto his lap.

She sighed. Max's lap looked very comfortable. But there wasn't room for both of them.

Cleo gave Max one grateful lick on the chin, then looked back at Maddie with a worried frown. Her furry brows were pinched together, her teeth were showing, but for once, not in a snarl.

"You're covered in dog hair," Max pointed out as his gaze slipped over Maddie's breasts.

"Oh." Maddie looked down and attempted to brush herself off, but the last thing she was concerned with was a few dog hairs.

Setting Cleo aside, Max said, "Go lie down."

Maddie assumed he was speaking to the dog.

Cleo gladly retreated to the couch and again settled herself there, yawning and stretching and sighing in relaxation.

Maddie smiled. "Let's be very careful not to mention that 'v' word again. I don't like seeing her upset."

Without warning, Max caught her beneath her arms and pulled her upward until she was on her knees between his open thighs. It was a very nice place to be. Her face tilted up to his, her hands clasped his shoulders for balance.

Max stared at her mouth, and said huskily, "You've convinced me."

Maddie's heart leaped. She was half-afraid to believe what she hoped he meant by that. "Convinced you...of what?"

"That a sexual fling between us wouldn't be meaningless."

Her fingertips dug into his shoulders—nice solid shoulders—and she held on in case he suddenly changed his mind. "This means you're now willing?"

"Willing, able and anxious."

Ohmigod, ohmigod, ohmigod. "Tonight? Right now?"

Max glanced toward Cleo, heard her snoring, and smiled. "All right," he said gently, and his eyes seemed to be peering into her soul. "If you're certain that's what you want to do."

Maddie was more than certain. She was insistent. Fanatical even. "Yes."

Lifting her, Max brought her face up even with his. The new position caused Maddie's belly to flatten against his groin and she had to swallow back a groan. He was hard again! Or was it that he was hard *still?*

That thought made heat curl through her in dizzying intensity.

Max caught her gaze, refusing to let her look away until the very last second when his mouth touched hers. Her eyes drifted shut. The damp heat of his mouth, the sultry scent of his hard masculine body, the feel of his large rough hands, all consumed her.

Maddie's last thought was: *Finally!* And then she couldn't think at all.

Chapter Four

MAX TASTED HER deeply, ready and willing to fall off the deep end. Damn, he'd had no idea that watching a woman coddle his dog could be such an aphrodisiac. He loved Cleo, had loved her from the second she'd tried to bite him while he carried her off the road. Seeing someone else love her was a heady thing.

He hadn't known anything was missing from his life until he'd brought Cleo home.

He hadn't known anything was *still* missing from his life, until he'd seen Maddie press her face into Cleo's yellow fur and squeeze her so tight that the dog had no breath left to growl.

Cleo had looked helpless against the emotional onslaught. Her feelings had mirrored his own.

Something insidious and sweet and warm expanded in his chest the second Maddie went to her knees by the dog, making Max's heart feel full to bursting.

The more emotional feelings blended with the sharp sexual desire he'd been trying so hard to ignore, leaving him with no way to resist her.

Max's hands trembled as he held Maddie a tiny bit away from him. Her eyes were heavy, sexy, the blue heated to a midnight hue. Damn but he wanted her.

And he knew in his gut that it wasn't just physical desire,

though physically he was so aroused his bragging about a lead pipe earlier was coming back to haunt him. He felt so heavy, his jeans were now painfully tight. But it was more than that; Maddie had nurtured his dog when no other woman even wanted to look at her, much less touch her.

Max had felt the dog's loneliness, her need for love behind her bristled warnings, and Maddie had seen it, too. She was a special woman, too special to let get away. He was already convinced that she'd be perfect to mother his dog. He had a feeling she'd be perfect for him, too. One way or another, he'd convince her to marry him.

What better way to start than by making her body need him?

Max brushed the corner of her mouth with the edge of his rough thumb. "Why don't you go get ready while I put our dishes away? I'll join you in five minutes."

Eyes wide, Maddie asked, "Umm... Get ready?"

She sounded scandalized, and Max couldn't help but grin. "You don't have to put on risqué lingerie or break out the oil. Just get rid of the excess dog hair clinging to your clothes. Maybe turn down the bed. That's all I meant." He added, "Most women like a few seconds alone to themselves."

She stared at him blankly and Max sighed. "You do have some sort of birth control on hand, don't you?"

"Uh..."

Max felt the urge to laugh with disbelief, or shout with frustration. "I gather by your long face that you don't?"

Maddie licked her lips. "I figured you carried condoms."

"Often I do. But not this time." Mostly because he knew the lack of protection would go a long way in deterring him from giving in. He was scrupulous about birth control, and didn't take chances. Period.

But now... "I could run to the drugstore."

Maddie's eyes were hungry as she stared at him. "How long will that take?"

"Half an hour, tops. Why? You have someplace to be?" The

thought that another man might be waiting in the wings tonight did not sit well with Max.

Maddie shook her head so hard her long blond hair whipped against his leg. "No! I'm just..." She shrugged, then gave him a wavering smile. "Impatient."

Max touched her cheek again. He couldn't seem to stop touching her. Her honesty was another turn on, nearly driving him over the edge. "I'll be quick." *As quick as humanly possible!* "I still have your key so I'll let myself back in. Go ahead and get ready and if Cleo wakes up, tell her I'll be right back."

Still she hesitated, and Max asked, "What is it?"

"You won't change your mind while you're gone?"

Tenderness exploded inside Max, mixing with the lust and the other swirl of emotions with combustible force until it was all he could do to force himself to his feet. He needed to join with her, and it was tempting to say to hell with protection. At the moment, lowering her to the floor and taking her right beside the table seemed like a grand idea.

"I won't change my mind," he promised.

The rain poured down in buckets soaking Max to the skin as he dashed to his truck. He drove faster than he should have, but for once it wasn't just Cleo waiting for him. No, now there was an adorable woman who displayed her brazen sexuality as often as she did her naiveté. He could barely wait to take her, to show her what her idiot fiancé obviously hadn't.

The lights from the all-night drugstore barely penetrated the constant rain. By the time Max was back in his truck with the paper bag on the seat beside him, every inch of him was dripping wet. Not that it mattered because he expected to be out of his clothes very soon. He was so hot, it was a wonder he wasn't steaming.

The apartment, as he let himself back inside, was quiet except for Cleo's snoring. Her back paws went through spasmodic jerks and her lips curled in a soundless howl as she dreamed of chasing some hapless critter. Max smiled affectionately.

In some ways, Cleo reminded him of Maddie. She was pushy and insistent one minute, in the next so sweet he wanted simply to hold her all night.

He couldn't hold Maddie all night. He'd have to leave so that Cleo was in her own home come morning. The dog had a problem that he doubted Maddie would care to experience.

If it wasn't for the doggy door Max had installed after the first two days of bringing Cleo home, all the carpets in his house would have been ruined. It wasn't Cleo's fault, so he'd never scolded her. She woke disoriented and nervous, and would run in circles trying to find her way out. Anytime she'd had an accident, she had looked heartsick about it, and strangely enough, embarrassed. So Max had ended up comforting her rather than scolding her.

As soon as Cleo had figured out the doggy door, she'd learned to hold on until she got outside. She'd still run around, baffled for a while, but eventually she'd hit the door and find herself in the backyard where trees and shrubs beckoned.

Max smoothed his hand over the dog, settling her back into a deep sleep without pesky rabbits or birds to provoke her, then he looked toward Maddie's bedroom. A bright light shone from around the partially open door. Max's stomach tightened in anticipation.

There was only one bedroom in her apartment. It was a nice place, though very small. The kitchenette led into the tiny dining room that led into a sitting area with a small television and a stereo system. Her bookshelves were filled with books, rather than photos or bric-a-brac. Her reading material displayed her intelligence, and as he imagined *Satisfying Alternatives to Intercourse* joining her other more academic texts, he winced. Perhaps after a few days of play, she wouldn't need the book at all.

Everything was decorated in floral patterns—cream-colored flowers, soft greens, hints of mauve. He liked it, and decided the small no-nonsense apartment suited her personality just right.

Dripping rain and gripping the paper bag, Max started toward that bedroom door and Miss Maddie Montgomery. He pictured her naked, in a sexy pose on the bed, her fair hair spread out over the pillow.

He pictured the smile on her face, the welcome in her dark blue eyes.

Holding his breath, Max pushed the door open—and jumped when Maddie let out a small shriek of surprise.

Clutching her heart, she said, "Ohmigod, you startled me, Max."

Max lounged in the doorway. "You were expecting someone else?"

Maddie wasn't naked, and she wasn't posed.

She wore a thin teal blue robe that fell to her knees and left the bottom half of her shapely legs bare to his view. Nice knees. And sexy calves. Small feet...

"No, of course not." She stepped away from the window where she'd been watching the storm. Nervously, she folded her hands over her flat stomach and shifted her bare feet. "You got here quicker than I thought and I didn't hear you come in."

He didn't tell her how much he'd hurried. "I was quiet so I wouldn't wake Cleo."

"She's still sleeping?"

"Like a baby."

Maddie's smile was all too obviously forced. Max knew he couldn't rush her, despite his clawing need and all her bravado. Every time she met his gaze, she blushed, so he looked toward the bed instead. She really did have a four-poster, he was amused to see. Would she actually carve a notch in the thick, smooth oak?

"I expected to find you in the bed."

The silky robe shimmered as she lifted one shoulder. "I wasn't sure you'd want me there."

Her reply surprised him, since she'd all but roped and

dragged him to the ground. "So," he said, flashing her a smile, "now my wants matter?"

"I thought you might prefer us standing against the wall, or perhaps bent over the chair."

Max couldn't hide his surprise.

"I'm not looking for the conventional wham-bam here, Max." Maddie took another step closer to him. "I was thinking along the lines of adventure." She shrugged.

She gestured toward the overstuffed flowered seat that held her dress. "It has padded arms on it, and a nice soft seat."

His tongue stuck to the roof of his mouth. As outrageous as her words were, they brought with them pictures of Maddie bent at the waist, her bottom in the air for him to cuddle and pet and kiss. He could almost see her, and that wasn't good for his libido.

Maintain control, maintain control, he told himself, repeating the advice that often graced his column. After a deep breath that didn't do a damn thing to slow the racing of his pulse, Max asked, "So you're looking to get kinky, huh?"

Maddie bobbed her head enthusiastically. "The way I see it, if I'm going to do this, I might as well go all out."

She was making him feel cheap, Max realized with astonishment, quickly followed by annoyance. He wanted their first time together to be romantic, not merely sexual. He'd never cared overly about being romantic before, but now he did, dammit. And romance wasn't likely if she insisted on getting risqué right off the bat.

He'd always thought there was a lot to be said for good old-fashioned missionary sex.

Keeping his expression and tone level, Max said, "Kinky it is. What would you like to try first?"

"I dunno. You're the supposed expert."

Supposed, ha! Going for the one thing Max knew for a fact would turn most women off, he said, "What about a ménage à trois?"

Her eyes widened. "You'd do that for me?"

Max nearly swallowed his damn tongue; her willingness threw him. He was beginning to think he'd made a huge mistake, and would have to walk out on her after all.

Then she took the final step that brought her body close to his and severely weakened his resolve.

With the most innocent expression he'd ever seen on a woman, she asked, "Do you know a guy who's willing, or do I get to pick him?"

Max jerked back a step. "A guy! I meant another woman."

Maddie gave him a mock frown. "No way! This is my show." Her smile proved she'd been teasing all along. "Why would I want to share you?"

Shaking his head, Max started to laugh. Maddie came close again to cover his mouth. "Shh. You'll wake up Cleo."

"I can't help it. You're so funny." Max pulled her against his chest, which effectively soaked her robe since his clothes were still dripping wet, and kissed her hard and fast. Maddie didn't complain. If anything, she hugged him tighter.

"How about," Max whispered against her smiling lips, "we get naked and climb into bed."

"To do things the conventional way?"

"It's a nice easy way to start, honey, I promise."

That seemed to appease her. Without missing a beat, she dropped the damp robe and turned her back on Max to climb into the large bed. *What a view!*

Heat roiled and welled beneath his skin. His control slipped a little, but he reined it in, determined to make this the best *notching* Miss Maddie Montgomery would ever experience.

As Max peeled off his clinging wet shirt, he couldn't stop himself from growling, "You have a gorgeous bottom, Maddie."

"Really?" Her face bright pink from her brazen display, Maddie scurried under the covers, then gave him a beatific smile.

Toeing off his shoes, Max added, "Really."

Her cheeks remained heated, but she watched as he dropped his pants, leaving his clothes and shoes in a sodden pile on the floor. He started for the bed.

"Turn around."

Max paused by the footboard. "Why?"

"I want to see if you have a nice backside, too."

Feeling a little self-conscious, Max obediently turned, and was startled by the sound of Maddie's low wolf whistle.

"Very nice," she said. "Now bring your hunky self to bed." She threw back the covers and patted the mattress beside her hip.

Chuckling at the uniqueness that was Maddie, Max settled himself beside her. He didn't have time to reach for her.

No sooner was he laid out flat than Maddie launched herself on top of him. Soft flesh moving against hard, silky hair against rough. Max barely had time to grab for a breath before her mouth covered his and her hands began mauling him again.

Max struggled to the surface of his turbulent lust. It wasn't easy because while his mind rebelled at a rushed, frenzied mating, his body was all for the idea.

A mauling had never felt so good.

"Maddie," he said, trying to hold her off. It wasn't easy. Maddie might be slender and delicate, but she was stronger than she looked.

She bit his neck, panting. "You're a tease, Max Sawyers. Stop teasing me and give it up."

Forcefully, Max held her back then flipped over to pin her to the mattress. "You want to wrestle, sweetheart? I'm game."

"There's no wrestling involved, you big ape, when you just hold me down."

Max knew there was a big goofy grin on his mug, but dammit, it felt good to be wanted so much.

"Why don't we talk a bit first," Max suggested, needing a distraction to regain some control.

Maddie shook her head. "I didn't get you into bed to *talk*."

He was starting to feel used again.

Being desired physically was great. Hell yes, it was wonderful.

But Max wanted to feel that she had picked him specifically, not just because of his body or his reputation. He needed to be reassured.

How lame for a macho stud! he thought in disgust.

Maddie had made it clear that she didn't want to get to know him, she just wanted "it."

Max seethed, wanting to tell her that he could give her more than sex, more than a warm male body in bed. But it sounded foolish. And unaccountably female. Gad. He wanted sex, for crying out loud! And up until a short time ago, sex without commitment was right up his alley.

But everything had changed.

Max rallied forth and said, "Okay, then let's decide on what type of kinky stuff you want to do."

"Everything." Maddie tried to get her arms free but couldn't. She finally subsided, staring up at Max with wide eyes shadowed by long lashes. Her hair was in an appealing tangle around her head, her cheeks were pink, her lips parted.

Max sighed. He was so hard he hurt, and he was getting harder by the second. "Spanking?"

Maddie's eyes widened even more. Good, at least *that* shocked her.

Then she said, "I doubt I could ever get you over my knees. You're too big."

That was one taunt too many.

Growling, Max abruptly sat up, making Maddie squeal as she realized she'd gone too far. But she didn't escape even halfway across the bed. With no effort at all, Max caught her by the waist and expertly flipped her across his naked thighs. Her long legs kicked and her soft white behind beckoned his hands. He couldn't resist palming her, squeezing gently.

At the touch of his hand on her behind, Maddie stiffened. "Don't you dare, Max Sawyers!"

The squirming bundle draped across his lap no longer sounded so derisive.

"Don't dare what?" Max asked. "This?"

"Max!"

His palm landed with a barely there thwack. Still she gasped and redoubled her efforts to get free.

"Max Sawyers! You stop it right now!"

Max easily controlled her. "You look mighty sexy like this, Maddie." He thwacked her again and she quit struggling to twist around and look at him.

"You think I look sexy?"

"You're naked," he explained reasonably. "Of course I think you look sexy."

She licked her lips. "You wouldn't hurt me, would you, Max?"

He turned her over and cradled her protectively in his arms. She was flushed, nervous and inflamed. Max absorbed it all, and felt that twisting inside his heart again. "Not even if you asked me to."

No longer fighting him, Maddie drew her left hand slowly over his shoulders. She tested his muscles, tangled her fingers in his chest hair, and when she looked at him, pure lust shone from her eyes.

Max bit back a groan. "Maddie…"

Leaning forward, she kissed his throat. "Please, no more teasing. I can't take it. I've been thinking about this forever, and now I want you too much."

"All right." At the moment, teasing was well beyond him. Hell, breathing took an effort.

"I love how you smell, Max."

Max tightened his hold on her. Finally, they were moving at a normal pace toward a proper goal. He dipped down to rub his cheek over the crown of her head. "I like how you smell, too, sweetheart. Sweet and soft and so very female."

"Female isn't a smell."

"Mmm. Female is most definitely a smell, a scent unique to every woman."

Her thumb brushed his nipple, stretching his control to the breaking point. "You know what I said about a small pistol?"

Max spread one hand over her behind, weighing the soft fullness in his palm. He nuzzled her cleavage. "You wounded me to my masculine core. I doubt I'll ever forget."

"I was teasing. There's nothing small about you at all, is there?"

Max met her gaze, and promptly lost the battle. Dropping backward onto the mattress, he allowed Maddie to settle herself on top of him. He gave himself up to her, relishing the kisses she rained over his face and throat and chest, wallowing in her tentative touch, the way she wiggled her pelvis against his straining erection.

He gave up trying to slow her down, and just went with his senses.

"Shh," Max told her when she cried out in surprise at the intimate touch of his fingers down her elegant spine, her generous bottom, and further. He traced around her most sensitive flesh with gentle fingertips.

Maddie reared up, stiffening her arms. "That...that feels good, Max."

"It should. If anything doesn't feel good, Maddie, I want you to tell me."

Eyes squeezed tight, teeth biting into her bottom lip, she nodded agreement.

"You're nice and wet." Max was so hot, his voice sounded disembodied, vague.

A groan broke past the restriction of Maddie's teeth as he continued to explore her, skimming over her delicate, swollen tissues.

Her rigid posture had brought her plump breasts right above his face and Max took swift advantage. Her nipples were dark pink, puckered and too enticing to resist. Max licked first, lazily stroking with the rough wet heat of his tongue, letting her know his intent. She trembled, her breathing now audible as she leaned forward, making it clear what she wanted.

Max drew her deep.

Maddie's hips jerked, causing his fingertips to slide over slick flesh.

"Relax for me, Maddie."

"Impossible."

Smiling, Max insisted, "It's very possible. And you don't want to wake Cleo."

"Okay. Okay. Okay…"

Max pushed one finger slowly, deeply inside her. Her feminine muscles gripped him in a tight silky vice.

"Okay!"

Using the only way he could think of to quiet her, Max kissed her hard. Maddie fell into the kiss, taking his tongue and giving back her own, consuming him, making him crazed with lust. He'd never had a kiss like this, inexperienced but so hungry, so generous and hot.

The gentle thrust of her pointed nipples on his chest was a seductive lure. Combined with her scent, stronger now that she was so excited, and the softness of her hair and skin licking over his heated flesh in dark sensual places, Max gave up. He knew she was ready, knew he was beyond ready, and decided it was time.

Getting Maddie to turn him loose took some doing though.

"Just let me get the condom," he urged.

Her fingernails bit into his shoulders, firing his lust further. "Don't leave me, Max."

"I'm not going anywhere except to the nightstand." He put her to the side and then got distracted looking at her body.

She was slim but shapely, her breasts rosy now with need, her stomach tightened, trying to hold in the sweet ache of desire. Her long legs shifted restlessly on the bed.

And her blond curls...they were damp and inviting.

Max bent and pressed a kiss low on her belly.

"Max!"

He rested his chin on her thigh. "You need to stop shouting, honey. Think of Cleo as a baby. If you wake her, she's not going to want to go back to sleep. Putting her outside the door won't help. She'll howl loud enough to wake the dead."

With dawning fury, Maddie said, "You've locked her out when you were with other women?"

A woman like Maddie could quickly grab a man's heart. She was aroused, wet and ready. Her breasts rose and fell with her deep heavy breathing and her skin was warmed to a rosy glow.

Yet she had the sensitivity to consider his dog's feelings.

Max gently stroked her thigh, high near her hipbones, and then very lightly, between.

"No," he whispered, bending to kiss her again. He hadn't been with many women since getting Cleo, mostly because Cleo hated them all and wasn't shy about letting Max know it. He'd tried, but having an hysterical dog on his hands wasn't his idea of fun. And the women had complained mightily when he'd chosen to calm Cleo over bedding them.

Selfish women.

Women unlike Maddie Montgomery.

"I tried shutting her out a few times," Max explained, letting his breath fan her skin, "so she wouldn't shed in my bed. She...ah, didn't like it. She really has this thing about closed doors, especially when she's on the wrong side of them."

Mollified, Maddie pulled a pillow over her face. When she spoke, her voice was muffled. "This will help. You can proceed now with what you...started to do."

Never before had Max suffered the combination of humor

and lust and tenderness. It kept him off guard with no way to protect his heart. Max gently urged her legs wider apart, then paused.

"What are you doing?" she mumbled from beneath the pillow.

With his heart in his throat and blood pulsing hotly through his veins, Max said, "Just looking at you."

The pillow lifted and Maddie's gaze met his. "Why?"

Touching her lightly with his fingertips, Max said, "Because you're so pretty and pink and ready for me."

The pillow slapped back over her face. "Oh."

Savoring the moment, Max kissed her softly, then as his hunger raged, not so softly.

Maddie's legs stiffened.

He teased her, teased himself, using his tongue, his teeth, and when she was sobbing beneath the pillow, her hands clenched in the pillowcase, Max drew her into his mouth and suckled her right over the edge.

The pillow proved inadequate to properly stifle her wild cries, but it helped enough. Thank goodness for small favors, Max thought to himself as he moved in a rush to the nightstand and ripped open a condom package. He couldn't have waited a minute more. Not a second more.

Maddie, her pillow now limp beside her equally limp body, got her eyes open enough to watch him sleepily as he slid on the protection and moved between her thighs.

Her hand lifted tiredly and stroked his shoulder. "That was...indescribable."

"Better than okay, huh?"

"Definitely—*oh!*"

Max tried to hold back as her body softened to accept him, as his erection slid deep inside her to be squeezed by hot, moist flesh. He growled low in intense pleasure. "Oh, yeah."

"Max?"

"Easy now, Maddie. Just a little more. Damn, you feel good."

She took two gasping breaths. "So...do you."

He pulled out, felt her hands grip his shoulders, her legs curl around his hips trying to keep him close, and he drove forward again.

Maddie tipped her head back on the pillow. "This is better than any damn feather!"

"You better believe it." Max gave up the fight and began a rhythm that supplied just the right amount of pressure, just the right friction. "Squeeze me, Maddie," he rasped. "It'll make it better for you. Tighter." He moaned. "That's it."

Holding him with arms, legs and hidden muscles, Maddie began to feel a part of him, a very necessary part.

Max meant to make the pleasure last, meant to give her a half-dozen orgasms so that she'd never be able to forget him, never be able to move on to the next man.

But it was already too late for him.

With a roar worthy of a wild beast, he came and Maddie joined him.

Unfortunately, their combined yells woke Cleo, who was highly affronted by their unseemly behavior.

And just as Max had predicted, she refused to leave the room.

Their night of debauchery was over.

Chapter Five

"WHERE'S THE BOOK?"

Maddie drew up short, staring back at the three women eyeing her so suspiciously. Darn, she'd forgotten all about the book!

Tossing her backpack—what she carried instead of a bothersome purse—into a seat, Maddie slumped onto the cracked leather couch. "I don't have it."

Bea snorted, making her white hair wobble precariously. Bea spent more time on securing her big hairdos than she did on anything else. "You mean it doesn't exist."

"Does, too," Maddie returned petulantly, then grimaced as Mavis and Carmilla shared a look. "I'll get the book. It's just that…well…" A big grin broke over her face and she leaned forward in excitement. "You guys were right!"

Catching Maddie's enthusiasm, all three women leaned forward. Silver hair blended with white blended with glaring red. Hands wrinkled from time and a working woman's life reached for Maddie.

Carmilla spoke first, her tone hushed with scandalized delight. *"You didn't."*

Bea laughed. "I'll bet she did! Just look at her. She's *glowing.*"

"Only one thing gives a woman a glow like that," Mavis

agreed, and she was grinning like a loon. "'Bout damn time, if you ask me."

"No one asked you," the other two replied, always too contrary to agree with Mavis's constant predictions.

Maddie let all three of them hold her hands, her wrists, her shoulder. "He's positively dreamy," she said. "A stud, just as you told me he should be."

"Give."

"Yes, every single detail, honey. I wait with bated breath."

Carmilla chuckled. "Mavis, there ain't a damn thing she can tell you that you haven't done a million times yourself, so forget the 'swooning young girl' act."

Mavis slanted Carmilla a venomous look that didn't mean a darn thing. Maddie knew they just loved to twit each other.

"Carmilla, darling, at sixty-eight, I *am* a girl compared to you."

Bea slapped her knee. As the oldest at seventy-five, she often played the peacekeeper. "She's got you there, old girl."

Maddie cleared her throat. "Do you three want to hear this or not?"

Mavis waved a hand. "Tell all."

"I did everything you said—well most of what you said. And he took me home just as you told me he would. It was a little rocky, but I finally won."

Carmilla blinked dark brown eyes. Her face was wrinkled and worn, but in a nice way, like a favorite pair of house slippers that only became more comfortable and appealing the longer you had them. "Whatd'ya mean, it got rocky? He didn't jump your bones?"

"Uh, no. I jumped his."

Mavis harrumphed indignantly. Her eyes spit green fire, which went well with her bright red hair. She resembled a beacon in the night, able to pull in any wayward male souls—which had been the point back when all her work was done at night. She kept the bright hair out of sentiment, and because the senior men still tended to flock to her like flies to honey. She had that special "oomph" or charisma—whatever you called it—that men never seemed to outgrow.

According to Mavis, she sometimes missed working the corner. Holding hands and behaving like a lady didn't suit her at all.

"What kind of man," Mavis demanded, "would have to be jumped?"

"He's a very good man."

"Honey, there ain't no such thing."

Bea swatted at Carmilla. "Don't tell her such a thing! Of course there are good men."

"Good for certain things, but she's not ready for love everlasting again so soon."

"For pity's sake, Carmilla, no one mentioned love everlasting!"

"Look at her eyes, Bea. That girl is smitten."

Everyone turned to stare deeply into Maddie's eyes. She squirmed and immediately felt defensive. "It's not like that at all! You know I've given up on that."

"After what your scumbait fiancé did? Hell yeah, you gave up. I still think you should let us contact a few old friends. I'm tellin' ya, Tiny would love to give your old beau a good goin' over."

Bea shook her head in exasperation. "You are so bloodthirsty, Carmilla."

Mavis snorted. "I agree with her. We should all rough him up, the miserable bastard."

Laughing, Maddie took turns giving each of them a hug. She always felt comforted by their fragile, warm embraces, given from the heart.

She'd been working as a counselor for several years now, and she'd made some friends along the way. She'd started with troubled teens, and gradually been shifted to older women. A lot of those women were now in homes with families and jobs, or doing volunteer work. But Mavis, Carmilla and Bee were aging rebels, women who refused to conform to society's strictures. They were fun loving and adventurous despite their fragile bones, and energetic in a way that belied their years.

They no longer needed her counsel, but they still liked to meet. And being with them helped temper the more stressful sessions Maddie had with abused women, or recovering alcoholics.

Maddie loved Carmilla, Bea and Mavis dearly. For her, they served as surrogate mothers, aunts, best friends and confidants all rolled into one. She admired them for what they'd survived, worried about them endlessly, and counted on them much more than they counted on her, though not a one of them would ever admit it.

She smiled at them. "Max is a good man, I promise. He's a hound dog, no doubt about that—which makes him perfect for my coming-out. But he's also honorable."

"All men," Carmilla said, "are hound dogs, some are just better at it than others."

Mavis raised a slim, drawn-on red brow. "So is this young man good?"

Maddie bobbed her head, making the women laugh. "Yeah." In a whisper, she confided, "He said I was sexy." Then, even lower, "And he seems to know all kinds of kinky stuff."

Carmilla gulped. "Kinky sexual stuff?"

Bea shook her head. "Of course she means kinky sexual stuff. What'd you think? That he wears his shoes backward?" Then to Maddie, "So what'd you do?"

"Nothing kinky," she rushed to reassure them. "He sort of lost control. But the good old conventional stuff was...well, *incredible.*"

"Well then," Bee said, setting aside her round glasses. "It's no wonder you're running a little late this morning."

Mavis signed. "I remember those mornings."

Carmilla nudged her hard enough to almost knock her off her chair. "Baloney. What you remember is the money on the nightstand, not a warm body in the bed."

Mavis grinned. "That, too."

It never ceased to amaze Maddie how open and...cavalier the women were about their hardships. To hear them tell it, life as a hooker had been a lark. But she'd talked with each of them enough to know that was simply their way of burying the past.

It sometimes broke her heart.

This time, as always, she hid her reaction with a smile. "Max didn't spend the night."

"*What?*"

"That cad!"

"I say we get hold of Tiny," Carmilla growled, "and let him teach old Max a few manners."

"It's not like that," Maddie hurried to explain. "You see, he has this dog."

Blank stares were the only response.

"The dog is adorable. Well, not physically. But she's very sweet. When she's not growling."

Mavis chortled. "Sounds like Carmilla."

"Ha ha."

Biting back her own laugh, Maddie said, "The dog has a...well, a bladder problem."

Bea leaned toward Mavis and said low, "I can certainly relate."

"Oh, for goodness sake, be quiet Bea!"

Maddie raised her voice to forestall the start of a new quarrel. "Max didn't want the dog to soil my carpet, so he went home."

"Afterward?" Mavis asked suspiciously.

Smiling, Maddie confirmed, "Yes, afterward." And in dreamy tones, "Way afterward."

"She's got that look again."

"Well," Maddie explained, "it was more wonderful than I'd ever imagined."

"Hurray!"

"'Bout damn time."

"Your damn ex-fiancé should be shot."

Maddie laughed out loud with the joy of it. She'd never imagined, never guessed, that sex could be so wonderful. Max had scandalized her with a few of the wonderful, incredible, sizzling hot things he'd done to her and with her.

But she wouldn't have had him stop a single one.

"So when are you seeing him again?"

At Bea's question, the other two got quiet, all of them waiting for her reply. Maddie forced a negligent shrug.

"I don't know."

"What the hell does that mean?"

"I'm sorry, Carmilla, but it's the truth. I'm not sure what to do now. Max is a confirmed bachelor, and I'm afraid if I get too clingy, it'll spook him."

"You assured him," Mavis asked, "that all you wanted was some good one-on-one experiences to store away for a rainy day?"

"Yes, I told him all that. I don't understand him. He seemed to really resist me, but then once things got going, he was..."

"Into it?"

"Yes."

"Typical man. Fickle, all of them." Mavis shook her head. "Why, I knew a guy once—"

Bea threw up her hands. "You knew lots of guys in lots of ways, Mavis. For cryin' out loud, let's don't go tromping down memory's bumpy lane right now. We need to figure this out for Maddie."

Carmilla crossed her arms beneath her massive bosom and said three words. "Let's call Tiny."

"I have a better idea," Mavis said, ignoring Bea because

she had obviously *wanted* to go down memory lane. "Forget about him."

Maddie bit her bottom lip. Though she knew it was probably best, and it *had* been her original plan, she didn't want to forget about Max. Not yet, maybe not for a long, long time.

Maybe not ever. *No,* she would *not* think that!

Bea patted her arm. "Now look what you've done, Mavis! You're going to make her cry."

"I'm not crying!" Maddie had no intention of getting maudlin over Max Sawyers. This was an adventure, an experience, a way to add lascivious excitement to her PG-rated life. She wouldn't let herself get hurt over it.

"Get rid of that long face, Maddie," Mavis said with a laugh. "I didn't mean forget about him forever. Just long enough to whet his appetite. If this Max fellow is anything like you say, he'll expect you to be after him now, wanting more of his sexy body and all the well-oiled parts. Well, throw 'em for a loop, I always say! Don't give him what he wants."

Carmilla gasped with glee. "Exactly! That's brilliant, Mavis!"

Mavis pretended to have a heart attack over the praise and wouldn't quit until Bea threatened to give her mouth-to-mouth resuscitation.

"Men always want what they can't have." Carmilla rubbed her hands together. "As long as you don't give it to him, he'll keep coming back."

"I already gave it to him."

"He'll want it again, and more."

"But..." Maddie wondered how to phrase her worry. Then she decided that with these three, delicacy wasn't needed. "I *want* to give him more."

"Music to my ears." Bea patted her hand and said, "You're a healthy woman, honey. Just tell him that. Sex—but nothing else," she warned. "It's the 'nothing else' that'll get his goat. I promise, it'll drive him plumb crazy and before you know it, he'll be the one chasing you."

"But wait at least a week," Mavis advised. "After a week, he won't know what to think! He'll be gnawing on his own insecurity. Oh, it'll be so sweet."

"I want to meet him," Bea suddenly declared. "Bring him around. I want to judge for myself if he's worth all this bother."

Maddie knew firsthand that Max was more than worth it, but she wanted to show him off to the ladies. She wanted them to see him and experience his charm.

"I could go to him in a week to get the book—"

Carmilla's rough laugh interrupted Maddie's plan. "A book that claims to have *Satisfying Alternatives to Intercourse* has to be drivel."

"Or an outright lie." Bea watched Maddie with a calculating eye as she delivered that insult.

Trying not to laugh, Maddie assured them, "It exists, and I have it on good authority that it's excellent."

"Bring it, and the young man. We'll check them both out."

"Yes, Mavis," Maddie agreed. "And then all three of you will owe me an apology."

There was a general round of grumbling over that prospect, then a snort of contempt, proving that not one of them planned to apologize at all. No, they just intended to meddle, but Maddie didn't mind. She could barely wait to see Max's reaction to them.

She figured if she could be cordial to his dog, dealing with Mavis, Carmilla and Bea ought to be a piece of cake.

SHE DIDN'T CALL, she didn't write...

Max paced the small confines of the bookstore, his temper high, his mood black.

His manly ego thoroughly damaged.

He'd written three columns on the evils of women-on-the-make, then had to destroy them. Truth was so often stranger than fiction, and no one would have believed that he was actually *complaining* about the situation.

In fact, he could barely believe it himself. But dammit, he'd bought a box of condoms just for her! He had three of the little silver packets in his wallet right now.

Yet she hadn't so much as blinked when he'd told her he couldn't spend the night a week ago. She hadn't offered him her phone number, hadn't invited him back, hadn't done anything but thank him.

And now he knew why.

Maddie truly had just been using him. One time. One lousy damn time and she was through with him. She had the number for the bookstore, and she knew Annie. She could have gotten his home number. But no. She'd ignored him without hesitation.

The hair on the back of Max's neck bristled. *How dare she?* He was no lady's conquest! He wasn't a man to be trifled with!

He had a good mind to storm over to her apartment and see for himself if she'd reduced him to a nick in the bedpost. Only...what if she was with another man when he showed up?

What if she took his visit as a sign of jealousy?

Max cursed and started pacing again. If he found a man there, he just knew he'd get rip-roaring mad and probably do something foolish—like punch the guy out.

And he sure as hell didn't want it to look like he was chasing her. Ha! The very idea was absurd. Women chased *him*, not the other way around.

Max sighed as he stalked the perimeter of the bookstore once again. It was bad enough to be in such a foul mood without having to deal with Annie's shop as well. But his little sister and Guy were off wallowing in premarital ecstasy, on a wedding planning venture that seemed to have no end in sight.

Guy insisted that Annie have the biggest and best wedding around. And his father agreed. They didn't know he had a job writing for the paper, so they probably thought they were doing him a favor, keeping him employed. Ha.

Curse them all.

Cleo whined, tilted her small head and gave Max a quizzical look. If he didn't know better—but he damn well did—he'd think Cleo missed Maddie, too. Impossible. The woman was too pushy to be missed by man or beast.

So why had Cleo been moping so much? Why had she been so maudlin? He loved Cleo, he really did, but it was almost repulsive to see her dragging her chubby little short-legged body around in a depression. He preferred her grumbling and snapping to the worried, unhappy look she'd worn since Maddie left.

Now he knew where the term "hangdog expression" had come from, because Cleo wore it all over her furry face.

"I'm fine, Cleo," Max bit out, "so quit frowning at me."

Cleo looked unconvinced. She whined again and laid her head on the floor, resting it on her front paws and staring up at Max with wrinkled brows and quivering whiskers.

"Stop fretting!" he demanded, unable to bear it a second more. "It doesn't suit you at all. Besides, I'm just stewing in my own juices."

"And what juices would those be?"

Max jumped at the soft, teasing female voice. Maddie stood there in the doorway looking sweet and sexy and happy to see him, as if a damn week hadn't gone by, as if she hadn't been ignoring him completely after taking him like a convenient body with no soul.

No, Max admitted to himself, that wasn't quite the way it had happened. She'd taken his body, yes—most thoroughly in fact—but she'd also grabbed his heart and soul with both fists.

It was unbearable.

Just looking at her hurt.

Cleo, the traitor, took one peek at Maddie and began leaping about in near maniacal excitement. Her snarls and growls actually mingled with happy woofs. Max glared at her.

Then her tail—a tail seldom seen since it spent most of its time curled safely against her belly—gave a one-thump wag of delight.

"Well, I'll be damned."

Maddie went straight to the dog, not even slightly put off by Cleo's mixed display of joy and wrath, and hugged her tightly. "Did you miss me, sweetie?"

Yellow fur clung to Maddie's hot-pink T-shirt, a T-shirt that read *Made In The Sun.* Cleo went so far as to lick Maddie's ear.

Oh yeah, Maddie with her long blond hair hanging free, her blue eyes smiling, would look very sweet under the hot sun. Naked. Open for him.

Max cleared his throat, angry at himself for responding to her. Sure, she loved all over his damn dog, but she'd barely said two words to him.

It was as if she hadn't missed him at all.

"Well, well," he murmured in his most sarcastic tone, "look what the cat dragged in."

At the word "cat" Cleo's ears lifted, her portly body trembled and she went bonkers. She snapped at the air and raced around the small bookstore, bumping into shelves and sticking her snarling nose into every small space, searching for the heinous feline creature.

Maddie frowned at Max. "Now look what you've done!" She rushed after Cleo, her white sandals clicking on the tile floor as she ran through a haphazard game of tag that had Maddie, too, bumping into bookcases before she finally got both hands anchored in Cleo's collar. "Shh. Shh. It's all right, Cleo. I promise, there aren't any other creatures here except us."

Cleo wasn't about to trust anyone and so the game continued. Maddie got dragged several feet before she gave up and released Cleo's collar, only to rush after the dog, explaining all the while.

Max sauntered off to the back room to get himself a cola. He was being ignored, so he figured no one would miss him. Let the two ladies have their fun. He'd ignore them right back.

He'd finished half the bottle of soda before Maddie again

appeared in the doorway. The tight tee outlined her breasts and her long legs were displayed under an itty-bitty white cotton miniskirt.

She looked good enough to eat, he thought. Then in the next second, he got hard.

"What are you doing?"

Max shrugged, the epitome of a man without a care. He ruined the pose, though, by grumbling, "Not a damn thing, why?"

"My, my," she said with raised eyebrows. "Surly this morning, aren't we?"

Surly? *Surly!* Max paused, thinking, Did real men act surly? Good grief, he didn't think so.

He mentally shook himself and gathered together his lauded control.

"Sorry," he uttered, once again sounding like himself, a man without a care, a man who excelled in deception. "I had a...late night."

There, Miss Montgomery, he thought, work that over in your conniving little brain.

Yawning hugely, Maddie said, "Me, too."

Max jerked to attention and demanded, "A late night doing *what?*"

"Working."

"Oh."

She gave him an impish grin. "What did you think I was doing?"

"Notching more bedposts?"

"And that would have bothered you?"

"Not in the least."

Her smile was smug and he wanted to kiss it right off her face. No sooner did the thought enter his mind than he decided, why not?

Max stalked her, his intent gaze letting her know exactly what he wanted, and Maddie began backing up as she chuckled.

"Cleo finally settled down." She giggled as she said it, and stopped abruptly when her back came up against the small cool refrigerator.

Max caged her in, flattening his hands on either side of her head. "She ran out of gas, that's all. Cleo can raise a racket for hours until she literally flops down exhausted."

"That exactly what she did! One second she was running around—"

Her words were swallowed up by his kiss. Damn, she tasted good. Too good. Even better than he'd remembered.

Max had almost forgotten how wonderful her soft mouth felt under his, how teasing her tongue could be, her delicious taste. "Mmm."

He lifted his mouth from hers and pressed soft, biting kisses down her throat. "You like hickeys?"

Maddie, breathing roughly, rasped, "Hickeys?"

"Love bites." He licked her throat. "Do you like them?"

"I...I don't know." Her hands clenched in his shirt, her hips pressed into his. "I don't think I've ever had one."

Max opened his mouth on her neck, right over her thrumming pulse, and sucked her skin gently against his teeth.

Maddie responded with a long, hungry groan.

Max made sure the mark would be low enough that she could cover it easily with her clothing, but she tasted so good he didn't want to let her go. He kissed her throat again and again, then moved on to her jaw, her ear.

Maddie panted. "This is wonderful."

She made him crazy. Max took her mouth hard in a voracious kiss, all the while his mind was churning. He knew he should hold back, knew he should set things straight with her. He couldn't. Not right now.

"Ever had a nooner?"

Maddie slowly blinked open her heavy eyes. "A nooner?"

Max cupped her cheek and smoothed her skin with his thumb. She was so soft. "It's afternoon. A great time to play."

Her eyes widened. "Play, as in...?"

"Make whoopee. Here. *Now.*" He wanted her so badly, just getting the words out was an effort.

Maddie glanced around the tiny back room where unopened boxes crowded the floors and file cabinets were squeezed into the corners. One small square table held a coffeemaker and was surrounded by three mismatched chairs. The miniscule refrigerator hummed against her backside. Max could feel the teasing vibration through Maddie, their bodies were pressed so closely together.

Most importantly, though, was the open door leading into the rest of the bookstore. Any customer coming in might be able to see them if they got close to the door. Max saw the confusion, the scandalized excitement that darkened Maddie's eyes.

She bit her lip. "Here?"

In one deft move, Max flattened her more securely to the refrigerator and pushed himself between her thighs. With a tilt of his head, he could see the front door, but no one coming in could see him unless they rounded the corner. Max knew she felt his erection, as well as the way his hands shook. But he didn't care. All he cared about was hearing her soft enticing groans again as she came.

"Here," he growled.

"Standing?"

"Standing. You offered this last time, remember? The only difference is that the fridge is nice and cool, and I swear, you'll appreciate that in a minute."

"Why?"

"Because I'm going to make you burn up."

"Oh." She touched his chest, looked around the room again. "I'm...I'm kind of wobbly," she said worriedly.

Max smiled. "I won't let you fall." Hell, his muscles were so tense, so tight, he was more likely to break than bend.

Maddie licked her lips slowly while her eyes searched his. "What if someone catches us?"

Kissing the corner of her sweet mouth, Max whispered, "It's an exciting thought, isn't it? Doing the forbidden? Taking a risk? But the door has a bell, remember? We'll know if anyone comes in." With a touch of demand, he added, "Trust me."

Her fingers gripped his upper arms, squeezing, caressing. "All right."

Breathing hard, Max held her gaze as he caught the hem of her miniskirt and slowly raised it. Maddie moaned.

"We need to get rid of your panties," he told her, knowing his words would work as foreplay, "so that I can touch you."

Maddie closed her eyes.

"You want me to touch you, don't you, Maddie? That's why you're here again." He'd have rather believed she'd missed him, but he was a realist. Fingers on her thigh, he asked, "You missed *this*, didn't you?"

She nodded, her chest heaving, her thighs trembling as Max ran his fingertips up and over her legs to her hips.

With no warning at all, he cupped her through the silky triangle of underwear.

"Why, Maddie Montgomery," he said softly, "you're already hot and wet." Max moved his fingers over the damp silk, outlining her swollen folds, then higher, stroking her through the material. Maddie gasped.

"Mmm," he said. "Right there, huh?"

She didn't answer, so he paused, keeping one finger pressed teasingly to the ultrasensitive spot.

Maddie's eyes opened and she stared at him, looking somewhat dazed. "Max?"

He loved hearing her say his name. "I want you to answer my question, Maddie."

She swallowed, drew a steadying breath. "What question?"

Her rasping voice shook; Max liked that. "Is this where you want me to touch you?"

He flicked gently, then deeply, and Maddie's hips jerked against him.

"Yes!"

"I want to see your breasts, Maddie."

She stared at him.

"Show them to me." This was Max's favorite game, taking charge, making specific sexual demands. And after the week he'd been through, waiting for her, hoping she'd call, thinking she never would, he especially liked it.

And she especially deserved it.

Looking undecided about what to do, Maddie again bit her lip. It was an innocently sexual expression that turned him on even more.

Max quit stroking her, making his demand. "Show me your breasts, Maddie."

She swallowed hard, then began inching up her shirt. She had on a barely there bra of matching hot pink, transparent and sexy as hell. Max bent toward her. "Keep the shirt out of my way."

Her nipples were hard points against the thin material and Max closed his mouth around her hotly.

"Max!"

He tasted her other breast, leaving both nipples covered with damp clingy fabric. Leaning back to enjoy his handiwork, Max said, "Nice. Pretty."

He didn't want to take a chance on being interrupted, so he decided not to stall any longer. Maddie's skirt was bunched around her waist, her T-shirt up under her chin. He slowly took a step back, and cautioned her, "Don't move."

She barely even breathed.

Nodding in approval, Max knelt down and pulled her panties to her knees.

The door chimed.

Maddie started to jerk away, but Max quickly rose and held her still. He covered her mouth with two fingers scented by her body. Against her ear, he said, "Don't you move a single muscle, sweetheart. Do you understand me?"

Panicked, her eyes huge, Maddie mumbled against his fingers.

"Shh. Trust me."

A heartbeat of silence passed while they stared at each other and the interruption he'd wanted to avoid became a real risk. Finally she nodded.

Just that quickly Max left the backroom, closing the door behind him. There was nothing he could do about his noticeable hard-on except hope the two female customers wouldn't look at him closely until he got behind the counter.

They didn't. They were too busy picking up their favorite romance novels. They discussed authors and new releases and made faces at the goofy clinch covers. In the short time he'd been filling in for Annie, Max had noticed that their biggest sellers were romances.

Luckily the customers didn't wake Cleo, but they did give her horrified stares. She was stretched out on the floor beneath a table, snoring.

Max ignored the ladies' aghast expressions and waited on them patiently. Maddie, he was certain, would have thought Cleo looked cute. She wouldn't have regarded the dog with distaste, but rather with that small, endearing smile of hers.

Max could just picture her still standing against the old refrigerator, her legs open, her hands fisted in her shirt, breasts bare, panties around her knees. She looked so sexy, so sweet. So impatient.

He had to shake those thoughts away or he'd embarrass himself.

It was a good ten minutes before the store was once again empty. Max took a deep breath, flexed his hands and rolled his head to rid himself of the worst of his tension. In the corner, Cleo lay sprawled in boneless languor, the most relaxed she'd been since she'd slept at Maddie's apartment. Since then, she'd been watching the doors, the windows, and Max knew she'd been waiting for Maddie.

Just as he had.

That sudden insight annoyed him enough that he quickly opened the back-room door and walked in.

Maddie was standing just as he'd left her.

Her tiny pink panties were still twisted around her knees and her nipples were still erect little points, telling Max that her thoughts hadn't veered from the sexual at all. She may not have missed him, but she'd missed what he could do for her. And she had come back to him. He'd build on that. For Cleo's sake.

Without a word, he knelt in front of her again. As if they hadn't been interrupted at all, Max traced a path up her thigh and asked, "You ready for me, Maddie?"

Her stomach clenched. "Yes."

Slowly, enthralled by the contrast of her moist pink flesh against his dark hand, Max inserted one finger inside her. Maddie didn't look away. Her legs parted as far as the panties would allow, straining against the bonds.

"Do you want me to kiss you?"

"Yes." Then, almost as an afterthought, "Please."

She no longer hesitated at all in her answers. Max's heart pounded hard, and his control was a thing of the past. Still with his finger inside her, gently probing, Max breathed in her musky scent, then opened his mouth over her in a voracious, consuming kiss meant to bring her desire to an acute edge.

Maddie's breath left her in a harsh groan. Her hands settled on his head, her fingers inadvertently pulling at his hair.

He didn't mind. He liked her unrestrained show of excitement.

Max brought her right to the edge, teasing, nibbling, kissing softly, then not so softly. He used his tongue in a never-ending, rasping stroke—then left her.

Quickly stripping her panties the rest of the way off, Max tucked them into his back pocket.

Max stroked her bare bottom as he explained, "Quickies

are sometimes an elusive thing for women," Max explained as he stroked her bare bottom. "They need more…preparation. More stimulation."

How the hell he was stringing so many words together when all he could hear was the roar of his own racing heartbeat, Max wasn't sure. Maddie neither wanted nor required explanations. But he wanted her enjoyment to be a foregone conclusion, and talking not only aroused her further, it helped to calm him so that he could see to her pleasure. He refused to take a chance on leaving her unsatisfied.

"You talk too much, Max."

Max smiled at the crackle in her voice, the way she held herself so still and ready. Her back was pressed hard against the door of the fridge, her hips tilted outward, legs spread. Her little belly was so cute, so inviting.

He unzipped his jeans in a rush, then pushed them below his hips. "When I come into you now, the friction will be just right."

He felt the heat of Maddie's intense gaze, watching him as he rolled on the condom. She reached for him when he stepped between her widely spread thighs.

She held him tight when Max instructed, "Put your right leg around my waist. That's it, a little higher. Now just… Umm. That's right." She was so wet, he sank easily into her. "Tilt your pelvis toward me more."

Maddie anxiously followed his instructions. "This is fairly kinky, isn't it?" she panted.

"Yeah." He'd win her over yet, he thought. He'd make her insane with lust, make her understand that there was a special chemistry between them. Max kissed her again, and intent on making her hotter with words, he whispered, "What did you think about while I was with the customers, sweetheart?"

"You," she whispered. "What you just did to me?"

"Yes?" Max could already feel his triumph. She'd wanted him to kiss her, to pleasure her. "What about it?"

"I thought about…doing that to you."

Max froze. His vision clouded.

Unconcerned with his reaction, Maddie persisted with her arousing admission. Her breath pumped in and out, making the words stilted, as she moved against him, pleasuring herself on his rigid body.

"I thought about being on my knees in front of you, of taking you into my mouth, tasting you and sucking on you the same way you—"

With a muffled shout, Max drove into her. He was a goner, coming even as he heard Maddie's soft chuckle of success. He let her laugh, because seconds later she was climaxing, her nails biting into his butt, his arms the only things keeping her upright.

It seemed as though they stood there for hours, propped against each other, both of them gasping for breath. And then the damn door chimed again and with a dark oath, Max pulled away from her.

Would nothing ever go as he planned with Maddie? Every time he intended to overwhelm her with sex, she managed to turn the tables on him. And now, instead of being able to discuss things with her, the store had suddenly become as busy as a bus station, repeatedly drawing him away. Max disposed of the condom, pulled up his jeans, and staggered on wobbling legs out to the counter.

Unfortunately, this customer was much more observant than the others had been. She took in his disheveled state, the heaviness of his eyes, and said with characteristic cheerfulness, "Why Max Sawyers, you reprobate. You've been fooling around in Annie's bookstore!"

Lace McGee Sawyers, his sister-in-law, knew sexual satisfaction when she saw it. As a sex therapist, she was well acquainted with the subject.

Max looked at her, frowned, then said over his shoulder, "You might as well come on out, Maddie. It's just Lace, and

I know without asking that she's not going anywhere without an introduction."

"At least I got here *after*," Lace said with a grin.

Max gave her his laziest look. "You're good Lace, but not good enough to be sure of that."

"Oh, I'm positive." She laughed, then hugged him tight. "Because otherwise you'd be throwing me out!"

Chapter Six

MADDIE WANTED to be a coward and hide, but more than that, she wanted to meet Lace McGee Sawyers. Lace was married to Annie's oldest brother, Daniel, the doctor. She'd never met Daniel, but Annie assured her that he was every bit as hunky as Max, just in a different, more somber way.

She straightened her clothes the best she could, considering her panties were still in Max's pocket. She could hardly believe what she'd just done; as far as memories went, that one was a keeper! But it was more than the sex, because Max was more. She would have enjoyed talking with him, asking how Cleo had been. She wanted to try to find out if he'd missed her at all because she'd definitely missed him.

But as per her original instructions, he'd shown her a good time. She knew that was for the best, but she still wished they'd had time to...cuddle.

Shoulders back, Maddie walked out of the room. She was prepared to be adult, to be cavalier about the experience. But then she drew up short.

Lace was wrapped around Max! And he didn't seem to mind! The cur.

It made Maddie so angry to see another woman holding him so closely, that she didn't even think, she just reacted.

"Just what the hell is going on here?"

Max eyed her over the top of Lace's platinum-blond head. At first his look was questioning, then quietly satisfied. He even grinned before setting Lace away from him.

"Cursing, Maddie? My, my."

He looked mighty pleased about something, but Maddie was more interested in Lace. The woman was drop-dead beautiful. A real knockout.

Maddie felt instantly deflated.

She had no idea what to say, how to defuse the situation so she could make a hasty escape. Cleo came to her rescue.

Slowly getting to her feet, Cleo started snarling and sniping and making vague threats at Lace.

Maddie smiled.

Cleo came to Maddie, sat on her foot, and growled at the other woman. Maddie, feeling somewhat vindicated, patted Cleo's head.

"I have no idea what that dog has against me." Lace looked at Max. "She still hates women?"

Maddie answered before Max could. "She doesn't hate *me*. She *likes* me."

Lace grinned. "So I see. I suppose, considering the fact that Max seems rather partial to you as well, it's a good thing."

Maddie, surprised at how nice and reasonable the other woman was being, said, "Uh…"

Lace stepped forward, keeping a wary eye on Cleo, and offered her hand. "Hi. I'm Max's sister-in-law, Lace."

Maddie had no choice but to accept the woman's hand. "Maddie Montgomery."

"So you're Maddie! Annie has told me all about you. I understand we have a lot in common."

Maddie looked at Lace's gorgeous, perfect figure decked out in a striking black silk dress that showed off her incredibly beautiful blond hair in stark contrast and said again, "Uh…"

"I'm a sex therapist," Lace explained, "and Annie said you

work with social services for planned parenthood and troubled teens on sexual issues?"

Max piped in, saying, "And I love sex. We all have something in common."

To Maddie's chagrin, Lace merely poked Max in the side, treating him like a little brother. "You're outrageous, Max. Don't embarrass your lady friend."

Max snorted. "As if that's even possible. In fact, it's generally Maddie who's embarrassing me. She's so…candid."

Maddie thought about kicking him. Cleo must have picked up on her thoughts, because she gave Max a disapproving whine.

Lace shrugged. "In our business you need to be candid. Maddie would hardly be effective at what she does if she sat around blushing and stammering."

Damn, Maddie thought. The woman was beautiful and intelligent and likeable.

Max threw his arm around Lace, making Maddie narrow her eyes. But then he said, "Maddie, did you know Lace has always treated me like I'm twelve? I swear, I'd try to flirt with her and she'd pat my head."

Lace rolled her eyes. "Don't let it bother you, Max. I was in love with your brother, remember?"

"But you didn't know it at the time."

A feline smile enhanced Lace's already perfect features. "No, but I did know that I wasn't in love with you."

"Heartless wench."

Maddie grinned. They carried on just like siblings. "It's very nice to meet you, Lace. I listen to your radio show all the time. It's wonderful."

"Thanks. Maybe we could have lunch today and get to know each other better? Are you free?"

Maddie wanted to, she really did. But she had a few things she'd already committed herself to. "Could we make it another time? I have…plans for today."

Max took a step forward, no longer looking amused. "Plans to do what?"

She couldn't tell him without ruining the surprise. Maddie peeked at Cleo, saw that the dog was on alert, and shrugged. "Just...some things."

Max ignored Lace, who stood there looking beautifully spellbound by the sudden tension in the air, and he growled, "Things involving *debauchery?*"

Maddie gasped. How dare he try to embarrass her in front of his sister-in-law. She raised her chin and lied convincingly, "Yes."

Max started to reach for her, but Maddie stepped away. "In fact," she said airily, her anger a near tangible thing, "I should be going."

It was the perfect exit line, but Maddie hesitated.

Max had her panties in his pocket. She was more than a little aware of being naked beneath her skirt. When she looked at Max, she knew he was aware of it, too. His look dared her to leave without them, and dared her to request he give them back.

Maddie lifted her chin. "Thanks for the..."

Max smirked at her, and even then he looked so handsome she wanted to drag him back into the other room.

"The what?" he taunted.

Maddie ground her teeth together. Lace silently watched them both, her gaze moving from one to the other. "Why, for the entertainment this afternoon, what else? I'd have been bored to tears otherwise."

Lace choked on a laugh.

Maddie turned to her. "How about lunch on Friday, Lace? Are you free then?"

With a beaming smile, Lace said, "That'd be wonderful. Shall I meet you here at eleven-thirty?"

Maddie nodded. "Sounds perfect. I'll look forward to it."

She waggled her fingers at Max. "See ya later, Max." Then

she went to her knees—carefully so that her skirt kept her naked behind well covered—and hugged Cleo. "I'll visit again soon, Cleo! And maybe next time you'll be able to stay awake."

Cleo's growl turned into a begrudging woof.

Maddie walked out without another word to anyone.

MAX WAITED until Maddie had rounded the corner outside the shop, then said in a rush to Lace, "Do me a favor, sweetheart. Watch the shop for a few minutes."

"Max! Where are you going?"

Max reached in his pocket for his keys, felt Maddie's silky panties still tucked in there, and smiled. "I'm going to follow her, of course."

Cleo ran to Max's side and growled her approval as Max trotted out the door.

Lace hurried behind them. "But...she looked ready to kill you, Max! Maybe you should give her a little time to cool down, after provoking her that way."

"Ha!" Max headed for his truck in the parking lot. "You should get to know Maddie better if you want to see the definition of provoking. Besides, if Maddie plans to do any more debauching, I plan to stop her."

"*More* debauching?"

He grinned despite his urgency to catch up to Maddie. "She's a wonderful debaucher."

Lace caught his arm. "Then why stop her?"

"Because she should be doing all her debauching with *me!*" Max reached his truck and jerked the door open. Cleo sprang inside and Max quickly buckled her into her doggy seat. He could just see the back of Maddie as she walked toward a small white compact parked on the opposite side of the street.

He turned to Lace, who leaned in his open door window. "I promise I'll only be a minute."

"This is my lunchtime, Max."

"I'll bring you back something Mexican."

Her eyes lit up. "Deal. But I only have an hour."

"Gotta go, sweets. I'll be back on time, I promise." Max gunned the truck and pulled out several lengths behind Maddie.

They didn't have far to go. In fact, they were still on the same street, but Max couldn't believe it when she pulled the little car into a parking space in front of a well-known fetish shop. Eyes agog, he said to himself, "No way."

Cleo whimpered.

"Can you believe this? What the hell is she up to?"

Cleo had no answer, only a worried frown.

"You stay put girl, and I'll go check it out. I'll only be a minute." Max adjusted both windows to let in enough breeze for Cleo to be comfortable, then slipped out of the truck. Maddie had indeed gone into the fetish shop, bold as you please.

Dashing across the street, Max sidled up to the enormous front window that was draped with a dark blue curtain, hiding all the scandalous material for sale. He could just barely see inside where the curtains didn't quite close all the way.

Maddie had gone down a long aisle, so Max opened the door and followed her in.

He heard her talking to a salesperson.

"I want it to be red leather. With colored gems and silver studs."

Red leather! Studs?

"I have just what you need," the salesman said. "Follow me."

Ha! Max thought to himself. He was the man who had what she needed, not some salesman. He slunk along, feeling like a very determined fool. When he peeked around the corner of a tall shelf holding a variety of adult magazines and books, he saw Maddie testing the strength of a thick red leather collar.

His stomach dropped to his knees.

He was outraged, scandalized—and horny as hell.

The salesman said, "Would you like to see the ankle and wrist cuffs as well?"

In her oh-so-innocent voice, Maddie asked, "Ankle and wrist cuffs? Really?"

The salesman—a young fellow with an array of earrings—gave her a smarmy grin. "They're padded with sheepskin so as not to abrade."

Maddie's beautiful blue eyes widened in fascination. "Show me."

Growling under his breath, Max made his way back up to the front of the store and skulked behind a display of soft velvet whips. Just what did Maddie think she was going to do with that paraphernalia? Max wondered. Then such an interesting parade of ideas flashed through his mind, he almost didn't notice when Maddie came to the counter to pay.

He was shaking too badly.

She had her back to him, so Max couldn't see her final purchases, but the bag she walked out with was enormous. Almost as enormous as the smile on her face.

Max stewed as he followed her, keeping a safe distance away so as not to be observed. She was actually humming. He could hear the happy, devil-may-care sound easily over the noise of the street.

He narrowed his eyes as he watched her get into her car. Oh, Maddie may have been making some fantasy-based plans in her creative little mind, but Max decided right then and there that her plans were about to change.

She'd just started the car when Max leaned into the window. "Maddie."

She squealed and jumped a good foot. With a hand over her heart, she said, "Good grief, Max! What are you doing here?"

Max smiled. *I've got you now, sweetheart.* "I was just picking up some lunch for Lace."

He saw Maddie's smile turn into a frown. "She's having lunch with you?"

"Yes."

"What," she demanded, "does her husband think of that?"

"My brother's not an ogre who chains a woman to his side." Then he admitted, "Besides, he knows he can trust Lace."

That gave her pause, and rightfully so, because it was apparent she didn't trust Max at all.

All she said was, "Oh."

"What are you doing here?"

Her face turned beet red. "Max." She looked around, as if someone might hear her, then said, "Actually, nosy, it's a surprise."

"A surprise for who?" That was the part that was getting to him. If she wanted to play sex games, Max was willing. As long as he was the only other player, and they played by his rules.

"For you, who else?"

Now that pleased him. Who else, indeed.

"Here, I have something for you." Max pulled her panties out of his back pocket and offered them to her.

With a horrified gasp, Maddie snatched the underwear from his hand and shoved them under the car seat. "You, Max Sawyers, are the most annoying, the most—"

Max cut off her diatribe with a smoldering kiss. When he finally pulled away, Maddie was soft and warm and smiling at him.

Amazing.

"I thought about keeping them," he murmured. "Sort of as a trophy."

Rather than taking offense, Maddie asked, "Like a notch on the bedpost?"

It was hard to smile. "Yeah. But then I kept thinking about you running around bare-assed all day and I knew it'd make me crazy."

Maddie looked at him through her lashes. "Crazy...how?"

"Crazy with lust. Crazy with wanting you again. The thing about nooners, they're the equivalent of an appetizer." He trailed one rough fingertip down the line of her throat to her shoulder, then to the swell of her right breast. "I want the full course."

Sighing, Maddie said, "Mmm. Me, too." But she added, "Not that this afternoon wasn't nice. Exceptional in fact." And with a small smile, "I loved it. Thank you."

Damn, she was about to bring him to his knees right there in the middle of the street. Max cleared his throat.

"I gotta go, babe," he said regretfully. "Lace only has so long for lunch."

As if only then realizing what he'd done to her, arousing her again then saying goodbye, Maddie scowled. "Cad. But I'm glad you're here. I meant to ask you two things before you made me mad enough to leave."

Max didn't want her dredging up her pique, so he said quickly, "Ask away."

Now, Max thought, he'd find out about the bondage stuff. She'd ask him how he felt about it, if he'd be willing. And of course, Max would be understanding, and cooperative and—

"Will you come to work with me tonight?"

Vivid sexual images faded away to nothingness. "Uh...to work?"

"Yes, I have meetings several times a week with different groups, and tonight's the night I get together with some really special women. I'd like you to meet them, and as we discussed, you could share some firsthand experiences."

"Uh, Maddie..." Max was positively horrified by the idea.

"Please Max." She blinked those sexy big blue eyes at him and Max felt himself melting. He'd have to remember to write a column warning men about the effects of big blue eyes.

"I already told them about you. And about the book. I'd

appreciate it if you could bring it along, too, since you...distracted me when I was there and I forgot to get it."

Max grinned. "Is that what the women are calling it these days? A distraction?"

Maddie returned his humor. "A very pleasant distraction, to be sure."

"Pleasant?" He snorted at her and pretended to be insulted. "I thought it was more like mind-blowing, climactic—"

Maddie purred, "Definitely climactic."

Her tone made his nerve endings riot. Max eyed the tiny back seat of her car and wondered if they'd fit...but no. Cleo was waiting in his truck. Damn.

If talking with young women who were complete strangers about sexual variety was what it took to see her again, Max figured he could handle it. After all, he had altruistic motives. Cleo needed Maddie. Today was proof of that.

But he wouldn't like it.

Grousing, he asked, "Where and when?"

"Thank you, Max!" Maddie shuffled through the glove box then handed him a business card with the address of the clinic printed on it. "Five o'clock, okay?"

Still uncertain of the whole idea, Max hesitantly nodded his agreement and took the card. Maddie reached out and caught his hand. She lifted it to her mouth and kissed his palm.

"And Max?" she whispered. "Would you want to come over to my apartment afterward?"

Desire snaked through him, nearly curling his toes.

That had never happened to him before. If one of his male readers had written to Max about curling toes, Max would have called him a weenie.

Now he had to reevaluate, because his toes were indeed curled.

And Max Sawyers was definitely not a weenie.

"No." The seductive teasing left Maddie's gaze, until Max

leaned close and murmured, "I want you in my bed this time, little tease."

Her lips parted.

Max kissed her gently, sealing their agreement. If Maddie wanted to try her dominatrix tricks, it'd be on his turf.

"We'll have dinner," Max told her, stroking her sun-warmed cheek, "then I'll drive you to my house." And he'd damn well keep her there all night, he decided. Maybe even for a week. Possibly for the rest of her life.

It was the least he could do for Cleo.

When Max got back to his truck, tapping the clinic's business card against his thigh, Cleo gave him a sullen look.

"I'm sorry, girl, did you miss me?"

Grudgingly, Cleo licked his chin.

"Thanks, Cleo. I needed that."

Max found out how true that sentiment was the second he stepped back into the bookstore. Lace practically pounced on him.

"Okay, what's going on?"

In no hurry to bare his soul, Max carried the Mexican food into the back room and placed it on the table. Cleo, smelling the food, stayed hot on his heels. So did Lace.

"What's going on with what?"

When Lace didn't answer, Max looked up to see her staring at the small refrigerator. It sat out of alignment, crooked instead of flush against the wall. He grinned.

Shaking her head, Lace said, "You're such a rogue. And quit smiling. I refuse to ask you anything about it."

"Great. Then let's eat." Cleo barked in agreement, making Lace jump. The two females kept a good deal of space between them.

Max knew if Maddie had been there, Cleo would have still been sitting on her foot.

Lace had only eaten two bites of her burrito before she said, "Why are you dodging Dan and Daniel?"

Oh hell, Max thought. He didn't need this today. "Lace…"

"No, don't start with your excuses. You're needed at the business and you know it. I've been patient with all this middle-child moping, but Max, it's time to move on."

Max glared at her, wondering how in the world he'd run head on into two such bullheaded women in one day. Through his teeth, he said, "I do not mope." And his damn toes didn't curl either. "The simple fact of the matter is, there's nothing for me to do at the business."

"There's all kinds of things for you to do!"

"Okay, let me rephrase that. There's nothing that I'm needed to do. You know I'd go crazy sitting in an office, crunching numbers or sitting in on board meetings. That's not my speed, Lace. I'd be like a fish out of water."

After glancing at her watch, Lace gobbled down the last of her food and stood. She crossed her arms and gave Max a calculating stare.

"What?" he asked, feeling uneasy about the way she seemed to dissect him with her gaze.

"Guy wants to spend more time with Annie now. You know he worked extra long and hard trying to keep himself occupied so he wouldn't think of her."

"Yeah, so? I gather it worked, given how long it took him to wise up and admit he loved her."

Lace nodded. "And you know Daniel has no spare time with the hours he puts in at the hospital."

"You're not going to guilt me into anything here, sweetheart, so you might as well give it up."

Lace ignored his interruption. "A lot of the workload that Guy's looking to get rid of involves travel."

Max couldn't quite hide his sudden interest. Damn, he missed traveling. He'd been born with a heavy case of wanderlust and missed being on the road. Even the simplest trip was a pleasure for him.

But since bringing Cleo home, he'd curbed all those tendencies. Cleo needed him. He rubbed her ears as he said, "You know I can't leave my dog. And there's no one she'd be comfortable staying with."

They both heard the ding of the front door and knew a customer had come in. Max stood, ready to wrap up their conversation. And Lace needed to get back to the radio station.

"Maddie could watch her," Lace suggested as she gathered up her purse.

Max put his arm around Lace and headed her toward the door. "What makes you think I want to leave Maddie behind either?"

Suddenly a big male body, taking up the entire doorframe blocked them. A low voice said, "Then take her with you. Take the dog with you, too. I'll pay for arrangements that'll accommodate all three of you. But Max, I want you in my company."

Max stared at Dan Sawyers, his mostly absentee father, a man who until very recently had retreated from life. Annie's engagement had given him new purpose and forced him out of his self-imposed exile. Max was glad; he wanted his father happy.

Things had just gotten very complicated.

Distracted, Max watched Lace slip out of the shop in a hurry. Dan stood there, looking determined and somewhat uncertain.

Cleo, the traitor, abandoned him to chew on a rawhide bone.

Never before in his entire life could Max remember his father asking him for anything. His brother Daniel had been the father figure, filling in when their mother died and Dan retreated from everyone, including his children. He'd provided for them and seen that their physical, medical and monetary needs had been taken care of. But every holiday he'd sought isolation, leaving their emotional care to Daniel.

Max respected his brother more than any man he'd ever known. For most of his life, he'd resented his father.

"Can I get you anything, Dad? I think there's some coffee left."

Dan appeared to let out a breath he'd been holding. "Coffee would be great. A little conversation would be even better."

"Strange. I didn't think you cared for conversation." Max wanted to hold on to his resentment, to nurture it. But his thoughts were softened by Maddie, and he was in too mellow a mood to be angry.

They each pulled out chairs at the table Max and Lace had just abandoned. Max poured the strong, stale coffee.

"I owe you a lot of explanations."

"No. You owe Daniel, not me. And you owe him more than lip service."

"I know." Dan turned his coffee cup this way and that, took a sip and then winced at the bitterness. "Daniel and I are working things out. It was grossly unfair the way I abandoned him to deal with everything." In a softer voice he added, "He's an exceptional man. I'm so damn proud of him..."

Max gulped down his own coffee. All his life he'd been known as the difficult one. Daniel was the oldest, the most mature, the patriarch of the family from the time he was a kid. Annie was a sweetheart, the only girl, the most loving. But Max...he'd indulged in mischief for as long as he could remember and as soon as he'd gotten old enough, he'd taken to traveling.

As if reading his mind, his father said, "I'd always thought you'd outgrow your love of travel, but Lace tells me it's a part of you."

Max shrugged. "I enjoy it, but I've given it up."

"You don't need to give it up. I meant what I said. Guy has never liked traveling or dealing with the chore of buying from our manufacturers. In fact, he threatened to leave the company unless I took an equal share of the responsibility."

"I see." It figured that his father would find a way

around accepting that agreement. "So you want me to fill in for you now?"

"Not at all."

Max held his cup a little more tightly. That wasn't what he'd been expecting to hear.

Smiling, Dan said, "Given the way I've behaved in the past, you have every right to your assumptions. But the fact is, I'm enjoying being involved again. I'm enjoying life again."

Heart softening, Max returned his smile. "I'm glad." Then he asked, "What brought about this drastic change?"

A small smile on his face, Dan said, "I got some good advice."

"That right?" Max sipped his coffee. "What kind of advice?"

Dan tugged on his ear. "Sexual advice." Before Max could quite assimilate that, he added, "I was assured that a little sex would improve my disposition greatly. I've decided it's worth a try."

Max choked on a swallow and was forced to spend several minutes regaining his breath. When he was finally able to wheeze again, he said, "Sex!" and with a rumble of blustering menace, "Did Lace fill your head with nonsense?"

"Nope." Dan grinned. "Got the advice straight out of the newspaper. From that guy who writes the column on sex."

Max promptly choked again. Dan stood to thwack him on the back several times, but it didn't help. Good God, he'd advised his own father to make whoopie!

The vague memory of an unsigned letter, which he'd answered in the column, slipped through Max's brain. It had been good advice, he thought. But not for his *Dad!*

"The thing is," Dan continued, as if his youngest son wasn't turning red and strangling to death, "I've been out of the loop too long, both personally and professionally. The personal end I can work on myself."

"Glad to hear it," Max managed. He knew for a fact he

couldn't offer any more suggestions, so it was a good thing his father didn't want any.

"But I'm too old to start dealing with the entire workload all at once. You have a way with people, Max. Everyone respects you and likes you."

The praise not only distracted Max from his father's first bomb, but it also warmed him from the inside out. That didn't sit well with him. At his age, he shouldn't want or need a father's approval.

But it felt good to get it just the same.

Dan watched Max a moment, then continued. "Guy hates to travel, I'm not up to it, and you like it. Also, because of all your traveling, you're up on which supplies are quality, and what's needed where. You've hiked, skied, trekked through Africa, spent weeks alone in the wilds of Canada... You'd be the perfect one to make purchase recommendations."

Max glanced at his watch. The shop would close in an hour, then he'd head home and shower, make sure Cleo was fed and comfortable—and be with Maddie again. He could hardly wait.

Curiosity got the better of him and he asked, "How much travel are we talking?"

"In the States, pretty regularly. But as I said, the company can afford to accommodate you in whatever way you want."

"I won't have Cleo closed up in a damn storage area. She wouldn't understand and it would upset her."

Dan looked at Cleo, who was now snoring loudly. He grinned. "We have a small private plane. She can ride with you."

Damn but the idea was appealing. The need to be on the move had been eating at him for weeks. And Maddie had claimed she wanted to travel...

Of course, she'd also claimed to want him only to notch her bedpost. He'd have to work on her.

Tonight, he'd wrap her in such a hot, sensual spell, she'd become addicted and gladly follow him around the country.

Ha, and Cleo would learn to fly.

Max cursed low.

"What does that mean, Max? Are you considering it?"

"I don't know. I was actually thinking of something else."

"The foreign travel?" Dan asked anxiously. "Because there won't be much of that. Just one or two trips a year to Mexico, perhaps Taiwan or China."

If Maddie stuck around, Cleo could stay with her. It'd be nice to have them both to come home to.

Max flattened his hands on the tabletop. "Actually, I was thinking of a woman I've met recently. I'm not too keen on the idea of running off and leaving her unsupervised. She's...well, she's enticing as hell. Without me around, there'll be a line of guys trying to take my place."

Dan blinked at Max, then threw his head back and laughed.

Max couldn't remember the last time he'd seen his father laugh. "Care to share the joke?"

Dan wiped his eyes, still chuckling, and managed to say, "You're in love! By God, that's wonderful. And Max, don't misunderstand, I'm thrilled!"

Love? Max shook his head. "I don't know her that well."

"So? I met your mother and within minutes knew she was my life."

"Maddie makes me crazy."

"That's a good sign. When I first met your mother, I couldn't decide if I wanted to kiss her or throttle her."

"I guess kissing won out, huh?" Max found himself smiling, too.

"Absolutely. And she was worth all the effort it cost me to win her over." Dan looked at Max, his face again solemn. "There've been a lot of lost years, son. I hope you can forgive me, but I can understand if you can't."

Without a single hesitation, Max said, "I forgive you." In many ways, he was beginning to realize the loss was more his father's than his own. He'd had Daniel and Annie and Guy...but his father had had no one and nothing but his grief.

"Thank you." Dan smiled in relief, then released Max and stood. "You do love her, son. I can see it in your face."

Also coming to his feet, Max said, "I don't know. It's not that easy."

"Love never is! But you're a good catch, so I'm positive she feels the same." Dan clapped him on the shoulder. "Think about the job. We really do need you there."

Grinning, Max said, "I'll talk it over with Maddie." Who knows, he thought, Maddie said she wanted to travel. Maybe the job would be a lure to help get her to commit.

At this point, Max was willing to try anything.

Chapter Seven

MADDIE WAITED outside the clinic for Max. She couldn't stop thinking about what he'd done to her, what they'd done together! It was so wonderful.

And she couldn't stop thinking about Cleo.

Darn it all, she missed the dog almost as much as she missed the man. They were both so special! How many young, handsome, virile, world-traveled men would have settled down to take care of a dog? A very needy dog.

Not many.

No two ways about it, Max was special.

And she was sunk.

Maddie collapsed back against the brick wall of the clinic. How much longer would she have with Max? A few days, a week? Admitting to herself that she'd gotten emotionally involved wasn't easy. She'd meant to keep things superficial, to gather up some memories without commitment, the same as so many others did. Her ex had accused her of being too prim, and she'd wanted to prove him wrong. But now, what he thought didn't matter.

Deep down where it really counted, which was in her own heart, Maddie had always known that she wasn't the type of woman for sexual flings.

Oh, flinging with Max was great. Superb in fact. But she

also wanted him to hold her. She wanted to talk to him and ask about his travels. Most of what she knew of Max she'd learned from Annie. And it wasn't enough.

Bea and Carmilla and Mavis swore she needed to hold out on him. Not sex, because Max could get that anywhere and from just about any woman. She needed to hold out on all those things she so wanted to give to him; affection and caring and...*love.*

Maddie groaned, knowing she was already too deeply involved to hold back on anything.

A bright yellow dandelion grew up through a crack in the sidewalk in front of the clinic and Maddie ruthlessly brought her sandal down onto it.

She could not love Max Sawyers!

A long, low whistle brought her head up. Max stood there, grinning like the devil, his dark eyes full of teasing good humor. "You got a thing about weeds, I gather?"

Maddie stared at him blankly. "What?"

"You looked like you had murder on your mind."

Maddie devoured the sight of him. He looked scrumptious in a casual white shirt and khaki slacks. His dark hair was windblown, his teeth white in his tanned face. Her heart did a flip-flop, and was followed by her stomach.

She couldn't give him love, but she could give him female appreciation.

Maddie threw herself at him. Max looked startled for just a second before Maddie got hold of his head and brought it down for her kiss. "I missed you, Max."

He gave a murmuring reply against her lips. "Hmm. I like this welcome."

"Everything we did this afternoon... I haven't been able to stop thinking about...it." She'd almost said *you* but that would have given too much away.

Max lifted his head, looked up and down the street and smiled at her. "We're being watched by about a dozen people."

"Oh!" Maddie quickly straightened. Good grief, she worked here. The last thing she wanted to do was put on a show.

"Did you put your panties back on?"

"Of course!"

"Spoilsport."

Oh, the way he said that. He could make her want him with just a whispered word. "Max, behave. You'll get me all flustered and then I won't be able to concentrate on the meeting."

When she started to turn away, he caught her hand. "Tonight, how do you want it? Conventional or kinky?"

"Max…"

"Hey, a man needs to make plans. So which is it to be, sweetheart?"

He obviously liked to fluster her, Maddie thought. She looked up at him, touched his bottom lip, and said, "How about both?"

Maddie felt his indrawn breath both from her touch and her reply.

"You little witch," Max said with something that bordered on admiration. "Both it is."

"I was just teasing!"

"I'm not." Max handed her the slim book she'd requested. "Have you read this thing?"

"Not yet. Why? Did you?"

"Bits and pieces. It was…interesting, but not always accurate."

"There you see! I knew your perspective would add a lot." She smiled at him.

Max groaned. "Let's go get this over with before I change my mind."

Catching his arm, Maddie led him into the old building and down the tiled hallways. "You're not nervous are you?"

"Nervous about speaking to a bunch of young women on sexual dos and don'ts? Why ever would I be nervous?"

His sarcasm was plain to hear.

"Um, Max, about the women…" Maddie started to explain to him that the women weren't exactly young, but as she pushed open the door to the conference room, Max froze. Her friends were already inside.

Mavis, dressed in a long flowing dress of bright cherry red that nearly matched her hair, sat with her feet propped up on another chair. She wiggled her foot in time to whatever music was coming through a set of headphones plugged into a portable CD player.

Bea, wearing jeans and a white ruffled blouse, paced, obviously deep in thought. And Carmilla was secluded in the corner talking to someone who sat behind her. Maddie couldn't see who it was.

Maddie cleared her throat and drew everyone's attention.

Max looked around the room, then at Maddie. Bending close to her ear, he whispered, "These are not young women, Maddie."

"Uh, no."

Bea gave Max a thorough once-over, then let loose with a wolf whistle.

Nodding in agreement, Mavis said, "Ho, baby. He's a hottie."

Bea added, "Our girl knows how to pick 'em, doesn't she?"

"Neither," Max said, his face bright red, "do any of these women look the least bit confused about anything sexual."

Bea said, "Ha!"

Mavis added, "You got that right, sweet cheeks." And she gave him a cocky grin.

"They're very nice ladies, Max." Maddie tried glaring at Mavis and Bea so they'd back off just a little. Max looked ready to make a run for it. "I promise."

Carmilla finally stepped out of the corner and a man rose up from behind her. He rose and rose and rose some more.

Easily six feet six inches, the man was enormously built and bald as an ostrich egg. He wore a black Harley-Davidson T-shirt with the sleeves cut off to show massive biceps. His right forearm sported an intricate tattoo of a naked lady. When he moved his arm—which he was doing now by flexing his knuckles—the naked lady danced.

Maddie gulped.

Max said with certainty, "That is no lady."

The big man started forward.

Mustering up her courage, Maddie tentatively tried to offer her hand, and instead found herself tossed behind Max's back.

Carmilla burst loose with a robust laugh. "Honey, your heart's in the right place, but you sure ain't up to taking on Tiny."

Maddie peeked around Max. "Tiny? That's really you?"

Eyes narrowed, Max turned to face her suspiciously. "Is this another one of your jokes, Maddie? Like that 'small pistol' business. Because there's nothing tiny about that guy. He's *huge.*"

Maddie giggled nervously. "You mean just like your roll of dimes?"

Max gave her a belligerent look and growled, *"Flashlight."* Then he jutted his chin and added, "Industrial size."

"Oh, yeah." She giggled again. "I remember now."

"I know him," Carmilla interjected, "and I can guarantee you he would never hurt Maddie." Then, just because Carmilla was so dang bloodthirsty, she added, "But I make no guarantees where you're concerned, young fellow."

Max snorted.

Scooting out from behind her erstwhile protector, Maddie said, "Tiny, it's so nice to finally meet you!" There had been times in the past year that she'd wondered if Tiny was real, or a romanticized figment of Carmilla's imagination.

The man was very real. Imposingly real.

And though he took Maddie's hand and kissed her knuckles in a curiously old-world gesture, he kept looking at Carmilla with adoring eyes.

Well, well, Maddie thought. She glanced at Bea, who

winked, and then to Mavis, who was still eyeing Max's more interesting parts.

"*Down*, Mavis," Bea suddenly said. "Apparently our Maddie is the jealous sort. Just look at her, her eyes are turning red."

Mavis looked and said, "I'll be damned. Even her nostrils are flared." Then to Carmilla, "Quit playing touchy-feely with your boyfriend and come look at Maddie."

It wasn't just her eyes that were red after that comment. Especially when Max, wearing a huge grin, peered directly into her gaze.

"Are you jealous, sweetheart? And here I didn't say a word when Tiny kissed your hand."

"So," Mavis said, sauntering forward. "You're the young stud Maddie has been telling us all about."

Max stiffened, then glared at Maddie.

Shrugging, she whispered, "I didn't tell them *everything*. I just…"

"She bragged on you, is what she did. And after that worthless creep she almost married, we were more than glad to hear it."

Max gave a parody of a smile. "What exactly did she tell you?"

Bea stepped forward and gave Mavis a warning frown. Then she turned her smile to Max. "Why, she told us you'd made her happy." Her smile lit up just a bit more. "And Maddie definitely deserves some happiness."

Things were out of control, Maddie decided. "Are we having a meeting today or not?"

"Not," Carmilla said. "We want to get to know Max better. That's more important."

"And it's for certain he can't tell us anything about sex that we don't already know," Bea added.

"After all," Mavis said with a sniff, "we got paid for our expertise."

Maddie whipped around to face Max, giving the women and Tiny her back. In a pleading voice, she said, "I'm sorry!"

Surprising her, Max touched her cheek and said, "For what?"

"I..." She felt confused and lost her train of thought. "I meant to tell you about this, about my friends..."

"They are friends, aren't they?" She nodded and he said, "I think that shows what a special woman you are, that friendship has grown from counsel meetings."

"Damn right," Carmilla said, and Bea added, "Best friends. She's like a daughter to us, and you should remember that."

Mavis laughed. "Calm down, Maddie. He's not afraid of three little old ladies. Are you, young man?"

Max looked over Maddie's head at the others. His eyes were lit with challenge. "Why don't we all sit down?" He threw his arm around Maddie, almost making her drop the book. "I'll wager there's a few things I can still enlighten you on."

Tiny smiled.

Carmilla snorted.

Bea and Mavis said in unison, "You're dreamin'!"

Maddie wished she could just crawl away. But Max had hold of her hand and his grip was unbreakable.

Oh, dear. This wasn't at all what she'd planned.

MAX WANTED TO laugh at the silly little sick look on Maddie's face.

Prostitutes! Who'd have thought she was counseling retired ladies of the night? He shook his head. One thing about Maddie, she never ceased to surprise him.

"You know," he said to Mavis, who seemed to be the most brazen, "I thought I was here to talk to young innocent girls who were either caught in an unexpected pregnancy or had troubled home lives."

"You didn't expect a bunch of old biddies, did you?"

"I didn't expect mature women, no."

"Maddie does counseling with women of all ages. The poor young girls you're talking about meet with her on Tuesdays."

"And they're lucky to have her," Carmilla told him. "They don't come any more compassionate than Maddie."

"Not to mention how smart she is, and such a good listener." Bea smiled fondly at Maddie.

Maddie had slipped down in her chair until her face was almost hidden behind the fall of her hair. She looked miserable by the turn of events.

But her long legs, thrust out in front of her looked incredibly nice. Max wanted to start kissing her slim ankles and work his way up. All the way up.

Until she was panting and moaning and... He cleared his throat.

"How many nights a week does she do this?"

Bea, catching his distraction with Maddie's legs, raised a brow and asked, "This?"

Max shook his head. "Have these meetings."

Carmilla perched herself on Tiny's lap. Tiny didn't seem to mind, if his big grin was any indication. "Two to three times a week," she said, "depending. Truth is, we should have quit bugging her years ago, but she's so much fun to talk to. Like the daughter none of us ever had."

Maddie was a nurturer, Max thought, seeing it in the older women's eyes. She didn't pass judgment on people, and she looked beyond the obvious. He knew that much about her because of how she'd so readily accepted Cleo.

"Did you know," Max asked, more than willing to work to meet the women's standards, "that men can literally become addicted to a certain woman's smell?"

Maddie's head lifted, her eyes filled with fascination.

Bea scoffed.

Carmilla looked at Tiny, who delicately sniffed her shoulder.

Mavis shrugged. "Where'd you hear such a thing?"

"I've read about it in medical studies. My brother is a doctor and my sister-in-law is a sex therapist."

That got a few raised brows. Max hid his smile. "Every woman's skin has a unique scent. A man's body can get used to that scent, and if the woman leaves him—" or dies, Max thought, as his mother had, and suddenly he understood his father much, much better "—then the man will suffer withdrawal. It's probably where the term heartsick came from. You *do* feel like you have a broken heart. And it really does hurt."

Max looked at Maddie. How would he feel if he could never hold her again, never kiss her again? In such a short time he'd become very addicted to her, her laugh, her smile, her compassion. And her scent.

What exactly had his poor father gone through, knowing the woman he loved had been taken from him forever?

The women were quiet, watching Max with new respect. Max knew they'd expected him to orate on sexual positions or some such nonsense. But he was smarter than that.

"Did you know," he asked, watching them all closely, "that sex is a natural pain reliever?"

They all straightened up to listen.

"It's true. Sex releases endorphins that relieve pain."

"Fascinating," Maddie said. "Annie told me a little about this."

"Annie manipulated the facts so she could seduce poor Guy." Before that, Max thought, he'd never known how creatively sneaky his baby sister could be, or how determined she was to have Guy as her own.

"My knee *has* been botherin' me," Tiny rumbled, and everyone laughed as Carmilla swatted at him.

"Both men and women," Max continued, pleased that he had their rapt attention, "have testosterone. And testosterone is the only proven true aphrodisiac."

"All right," Bea said, "you win. I didn't know any of that."

Carmilla bobbed her slim eyebrows. "Want us to tell you some of what we know?"

Lounging back in his chair, his arms spread wide, Max said, "Sorry girls. I already know it all."

Maddie threw the book at him, which he handily caught, while the others all hooted and made lewd observations. Max blew a kiss at Maddie and said, "I'm having fun, doll. You should have introduced me to your friends earlier."

While Maddie sat there looking openly pleased with him, Max passed the book over to Tiny. "You should check that out. Especially chapter six."

Tiny looked at the book. Max hoped like hell the guy could read! Then Tiny flipped through a few pages and grinned. "Interesting stuff, huh?"

"Real interesting."

Carmilla tried to grab the book, but Tiny held it out of her reach. "If you want to know what it says, you'll have to let me read it to you."

"Is that a dare?" Carmilla asked.

Tiny looked at Maddie. "Would you mind if Carmilla and I took off a little early? Now that I'm finally with her again, I'd like to get her to myself just a bit."

Maddie looked at the couple with dreamy, romantic eyes. "Of course I don't mind!" She sighed. "I think it's very sweet of you."

Carmilla had silver hair and faded brown eyes, but in that moment, she looked like an excited young girl. Max wanted to imitate Tiny and pull Maddie into his lap, but she stayed out of reach for the next ten minutes.

It wasn't until after Carmilla had gone and Bea and Mavis and Maddie had shared speculation on what might come of the relationship, that Max was able to really get her attention again.

He caught her close and kissed her. The older women chuckled and urged Max with ribald suggestions.

Maddie hid her face in his chest once he released her.

"So," Max asked, "which of you lovely ladies does the incredible slogans?"

Bea, looking flattered, primped with her white hair. "That would be me."

"Care to talk business for a moment?"

Bea glanced at Mavis and Maddie and then, blushing like a schoolgirl, said, "Sure. That'd be fine," and with just a touch more hesitation, "right now?"

"It's a simple proposition."

"I know all about *those*, honey!"

Max smiled. "Not that kind." He really enjoyed the women's ease and comfort with their pasts. They were obviously no longer in the flesh business, and just as obviously not about to make apologies. They were strong, blunt women, and he respected that.

"I just agreed to do some work for my father," Max said. "It'll involve traveling and purchasing." Out of the corner of his eye, Max watched Maddie make a sudden jerky move. He glanced at her, and saw that her eyes had flared, her cheeks had gone pale. He started to ask her what was wrong, but then she lowered her head to stare at her hands.

Max cleared his throat. "Once I agreed to the job, I got to thinking about other parts of the business. We deal in sporting goods and outdoor recreations like rock climbing and kayaking and such. A lot of the equipment we advertise is geared toward a younger crowd. I'm thinking your slogans may be the perfect way to draw attention to them."

"Oh, this could be fun," Bea said, and her blue eyes were alight with excitement.

"Why don't you think on it, maybe come up with a couple of samples, and we'll present them to my father to see what he thinks."

"I'll get right on it!" Bea sauntered away, murmuring to herself, already working on thinking up ideas. Watching her,

Max noticed that she was slim despite her age, and had a rather stately walk. It dawned on him that Carmilla and Mavis were the same, though Carmilla had a very lush figure and Mavis was bordering on petite. They each had to be in or near their early seventies, but they had the attitudes and personalities of women much younger.

He wondered what his dad would think of them. He could hardly wait to introduce him to Bea. Now that his father was reentering the world, he could use a little shock therapy.

Mavis held up her hands. "I guess this makes me the third wheel."

"Not at all!" Maddie tried to stop her from leaving, but Mavis waved her off.

"I have a date anyway, honey, so don't worry about me."

Max cocked a brow. "A date?"

Maddie gave him a look. "Mavis is very popular among the retirees."

"Mmm-hmm," Mavis agreed. "Tonight I'm doing up the town with a very handsome widower." She leaned forward and confided, "He's six years younger than me! Only sixty-two. Isn't that delicious?"

Max held his humor in check and gave Mavis a hug. She was an easily likeable woman and he wished her a good time. He imagined the widower would have his hands full this night.

Once they were alone, Max asked Maddie, "You all right?" She was still too quiet and far too distracted. If she was thinking of the coming night and what she'd do with the stuff she'd bought at the fetish store, he'd gladly enlighten her to new plans.

"Yes, I'm fine."

He didn't believe her. Something was making her clam up, and Max decided he'd find out exactly what it was once he had her safely ensconced at his house. He took her hand and started her toward the door.

"You ever frolicked in a hot tub, Maddie, honey?"

Her steps faltered. "A hot tub?"

"In my backyard."

"But...it's too cool for that."

"Oh ye of little faith. I promise to keep you plenty warm enough. Hot even." Max leaned down to her ear and nipped her earlobe. "Burning up, in fact," he rasped.

They walked outside and Max started to lead her to his truck. Maddie held back. "I'll drive myself and meet you there."

No way. Max intended to keep her until he returned her to her home himself. If she was without a car, his odds were a lot better of succeeding. "Why bother," he asked. "Your car will be safe enough here."

"But..." She hesitated, then said, "Okay, just a second." Jogging over to her car, she unlocked the trunk and got out the bag he'd seen her purchase at the fetish shop. He thought of that damn collar and wanted to howl.

"Whatcha got there?" Max asked as she approached him again, the bag clutched tightly in her little fist.

Maddie grinned. "It's a surprise, remember? I promise to show you later tonight."

Oh, she'd show him all right. Max could hardly wait.

Once she was seated inside, the bag on the floor at her feet, Maddie looked at him. "Max?"

"Yes?" He hoped she'd ask for details on the hot tub, and then he intended to tantalize her with a blow-by-blow description of what he'd do to her, how he'd do it. The fun they'd both have.

"Do you taste the same as I do?"

The truck lurched hard as he pulled out into traffic. "Do I *what?*"

"Taste the same?" Maddie smoothed her skirt and settled herself comfortably in the seat. "I've been thinking about it all day. I don't mind if we play in the hot tub for a while, but when I taste you, I think we should be inside." As if sharing a confidence, she said, "I don't want to take a chance on a neighbor seeing us or something."

Max said, "Uh..." his mind still way back there on the tasting business.

She peeked at him. "I'm shy."

Max almost missed the turn onto the main street. "You intend to—" the words were so arousing, they would barely leave his tight throat "—*taste* me?" He hoped like hell she meant what he thought she meant.

Leaning slightly closer, Maddie put her small hand on his thigh. "Yes. Just like you tasted me." And then her hand tightened, squeezing his leg perilously close to a now very noticeable hard-on, and she added in a whisper, "Everywhere."

Max pushed down on the gas pedal.

"Slowly, Max, just as you've shown me." Her fingers drifted up his thigh, and he held his breath. Then they moved down to his knee. He groaned in disappointment and relief.

"Faster at the end though." Her fingers drifted upward again. "That's the right way, isn't it?"

Max locked his jaw to keep from panting with sensual pain. He could almost feel her mouth on him, her small pink tongue playful. He gulped.

Okay, so she wanted to play with bondage. No big deal. He could handle that, especially if it got her this enthusiastic.

She wanted to taste him.

Max felt like a Victorian maiden, ready to swoon. He concentrated hard on keeping the truck on the road so they didn't end up in a ditch.

Other women had riled him, aroused him, made him burn. What Maddie proposed had been done to him before. Hell, he'd done just about everything a man could do with a woman, and always enjoyed himself. So why was he shaking now? Why was he going alternately hot and cold with the excitement of it, the utter lust?

And dammit, his toes had just curled again.

Admittedly, he was in deep—and worse, he loved every minute of it.

Chapter Eight

THEY SNUCK into his house like thieves. Cleo, proving herself to be a miserable guard dog, was snoring too loudly to hear them. One small light shone from the kitchen, and the glow filtered into the living room where the dog sprawled across an enormous beige leather couch. Her tongue lolled out one side of her mouth, with spittle running down the couch cushion.

"She gets nervous in the dark," Max said. "So I always leave a light on for her."

Maddie's heart again performed that strange little softening for this man and his beast. "She's not much good at protecting you."

Max gave her a solemn nod. "I'd rather protect her anyway."

He was such an incredible man. And she wanted him so much.

She was also falling in love with him. Damn. Double damn.

It had just about killed her when Max claimed he'd be traveling again. She wanted to travel, too, and see the whole world. But she'd gladly have stayed in Ohio the rest of her life with Max. At first that idea hadn't appealed at all. When he'd said he'd given up traveling, she'd wanted to bemoan his decision. She didn't understand how anyone could not want to see the world, especially a man known for his wanderlust. Now she hated it that he'd leave her.

Maybe his life wasn't as settled as he'd claimed.

Soon he wouldn't have time for her anymore.

Maddie held close to the waistband of his slacks and followed him down the darkened hallway. She was here with him now, and the night was still young. Rather than regret the coming future, she should take advantage of the moment to get the most out of every second she could.

Max's house was beautiful on the outside. A mixture of Mediterranean tiles and stucco and lush landscaping. It wasn't enormous, but it was isolated, on a cul-de-sac, apart from the other houses and far more private.

The inside was too dark to distinguish precise colors, but the rooms were open, flowing into one another. The furnishings were sparse and everything appeared to be spotless. Max pulled her into his bedroom and softly closed the door.

Maddie thought of what she wanted to do to him, and how he'd react. Her stomach knotted with excitement and she licked her lips.

In the very next instant, she found herself pinned to a wall being kissed silly.

Max closed both hands over her breasts, moaned sharply, then parted her legs with his knee. He was hard, pulsing against her belly. Maddie tore her mouth away. "Max!"

Ruthlessly, he recaptured her lips. "I need you, Maddie. Right now."

She dodged him again. "I have plans!"

He groaned and pressed his face into her neck. "Your plans are what have me coming apart. Maddie, I don't know if I could bear it."

Smoothing his back, smiling quietly to herself, Maddie said, "Now Max. You're a stud, remember? Surely there's nothing I can do to you that you can't handle."

He bit her shoulder, making her yelp, then he straightened. "All right. If you're going to challenge me then I suppose I have to prove myself." He stepped away from her for a second to flip on a bedside lamp. The light was gentle, soft, just barely touching a king-size bed that was unmade and looked very comfortable.

She met Max's gaze and said, "Oh good. Now I can see you better."

His eyes nearly crossed. He took a deep breath, flexed his fingers, and then said, "Okay I think I'm ready." But as she reached for his belt he said, "No wait! It'd be better if you got undressed first."

Maddie blinked at him. "Why?"

Voice dropping an octave to where the guttural sounds stroked up and down her nerve endings, Max said, "I'll be distracted by your gorgeous bod and might be able to control myself better."

Might be able to control himself? Did that mean he was losing his control? Maddie smiled. She really liked the idea that she could push his buttons. "All right."

With Max watching her closely, his gaze a hot caress, she stripped off her clothes. She loved how he looked at her, how his muscles tensed and his high cheekbones colored with arousal.

She'd never experienced a man looking at her with so much intensity. Her fiancé never had, and she was very glad that she'd found out about him before she'd foolishly gotten married. Otherwise she wouldn't be here with Max now, and just the thought of that left her empty.

When she was completely naked she slowly stepped up to Max and undid his belt buckle. "You promise you're going to behave now, right?"

"Yes." Then he groaned as her hand slipped inside his open fly. "I'm such a liar," he gasped. "Hell no, I'm not going to behave. You're naked. You're talking about doing lecherous things to my body!"

"I'm not just talking Max. I'm going to do them."

He nodded, resigned and anxious. "Right now, I'm just concentrating on my legs."

Maddie slowly stroked him through his briefs. He was hard, throbbing and impossibly large. "Your legs?"

"Yes," he croaked. "I have to remember that I have them so I don't fall down."

Maddie chuckled. "Let's get rid of your shirt."

Before she could reach for it, Max had already whisked it over his head. It went sailing across the room to a darkened corner. Without her instruction, he kicked his shoes off and they thumped somewhere behind her.

Knowing she'd make him crazier, Maddie went to her knees in front of him. She removed his socks, teasing him by taking her time. Lastly, her hands curled around the waistband of his khaki slacks. She pulled both his pants and his underwear down, then ordered, "Step out."

He did, and Maddie looked up the tall, hard length of his body. Her nipples pulled tight and her belly tingled. He was so gorgeous, all male, rigid and strong and his scent...she leaned forward and kissed his abdomen, then drew his smell deeply inside her lungs.

Max's fingers settled into her hair, gently cradling her head. "Maddie." His voice was hoarse with strain.

Her fingers could barely circle him, holding him close at the base of his erection. She could feel his heartbeat there, matching her own. With her other hand she explored his firm backside, the iron hard muscles of his thighs, the soft tender weight below his shaft.

Max shook, his breath a gasping sound in the otherwise quiet room.

She kissed his right thigh, the smooth taut skin of his hipbone. His fingers tightened, inexorably guiding her to where he wanted to feel her mouth.

Suddenly overwhelmed with a need to please him and herself, Maddie obliged and without warning, without so much as a single peck to warn of her intent, she drew him deep. As deep as she could.

His taste was incredible, hot and salty and alive. She swirled her tongue around him, amazed at how seducing him was seducing her as well.

Max jerked hard, his head back, his fingers now tight, holding her close. He moved, once, twice, then cursed low. "I can't, Maddie."

She withdrew a bit, licked the very tip of him, and said, "Yes, you can."

He howled, sounding much like a wounded wolf. "You don't get it, baby." She could barely understand him, his words were so raw. "I'm about to—"

Thrilled with her success, Maddie said, "Please do," and enclosed him in her mouth once again.

A heavy beat of stillness enveloped them, not a sound, not a heartbeat. And then Max broke. Maddie nearly cried out with the excitement of it. She hadn't known a man could be so untamed in his pleasure, so hot and free.

Maddie continued tantalizing him until his legs went limp and he dropped to his knees in front of her. He sat back, still panting, then met her anxious gaze and gave her a breathy laugh.

"You're dangerous," he whispered, and pulled her close. There on the floor he held her, giving her all the cuddling she'd wanted, until the trembling had left his body and he could breathe again.

And then he got even.

MAX WATCHED Maddie sleeping the next day. It was early afternoon, but she showed no signs of waking. Her blond hair was twisted onto his pillow, and her bottom was beautifully bare. He smiled. He wanted to touch her, but more than that he knew he needed to let her sleep. After the stunt she'd pulled last night, he'd kept her awake till well past dawn.

And even then he hadn't been appeased.

Maddie was simply different. Better. More. Deeper and sweeter and more consuming. He'd never tire of her. He knew that now.

What to do? Having her around would provide the perfect home life for Cleo. And for him. He needed her to commit to him, but she claimed to be against marriage.

All night long, she'd reveled in their intimacy, but not once had she hinted at an emotional connection.

Quietly, Max slipped from the bed and went to the kitchen to get juice. He'd wake her, they'd talk, and hopefully he could find some chink in her armor, some way to make her stop distrusting marriage, and to give him a chance to bind her to him.

MADDIE AWOKE to the shifting of the bed and warm breath drifting over her bare hip. She smiled even before she got her eyes open. "Mmm," she mumbled with a languid stretch that found plenty of sore muscles from the newest night of debauchery. Max was just so damn good at debauching. A master.

"Not again, Max," she moaned, knowing she needed a warm shower before she could even think of going another round.

She twisted to face him, then jumped a foot when Cleo met her with a loud bark. She was naked in front of the dog!

Dreadfully embarrassed, Maddie jerked the sheet up off the floor to cover herself. The bed was destroyed, the sheets pulled loose, the spread totally gone. Both pillows were in the middle of the bed and Maddie blushed when she remembered why. Max had propped her up like a pagan offering, then made her feel pagan with the carnal way he'd enjoyed her body.

Cleo came the rest of the way into the bed, a little hesitant, keeping her head low, her tail well hidden, and Maddie felt emotions rise to choke her.

Scooting so that she was more or less sitting in the bed with the sheet around her sarong-style, she opened her arms to Cleo and the dog lumbered onto her lap.

It was the first time Cleo had come to her so openly, and it broke Maddie's heart. Maddie squeezed the dog tight as tears seeped from her eyes. She loved the ugly beast as much as she loved the magnificent master.

She wanted them both. She wanted them forever.

Yet she'd argued with Max, insisting on no more than a notch on the bedpost.

"Oh Cleo," Maddie wailed softly, "what am I going to do?" Last night had been the stuff dreams were made of, and Max thought it was all a lark, a way for her to gain sexual experience.

She certainly didn't disdain what she was learning sexually. No way. Max was a remarkable lover, natural and intense and so clever. Very clever.

But she cared about more than their physical relationship. She cared about all of him, his humor and his honor and the way he loved. He gave Cleo his whole heart, and he hadn't hesitated at all to befriend Carmilla, Bea and Mavis.

He was so easy to love, darn it.

More tears trickled down her cheeks, and Cleo whined. She licked Maddie's face, then began to wail.

The dog had the worst morning breath Maddie had ever smelled, but it didn't matter. They comforted each other, and it broke Maddie's heart to admit she had played a dumb game and lost. She'd thought she could cavort in sexual frivolity with Max and just walk away more experienced. She should have known after seeing Max with Cleo that he wasn't a man who could be played with.

And he wasn't a man who women willingly walked away from.

Maddie rocked the dog, holding her pudgy body tight. Cleo shifted around anxiously, throwing her head back and really getting into the maudlin mood of it. The more Cleo whimpered, the more tears ran down Maddie's face to mat in the dog's scruffy fur. The more Maddie hugged and cuddled the dog, the more Cleo moaned and yowled.

Max came running into the room. He carried a tray with two glasses of orange juice on it and a look of befuddlement on his face. He stopped in the doorway and glared when he saw the two females huddled on the bed making enough racket to wake the entire street.

"What the hell is going on?"

MAX LOOKED AT Maddie's tear-streaked face with alarm. Good God, she didn't cry well. Her nose was red and swollen, her eyes puffy. Her cheeks were blotchy.

He wanted to hold her in his lap and beg her not to cry. First she'd curled his toes, and now she was ripping his guts out.

More softly, he asked, "What's all the caterwauling about?" He set the tray down on the nightstand. "Maddie? Are you hurt?"

She hid her face in the dog's fur. When he started to touch her, Cleo issued a low growl of warning, then snuffled her nose into Maddie's neck.

"Well, I'll be." His damn dog had switched loyalties. Max shook his head. Good thing he loved Maddie, too. *Love.* What a tricky thing to happen to a guy.

From now on, when he wrote his column, he'd be a lot more understanding with the poor saps who got themselves tangled up in the emotion. It was damn hard to deal with, setting his heart on fire and turning his brain to mush. Everything he'd always thought he knew about women now seemed insignificant, all because he hadn't yet known Maddie. Which meant he hadn't known much at all.

Oh sure, he could make little Maddie scream with pleasure, but could he make her say, "I do"? He hadn't believed in love at first sight. He hadn't been all that sure that love existed at all, at least not the type of love that had stolen his father from him, the type of love that had turned his sedate older brother into a caveman and their friend, Guy, into a ball of distraction.

Max had honestly believed that if love existed, it needed time to grow, to stew and ferment and get real sticky. But hell, almost from the second he'd seen Maddie, his heart had known she was different. He tried to claim it was just his body talking—because she was one sexy little number—but no. It had been his heart attempting to warn his head, and now he had a wailing woman in bed with his dog and a bad case of uncertainty.

When Maddie lifted her face again, Max stared in horror. She had dog hairs stuck to the tear tracks on her cheeks. She looked to be in the throes of a transition from woman to werewolf.

She sniffed loudly. And wetly. "I'm sorry, Max."

Feeling his way, Max ventured, "For what exactly?"

"For—" She sniffed again and Cleo whined in sympathy "—for carrying on so."

Max sat on the edge of the bed and ignored Cleo's protective bluster to scratch her ear. "Care to tell me what you're carrying on about?"

Maddie nodded, but then said, "You'll hate me."

"Oh, hon." He picked off a few of the dog hairs clinging to her cheeks. "I could never hate you."

"I love you."

Max drew back, nonplussed. "What?"

"See! It's awful!" Her face went back into Cleo's fur and Cleo glared at him.

Max got his mouth to close while wondering if he'd heard right. He felt mired in confusion. Cleo continued to give him dirty looks.

Max needed to take this slowly. If Maddie really was confessing to what he thought she might be confessing to, she sure as hell wasn't happy about it.

"Here, sweetheart. Drink a little juice." A totally inane thing to suggest, but at the moment nothing more brilliant came to him.

Maddie wrinkled her red nose up and turned away. "I can't drink cold in the morning. I need coffee. Hot black coffee."

"Oh." Max frowned at her. "The caffeine is bad for you."

Maddie blinked spiked wet lashes and then her face crumbled again. "What does it matter," she wailed. "Everything is ruined now anyway and I love Cleo so much."

So now she loved Cleo, too? Max looked around his room for inspiration. There was none to be found.

Making a sudden decision, he said to Cleo, "You gotta go out, girl?"

The dog abandoned Maddie's secure hold in the blink of an eye and began anxiously circling Max's feet. Max threw the sheet off the bed, lifted Maddie in his arms, and started out of the room.

"Max! What are you doing?"

He didn't slow down. Cleo danced along beside him, her tubby body jiggling as he headed for the back door. "You look like hell in the morning, Maddie, did you know that?"

She pressed her face into his shoulder, sharing some of the tear-soaked dog hairs. "Yes. But it doesn't matter."

"Caffeine doesn't matter, how you look doesn't matter. What does matter, sweetheart?"

She started to answer, then gasped loudly as he slid the patio doors open and stepped outside. Cool April air washed over their naked bodies. Cleo shot past, running into the yard beyond the privacy fence and barking with the sheer joy of going outside. She found her deflated plastic ball in the yard and trotted it back to Max.

"Just a second, girl. I have my hands full."

Maddie clutched at him. Her red-rimmed eyes were huge and her face was pale. "What are you doing?"

She sounded squeaky, all aghast at being outside in the buff.

"I promised you the hot tub. But then you distracted me with that incredible mouth of yours." Color rushed back into her cheeks, making Max smile. "The water's warm, so prepare yourself."

Maddie tried to keep a death grip on his neck, but Max lowered her into the frothing water of the hot tub. She looked around, and when she realized they were hidden completely by tall trees and the fence, she relaxed. Her gaze was still anxious as she watched him throw the ball for Cleo.

Max climbed into the tub and joined her. "I forgot about this," he said as he lifted her into his lap and positioned her to recline back against his chest. "And didn't you forget about something, too?"

Maybe if he could distract her from her tears, Maddie would tell him she loved him again. More calmly this time, so that he could believe it.

Maddie held still as Max cupped her breasts beneath the churning water. She caught his wrists and pressed his hands closer still. "What did I forget?"

"You said you had a surprise for me," Max reminded her.

"Oh!" She twisted around to face him. "I forgot after...well, after you did what you did."

"What I did?" Max teased, glad to see she'd stopped crying for the moment. "What about what you did."

Her ravaged face softened. "I loved what I did. You taste so good, Max, and it was so extraordinary to watch you—"

Max clapped his hand over her mouth. "Shh," he warned. "I always wake up horny, and having you here makes it especially bad because I've been wanting you since before I even opened my eyes. Don't torture me now, okay?"

Maddie nodded and when he lifted his hand she asked, "Always?"

He grinned. "Yeah."

She bit her lip, and her gaze tried to see him below the

water, but the bubbles made that impossible. Finally she sighed. "Okay. Can I go get my surprise now?"

Max stalled. "Uh, now?" He looked around. The yard was secluded, but he wasn't sure he wanted to get into anything too frisky out in the open that way. "What about waiting until we—"

Before he could finish, she'd scrambled out of the hot tub—giving Max a delectable glimpse of her pale round bottom—then darted for the door. She was back in less than half a minute with her bag.

Max stiffened, anxious and turned on and curious.

To his surprise she called Cleo to her and the dog came running, her tooth-punctured ball clamped in her mouth. Cleo growled and grumbled and groused as she approached Maddie, but her tail was out and wagging. Max leaned back into the water and felt contentment swell inside him.

Life was good with his dog happy and his woman making him crazy with lust.

All he had to do was figure out this love business.

"Come here, Cleo," Maddie was saying and she seemed oblivious to her nakedness now. Max was far from unaware. The chill of being wet and in the cool air had Maddie's nipples drawn tight. He could almost taste her.

Reaching into the bag, Maddie lifted out the ornate collar. Red leather, with colorful studs, just as she'd ordered.

"Isn't it beautiful?" she asked Max. "I couldn't find anything pretty enough for Cleo at the pet store, but I'd noticed her collar was looking a little old."

Max stared at the decorative, gaudy fetish collar and wanted to roar in hilarity at his own misconceptions.

He also wanted to moan out his disappointment. Though at first he hadn't been too keen on getting kinky, he'd kind of gotten used to it.

"She didn't like for me to mess with it," Max explained, nearly choking on his suppressed laughter.

Maddie nodded. "This one is pretty. I found it at a...specialty shop. She'll like it. It looks fit for a queen."

A queen indeed, Max thought.

Cleo held perfectly still as Maddie removed the old leather collar and replaced it with the new. Once Maddie was done, the dog cast a nervous, uncertain glance at Max, which made him wonder if she knew where it had come from.

He not only had a kinky woman, but now his dog looked a bit risqué as well.

Max was grinning too much to reassure Cleo, so she looked away and shook her head. The collar was butter-soft red leather and sparkled with multihued faux gems and shining studs. Cleo's rough yellow fur stuck out in clumps around it.

Still clutching her bag and looking at the dog, Maddie backed up next to where Max lounged in the tub. She sighed dreamily. "Doesn't she look wonderful?"

Max looked at Maddie, his heart feeling as swollen as his male parts always did when she was around. The combination was explosive. "Yes, she does."

Cleo again shook her head to get a feel for the collar, woofed in acceptance, then grabbed up the hapless ball. With a snarl, she ran off to do battle, slinging the ball away then snatching it back again for more punishment.

Max reached out of the tub to hook his arm around Maddie's hips. "You'll never guess what I thought you had in that bag."

When he recalled his heated visions of bondage and dominance games, Max's pulse raced. There would still be time to play those games, he decided. He'd find the time.

Maddie's eyes were hot when she looked at him again. Of course, they were still swollen and red, too, and dog hair clung tenaciously to her cheeks and forehead. "You won't guess," she purred, "what I *do* have."

Lust surged upward, nearly obliterating everything else. Max sat up on the bench in the tub, retaining his hold on Maddie, and said, "Tell me."

Smiling wickedly, she pulled out a large white feather and whisked it around in the air. "I found this when I bought the collar and couldn't resist. I've decided I want to try it."

Max eyed the feather. "On what?"

"On *you.*"

His stomach clenched hard and he met her gaze. "Because that's what your ex-fiancé was doing?"

"No." She leaned down and kissed the end of his nose, then whispered, "Because the idea of having you tied up and at my mercy is very appealing."

Max tried to peek into the bag. "What else do you have in there?" No way would he let her use the damn feather on him, but using it on her might be fun.

Maddie held the bag away, then lifted out a velvet mitt. "This is for stroking."

"Ah." He knew just where he'd use it on her, too. "Anything else?"

Not quite meeting his gaze, Maddie mumbled something, and Max said, "What's that?"

She mumbled again, scuffing her bare toe along the edge of the hot tub.

Max tipped up her chin, curiosity humming thickly through his veins. "What else did you buy, honey?"

Maddie hesitated, then reached defiantly into the bag and withdrew a sexy little barely there camisole of cream lace. It had interesting cutouts where her nipples would be, and ended at about her hipbones. Max shuddered, just imagining Maddie decorated with that bit of fluff.

"Nice," he rasped.

Maddie clutched the camisole to her chest. "Really?"

"Oh yeah." Forcing his gaze to her face, he said, "You'll look great." Then he added, "But no better than you do standing here right now, buck naked with dog hairs sticking to your skin and your hair all mussed."

She frowned.

He meant it.

Max reached for her. "Come here, sweetheart. I want to talk to you."

She dropped the feather and the lingerie onto a lawn chair and climbed back into the tub with a splash. When she started to sit beside him, Max again brought her onto his lap—facing him this time.

Max cupped the water in his palms and rinsed her cheeks, her chest, until the dog hairs were gone and all that was left was the effects of her tears. He supposed Maddie was one of those women whose eyes stayed puffy for hours after crying. He didn't mind.

He kissed her chin, her nose, her soft mouth. "Why were you crying, honey?"

Maddie played with his chest hair. "I already told you."

"Because you love me?" Max had never felt vulnerable before, but he felt totally exposed saying the words to Maddie now. If he had heard her wrong, if she denied them, he wasn't sure what he'd do. His heart rapped sharply, clapping against his ribs.

She bobbed her head. "Yes."

"And that's a bad thing?" He wanted her to look at him, but she kept averting her face.

"It hurts." She peeked at him, then pressed herself hard against him with a bear hug. "I don't want to put any other notches on my bedpost."

"Thank God." Max returned her hug.

"I don't want you to leave me, either, but I promise I won't be a pain about it. If you...if you want to see me occasionally still, I think I'd like that."

"Maddie, where is it you think I'm going?"

"You took the job with your father." She squeezed him so hard she nearly choked him. "You're going to be traveling again."

"A little." Max stroked her back, then her soft bottom. "And only if you and Cleo can come with me most of the time."

Maddie bolted back so hard she lost her balance and toppled off Max's lap. Her head went underwater then she reappeared with a sputter. Max caught her beneath the arms and lifted her.

"For crying out loud, Maddie! What are you doing? Trying to drown yourself?" He wasn't sure he liked such a volatile reaction to his suggestion.

Maddie spit out chlorinated water and wheezed, "You want us to travel with you? Really?"

The tension that had been squeezing his heart started to ease. Max grinned. "Yeah, really. Cleo needs me too much to be left behind very often. And I'd only leave her with you, anyway. No one else."

Her smile was beautiful, brighter than the afternoon sun lighting the yard. "You trust me that much?"

Max nodded. "When I go places too far for Cleo to go along, I'll have to leave her behind. I'd feel better knowing she's with you, because she loves you."

Maddie looked toward the yard where Cleo was performing the strange act of dragging herself forward with just her front legs, scratching her behind on the ground. Maddie chuckled. "I love her, too, and I'd be happy to watch her for you."

"Here?" Max ventured, pushing just a little. "Because she'd be most comfortable in her own house."

With a wary stillness, Maddie looked at Max. "Okay, if that's what you want."

Max shoved aside his uncertainty—as any manly man would do—and stated, "You know, if you're going to be staying here sometimes, you really ought to get over this silly aversion you have to marriage and give the idea some thought. I mean, you said you love me, and you said you love my dog. Right?"

Maddie's bottom lip quivered. Oh hell, Max thought. If she

started crying again he didn't know what he'd do. Her eyes would end up swollen shut.

Maddie gulped. "You…you'd want to marry me?"

He never hesitated. "Yes. I told you all along that I was through with short-term affairs. But I swear, baby, I'd never cheat on you. Not like your ex did. So if that's what's worrying you—"

"Do you care about me, Max?"

She looked so uncertain, Max grabbed her up close and kissed her breathless.

"Care about you? I'm crazy nuts for you."

"You are? It's not just sex?"

"I've loved you," Max growled against her mouth, "almost from the moment you threw yourself against the bookstore's door. And by the time you fell inside on the floor, I was a goner."

Maddie made a small sound of surprise and he kissed her hard again. Damn, he didn't ever want to stop kissing her.

"I love how you taste, how you laugh, the crazy clothes you wear and the incredible things you do to my body. Hell, yes, I love the sex. And so much more. I especially love the way you take all the bluster away from Cleo and how you accept your friends and give so much of yourself. I kept telling myself that you'd be perfect for Cleo, but the fact is, you're perfect for me."

"Oh Max." She sniffled loudly.

"I need you, Maddie. I already told my father that I didn't want to travel and leave you behind. Not even for a few days. Not when I don't have to."

She pushed against his chest and sat up to face him. Being that she was on his lap, there was no way she could miss his erection.

She smiled. "I don't want you to put off a great job with your family just because of me. As long as I know you're coming back, I'll be happy."

Max cupped her cheek. "As long as I know you're here waiting for me, I'll be coming back."

Maddie reached beneath the water and encircled his erection. "Too bad I don't want to get the velvet glove wet."

Max groaned. But he caught himself before succumbing. That thought amused him enough that he could fight off the lust. For just a moment. "I have another job you should probably know about."

Dismayed, she paused in her attention to his body and said, "More travel?"

"No, writing." He explained about the column he did for the magazine and to his surprise, Maddie glared at him.

"I read that column! You're always so cynical!"

"I was uneducated."

"Ha! You know more about women—"

"Their bodies, yes. But you've taught me about my own heart."

Her frown melted away. "Oh, Max." She kissed him, then asked hesitantly, "No one knows you write that column?"

"No, and I'd like to keep it that way."

Maddie grinned in relief. "Me, too. I'm finding I'm the jealous sort—which is new for me—and I just know if anyone found out that you write—"

A familiar female voice intruded. "Well, well. Someone go get my shotgun." Mavis sounded highly amused.

Max looked up and saw two of Maddie's friends standing just inside the gate to the privacy fence.

Bea caught his eye and added, her own voice heavy with humor, "Is it legal to carry on out in the open like this?"

Maddie screeched and slipped neck deep into the water. Unfortunately, she went between Max's legs and used his left thigh as an added shield. There was no way he could duck. A quick survey showed that his modesty was intact, thanks to the bubbling water and Maddie's shoulders.

"Bea, Mavis," Max said, trying not to lose his cool at the sudden turn of events. "What are you two doing here?"

Bea held out her arms in a grand gesture. "We came to tell

Maddie that Carmilla is eloping! She and Tiny are heading to Las Vegas tonight and Carmilla expects a party when she returns."

Maddie jostled around with joy, almost forgetting her state of undress. "That's wonderful!"

Mavis laughed. "Yeah, she always talked about Tiny, but she figured he'd forgotten about her. Not so. She used your young fellow here as an excuse to get in touch with him again, and nature took care of the rest."

Bea tipped her head at Max. "Looks like nature has been working on the both of you, too. So tell me, when's the wedding?"

"Just as soon as I can arrange it," Max said, and then his father stepped out of the house.

"Wedding! Why Max, that's wonderful." Dan didn't look the least bit surprised to see his youngest son making merry in a hot tub with a naked young lady. He stepped out of the open patio doors and then caught sight of Mavis and Bea. He stopped stock-still, looking spellbound and tongue-tied. "Uh, hello."

A very slow smile spread over Bea's face as she looked him over. She winked, then said in an aside to Mavis, "Dibs."

Cleo suddenly noticed the crowd and began barking. Deciding she needed to protect her master she not only charged the newcomers, she put herself between them and her human family.

She leaped right into the hot tub.

MADDIE KNEW her face was still red. Red and swollen. But she was so happy, it didn't matter. Max loved her. He wanted to marry her. Life couldn't get much better.

She and Cleo were both drier now, except for their hair. Maddie had already combed her own and she sat on the floor, Cleo lying in front of her, while she untangled the dog's fur. Everyone else was gathered at Max's kitchen table. Dan had insisted on coffee and Mavis and Bea had seconded his vote. They all sipped a fresh cup, except for Max.

Dan, who could barely keep his eyes off Bea—which she obviously loved—said, "I came by to see if you'd be ready to travel as early as next weekend." Sheepishly he admitted, "Now that I've finally gotten your agreement to join me in the business, I don't want to take any chances on you backing out."

Max, wearing only a pair of jeans and looking sexy enough to kill, leaned against the counter drinking juice. "Where to?"

"Minnesota. You'd have this whole week to get acquainted with the product and the price list." Dan added hurriedly, "And of course your young lady and the dog are more than welcome to go along."

Cleo snarled at Dan. She wasn't the least bit happy having the house full, but Maddie was keeping her calm.

Max glanced at Maddie and she smiled. "I'm free."

Max smiled, too, his look intimate enough that Bea and Mavis raised their brows and snickered. Dan gave both women another quick glance, then shared a small grin with Bea.

Max clapped his father on the back, drawing his attention away from Bea. "That'd be fine, then. I'll be there bright and early tomorrow."

Dan sent Maddie a look of gratitude. "I can't tell you how wonderful it is to meet you, young lady. And I'm thrilled you'll be joining our family. Annie speaks very highly of you, and Lace has been singing your praises, too."

Maddie felt ready to burst with happiness. Then Mavis stood. "All this lovey-dovey stuff is killing me. I wish you all well, but I'm much happier playing the field."

Max grinned at her. "Another hot date tonight?"

"Every night, sweetie."

Bea clasped Dan's arm. "Why don't you let me take you to lunch, sugar? Your son suggested I show you some of my slogans."

Dan glanced at Max, his brow raised in question.

"She's good, Dad. Very good."

Bea gave a feline smile. "And I write great slogans, too."

Dan choked, but quickly recovered. "Why, yes, lunch sounds very nice."

Max shook his head. It seemed his whole world had gotten turned upside down in a relatively short time.

His brother had married, his sister had married—which included a long-time family friend getting hitched, too. Maddie had burst into his life and practically stolen his dog from him.

He glanced at her to see Cleo sprawled over her lap in bliss while Maddie bent to the task of combing out the tangles in the dog's seldom seen tail. Maddie's brows were drawn in concentration, her eyes still swollen, her nose still red.

Damn he loved her.

And now his father was actually smitten with a woman.

Max waited impatiently until everyone had left the house. Cleo whined at the back door and Maddie let her back out to fight with her ball. Dog hairs were all over Maddie's fresh clothes, but thankfully there were none on her face. She went directly to Max and held him.

Max said, "Will you marry me soon?"

"As soon as you like."

He grinned. "An agreeable woman. What a lucky cuss I am." Then he added, "Now, about that bag of goodies you brought…"

Maddie looked up at him and smiled. "Thank you, Max."

"For what, sweetheart?"

"For being a reprobate. For being a kinky, macho, adorable, loveable man." She kissed him gently. "And mostly for being all mine."

Max lifted her in his arms. "Being all yours is my pleasure. In fact, I insist on it." He started toward the bedroom. "As for the rest, I think we need to explore the kinky part just a bit more."

He bobbed his eyebrows at Maddie and she laughed, saying, "Now where did I leave my feather?"

His life was complete.

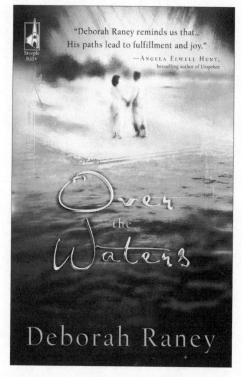

Imagine not knowing if your next meal may be your last.

This is the fate of Yelenda, the food taster for a leader who is the target of every assassin in the land. As Yelenda struggles to save her own mortality, she learns she has undiscovered powers that may hold the fate of the world.

Available wherever
trade paperbacks
are sold.

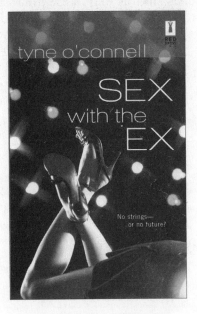